NEW BLOOD

**OTHER BOOKS FROM DIANE RAETZ
AND PATRICK THOMAS**

IN THE MYSTIC INVESTIGATORS SERIES:

ONCE MORE UPON A TIME

PARTNERS IN CRIME
(FORTHCOMING)

**PADWOLF PUBLISHING BOOKS
FROM PATRICK THOMAS**

IN THE MURPHY'S LORE SERIES:

TALES FROM BULFINCHE'S PUB

FOOLS' DAY

THROUGH THE DRINKING GLASS

SHADOW OF THE WOLF

REDEMPTION ROAD

BARTENDER OF THE GODS

NIGHTCAPS

EMPTY GRAVES: TALES OF ZOMBIES

FAIRY WITH A GUN:
THE COLLECTED TERRORBELLE

DEAD TO RITES:
THE DMA CASEFILES OF AGENT KARVER.
WITH C.J. HENDERSON AND JOHN L. FRENCH

NEW BLOOD

Edited by
Patrick Thomas
and Diane Raetz

PADWOLF PUBLISHING

For Erin and Colin

New Blood
Like Part of the Family © 2010 Jonathan Maberry
By Any Means © 2010 Danielle Ackley-McPhail
Tequila Sunset © 2010 Brad Aiken
Whispers During Still Moments, revised © 2010 Linda Addison,
    originally published in *Dark Thirst* © 2004, Pocket Books.
Holiday's Bite © 2010 W. H. Horner
Lo'Pontogo Madness © 2010 T.L. Randleman & Neal Levin
Box Lunch © 2010 James Chambers
Kashrut © 2010 Bernie Mojzes
The Vampire Escalator of the Palisades Promanade © 2010 Hildy Silverman
Love and Other Excuses © 2010 Terri Osborne
The View Never Changes © 2010 KT Pinto
Cauterize The Wound © 2010 Jeffrey Lyman
If At First You Don't Succeed... © 2010 C.J. Henderson
Tripp's Raid © 2010 John Sunseri
Cannibalistically Incestous
Vampire Penguin from Coney Island © 2010 Diane Raetz & Patrick Thomas

Padwolf Publishing, Inc.
www.padwolf.com

ISBN: 978-1-890096-44-1
Printed in the U.S.A.
First Printing.

Cover Design/Art: Patrick Thomas, www.patthomas.net
Interior Design: Danielle McPhail
Sidhe na Daire Multimedia, www.sidhenadaire.com
Interior Art: Linda Saboe, www.croneswood.com

Contents

Like Part
of the Family

By

Jonathan Maberry

"My ex-husband is trying to kill me," she said.
She was one of those cookie-cutter East Coast blondes. Pale skin, pale hair, pale eyes. Lots of New Age jewelry. Not a lot of curves and too much perfume. Kind of pretty if you dig the modeling-scene heroin chic look. Or if you troll the anorexia twelve-steps or crack houses looking for easy ass that's so desperate for affection they'll boff you blind for a smile. Not my kind. I like a little more meat on the bone, and bit more sanity in the eyes. This one came to me on a referral from another client.

"He actually try?"

"I can *tell*, Mr. Hunter."

Yeah, I thought and tried not to sigh. *What I figured.*

"You call the cops?"

She shrugged.

"What's that mean? You call them or not?"

"I called," she said. "They said that there wasn't anything they could do unless he did something first."

"Yeah," I said. "Can't arrest someone for thinking about something."

"He threatened me."

"Anyone hear him make the threat?"

"No."

"Then it's your word."

"That's what the police said." She crossed her legs. Her legs were on the thin side of being nice. Probably were nice before drugs or stress or a fractured self image wasted her down to Sally Stick-figure.

Skirt was short, shoes looked expensive. I have three ex-wives and I pay alimony bigger than India's national debt. I know how expensive women's shoes are. I was wearing black sneakers from Payless. Glad I had a desk between me and her.

"Your husband ever hurt you?" I asked. "Or try to?"

"*Ex,*" she corrected. "And…yes. That's why I left him. He hit me a few times. Mostly when he was drunk and out of control."

I held up a hand. "Don't make excuses for him. He hit you. Being drunk doesn't change the rules. Might even make it worse, especially if he did it once while drunk and then let himself come home drunk again."

She digested that. She'd probably heard that rap before but it might have come from a female case worker or a shrink. From the way her eyes shifted to me and away and back again I guessed she'd never heard that from a man before. I guess for her men were the Big Bad. Too many of them are.

It was ten to five but it was already dark outside. December snow swirled past the window. It wasn't accumulating, so the snow still looked pretty. Once it started piling up I hated the shit. My secretary, Mrs. Gilligan, fled at the first flake. Typical Philadelphian –they think the world will come to a screeching halt if there's half an inch on the ground. She's probably at Wegmans stocking up on milk, bread and toilet paper. The staples of the apocalypse. Me, I grew up in Minneapolis, and out in the Cities we think twenty inches is getting off light. Doesn't mean I don't hate the shit, though. A low annual snowfall is one of the reasons I moved to Philly after I got my PI license. Easier to hunt if you don't have to slog through snow.

"When he hit you," I said, "you report it?"

"No."

"Not to the cops?"

"No."

"Women's shelter?"

"No."

"Anyone? A friend?"

She shook her head. "I was…embarrassed, Mr. Hunter. A black eye and all. Didn't want to be seen."

Which means there's no record. Nothing to support her case about ex-hubby wanting to kill her.

I drummed my fingers on the desk blotter. I get these kinds of cases every once in a while, though I stayed well clear of domestic disputes and spousal abuse cases when I was with Minneapolis PD. I have a temper and by the time they asked for my shield back I had six reprimands in my jacket for excessive force. At one of my IA hearings the captain said that he was disappointed that I showed no remorse for the last 'incident'. I busted a child molester and somehow while the guy was, um, resisting arrest he managed to get mauled and mangled a bit. The pedophile tried to spin some crazy shit that I sicced a dog on him, but I don't *have* a dog. I said that he got mauled by a stray during a foot pursuit. Even at my own hearing I couldn't keep a smile off my face to save my job. Squeaked by on that one, but next time something like it happened—this time with a guy who whipped his wife half to death with an extension cord because she wasn't 'willing enough' in the bedroom—I was out on my ass. He ran into the same stray dog. Weird how that happens, huh? Long story short, I already didn't have the warm fuzzies for her husband. We all have our buttons, and when the strong prey on the weak all of mine get pushed.

"Did you go to the E.R.?"

"No," she said. "It was never that bad. More humiliating than anything."

I nodded. "What about after the divorce? He lay a hand on you since?"

She hesitated.

"Mrs. Skye?" I prompted.

"He tried. He chased me. Twice."

"*Chased* you? Tell me about it."

She licked her lips. She wore a very nice rose-pink lipstick that was the only splash of color. Even her clothes and shoes were white. Pale horse, pale rider.

"Well," she said, "that's where the story gets really...strange."

"Strange how?"

"He –David, my ex-husband—*changed* after I filed for divorce. He's like a different person. Before, when I first met him, he was a very fastidious man. Always dressed nicely, always very clean and well-groomed."

"What's he do for a living?"

"He owns a nightclub. *The Crypt*, just off South Street."

"I know it, but that's a Goth club right? Is he Goth?"

"No. Not at all. He bought the club from the former owner, but he remodeled it after *The Batcave*."

"As in Batman?"

"As in the London club that was kind of the prototype of pretty much the whole Goth club scene. David's a businessman. There's a strong Goth crowd Downtown, and they hang together, but the clubs in Philly aren't big enough to turn a big profit, and not near big enough to attract the better bands. So, he bought the two adjoining buildings and expanded out. He made a small-time club into a very successful main stage club, and he keeps the music current. A lot of post-punk stuff, but also the newer styles. Dark cabaret, deathrock, Gothabilly. That sort of thing. Low lights, black-tile bathrooms, bartenders who look like ghouls."

"Okay," I said.

"But this was all business to David. He didn't dress Goth. I mean, he wore black suits or black silk shirts to work, but he didn't dye his hair, didn't wear eye-liner. Funny thing is, even though he was clearly not buying into the lifestyle the patrons loved him. They called him the Prince. As in Prince of—."

"Darkness, yeah, got it. Go on."

"David was more fussy getting ready to go out than I ever was. Spent forever in the bathroom shaving, fixing his hair. Always took him longer to pick out his clothes than me or any of my girlfriends."

"He gay?"

"No." And she shot me a 'wow, what a stereo-typically homophobic thing to say' sort of look.

I smiled. "I'm just trying to get a read on him. Fastidious guy having trouble with a relationship with his wife. Drinking problem, flashes of violence. Not a gay thing, but I've seen it before in guys who are sexually conflicted and at war with themselves and the world because of it."

She studied me for a moment. "You used to be a cop, Mr. Hunter?"

"Call me Sam," I said. "And, yeah, I was a cop. Minneapolis PD."

"A detective?"

"Yep."

"Okay." That seemed to mollify her. I gestured to her to continue. She took a breath. "Well...toward the end of our relationship David stopped being so fastidious. He would go two or three days without shaving. I know that doesn't sound like the end of the world, but I never saw David without a fresh shave. Never. He carried an electric razor in his briefcase, had another at home and one in the office at the club. Clothes, too. Before, he'd sometimes change clothes twice or even three times a day if it was humid. He always wanted to look fresh. Showered at home morning and night, and had a shower installed in his office."

"I get the picture. Mr. Clean. But you say that changed while you were still together?"

"It started when he fell off the wagon."

"Ah."

"When I met him he said that he hadn't taken a drink for over two years. He was proud of it. He thought that his thirst –he always called it that—was evil, and being on the wagon made him feel like a real person. Then, after we started having problems, he started drinking again. Never in front of me, and he always washed his mouth out before he came home. I never smelled alcohol on him, but he was a different person from then on. And he started yelling at me all the time. He called me horrible names and made threats. He said that I didn't love him, that I was just trying to use him."

"I have to ask," I said, being as delicate as I could, "but was there someone else?"

"For me? God, no!"

"What set him off? From his perspective, I mean. Did he say that there was something that made him angry or paranoid?"

"Well...I think it was his health."

"Tell me."

"He started losing weight. He was never fat, not even stocky. David was very muscular. He lifted a lot of weights, drank that protein powder twice a day. He had big arms, a huge chest. I asked him if he was taking steroids. He denied it, but I think he was trying to turn into one of those muscle freaks. Then, about a year and a half ago he started losing weight. When he taped his arms and found that his biceps were only twenty-two inches, he got really angry."

"David has twenty-two inch biceps?" Christ. Back in his Mr. Universe days, Arnold the Terminator had twenty-four inch arms, fully pumped. I think mine are somewhere shy of fifteen, and that's after three sets on the Bowflex.

"Not anymore," said Mrs. Skye. "He lost a lot of muscle mass. Really fast, too. I was scared, I told him to go to a doctor. I thought he might have cancer."

"Did he go to the doctor?"

"He said so...but I don't think he did. He kept losing weight. After six months he didn't even have much definition. He was kind of ordinary sized."

"Was he drinking by this point?"

"I'm sure of it."

"That when he started putting his hands on you?"

"Yes. And he became paranoid. Kept trying to make it all my fault."

"How long did this go on?"

"Well...after the first time he, um, *hurt* me, I gave him a second chance. After all, he was my husband. I figured that he was just scared because of his health. But then it happened again. The second time he knocked me around pretty good. I couldn't go out of the house for a few days."

"Was that when you left?"

It took her so long to answer that I knew what her answer would be. I've done too many interviews of this kind. If self-esteem is low enough then victimization can become an addiction.

"I stayed for two more months."

"How many times did he hurt you during that time?" I asked.

"A few."

"A few is how many?"

Another long pause. "Six."

"Six," I said, trying to put no judgment in my tone. "What was the straw?"

She looked at her hands, at the clock, at the snow falling outside. If there'd been a magazine on my desk she would have picked it up and leafed through it. Anything to keep from meeting my eyes. "He choked me."

"I see."

"It was in the middle of the night. We were...we were..."

I almost sighed. "Let me guess. Make-up sex?"

She nodded, but she didn't blush. I'll give her that.

"He'd been sweet to me for two weeks straight without getting mad or yelling, or anything. He acted like his old self. Charming."

She finally met my eyes.

"David has enormous charisma. He makes everyone like him, and he always seems so genuine."

"Uh huh," I said, wondering how that charm would work on a black-jack across his teeth.

"We sat up talking until late, then we went to bed. And in the middle of the night...things just started happening. You know how it is."

I didn't, but I said nothing.

"I was, um...on top. And we were pretty far into things, and then all of a sudden David reaches up and grabs me around the throat. I thought for one crazy moment that he was doing that auto-whatever it's called."

"Autoerotic asphyxiation," I supplied.

"Yeah, that. I thought he was doing that. He talked about it once before, but we'd never tried it. He's really strong and I'm pretty small. But...I guess I thought he was trying to change things, you know? Create a new pattern for us. A fresh start."

Naivety can be a terrible thing. Jesus wept.

"But it wasn't sex play," I prompted.

"No. He started squeezing his hands. Suddenly I couldn't breathe. It was weird because we were so close to...you know...and David kept staring at me, his eyes wide like he was in some kind of trance. I tried to pull his hands apart, but it just made him squeeze tighter. That's when he started calling me names again, making wild accusations, accusing me of destroying his life."

"How did you get away?"

Her eyes cut away again. This was obviously very hard for her.

"I threw myself sideways and when I landed I kicked him in the, um...you know."

I smiled.

"Good for you," I said, but she shook her head.

"I grabbed my clothes and ran out. Next day I drove past the house and saw that his car was gone. I had a locksmith come out and change all the locks and change the security code on the alarm. I hired a messenger company to come and take a couple of suitcases of his clothes to the club. Next day I rented a storage unit and hired a moving company to take all of his stuff there. I used the same messenger service to send him the key."

"I'm impressed. That was quick thinking."

"I...I'd already looked into that stuff before. Until that last stretch where he was nice I was planning to leave him. I'd already talked to my lawyer, and I filed for divorce by the end of that week."

"What did David do?"

"At first? Nothing except for some hysterical messages on my voice-mail. He didn't try to break in, nothing like that. But after a while I started seeing his car behind mine when I was going to work."

"Where do you work?"

"I'm a nurse supervisor at Sunset Grove, the assisted living facility in Jenkintown. Right now I'm on the four to midnight shift. I've spotted David's car a lot, sometimes every night for weeks on end. I've seem him drive by when I'm going into the staff entrance, and he's there again when I get back home."

"What makes you think he's planning to do more than just harass you?"

"He's said so."

"But—."

"He didn't say or do anything at first...but over the last couple of weeks it's gotten worse. About three weeks ago I came out of work and stopped at a 7-11 for some gum, and when I came out he was leaning against my car. I told him to get away, but he pushed himself off the car and came up to me, smiling his charming smile. He told me that he knew who I was and what I was and that he was going to end me. His words. *'I'm going to end you'*. Then he left, still smiling."

"Did anyone see this?"

"At one in the morning? No."

Convenience stores have security cameras, I thought. If this thing got messy I could have her lawyer subpoena those tapes. I had her write down the address of the 7-11.

"That's how it went for a couple of weeks," she said. "But last night he really scared me."

"What happened?"

"He was in my bedroom."

"How?"

"That's it...I don't know. The alarms didn't go off and none of the windows were broken. I heard a sound and I woke up and there he was, standing by the side of my bed. He's really thin now, and as pale as those Goth kids at his club. He stood there, smiling. I started to scream and he put a finger to his lips and made a weird shushing sound. It was so strange that I actually did shut up. Don't ask me why. The whole thing was like a nightmare."

"Are you sure it wasn't?"

She hesitated, but she said, "I'm positive. He pointed at me and said that he knew everything about me. Then he started praying."

"Praying?"

"At least I think that's what he was doing. It was Latin, I think. He saying a long string of things in Latin and then he left."

"How'd he get out?"

"The same way he got in, I guess...but I don't know how. I was so scared that I almost peed myself and I just lay there in bed for a long time. I don't know how long. When I finally worked up the nerve, I ran downstairs and got a knife from the kitchen and went through the whole house."

"You didn't call the cops?"

"I was going to...but the alarm never went off. I checked the system...it was still set. I began wondering if I *was* dreaming."

"But you don't think so?"

"No."

"Why are you so sure?"

She fished in her purse and produced a pink cell phone. She flipped it open and pressed a few buttons to call up her text messages. She pointed to the number and then handed me the phone.

"That's David's cell number."

The text read: *Tonight.*

"Okay," I said. "Let me see what I can do."

"What *can* you do?" she asked.

"Well, the best first thing to do is go have a talk with him. See if I can convince him to back off."

"And if he won't?"

"I can be pretty convincing."

"But what if he won't? What if he's...I don't know...too crazy to listen to reason?"

I smiled. "Then we'll explore other options."

The Crypt is a big ugly building on the corner of South and Fourth in Philadelphia. Once upon a time it was a coffin factory—which I think would have been a cooler name. Less trendy and obvious. The light snow did nothing to make it look less ugly. When we pulled to the corner, Mrs. Skye pointed to a sleek silver Lexus parked on the side street.

"That's his."

I jotted down the license plate and used my digital camera to take photos of it and the exterior of the building. You never know.

"Okay," I said, "I want you to wait here. I'll go have a talk with David and see if we can sort this out."

"What if something happens? What if you don't come out?"

"Just sit tight. You have a cell phone and I'll give you the keys. If I'm not out of there in fifteen minutes, drive somewhere safe and call the name on the back of my card." I gave her my business card. She turned it over and saw a name and number. Before she could ask, I said, "Ray's a friend. One of my pack."

"Another private investigator?"

"A bodyguard. I use him for certain jobs, but I don't think we'll need to bring him in on this. From what you've told me I have a pretty good sense of what to expect in there."

As I got out my jacket flap opened and she spotted the handle of my Glock.

"You're not...going to *hurt* him," she asked, wide eyed.

I shook my head. "I've been doing this for a lot of years, Mrs. Skye. I haven't had to pull my gun once. I don't expect I'll break that streak tonight."

The breeze was coming from the west and the snow was just about done. I squinted up past the streetlights. The cloud cover was thin and I could already see the white outline of the moon. Nope, no accumulation. Typical Philly winter.

I crossed the street and tried the front door. Place didn't do much business before late evening, but the doors were unlocked. The doors opened with an exhalation of cigarette smoke and alcohol fumes. There was probably a anti-smoking violation in that. Something else to use later if I needed to go the route of making life difficult for him.

It was too early for a doorman, and I walked a short hallway that was empty and painted black. Heavy black velvet curtains at the end. Cute. I pushed them aside and entered the club. Place was huge. David Skye must have taken out the second floor and knocked out everything but the retaining walls of the adjoining properties. The red and white maximum occupancy sign said that it shouldn't exceed four hundred, but the place looked capable of accommodating twice that number. Bandstand was empty, so someone had put quarters in to play the tuneless junk that was beating the shit out of the woofers and tweeters. Whoever the group was on the record they subscribed to the philosophy that if you can't play well you should play real god damn loud.

There were maybe twenty people in the place, scattered around at tables. A few at the bar. Everyone looked like extras from a direct-to-video vampire flick. The motif was black on black with occasional splashes of blood red. White skin that probably never saw the sun. Eyeliner and black lipstick, even on the guys. I was in jeans and a Vikings warm-up jacket. At least my sneakers and my leather porkpie hat were black. Handle of my gun was black, too, but they couldn't see that. Better for everyone if nobody did.

The bartender was giving me *the look*, so I strolled over to him. He knew I wasn't there for a beer and didn't waste either of our time by asking.

"David Skye," I said, having to bend forward and shout over the music.

"Badge me," he said.

I flipped open my PI license. "Private."

"Fuck off," he suggested.

"Not a chance."

"I can call the cops."

"Bet I can have L and I here before they show. Smoking in a public restaurant?"

Another smartass remark was on his lips, but he didn't have the energy for it. He was paid by the hour and this had to be a slow shift for tips. I took a twenty from my wallet and put it on the bar.

"This isn't your shit, kid," I said. "Call your boss."

He didn't like it, but he took the twenty and made the call.

"He says come up." The bartender pointed to another curtained doorway beside the bar. I gave him a sunny day smile and went inside.

There was a long hallway with bathrooms on both sides and a set of stairs at the end. I took the stairs two at a time. The stairs went straight up to his office and the door was open. I knocked anyway.

"It's open," he yelled. I went inside and as I looked around I hoped like hell that the office décor was not modeled after the interior landscape of David Skye's mind. The walls were painted a dark red, the trim was gloss black. Instead of the band posters and framed *'look at who I'm shaking hands with'* eight-by-tens, the walls were hung with torture devices and S and M clothes. Spiked harnesses, leather zippered masks, thumbscrews, photos from Abu Graib, diagrams of dissected bodies. A full-sized rack occupied one corner of the room and an iron maiden stood in the other, one door open to reveal rows of tarnished metal spikes. The only other furniture was a big desk made from some dark wood, a black file cabinet and the leather swivel chair in which David Skye sat. He wore a black poet's shirt, leather wristbands, and a smile that was already belligerent.

"Who the fuck are you and the fuck you want?"

The man was a charmer. I could just taste the charisma his wife had mentioned flowing like sweetness from his pores.

I flipped my ID case open. "We need to have a chat. It can be friendly or not. Your call."

"Go fuck yourself."

So much for *friendly.*

"That whore send you?" he demanded.

I smiled but didn't answer.

He had a handsome face, but his wife was right when she said that he'd lost weight. His skin looked thin and loose, and he had the complexion of a mushroom. More gray than white.

"Did my wife send you?" he said, pronouncing the words slowly as if I'd come here on the short bus.

"Why would your ex-wife send me?"

His eyes flickered for a second at *'ex*-wife'. I strolled across the room and stood in front of his desk. He didn't get up, neither of us offered a hand to the other.

"She makes up stories," he said.

"What kind of stories?"

"Bullshit. Lies. Says I slapped her around."

"Who'd she say that to?"

He didn't answer. He did, however, give me the ninja secret death stare, but I manned my way through it.

"What are you supposed to be," he said.

"Just what the license says."

"Private investigator. Private *dick*."

"Yes, and that was funny back in the 1950s. Why do *you* think I'm here?"

"She's probably trying some kind of squeeze play. The club's doing okay, so she wants a bigger slice."

"Try again," I said, though he might have been right about that.

"Oh, I get it....you're supposed to scare me into leaving her alone."

"Do I look scary?"

He smiled. He had very red lips and very white teeth. "No," he said, "you don't."

"Right...so let's pretend that I'm here to have a reasonable discussion. Man to man."

Skye leaned back in his chair and stared at me with his dark eyes. It was a calculating look and I'm sure he took in everything from my slightly threadbare Vikings jacket to my cheap black sneakers. Put everything I was wearing together and it would equal the cost of his shirt. I was okay with that. I don't dress to impress. Skye, on the other hand, smiled as if our mutual understanding of my material net worth clearly made him the alpha.

I smiled back.

"What does she want?" he asked.

"For you to leave her alone."

"What is she afraid of?"

"She thinks you're trying to kill her."

"What do *you* think?"

"What I think doesn't matter. I'm not a psychic, so I don't know whether you're trying to kill her or if you're playing some kind of mindgame on her. Whatever it is, I'm here to ask you to lay off."

"Why should I?"

"Because I asked real nice."

He smiled at that.

"Because it's illegal and I could build a harassment case against you and you could lose your club and sink a quarter mil into legal fees. Because I know inspectors who can slap you with fifteen kinds of violations that will hurt your business. I can have your car booted by *accident* three or four times a week, every week."

"And I could have you killed," he said, the smile unwavering.

"Maybe," I said. "You could try, and I might fuck up anyone you send and then come back here and fuck you up."

"Think you could?"

"You really want to find out?" When he didn't answer, I took a glass paperweight off his desk and turned it over in my hands. A spider was trapped inside, frozen into a moment of time for the amusement of the trinket crowd. I knew he was watching me play with the paperweight, wondering what I was going to do with it.

I put it back down on the desk.

"Really, though," I said, "how long do we need to circle and sniff each other? We don't run in the same pack and I don't give a rat's ass what you do, who you are, or how tough you think you are. We both know that you're either going to stop bothering your ex-wife and go on with your life; or you're going to make a run at her—either because you have some loose wiring or because I'm pushing your buttons by being here. If you back off, we're all friends. I'll advise my client not to file a restraining order and you two can let the divorce lawyers earn their paychecks by kicking each other in the nuts."

"Or...?" he asked. Still smiling.

"Or, you don't back off and then this is about you and me."

"Nonsense. You're no part of this. This is about me and—."

I cut him off. "I'm *making* this about you and me. Maybe I have a wire loose, too, but once I tell a client that I'm going to keep her safe, I take it amiss if anything happens to her."

"'Amiss'," he repeated, enjoying the word.

"But that's a minute from now. We're still on the other side of it until you give me an answer. What's it going to be? You leave her alone? Or this gets complicated."

"What were you before you started doing this PI bullshit?"

"A cop."

He grunted. "You sound like a thug. An asshole leg-breaker from South Philly."

"Thin line sometimes."

He steepled his fingers. It was one of those moves that looked good when Doctor Doom did it in a comic book. Maybe in a boardroom. Looked silly right now, but he had enough intensity in his eyes to almost pull it off. He gave me ten seconds of *the stare*.

I stood my ground.

His cell phone rang and he flipped it open, listened.

"I'm in a meeting," he said and closed the phone.

His smile returned.

I heard the footsteps on the stairs even though they were quiet.

I sighed and turned. There were four of them. All as pale as Skye, but much bigger. "Really? You want to play that card?"

"It's one of the classics. Though, to be fair, it'll be more than a typical beating. I...hm, am I wrong in presuming you *have* had your ass kicked?"

"That cherry was popped a long time ago."

The four men entered the room and fanned out behind me.

"So, our challenge, then," Skye said, "is to put a new spin on this. Something surprising and fresh so that you'll be entertained."

"Mind if I take my jacket off first?"

"Go right ahead."

I heard a hammer-cock behind me.

Skye said, "You can put your jacket on my desk here, and take off your shoulder holster and put that—and your piece—on top of it."

"Sure, whatever," I said. I shrugged out of the jacket. I bought it the year the Vikings took their eighteenth division title. I'll but a new one if they ever win the Super Bowl. Or when pigs sprout wings and learn to fly, whichever comes first. I folded it and set it down, unclipped my shoulder rig, set that down. If I was going to ruin my clothes, then at least nothing I was currently wearing had sentimental value.

I leaned on the desk. "Let's agree on a couple of things first, okay?"

"Sure," he said with a grin.

"When I'm done handing these clowns their asses, then you and I dance a round or two."

"That would be fun," he said, "but I doubt I'll have the pleasure."

"Second, if I walk out of here on my own steam, then it's with the understanding that you will leave the lady alone."

"If you walk out of here? Sure. But, tell me something," he said, and he looked genuinely interested, "why do you care? What is she to you?"

"Maybe I'm the possessive type, too. Maybe now that she's asked for my help, it's like she's part of the family. So to speak."

"Part of the family? You fucking kidding me here?"

"Nope."

"You Italian? This some kind of dago thing?"

"I said it's *like* she's part of the family. My family," I said, "and I protect what's mine."

"That's it? It's just a macho thing with you?"

"No, it's more than that," I admitted. I gestured to the torture and pain motif in which his office was decorated. "But, seriously, I doubt you would understand."

"Mmm, probably not. I'm not into sentimentality and that bullshit. Not anymore."

"What happened? What changed you?"

His smiled faded to a remote coldness. "I learned that there was something better. Better than family, better than blood ties. Better than any of this ordinary shit."

"You found religion?" I said.

"It's a 'higher order' sort of thing that I really don't want to explain and I doubt *you'd* understand."

"I might surprise you."

"I don't think that's possible. But *we* might surprise you. In fact I can pretty fucking well guarantee it."

"Rock and roll," I said.

I straightened and turned toward the four goons. They took up positions like compass points. The office was big, but not big enough to give me room to maneuver. They were going to fall on me like a wall, and they knew it. The guy with the gun even snugged it back into his shoulder rig. They were *that* confident, and they were smiling like kids at a carnival.

"You shouldn't have bothered Mr. Skye," said the guy in front of me. He was the guy who'd holstered his gun. He stood on the East point of the compass. "You should have—"

I kicked him in the nuts. I really didn't need to hear the speech.

I'm not that big but I can kick like a Rockette. I *felt* bones break and he screamed like a nine year old girl. Dumbass should have kept his gun out.

I stepped backward off of him and put an elbow into West's face. It had all of my mass in motion behind it. That time I heard bones break and he went down so fast that I wondered if I'd snapped his neck.

That left South and North. South spent a half second too long looking shocked, so I jumped at him with a leaping knee—the only Muay Thai kick I know—and drove him all the way to the wall. By the time North closed in I'd grabbed South by the ears and slammed him skull-first into a replica of a torture rack. Blood splattered in a Jackson Pollack pattern.

I pivoted and rushed to intercept North who was barreling at me with a lot of furious speed; so I veered left and clothes-lined him with my stiff right forearm. He did a pretty impressive back flip and landed face down on the black-painted hardwood floor.

If this was an action movie everything would switch to slow motion as the four thugs toppled to the ground and I turned slowly looking badass, to face the now startled and unprotected villain.

The real world is a lot less accommodating.

I caught movement behind me, figuring it for Skye going after my gun, so I whirled and made ready to launch into a diving tackle.

Only it wasn't Skye.

It was East and West getting to their feet. West's face was smeared with blood from his broken nose, but he was smiling. As I watched he took his nose between thumb and forefinger and *snapped* it into place, then spit a hocker of blood and snot onto the floor.

North was chuckling as he rose; and behind me I could hear South shifting to stand behind me again. I turned in a slow circle. They were all smiling. They shouldn't have been *able* to. They should have been sprawled on the floor and I should have been giving some kind of smart-ass speech as I closed in to lay a beating on Skye. That was the script I'd written in my head.

What the hell was this shit?

"Surprise!" said Skye dryly.

"What the hell are these fuckers *taking*?"

"You wouldn't believe me if I told you."

"Try me."

"Blood," he said.

"What the—"

And I looked more closely at the smiles. Lots of white teeth. Lots of long, pointy white teeth.

"Oh, balls," I said.

"Yeah, kind of cool, huh?"

"Vampires?" I said.

"Yeah."

"Actual vampires."

Skye laughed. The four—well, let's call a spade a spade—*vampires* laughed with him.

Even I laughed.

"Geez. When shit goes wrong it goes all the way wrong, doesn't it," I said.

"On the up side," said Skye, "you did win the first round. Nice moves."

"Thanks."

The four of them circled me. My pulse jumped from 'uh-oh' to 'oh shit'. It was cold in his office but I was starting to sweat pretty heavily.

"I guess I shouldn't be surprised," I said. "You're one, too? Am I right?"

"A recent convert," he admitted.

"So...that whole weight lose, going all weird on the missus that was—-?"

"A transition process. It's not like they show in the movies, you know. Takes weeks. The whole metabolism changes."

"No kidding."

One of the vampires faked a lunge to psyche me out and I jumped a foot in the air. I'm pretty sure I didn't yelp like a Chihuahua, but I wouldn't swear to that in court. They all laughed at that, too. I didn't.

"Which explains why you lost all that weight."

"Who needs steroids and free-weights," he agreed and spread his hands. "This package comes with honest to God super strength. I'm like Spider-man and Wolverine rolled into one. Super strong and I heal from damn near anything."

"Could you be more specific on that last point?"

"Cute."

"Worth a try." I looked at them, at their grinning, evil faces. My nuts were trying to crawl up inside of my chest cavity. I mean...*fucking vampires?*

"Weird thing was," I said, "I was starting to build a case in my head about your wife. You losing weight and getting pale, blaming her for it all, saying you know what she is…is she a vampire, too? Is she the one who bit you?"

Skye laughed. "Christ no. And she's not a succubus either. She's just a nagging, soul-draining, passive-aggressive codependent bitch."

"Wow. You're really a chauvinistic prick, aren't you?"

"Better than being pussy whipped."

I dropped it. I had bigger fish to fry than trying to bring this macho jackass into the Twenty-first century. Namely the fact that I was in a roomful of vampires.

I know I keep harping on that, but really…it's not the sort of shit that happens all the time to me. Or, like…*ever.*

"Say, man," I said to Skye, "any chance we can roll back this tape to the point where we were still friends? I just walk out of here and we all call it a day?"

Skye made a face as if pretending to consider it. "Mmm…no, I don't see that happening."

"You want to make a deal of some kind?"

"Nah," he said. "You got nothing I want. Except the O-positive."

"AB neg," I corrected.

"Never tried that."

"You wouldn't like it. Goes right to your hips."

The wattage on his smile was dimmer. Jaunty banter can buy only so many seconds and then it's back to business.

I tried to keep my face neutral, but my pulse was like a jazz drum solo.

"I'm going to throw something out here," I said. I could hear a tremor in my voice. Fuck it.

"Oh, please." He gestured to the four killers and they started forward.

"Wait! Just hear me out. What have you got to lose?"

The thugs looked at Skye. West gave a 'why not?' kind of shrug.

Skye sighed. "Okay, what is it? Last words? A little begging?" he suggested.

"Mm, more like last threat."

"This I got to hear."

The five of them looked genuinely interested.

"Okay, so here you are, five vampires. That's some really scary shit, am I right? I mean creatures of the night and all that."

He nodded, nothing to disagree with.

"To most people that's enough to make them go apeshit crazy. I mean…vampires. Not your everyday thing. It opens up all kinds of metaphysical questions. If vampires exist, what *else* does. If there are supernatural monsters, does that mean God and the Devil are real. You follow me?"

"Sure. We get that a lot."

"And I'm outnumbered here. Five to one. Tough odds without you fellows being the undead. So…why ain't I scared?"

His eyes narrowed.

"I mean, yeah, my pulse is racing and I'm sweating. But do I look as scared as I should be? I don't do I? Now…why is that?"

"So you put up a good front. It'll be a good anecdote later," he said. "For us."

"Maybe he's got a hammer and stake," suggested West.

That got a laugh.

"Nope."

My heart rate had to be close to two hundred. It was machinegun fire in my chest.

"Coupla garlic bulbs in your pocket?" asked East.

"Nah. I don't even like it on my pizza."

"You don't have any backup," said North. "And you don't got your gun."

My blood pressure could have scalded paint off a battleship. I wiped sweat off my brow with my thumb.

"Okay, jokes over," snapped Skye. "What's the punch line here? Why aren't you as scared as you should be?"

I smiled.

"I'll show you."

The first time it happened, way back when I was thirteen, it took almost half an hour. I screamed and cried and rolled around on the floor. First time's always the hardest. Each time since it was easier. My grandmother and her sister could do it in the time it took you to snap your fingers. My best time was during a foot chase back when I was with Minneapolis PD. I was running down the guy who'd beaten his wife with the extension cord. He saw me coming and ducked into his apartment, I kicked the door and he came out of the bedroom with a gun and opened up. I went through the change in the time it took me to leap through the doorway. Like the snap of my fingers. One minute me, next minute *different* me.

I tore the shit out of him. I lost my badge and pension and had to make up all sorts of excuses. On the plus side, I didn't die, which *would* have happened if I hadn't managed the change so fast. I'm only mortal when I look like one.

That night in Skye's office wasn't my best time. Maybe third or fourth best. Say, two, three seconds. It felt like an explosion. It hurts. Feels like my heart is bursting, like cherry bombs are detonating inside my muscles. It starts in the chest, then ripples out from there as muscle mass changes and is reassigned in new ways. Bones warp, crack and re-form. Nails tear through the flesh of my fingers and toes, my jaw shifts and the longer teeth spike through the gums. It's bloody and it's ugly and it hurts like a motherfucker.

But the end result is a stunner. A real kick-ass dramatic moment that wows the audience.

I think all four of the thugs screamed. They jerked back from me, looks of shock and horror on their faces. If I wasn't so deeply into the moment I would have smiled at the irony. Monsters being scared by a monster.

I crouched in the center of the room, hands flexing, claws streaked with blood, hot saliva dripping from my mouth onto my chest.

It would have been cool and dramatic to have said "Surprise!" to them the way Skye had said it to me, but my mouth was no longer constructed for human speech. All I could do was roar.

I did.

And then I launched at them.

Vampires are strong. Four or five times stronger than an ordinary human.

Werewolves?

Hell, we're a whole different class.

I slammed into West with both sets of front claws. He flew apart like he was made of paper and watery red glue. North and East tried to take me high and low, but they'd have done better to try and run. I brought my knee up into East's jaw as he went for the low tackle and his head burst like a casaba melon. I caught North by the throat and squeezed. Red geysered up from the stump of his neck as his head fell away. South backed away, putting himself between me and Skye, arms spread, making a more heroic stand than I'd have thought. I tore the heart from his chest. Turns out, vampires *need* their hearts.

Skye had my gun in his hands. He racked the slide and buried the barrel against me as I leaped over the desk. He got off four shots. They hurt.

Like wasp stings.

Maybe a little less.

I don't load my piece with silver bullets. I'm not an idiot.

He looked into my eyes and I would like to think that he saw the error of his ways. Don't fuck with the innocent. Don't fuck with my clients. My clients are *mine*, like members of my pack. Mess with them and the pack leader has to put you down. Has to.

So I did.

She saw me coming from across the street, her face concerned and confused. I was wearing a different pair of pants and different shoes. My own had been torn to rags during the change. Stuff I was wearing used to belong to the bartender. He didn't need them anymore. He'd been on the same team as Skye and the four goons.

I opened the door and climbed in behind the wheel.

"Are you all right, Ro?" she asked, studying my face. "Are you hurt? Is that blood?"

I dabbed at a dot on my cheek. Missed a spot. I pulled a tissue out of my jacket pocket and wiped my cheek.

"Just ketchup," I said.

"You stopped for *food*?" she demanded, eyes wide.

"It was on the house. I was hungry. No biggie."

She stared at me and then looked at the club across the street. The snow was getting heavier, the ground was white and it was starting to coat the street.

"What happened in there?"

I put the key into the ignition.

"I had a long talk with your ex. I told him that you were feeling threatened and uncomfortable with his actions, and asked him to back off."

"What did he say?"

"He won't be bothering you anymore."

"Just like that? He agreed to leave me alone just like that?" She snapped her fingers.

"More or less. I told him that I had some friends on the force and in L and I, and made it clear that I could make his life *more* uncomfortable than he was making yours. He didn't like it," I said, "but..." I let the rest hang.

"And he *agreed*?"

"Take my word for it. He's out of your life."

She continued to study me for several long seconds. I waited her out and I saw the moment when she shifted from doubt and fear to believe and acceptance. She closed her eyes, sagged back against the seat, put her face in her hands and began to cry.

I gripped the wheel and looked out at the falling snow, hiding the smile that kept trying to creep onto my mouth. I was digging the P.I. business. Fewer rules than when I was on the cops. It allowed me to be closer to the street, to go hunting deeper into the forest.

Even so—and despite what I'd said to Skye—I *was* pretty rattled that he'd been a vampire. I mean, being who and what I am I always suspected other things were out there in the dark, but until now I'd never met them. Now I knew. How many vampires were there? *Where* were they? Would they be coming for me?

I didn't have any of those answers. Not yet.

I also wondered what *else* was out there? I could feel the excitement racing through me. I wanted to find out. Good or bad, I wanted to find out.

I reached out a hand and patted Mrs. Skye's trembling shoulder. It felt good to know that one of the pack was safe now. It felt right. It made me feel powerful and satisfied on a lot of different levels. I knew that I was going to want to feel this way again. And again.

The snow swirled inside the thickening shadows. Inside my head the wolf howled.

By Any Means

By

Danielle Ackley-McPhail

"We declare our right on this earth...to be a human being, to be respected as a human being, to be given the rights of a human being in this society, on this earth, in this day, which we intend to bring into existence *by any means necessary.*" *Malcolm X*

His mind was still his own. Very little else was.
Jean-Paul Marot was having a very bad day.

"Okay, now manipulate the upper right limb for me." The cold, clinical voice belonged to First Technician Nigel Burton, his own personal demon. "Focus...concentrate on the particular servo you wish to activate. Visualize the limb lifting, contracting, extending. Flex each digit."

If Jean-Paul had still had teeth, he would have ground them. He bent his will to making the arm complete the actions requested not because he wished to comply, but to get the man to shut up and go away. There was a sizzle and a spark; he jerked in reaction and somewhere metal clanged against metal as his foot flexed, contrary to his intentions.

The coolness was no longer evident as Burton cursed. "Will you focus! I would like to get out of here some time this cycle!"

Not willing to answer aloud, to hear the grating sound of his new voice, Jean-Paul pictured the arm going through the requested sequence, both heard and sensed the gentle *whir* of the servos, the soft hiss of the rods extending and contracting through the thin, amorphous alloy sheath that mimicked the Palmar carpal ligament. This time the limb performed as intended. And he had to admit, the movement was smooth, the mechanical sounds nearly nonexistent to even augmented hearing. He was, apparently, a well-oiled machine.

And he hated it.

"Excellent; well, that's in order," Burton murmured more to himself, than anyone else. "Tomorrow, the optics and I'm done."

Done? Then what? Jean-Paul was about to question the man, but he did not get the chance. There was a click somewhere from behind his metal chassis and as the sound faded he could sense the internal leads connected to his motor functions retracting. With each coiling millimeter of encased wire he could sense the pending disconnect. *No! Damnit, no!* But the cry was silent, his vocal processors already powered down.

Jean-Paul was left suspended in darkness, deprived of all senses but his thoughts.

"Now, please note the advancements in this prototype..."

The voice came up out of nowhere, like the blast of a foghorn point blank to the ear. Jean-Paul would have flinched, but apparently whatever process had restored his hearing had not progressed far enough to allow him control of any mobility functions. He couldn't even scream, though that had not stopped his thoughts from doing so in the long hours of darkness. The urge to pant, to flood his body with oxygen in preparation for fight or flight, was strong. Too bad he was no longer capable. He was quickly learning that unacted-upon autonomous responses flooded the brain with chemical components. The affect was something less than comfortable when he had no way of dispersing them.

Apparently, Burton had not yet been back to engage his optics, but maybe Jean-Paul could regain some mobility. Calling to mind the exercises of the day before, he focused on the leads slowly uncoiling, willed them a bit more speed; visualized the connectors engaging. Of course, that part of him didn't seem to work that way. There was no noticeable effect as the voice he'd awaken to droned on. "...constructed of an amorphous alloy which we process and cast on site..."

He couldn't help but listen as the voice catalogued his new body's attributes; phrases such as high-yield strength, high corrosion- and wear-resistance, and superior elastic limits were bandied about. The buzz words "minimal costs" and "long-term serviceability" followed.

Despair fed the chemical mix swirling about Jean-Paul's brain.

Long-term servitude was more like it. That was the first reality he had learned on reawakening to the irrevocably altered life he now possessed. The sole survivor of a catastrophic failure in the orbital mines where he was employed, he had been given two options: die a horrible, lingering death for which his parents would inherit a hefty debt, or authorize the transfer of his brain to the developmental exoskeleton in which he was now housed, which would then provide him the opportunity to work off his medical care and the cost of said interment, thus sparing his parents the burden. Some choice…

When the Corporate voice reached the part in his spiel about profit-and-loss calculations and the potential for a secured and dependable work force, Jean-Paul once again had the urge to grind his non-existent teeth.

"Now, Jean-Paul," the voice addressed him for the first time as his internal leads finally completed reengagement. "If you will demonstrate for our guests…" This time the urge was to forcefully grind *the voice's* teeth together as Jean-Paul was ordered to jump through proverbial hoops for the investors, but even as the thought occurred to him, some chemical flooded his preservation mixture and all he could do was comply.

Whoever said slavery was abolished had no dealings with the Corporation.

Weeks went by, then months; all blended together as Jean-Paul adapted to his new life.

It wasn't really too different from the old one, if a bit more isolated. Once he had functionality back, and learned to manipulate the cybernetic exoskeleton and correctly interpret the augmented sensory data, he was filtered back into the mining crews.

There he was…a hulk among strangers. All the miners from his shift had had the good fortune to not leave the accident site in any semblance of life. Each had gone peacefully to their graves, so to speak, while he'd ended up in R&D. This new batch of rockhounds didn't even know he'd once had a face just like theirs. To them he was mindless mech, nothing but metal muscle. He accepted his pick and his drill and was inserted, usually alone, into the dig sites where the robotic extractors couldn't go. He didn't mind; this way he didn't have to face the others talking around him as if he wasn't there.

The nice thing about having a super-strong exoskeleton and precious little cellular matter—pretty much all that was left of the original him was his brain—Jean-Paul could work long hours as if they were nothing, and process more rock than any full crew. Still, he had to eat, after a fashion.

Just about the time his power packs were running down, a hail came over his internal comm.

"Hey, ultraman, time to check the fluids and top off the tank."

"Acknowledged," Jean-Paul responded. Gathering up both his tools and the bulging sack of ore he'd extracted, he hiked out of the pit and over the short distance to the landing platform. As the shuttle touched down, he mentally heaved a sigh. His solitude had been comfortable. Caught up in the manual labor, he'd almost forgotten the change in his fate; well...as long as he didn't look too closely at his limbs...or the mounds of ore that would have taken weeks or the intervention of heavy equipment to extract. That was when he couldn't ignore the fact that he *was* heavy equipment now. Believe it or not, he missed the bone-weary ache of shifts past.

The loading ramp lowered and Jean-Paul joined the rest of the crew on the shuttle. Silence enveloped the personnel compartment as he dumped his gear and stowed his haul. When he turned there was a whole spectrum of expressions on the other miners' faces. Awe, resentment, fear, curiosity...even envy. They ran the gambit, but not one of the men voiced what was on their minds. With another mental sigh, Jean-Paul moved to the alcove at the rear of the compartment, a recent addition tailored to his new physique. The trip back to the station was silent.

There was nothing comfortable about it.

Burton was nowhere in sight as Jean-Paul entered the R&D lab. Maybe things were looking up.

"Hello," a soft, even friendly voice spoke from behind him. He turned a bit abruptly, scrambling with his gyros to regain his center. Just visible beyond the edge of the door a female technician appeared to be cataloging supplies. She was cute and young and completely beyond him in all ways that mattered. Jean-Paul just stared, appreciating the sway of her silky brown ponytail, and trying to keep his mind off the theoretical sway of her hips. He couldn't manage anything else.

"I said, hello," she repeated with a gentle grin as she turned to look over her shoulder with eyes blue enough to be compared to the sky if there had been one.

"W-where's Burton?" He could have throttled himself. Like he cared where the prick was. The man had never once directed a personal comment at Jean-Paul, never bothered to hide his loathing.

She just looked at him, kind of like his mother would have if she'd caught him acting so socially inept. "Sorry...hello." he finally manage, cringing inside at the flat, harsh tones. They hadn't wasted any resources on cosmetic applications when they'd tooled him together.

"First Tech Burton is on sick leave; I'm covering his shift, Mr. Marot," she answered his original question with a pleasant, open expression on her face, as if all were completely normal with this encounter. "My name is Chloe Kendall, lowly lab tech."

Jean-Paul could not speak. He was drowning in the chemical response that would have tightened his chest, had he still had one. This was the first respect shown him since he'd half waken up on the operating table and been forced to chose his own Hell. Slowly, carefully, he focused on his arms, his hands. Worked the servos, careful flexing in an effort to rebalance his mix. "Nice to meet you, Tech Kendall."

"Chloe will do, unless you object...or Kendall, if that's more comfortable for you." She continued without waiting for a response. "So, time for dinner, is it? Just a few more minutes, I need to inspect your seals and gaskets first..."

Her comment was so easy, so natural; it left him feeling as if his gyros still spun out of his control. He sat were she indicated and prepared himself for the uncomfortable process. The back of what constituted his head retracted with a whisper. Kind of silly, but he felt naked. Couldn't be barer than he was now, without becoming a smear on some microscope slide. It didn't seem to faze Kendall, though.

When Burton had seen to this, Jean-Paul hadn't bothered to ask any questions. The man never would have answered; that would have required him to acknowledge that the cybernetic unit he serviced contained a human being. But Kendall...maybe she wouldn't mind a question or two...

"What...what is the preservation mixture?"

Kendall remained silent, but he could hear her bustling behind him. On his part, at least, the silence was strained. Was she unresponsive because her task required total concentration? Or because he's overstepped himself? Worse, was it because she wasn't overly eager to be the one to educate him in the means by which his survival was maintained? His thoughts wanted to scream again, this time at a different type of darkness.

Finally, he could sense the braincase sliding closed. His hope retreated into its own shell along with it.

"Okay, ready to start?" Kendall's demeanor *seemed* to acknowledge Jean-Paul's humanity, but she still didn't answer his question. He nodded and vowed to maintain his silence. She crossed in front of him and took something that resembled an oversized, dual-compartment IV bag from the ambient temperature suspension unit. One compartment was full of a lightly tinged, clear fluid, the other was empty.

The bag, holding something between four or five pints of fluid, went on a secure pole mount next to the bench where he sat. Kendall reached beneath his chin for the dual-connector umbilical. That he understood. The one connector fed the replacement fluid to the compartment housing his brain; the other drained what was already there into the empty side of the bag for ready disposal. The process wasn't perfect. There was some mixing of the new with the old, but nothing of much concern given the amount of contaminants regularly floating around in an unaltered human's system. Yeah, the process he understood, but the mix itself... that was a mystery.

He watched as she flipped the release. It was unsettling. The changing of the fluid was the only truly physical sensation he felt anymore. Not the most comfortable realization. Any other feeling was transmitted from mechanical sensors distributed at key points of his exoskeleton...more like a cat's whiskers than traditional nerve endings.

"Well, to simplify, it's basically nutrient-infused plasma."

Jean-Paul actually jerked as Kendall's comment drew him out of his thoughts. He had given up on her answering his question.

"*Woh*, watch it..." She braced a hand against his shoulder, gently pressing him back into place. "You're not quite done yet, and I don't feel like cleaning that goop up."

There was a grin on her face that softened the quip. He wished he were still capable of grinning back. This was the first time he had the desire to smile since he'd waken up; seemed such a waste to not be able to follow through. "Thank you," he answered, instead. "Plasma...from blood?"

"Yes, exactly. They even have to use the real stuff," she went on. "The synth variety is fine for supplementing a blood supply, but the brain can't be sustained on it alone. There's some necessary element they can't replicate.

"Whole blood would work, too," she added, a thoughtful expression on her face, "but Medical gets dibs on that."

He didn't want to think about someone else's blood cradling... feeding his brain. Bad enough his body wasn't his own. Plasma was sanitized, he could deal with that; a steady diet of someone else's blood...that was a nightmare.

They remained silent as the process completed. Jean-Paul could feel the difference the new mixture made. His brain was hungry for it, his thoughts raced with renewed energy. He was ready to take on the world. And yet, as the final drops trailed out of the bag, and he watched Kendall go about detaching the umbilical, dread already started to sour the mix. If things went as they did when Burton was on duty this was where she switched him off.

"Don't. Please..." The words came out toneless, but every ounce of desperation bouncing around his brain powered them. For once, his new body responded seamlessly as he stood.

Kendall hesitated, her hand just above the remote shutdown. "Corporate will notice the excess power consumption, someone will investigate."

"No, I won't move... I just want to listen, the drain will be minimal," Jean-Paul promised, praying fervently the woman would have mercy to go along with the compassion she'd already shown him. There was no telling when such an opportunity would arise again. Burton loathed him, took pleasure in throwing the cut-off switch; knew that deep within the metal alloy housing Jean-Paul's mind screamed every conscious moment until he was switched back on.

"Listen to what?" Kendall asked.

"Anything...everything," Jean-Paul answered. His hearing was sensitive enough that conversations several floors down were just barely audible to him, despite the station's sound-dampening measures. What was being said was indecipherable, but as evidence he wasn't alone and disconnected, the words were priceless. "Just don't leave me locked inside my head. You have no idea..."

Or maybe she did. There was a look of deep understanding in her eyes. Instead of initiating shutdown, Kendall crossed to the work bench across the room.

"What's a little drain?" her voice was kind, with an edge of regret, as she turned the knob on a portable sound system one of the other techs had left behind. "Sit back down, and tell me when you can hear this." She edged the knob up until Jean-Paul lifted a servo-powered hand. It was below audible levels for conventional hearing, but to him, it was literally music to his ears.

"Thank you."

Jean-Paul didn't see Chloe Kendall again. But each time he returned for his weekly change-out and encountered Burton, he cherished her memory anew. For the knowledge she had given him, of course, but even more so for what she had done for him; the woman had restored his sense of his own humanity. Now, when Burton's hand reached for the cut-off switch, Jean-Paul merely retreated into the memory of his encounter with Kendall. In his head, he even made new ones as he and Chloe danced to music only he could hear, or simply sat and talked like one human being to another. The urge to scream was still there, but not so much that he couldn't resist it.

Mostly, though, Jean-Paul spent his time out in the mines, earning off his debt faster than anyone in Corporate would admit. He no longer worked completely alone—there weren't nearly enough sites inaccessible to heavy machinery to make that practical. And thanks to Kendall, he no longer accepted the role of metal muscle. Upon occasion he was even known to talk.

Upon occasion, the other miners even answered.

"Hey, Franklin," he called out to the foreman in the middle of his current shift.

Across the tunnel one man raised his head from where he bagged the raw ore that had been dumped out of the robotic extractor. They'd already emptied the Chomp's hopper twice, and similar bundles were stacked everywhere, awaiting offload to the shuttle. The mine was crowded with them, but Corporate like to minimize pick-ups. Miners just had to deal. "What's up, JP?"

"I'm hearing something odd...a vibration in the rock wall...or something off in the Chomp...I can't tell, which. It's too low-frequency for me to place." Around him the other men shifted uncomfortably, casting glances over their shoulders, looking around at the markers on the wall to see how far they were from the mine entrance. There hadn't been any trouble since the collapse that had radically changed his life. All that meant to them, though, was that trouble was overdue. Several of the others gave Jean-Paul dark looks. Miners were a superstitious lot, time and technological advancement certainly hadn't changed that. Not for the first time, Jean-Paul wondered if his survival of the last incident had been luck, or curse.

Franklin, however, merely gave a nod in thanks. "Hey, Antonetti, check the readings; I want scans of the mine tunnel out to fifty meters on all axes." He turned toward the extractor, affectionately called the Chomp, and caught the eye of the mine tech monitoring its progress. "Power the beast down, Otto, give me a diagnostic while we're waiting for the scans.

"Everyone else, settle in for your fifteen," Franklin ordered the crew.

The men mostly hunkered down against the nearest bundle of ore, their eyes closing as they pulled rations from their pocket and methodically chewed, half sleeping through the meal as if they weren't sure which one they needed more. Jean-Paul simply walked from one end of the tunnel to the other, still trying to pinpoint the anomaly that had set all this in motion. It was no use, though. His hearing may have been augmented, but it was still processed by a human brain. He'd lost the sound sometime about when everything was shut down, unfortunately that still didn't help pinpoint the culprit.

"Everything looks clear, boss," Antonetti reported to the foreman. A similar response came from Otto. Jean-Paul was glad to hear nothing was showing up. Of course, he didn't relax any. Just because trouble didn't register, didn't mean it wasn't there.

Fifty meters, apparently, hadn't been enough.

Five meters past that point the faint creak at the threshold of Jean-Paul's hearing culminated in a pop. That, of course, was drowned out by the rumple of protesting rock. Beneath their feet, the mine debris began to dance; dust filled the air.

"Back! Everybody get back!" Franklin barked the order, waving his crew toward the distant mine entrance behind them.

Jean-Paul's sensors detected noxious compounds seeping into the air supply heavy enough to make him glad he no longer had a sense of smell. Fortunately, his system filtered such things out. Around him, the other men hadn't quite realized, though their breath came a little more labored, punctuating the mine's rumbles with sharp coughs.

The mining equipment, with the exception of the emergency packs, was abandoned in place as they all turned and fled, as any good mine rat had the sense to do. Only Jean-Paul couldn't keep up. His exoskeleton wasn't designed for running or rapid movements. Shuffling along at the rear as best he could, he watched in horror as the tunnel ahead began to rain down dust. First fine puffs. Then steady streams. The coughing intensified.

Sound was peculiar below ground, surrounded by rock and heavy minerals. Contained, with plenty of angular surfaces to distort and echo. So hard to tell which way it came from.

"Stop." But Jean-Paul wasn't designed to yell, either. No one heard, or if they did, no one paid attention. They did enough yelling of their own, though, as the rock beneath them rumbled a bit more. Dust came down in a sheet on their heads, followed closely by the roar of the collapsing tunnel.

Not again. The front edge of the fleeing group disappeared beneath a cascade of ore. Antonetti and five others vanished from sight. The second tier scrambled back, encountering the odd boulder from above, but escaping alive, if less intact. Four men were left, not counting Jean-Paul, Franklin and Otto among them. They scrambled back toward him, groaning and hissing as the unstable tunnel above them threatened further collapse.

"Back to the Chomp, now," he ordered, though it was not his place. No one argued at his taking charge; Franklin could barely stand and his eyes were glazed. There were signs that he had taken a blow to the head. The others were equally hampered by panic and shock. Jean-Paul lifted the foreman as carefully as he could and moved back down the tunnel to the rock extractor. "Quick, we have to get the hopper emptied before the rest of the tunnel goes."

The men complied despite clear injuries that had to have made the effort excruciating, Jean-Paul set Franklin down where he would be sheltered by the extractor and then added his metal muscle to the task at hand.

There was barely room for the men inside the cleared compartment. None at all for Jean-Paul. If there was any chance he could dig his way out, he would have, but it was too likely disturbing the cave-in would bring the rest of the tunnel down. Instead, he huddled in the lee of the larger machine and prayed the mountain was done falling on them.

Perhaps he wasn't thrilled with his current life, but he found he wanted to keep it nonetheless.

It took six days for most of the men to die. Injury...deprivation... despair. Each took their toll as faces grew gaunt beneath their veil of rock dust. The water gave out on day four, as only one emergency pack made it back to the hopper. By day five, the power pack on the comm lost its charge, cutting them off from any contact with the rescue crews. The despair grew plenty thick then.

As each man was lost, Jean-Paul bundled the bodies in the ore sacks and slid them in the space beneath the extractor. Finally, at day seven only Franklin was left. There was now plenty of room for both of them in the hopper.

"Do you hear them yet, JP?"

"Hard to tell through all the rock, sir," Jean-Paul answered his foreman. "But I believe so." For once he didn't mind that his vocal processors were incapable of inflection.

Made it easier to lie.

"Good...good..." Franklin's words slurred. "So thirsty..."

He wondered how long the man would last. There was no need to touch Franklin to know he was burning up. Jean-Paul was starting to have a hard time of it himself. His power pack was in the red zone, with perhaps two days left if he restricted his movement. As for his preservation mixture, it was feeling pretty thick. It was getting harder to think and, if he wasn't mistaken, he'd begun to crave plasma.

As Franklin fell into unconsciousness, Jean-Paul found himself toying with the connectors of his umbilical. Flashes of his conversation with Kendall drifted through his mind, particularly one comment she'd made: *Whole blood would work too...*

Without intending to, he began to keen. His mind recoiled violently at the thoughts that rose unbidden. If he'd still had a stomach he would have heaved. Despite his need to conserve, he got up and left the hopper. Was it desperation, or could he hear a faint scratching on the far side of the rubble pile? He prayed as he had not done since before his new life. Again a faint sound; and the barest bit of hope rekindled.

Turning to take the news to Franklin, Jean-Paul suddenly found himself tumbling sideway. The only way to describe it was a dizzy spell. He fought to focus. The exoskeleton was a bitch to steer when his mind was loopy. He managed to keep himself off the ground, but fairly staggered back to the hopper.

"Hey, Franklin..." he started, but darkness flooded his optics and he found himself on his knees, gripping the raised hatch of the hopper to stop himself from sliding all the way down. What could only be described as a ravenous hunger took over... A new chemical flooded his brain, something foreign and insistent. Artificial. It kind of reminded him of the investors' demonstration, where his violent impulses had been suppressed, what seemed like ages ago. The craving reared up once more, crippling him. This impulse was clear: Survive.

His soul screamed, even as his hand reached up and withdrew the umbilical. He watched as it extended, completely independent of his own desire; moaned as the feed half of the connector slid into Franklin's carotid artery, the drain half merely dangled.

This couldn't be happening...he didn't want to live this bad! Of course, he should have known the Corporation would protect their investment by any means necessary, though he doubted they would have anticipated this.

Letting go of the hatch, Jean-Paul allowed himself to slump to the ground, desperately wishing the connector would fall out. But no, the greedy little bloodsucker hung on. He was forced to watch as the deep red fluid flowed toward him, and the murky, yellowed preservation mixture drained down the side of Franklin's neck. Somehow the man never woke up, though a part of Jean-Paul noticed even yet the shallow rise and fall of his chest.

More and more he saw himself as the monster they had made him. A parasite preserving his own pathetic life.

He wanted to be sick.

He wanted to die.

He wanted to deny how absolutely invigorated he felt now that the process was done. If he'd thought fresh plasma was rich, what he experienced now was like euphoria. Reaching out, he tugged on the umbilical. A crimson trail ran down the front of his chassis from the connector, residual he'd never noticed before when it was just plasma. It was quickly obscured by the spray of lifeblood spurting from across the compartment. He tore his gaze away from the evidence of his horror, looking instead toward Franklin.

Revulsion and guilt sent their chemical cocktail swirling through his stolen blood. Jean-Paul yanked over the emergency pack and frantically tried to administer a pressure bandage before his savior bled out. His "hands" were too clumsy, the skin too slick. He could hear more than feel as fragile cartilage gave way beneath his efforts. Falling back against the compartment wall, Jean-Paul's tortured moan came out in one long, continuous tone. He couldn't manage anything more.

His spirit wanted to retreat into the darkness he'd previously loathed, to hide from this reality. But that wasn't possible, and he just sat there, optics trained on Franklin, with only one thing to be grateful for: there was no longer any chance the man would meet the same ill fate that had brought Jean-Paul to this pass.

Now fully alert, his brain was assaulted by sensory input he'd been too fogged to process before. He began to notice the sound of shifting rubble, and the faint cries of the crews. They weren't close...perhaps ten, twenty meters from breaking through, from the sound of it. If it wouldn't have place them in danger, he would have brought the rest of the tunnel crashing down on the evidence of what he'd done, himself included. Only that was not an option, even if whatever chemical corporate had programmed into him would let him carry out the act, he would not be responsible for taking even more lives.

Oh God, he prayed. *Please don't let Kendall be among the rescue crew.* He couldn't stand if she were to see him like this. Bad enough his sense of his own humanity was shattered; he couldn't bear to see the same loathing reflected in her eyes.

He still didn't scream...but he couldn't help but cry.

Tequila Sunset

By

Brad Aiken

"Ouch!" Sarah's hand shot up to rub the sting from her neck, and felt the warm trail of stickiness oozing along her skin.

Twisting away from the comfort of her overstuffed down pillow, she looked curiously at the man lying next to her. "Did you just bite me?" She brought her blood-tinged hand up between them, confirming with a glance what her mind held in disbelief. "I can't believe you just bit me. What the hell's wrong with you?"

A youthful man of not-so-rugged proportions leaned over her, smiling serenely. "Oh, come on. It was just a little love nibble."

She studied his face. "I don't even know who the hell you are."

His smile wilted. "But last night..."

"Hell, I was drunk as a skunk." She ran her hand through the thick mat of sandy brown curls surrounding her face, oblivious to the streak of dark purple her fingers made along the way. "All I remember is how cute you looked sitting at the bar." She looked him over slowly, starting at the head and working her way down, lifting the sheet just enough to take a peek. "Obviously, I was drunker than I thought."

His big brown eyes drooped. "You *must* remember. I told you *everything* last night." He waited for some sign of revelation, but none came. "How could you forget? After I finished, you winked and told me you knew there was something special about me the moment you saw me. I figured you thought I was joking, so I went through it all again to make sure, but you didn't say another word. You just took my hand and held on tight until we were up here tearing each other's clothes off. It was magical."

"For you maybe."

"Hey, you had a good time too."

She shrugged. "I'll have to take your word for it. What the hell did you tell me anyway? If I ever hear it again, I want to be sure not make the same mistake."

He grimaced. "You really don't remember, do you? I guess I should have known you were only OK with it because you were stone drunk."

Sarah shifted her body and propped herself up on an elbow. "So what's your big secret? You might as well tell me; you're already in my bed."

"You'll just think I'm nuts."

"Then why did you tell me last night?"

"I thought maybe you were different."

"I like to think I am. Go ahead, spill it. Who knows? I fell for it once, maybe you'll get lucky again."

He sighed deeply. "All right, here goes." He cleared his throat. "I'm a vampire."

She laughed and fell back into the sheets. "No...really, what is it?"

His jaw clenched tightly without breaking even the slightest of smiles.

Sarah's grin faded. "You are *seriously* deranged."

The big brown eyes studying her sunk under a furrowed brow. "But I love you."

Sarah rose, pulling off the top sheet as she did, wrapping herself tightly in the white silk. "Get your stuff and get out of here." She walked to the window by the bed and opened the curtains.

The morning sun hadn't yet peeked over the horizon, but the room began to glow with the approaching day. He turned away from the window and winced, bloody fangs hanging over his bottom lip.

"Shit!" Sarah jumped back, and the sheet fell to her feet.

He smiled. "Wow. Even better in the light."

Sarah scurried to pull the sheet around her, clinging to it tightly as she rose to her feet. She looked back as he finished licking his fangs clean.

"Take those things out, you fruitcake. I can't believe you stuck them in me."

He wiggled them firmly. "Can't..." They didn't budge. "See?"

She approached cautiously and gave them a firm tug.

"Ouch!" he yelped. "That hurt."

As the room began to brighten, the sharp teeth began to recede.

"Shit." She jumped back again, this time being sure not to expose herself. "You're serious...shit."

"Of course I'm serious," he pleaded. "About that and about my love for you. Nothing else matters."

"How about that I don't love you?"

"You just don't know me yet."

"Thank God."

"That hurts."

She reached for the bite mark on her neck. "So does this."

"Yeah," he sighed. "I remember when I first got mine."

"You mean...I can't believe I'm asking this, but does this mean..."

He nodded. "Fraid so. Sorry, I thought it was what you wanted."

"Are you nuts? Didn't it occur to you to ask me when I was sober?"

"I was kinda blitzed myself. But I do love you and once you get to know me, you'll love me too. I'm irresistible." He grinned, and with the fangs having receded to normal teeth, didn't look half bad. "That's all that matters."

"How about the fact that I'm afraid of the dark? Utterly, panic-inducing, psychopathically *petrified* of the dark."

"Well...that *could* be a problem." He looked down.

"Ya think?"

The pain in his pale face was increasing by the minute. "Got a closet I can crash in for the day?"

Sarah threw her hands up. "What the hell." She walked over to her bedroom closet and opened the door. "Just don't touch the lingerie or I'll fry you myself."

He nodded and came up beside her. "Ooh, a walk-in. Mind if I take the top shelf back there?"

"Knock yourself out."

"Thanks."

"I meant that literally."

"Sense of humor. I love that in a woman." He walked into the closet without looking back to see Sarah roll her eyes.

She grabbed the clothes she needed for work, then started to shut the door. She stopped abruptly. "By the way, what's your name?"

"Bram."

She didn't even try to hold back the laughter. "Right."

"No, really."

"Let me guess...Stoker, right?"

"Nah. Bernstein. My parents had my life planned out from day one. It's a Jewish thing."

She shook her head. "So are you gonna turn into bat now, or what?"

"Later." Bram looked around the closet. "You have a shoebox or something in case I need to...you know..." Sarah stared blankly. "I'm gonna be in here a while."

"Ahh." Sarah pointed to a box in the corner. "Just make sure you take the shoes out first." She eyed him as he stood with his hands folded in front of his waist. "So...when are you going to do the bat thing?"

"It's really not polite to watch."

She cocked her head. "I don't know who's nuttier, you or me." She bit down on her lip so hard, a trickle of blood ran from the spot.

His black eyebrows scrunched together, making a streak across his white chalkboard of a face. "That's not very nice."

"Sorry."

The frown morphed into a smile. "Unless it's an offer," he winked.

"No...*God* no...Sorry." Her faced turned red.

It's was Bram's turn to laugh.

Sarah didn't. "This is all just a hoax, isn't it?"

"No hoax."

"Then when am I gonna...you know..."

"Not for a while." He shook his head. "It takes about three weeks. You won't even start to feel anything for a few days yet. Might want to put in for the night shift though."

"Cute." She slammed the door on his grinning face.

"Hold it!" Sarah called out as she raced through the oversized revolving door to the Bella Lugo Apartments where she'd been living for the past three years.

A thick hand shot out from between the closing doors, and they sprung open.

"Thanks," she said as she walked in, pulling off her wool cap.

A squat elderly man with graying sideburns and little else on his age-spotted head nodded pleasantly. "Long day, huh?"

"You don't know the half of it," she sputtered, tucking her gloves and hat into the pockets of her full-length black wool coat. "Bad enough you gotta find your way home in the dark at 5 o'clock, but it's cold as a witch's..." She stopped herself and eyed the kindly gentleman with a blush.

"They were cold when I was your age too, honey."

Sarah laughed through rosy cheeks. The elevator dinged as it came to a halt on the thirteenth floor. "Well, this is me," she chirped. "Have a nice evening." She scurried out, rounding the corner to the right without looking back and made a bee-line for apt 1313, crossing her legs and bouncing in front of the door as she reached for her keys. The door flew open with a twist of the wrist, and Sarah threw her coat on the foyer credenza as she raced towards the bathroom. It wasn't until she was washing up that she was lured by the scent of fresh basil and garlic wafting in through the crack under the door.

She twisted her hair into a thick pony tail and pulled it over her right shoulder, holding on with both hands as she walked slowly toward the kitchen. She stopped abruptly at the archway to the dining room. The table was set with her grandmother's fine china and silver atop a white lace linen cloth; two crystal wine glasses filled with Merlot were perfectly spaced on either side of the half-filled bottle resting on an embroidered gold felt doily in the center.

As she stood, speechless, Bram stepped out of the kitchen and smiled. He had on the same clothes he'd worn to the bar last night, a pair of new denim jeans and a powder blue turtleneck that minimized the pallor of his skin. His black hair shined with a dab of gel holding it in place and his deeply set brown eyes were strong but serene.

"Well," Sarah whispered, "don't *you* clean up nice."

Bram grinned a mouthful of polished white teeth.

"Oh, God. I'm a mess." Sarah started to fuss with her hair. It was futile without a mirror. She gave her black knit sweater a tug at the bottom, then one final sweep of both hands to smooth back her curls. "Don't you know a woman needs some lead time to get beautiful?"

He laughed. "Please. Don't change a thing."

Sarah breathed in the aroma. "Garlic?"

"Myth number one about vampires," Bram said. "We love garlic. Garlic bread, garlic pesto sauce, cloves of roasted garlic on toast. OK, raw garlic, maybe not so much. But garlic butter sauce over linguine, served with a fine Merlot..." He kissed the tips of his fingers, and flung the kiss into the air. "Please," he motioned her to sit and handed her a glass of wine.

She looked up at him dubiously as he tapped his glass against hers. "And for the main course...steak tartar?"

"Heavens no." His face squinched up. "I'm a vegetarian."

Sarah's mouth dropped open. "Myth number two?"

"Nah," Bram whispered, "I'm just weird."

Sarah laughed.

"We eat the same stuff after we turn as we did before. The blood sucking is myth number two. The only time we bite is to start the transition for our soul mates. It's an enzyme we inject that does the trick. No sucking of blood."

Sarah looked dubious.

He shrugged. "Sorry to disappoint you."

"Anything but." She eyed the spread on the table. "You mind? I'm famished."

He piled a generous helping of pasta on her plate, then sat across from her. "After you, mademoiselle."

"Very charming, Bram, but I'm still not ready to forget that you bit me."

"Nor should you, my dear."

The days passed quickly. Sarah tried to send Bram on his way after that first dinner, but he convinced her she'd need him when she started to turn. She was less than thrilled, but acquiesced, and as the days passed, came to look forward to his gourmet cooking and charmingly quirky company.

"Right on time." Bram greeted Sarah at the door and took her coat.

She inhaled deeply. "Umm…Portobello Marsala! You make it very hard to hate you, you know."

Bram just smiled.

"So Bram?" She looked into his eyes. "How come I still don't feel it? I don't' feel a bit different than the day you bit me."

"Don't know. You should be starting to feel pretty irritable when you go out in the sun by now. Nothing?"

"Nada."

"Hmph." He scratched his head and winced.

Sarah noticed a patch of red on his forehead and reached up to tilt it down so she could take a closer look. "What's this?"

"You could have told me you had a sunlamp in the master bath."

She pushed his head away. "Serves you right for going in there."

"I just needed some soap. The guest bath was out."

"Oh. Sorry."

Bram shrugged. "I'll live."

"So what about me? What's going to happen to me?"

"I'll call my doctor tonight and see what he says about the transition. His office opens at one."

"AM?"

"Of course. Wouldn't be a very busy practice if people had to go out in the sun to get there. Maybe he can recommend a good shrink to help you with that darkness phobia too."

"I'll use a flashlight," she muttered.

Sarah found herself getting progressively more tired as the week wore on. Not that she felt any substantive difference, but Bram was a bundle of energy, and she couldn't resist his infectious enthusiasm in showing her nightlife all over the city; people and places she never knew existed.

Friday night was a welcome relief. It had been exactly one week since first bite, and she dragged herself home from work, thankful for the rest promised by the upcoming weekend. Bram greeted her at the door as usual.

Sarah handed over her coat. "So, what did your tooth fairy say?"

Bram looked confused.

"You know, that doctor of yours. Weren't you going to see him last night after you dropped me off?"

"Ah. Yes. He was stumped."

"Great."

"He asked me to get a blood sample."

She put her hand to her neck. "Oh no you don't."

"From your arm."

"Oh." Sarah eyed him. "You?"

"I was a lab tech once upon a time; night shift at the blood bank."

The laughter poured out. "Talk about your kid in a candy store."

He frowned. "I told you we don't do that."

"Not even a little?"

He frowned harder.

"Sorry," she blurted between giggles.

Bram pulled out a syringe. "So where do you want to do this?"

"How about in *your* arm?"'

He shook his head. "Come on. It'll just take a couple minutes. I'm good at this...really."

He took her hand and led her into the kitchen. Sitting adjacent to her, he placed her arm on the table, applied a tourniquet, and drew the blood with ease.

"Humph," she nodded. "You *are* good. So how long will it take?"

"About a week."

"A week? Where the hell is he sending it? China?'

He shook his head. "Nah. Transylvania. "

The weekend was a series of all-nighters. Bram took her to clubs she never dreamed she'd be able to get into, sneaked her into the Museum of Fine Arts through a hidden corridor, where they had the whole place to themselves at three in the morning, and wined and dined her at penthouse clubs that were open all night. She could never tell the vamps from the mortals, but they all seemed to know Bram. She felt like a celebrity, and he treated her as if he had a window into her soul.

She called in sick Monday morning, and then every day that week.

"Aren't you worried about losing your job?"

"It sucks anyway."

Bram was rarely at a loss for words, but he sat solemnly, studying the room. "That really was very thoughtful." He motioned to the black-out blinds she'd had installed on all the windows.

Sarah shrugged. "I figured I'd need them soon enough; that closet doesn't look so big when you think of it as a bedroom."

"Yeah, about that." He stared at the floor. "Dr. Price called. He got the results. Seems I screwed up."

She looked up at him. "Oh, no. You are *not* jabbing me with that needle again."

"No, no. I didn't mean that. The sample was fine."

"What then?"

"I guess I drank a few too many Tequila Sunrises the night we met."

"We both did. So what?"

"Doc says they screw up the enzyme. It gets deactivated by the Sunrise."

"So? We'll try again. Bite me."

Bram looked up. "Excuse me?"

She winked. "Bite me, dough boy."

He was in shock.

"Yeah," she shook her head, "I can't believe I'm saying it either. But these past two weeks...for the first time in my life, I'm living. Doing this forever sounds pretty good to me, and doing it with you..." She leaned over and gave him a kiss.

A tear welled up in his eye.

Sarah put her hand on his. "Aren't you happy? Isn't this what you wanted all along?"

"Of course it is. Only I never thought you'd feel this way...not really. I was just hoping for forgiveness."

"Got more than you bargained for, huh?"

"More...and less."

Sarah backed away. "Great!" she yelped. "Now that you've got me, game over. Is that it?"

"No, Sarah." He stood and moved toward her, but she shrugged him off. "You've got it all wrong. I want you more than anything."

"Then bite me."

"It won't work."

"Why? You've been out drinking again? I don't buy it."

"When the enzyme was injected the first time, it wasn't just deactivated. It formed an immune complex."

"Huh?"

"You're immune, Sarah. Even if I bite you again, if *any* vampire bites you, you can't be turned."

"You mean I'm stuck like this forever?"

He nodded wearily.

"But I can't live like that again."

"Isn't that what you really wanted?"

"Yeah, at first. But now you've ruined all that. I love you, you moron. Don't you know that? The enzyme may not have worked, but you transformed me anyway. I can't go back to the way I was."

He looked into her eyes. "I'll be here for as long as you'll have me."

"And what? I work days, you work nights and we share an occasional meal in between?"

He shrugged. "Money's not a problem. You don't have to work."

"Thank God. I was dreading going back to my boss to grovel. But still, what about when I get old? Don't you stay young forever, or is that another myth?"

"No myth. You'll just have to settle for a younger man."

"That's not what I meant."

He smiled. "I know."

"No way to get that enzyme to kick in?"
"Nope."
Her head drooped. "Damn."
"Sorry."
"Ah well, it's only eternal life."
They sat quietly side by side, staring at the wall.
"So," Sarah said with a sigh. "Got plenty of money, huh?"
"Yup."
"Good. We're going to need a bigger closet."

Whispers During Still Moments

By

Linda Addison

"I need to tell you something," Adina said, straddling her latest victim on the dank ground in the alley. He had been handsome, with a strong chin, high cheekbones. Arrogant in his tailored blue suit and perfect hair cut when they met at the Greenwich Village wine bar earlier in the evening. The designer sunglasses tucked away in his suit pocket were going to look good on her.

His ruined face gurgled. Blood dribbled from the sides of his mouth, streaking his blond hair. She didn't usually eat meat, but his kiss had been so sweet, his tongue so tender, she had to take it. More importantly, his eyes were still intact, though glazed over by blood loss.

"Don't go yet, listen . . ." Adina said softly, leaning close to him, licking the blood from his face. It was cooling in the night air, but it was still savory. She whispered in his right ear, in her native African Amharic language, giving him part of the secret. "Fumiya ayzie, kambui sipo."

Trembling with release, she growled, ripped his throat and drank his warm blood. The ritual filled her body with tingling energy. As Adina swallowed his sweet blood her organs revived, her internal systems from nervous, endocrine to her muscles and skin became younger, stronger, as if she were connected to the endless force of the Earth itself. This was the gift granted to first generation vampires by the Whisper, their secret to apparent immortality.

She stretched, enjoying the increased vigor, wiping the

blood from her mouth, licking it from her hands. A scent made her glance into the shadows of the buildings. The sweet, sour smell made her stomach twitch. Something ran away.

She jumped up and chased the figure down the alley, but it was gone by the time she reached where the darkness ended and the street lights of the Village intruded. The sidewalk was full of people. Standing in the shadow of the building, she couldn't tell which way the creature ran. The smell, the hot tendril of its motion simply stopped as if it had disappeared into thin air, not something a normal human being could do.

She licked her lips, the taste of the watcher's scent was a first generation vampire. That odor was familiar, it had been stalking from a distance but tonight came closer. The sensation of ants crawling under the skin of her neck and scalp tickled her as the thing ran away. Once it hit the street her physical sensing of it abruptly ended. This wasn't a First. There was none of the maniac anxiety building inside of her, a typical reaction when one First met another.

The scent was primal, even though it wasn't an animal. The being wasn't a normal human. They couldn't run that quickly. Could the thing have been a Remade, a human made into vampire by a First?

Adina walked back to the body. She rubbed the back of her neck, tingling danced lightly up and down her spine, another feeling she had when near another First. Whatever creature was, Adina had been so engrossed in the ritual and feeding that she hadn't perceived being observed before. It dared to come so close Adina could still tastes the thing's body heat where it had huddled in the shadows. A shiver went through her, how did the strange being elude her? She would have to be more careful. Even a First could be destroyed.

She used the dead man's clothes to wipe the blood splattered on her black leather halter, bare midriff and leather pants. The blood didn't come out of her belly button and silver belly ring easily, but what little was left wouldn't be obvious against her dark, brown skin. After shoving the man's body into a large trash bin, she put on her black leather jacket and his sunglasses.

She patted her close-cropped hair in place and straightened her clothes. The alley was quiet, with only the sound of rats scratching in garbage, the wind moving scraps of paper, and the distant murmur of traffic disturbing the peace.

Adina walked out of the alley rejuvenated and intoxicated. The Fall air was cool, so good against her body, running warm with fresh blood. The Village street was crowded with people out for dinner, movies, or just enjoying the crisp air of September. They reminded her of flies flitting around dead carrion, feeding off the remains of an Earth they had little regard for, rushing through their days. So many of them. So much food.

Two thousand years earlier she had been too aware of their lives, but the millennia had worn away her bond to them. Once she had cared for people, those in Sama, her home village in the Wello region of Central Africa. In time, everyone she cared about died. Each loss, each love ended by illness, old age or disinterest wore her heart thin. She questioned more than once the point of caring for anyone, of falling in love, until the pain and sadness were no longer worth it.

The last time she loved one of them was hundreds of years ago. Tacuma had dark sad eyes, a quiet voice, beautiful dark brown skin and strong shoulders that Adina loved to caress and kiss when they walked together. She was convinced he knew there was something different with her, but Tacuma never questioned Adina. Not when she went on excursions at night, not even when she asked him to leave his village and move to an unpopulated area. Moving was the only way she could hide the fact that she didn't age.

Tacuma truly loved Adina and would do anything she asked, without questioning the reason. Every time she looked in his eyes she saw his death, so Adina ended the relationship with him. She closed her heart and accepted the Earth as her only partner.

The patterns of people's birth, life and death flickered through time over the years, like fire flies. Humans managed to add some years to their life span over the last thousand years, but death still came soon in comparison to her life. Hunting and feeding became the center of her pleasure. The Earth and the Whisper didn't change, her only true friends.

Adina walked slowly through the crowded streets, the rushing of blood singing to her like the river of her home village hundreds of years ago. Occasionally when a man or woman glanced at her, blushed or took a deep breath as they passed by, their heartbeat quickened. They couldn't always know why they reacted to her, unconnected to their animal spirits. Although their minds didn't know they were prey, their bodies did.

Adina closed her eyes for a moment and continued walking. Even with no sight she could sense them like the warmth of bright lights. Easy to avoid, blood running in their bodies like electricity. She licked her lips, sucked in air for a deep breath—their scent spread on the Earth like an infection. Food, gasoline, cologne, garbage, leather, cotton, rubber of their clothes and shoes was thick in the air. It was disgusting.

She fingered the gold figure on the chain around her neck, the symbol of Mercury, fire, like her, the great destroyer, cleanser of the Earth. The heels of her boots clicked against the concrete sidewalk, but underneath the Earth waited. She could feel it, her oldest companion, next to the Whisper in her dreams. She sighed. Whether they were a blessing or a curse didn't matter. she could no more control the Whisper than she could the Earth or her blood hunger.

Adina felt someone watching from a distance, probably the creature from the alley. She had the same tingling in her neck and spine. It wasn't a First, but there was something about how sensitized she felt to its presence that was similar to being in the vicinity of another First.

She stopped in front of a clothing store and looked at the people passing by reflected in the window. She saw nothing unusual about anyone. Whoever it was could be across the street or blocks away. How was she being blocked from targeting its position? This was no normal human.

In the past she had been followed by a Remade, who had been studying her, hoping to find some way to live the extended, virtually immortal lives of a First, wanting desperately to link into the Whisper. Adina killed her when the Remade wouldn't leave her territory.

This thing watching her now was different. There was impressive power in it. Nothing had challenged her in hundreds of years. This could be interesting.

Taking her time pretending to window shop, Adina walked down Eighth Street towards the West Side. The side streets were quieter. People were home in the apartments over the closed shops, and all the sidewalk action was along the main avenues and streets, where the restaurants and clubs were located.

There was a deep growl from an alley between two buildings on an off street. Normal humans couldn't hear the sound over the city noise, but it vibrated clearly in Adina's ears. Curious, Adina turned into the small empty street and followed the growl down the alley. She crept up on a tall African-American man with thick, long dread locks holding a knife to the throat of an short, older Hispanic man with his hands bound behind his back. The bound man's sharp features were contorted in pain.

A quick rush of adrenalin made her tremble slightly, her reaction to being near a Remade. The older man was a vampire, his growl a call for help. His acrid scent permeated the alley with fear and disorder. This level of chaos usually came from a vampire created in less than a year and with little guidance from his Maker. No wonder he had been captured.

"Tell me where, now," the younger man said, letting the knife draw more blood. The dark blood of the Remade surged out of the neck wound like thick gravy, joining the puddle of blood on the ground. Judging from the thick constancy of his blood, Adina would guess he hadn't fed in a while. The young man was bleeding out the vampire.

Adina frowned. The blood of Remade was bitter. She had tasted one once, before killing it.

The older man wavered and looked in her direction, his dark, deep-set eyes locking onto hers, pleading for help. The knife-holder glanced quickly in the same direction but returned his attention to the vampire. Adina was in the shadows of a building and knew he couldn't see her. This wasn't the person watching her earlier, he was a normal human being with no apparent special abilities other than being cunning enough to capture an incompetent Remade.

She shook her head and growled so low the human couldn't hear her, but loud enough for the vampire to get message. He slumped to his knees. It was clear he understood Adina wouldn't help him.

Adina slipped away. Whatever the young man's mission, let him kill the vampire. She didn't want the competition in her territory anyway. Hopefully he wasn't stupid enough to cross paths with her. But if he did she'd consider adding him to the collection she kept in her basement. She smiled. Of all humans, vampire hunters were her favorite to play with.

Chun Zhang kept his distance, even though he suspected Adina sensed him watching. He wasn't prepared to face her yet. Firsts were acutely aware of their surroundings. He needed to have a good sense of her movement around the city. Her feeding ritual was the same as the few other Firsts he had observed. He wanted to check out her house. This would be harder now that she knew he was trailing her, but not impossible.

When she ducked into the alleyway he considered following, but didn't believe she was going to feed twice in one night. Even from two blocks away, he could feel she was sated. Instead, Chun maintained his distance, retained the hot tendril of psychic energy he picked up from Adina and made sure he didn't project his exact location. Chun was very good at finding lost people, and even better at tracking Firsts once he had a taste of their energy. Usually he needed to be in physical contact with something of the person, but the psychic energy of a First when feeding was so strong he could shadow them without ever touching anything of theirs.

He felt guilty, as always, at having seen her kill. That never changed. But he couldn't have saved the young man. No point in thinking about that. He had to keep his mind on the mission: destroying her. This was a first generation vampire, rare and powerful. He needed to capture the ritual words she gave her dying victims before finishing her. The more words he collected, the closer Chun got to being able to use that power against them and perhaps even become fully human again.

He fought the dread that crept into his gut when he thought of using the words. But the fourth Noble Truth of Buddhism gave him reason to hope: to end suffering he must change the way he thinks and perceives. He had to believe learning how to use these words would end much suffering. There was little else to hope.

He couldn't get close enough to hear what she whispered tonight, even with his enhanced hearing, but Chun could tell it wasn't English. Probably her native African language. Following her from a distance for a few weeks, he watched her shop for clothes and jewelry, up town and down. She called herself Adina, which meant She Has Saved in Amharic. A fitting irony.

It made him sick to see men and women alike attracted to her, when at any moment they could become her next meal. Not that she wasn't attractive in her own right, with her long muscular limbs, wide hips and skin the color of coffee beans, her almond shaped brown eyes and full mouth that were on the verge of smiling, all the time. She walked with a roll of her hips that often drew attention, like a ship cutting through ice floes, people noticed her when she passed. Although she could be hundreds of years old, she looked barely twenty years old. After feeding she shone with life, the life of her latest victim.

Whether he liked it or not, the cost of destroying a First was to watch a few fellow humans die. Nisi, his teacher and his love, had made that clear. She'd called a few days ago to say she would be in town this week. He needed to see her. Nisi made him feel human. Their love, even with the distance their work required, gave him reason to continue. Although he was stronger and faster than a normal human, Chun suspected he might need Nisi's help with this First.

In the long run, destroying one First saved many humans and broke another link in the making of other vampires. This is what he had to keep in mind. Humans had a better chance of surviving the vampire plague if the First could be eradicated.

A shudder went through him, a sharp pain throbbed in his forehead. One of his debilitating headaches erupted. Time to go home. Once the headache started, there was a good chance the rest of the seizure would come and he didn't want to be on the street when that happened. He hailed a taxi.

Home was a small, two story building tucked in the downtown meat district. The building was perfect with its old fashion coal furnace and thick brick walls. Blocks away from the residential area, it was full of activity during the day and deserted at night. The perfect place for him to live, far enough away from vampire hunting grounds, especially a cocky First. They rarely felt the need to hide in the dark corners where humans didn't go. They enjoyed flaunting their virtual immortality, sometimes even becoming part of social circles that made them visible to anyone looking for them. Adina owned a small house off a private courtyard in an upscale part of the city. She practically glowed with over-confidence.

Chun stumbled into the kitchen through the side entrance of his house, locking the inner and outer doors. Ping, his dog, a large white and grey German Shepherd Wolf mix, padded down the hall to meet him. Chun reset the perimeter alarms before going down the stairway in the kitchen, to the basement to collapse on a small bed. Ping whimpered, sensing the attack and nudged him gently with her nose.

"Good girl," he slurred through the pain, patting her head.

Chun pulled open the drawer of the small table next to the bed and took one of the capsules out of the jar. He popped the pill into his mouth, took a gulp of water from a water bottle, shoved his plastic mouthpiece in and curled up on the bed. Ping laid down on the floor, next to his bed, waiting for the attack to end.

He wasn't sure the ground herbs in the capsules helped, but Lucky Falcon, the Navaho doctor promised they wouldn't make him feel worse and they could assist the recovery process, so Chun promised to take them.

He couldn't go to a regular doctor and tell them that the blood of a vampire, mixed in with his own, periodically became dominant, and as this blood entered his brain Chun had seizures. On the other hand, it was also the same infection that gave him the abilities to be an efficient hunter of their kind. *What doesn't kill you, makes you stronger.*

The storm exploded in his body. The seizures began as the vampire blood fought to take over his blood stream. Kidneys, liver, heart, lungs, every major organ resisted the blood that now flowed through them. His mind floated into a dream-like state, away from the gripping headache and spasms. His thoughts drifted from words to images and memories, swinging back and forth in time as the attack blossomed into full force.

. . . Chun as a child, in China, riding high on his grandfather's shoulders, his grandmother scolding them to be careful, looking up at clouds shaped like dinosaurs . . .

. . . in their first home in California, aluminum siding and clean cement sidewalks, a mountain of leaves in their backyard in the fall . . .

. . . Chun in college, his heart skipping a beat when he first saw Tina . . . sitting on the bed on their wedding night, the room filled with candle light and the scent of fresh roses, Tina so beautiful he had tears in his eyes,. . . walking on the beach with his wife at night . . . his mother cooking meat dumplings . . . blood . . . everywhere . . . blood . . . the man knocking him out with one hand while sucking the life out of his wife . . . someone singing Happy Birthday in a dark room . . . coming to lying next to his wife's body . . . her blood soaking into his clothes, a pale man kneeling over Chun drawing on his chest with her blood . . . cutting into a rare steak, the blood seeping onto the plate in the shape of a leaf . . . the sharp pain of a bite through his skin, his scream . . . Tina throwing her wedding bouquet in the air, the white roses arcing in the air . . . "she died too soon. You must listen, I have something to tell you" the man said to Chun and then whispered in Chun's ear in French, "avec envie, légèrement". . . blood . . .the vampire's face covered in his wife's blood, shuddering with pleasure as he caressed Chun's neck, baring his teeth for the last bite . . . red, white and green balloons in a bright blue sky . . .a glint of metal, the vampire's head falling from its body . . . his wife's laughter . . . blood . . . a large brown-skinned woman standing over Chun with a sword . . . blood . . .

Ping licked his hand, recognizing the end of the attack. Chun slowly sat up and took a couple of sips from the water bottle. He knew better than to stand up immediately. It usually took him about twenty minutes to fully recover. He put his head down and breathed slowly, waiting for his body to readjust as the vampire blood became passive again.

Nisi, his savior. She had destroyed the First that killed his wife and had almost killed him. Unfortunately, her blow had spilled the vampire's blood into Chun's open wounds, infecting him. It wasn't her fault; she'd thought him dead. He would have died, but the First's blood bought him back to life.

Nisi had easily carried him to her car that night, and to her home. She was strong enough to cut off the head of a vampire, and yet gentle with him. Realizing that regular doctors wouldn't know how to treat his wounds, Nisi called a neighborhood doctor, Lucky Falcon, to guide him back to life. Falcon was a Navaho healer, trusted by her and well versed in the traditional and untraditional methods of curing people.

Within a few days Chun had miraculously recovered from most of the wounds. Nisi told him what she knew about vampires. Chun would have thought her mad if he hadn't been through the hell of the past few days. He couldn't deny the violent memory of the attack, or the way he had changed. Everything was different.

Laying in her bed, Chun knew where Nisi was in the house, and when she left. Wrapped in her sheets, he could feel her move through the city, as if a string was attached between them. One of the many things that had changed since the vampire attack.

Nightmares filled his dreams when he slept, images of faceless, maimed bodies, screams and moans forced him to wake in a sweat. Once awake, voices filled his head, like the walls had disappeared and he was hearing conversations from the houses in the neighborhood. If he woke in the middle of the night, he could walk through the house in the dark and see everything clearly. One day he tripped on the way down the stairs and grabbed the wood railing, pulverizing the wood. There were times he had felt as if he was losing his mind, the experiences he had couldn't be real.

Falcon stopped by almost every day, checking Chun's wounds and talking to Nisi. Chun could hear them clearly, even when they were on another floor. When Nisi began telling him what she knew about vampires and hunting, he told her about the new sensations.

"I knew you were changed by the blood," Nisi had said, as they sat on her couch. "No one heals as fast as you did, except - -"

"One of them?" Chun said. "I've heard every word you and Falcon have said. I know you're afraid I'll change into one of them."

Nisi caressed his arm. "In the beginning, but now we know you're still human."

"But I'm different."

"Yes, stronger, your hearing, sight, all more like them, but no blood hunger." Sunlight streamed from the window over them. "You can still walk in the daylight."

"So far," he said.

She shook her head. "I don't think it'll happen and Falcon agrees with me. He needs better equipment to test your blood, but he's convinced the fact that the vampire was killed as the blood entered you prevented the complete transformation from happening. It may also be something special about your blood, he's not sure. But he's pretty certain you aren't going to change into a Remade vampire. "

"If I do become one of them, you have to destroy me. I couldn't stand living like the monster who killed my wife."

Nisi nodded. They held each other. The scent of lavender water she wore surrounded him like a warm blanket.

The three of them spent the next few weeks discovering how the mix in his blood had altered Chun. He was stronger, faster, and could heal quicker than regular humans. All of his senses were heightened. If he was physically in contact with someone's belongings, he could track them.

"You're almost a superman," Nisi told him a couple of weeks later. They laughed together. It was not long after that Chun asked her to teach him about killing vampires.

When he told Falcon the words the vampire whispered, he had his first seizure.

He came out of it with Falcon and Nisi sitting by his bedside.

Falcon shook his head and said in Navaho, "Ant iihnii." Witch people.

"The Firsts each have a spell that keeps them strong and young," Falcon said. "Sounds have power. The power speaks to the blood, the blood to the body. This is how the First live forever. You have that blood in you now. This curse saved you. Everything has light and dark to it. Perhaps you can use this to find the weakness to their strength, a way for us to destroy them."

"Falcon, you know I don't believe in the idea of magic words," Nisi said, helping Chun drink water. "I believe in the sword that spills their blood. This whispering ritual is just something they do."

"It doesn't matter what you and I believe. There was a time when you didn't believe in vampires. Chun's new abilities may be the way to another weapon."

He turned to Chun. "You know the truth in your blood, in the words you spoke, yes?"

Chun nodded slowly.

"But I'd like to learn the sword in the meantime," Chun said, smiling at Nisi.

Nisi taught him how to handle a sword, and what she knew about First generation vampires and the Remade. This woman from a farm in North Carolina didn't look anything like the cliche of a vampire hunter from the movies. Just a little taller than he, she was stocky, wide with muscle, with strong, large hands gentle as butterfly wings over his body and capable of swinging a steel sword with the accuracy of a samurai. Her short brown dread locks made her look fierce as they practiced the fighting forms.

In those weeks of training she also healed his heart. Somehow, in facing the desperate future they would live as hunters, they found a place in each other's soul. Her eyes reflected a deep loss. She hadn't talked about it, and he didn't need her to, unless it would ease her pain.

When they made love, Chun wanted to fall into her body like water and become the air in her lungs, the perspiration, slick and warm on her smooth skin. Every kiss, nibble, caress between them sent tingling through his spine. They took their time, stroking the kindled passion until they were intoxicated with desire.

Touching her soft skin with his lips was enough to arouse him, and take his breath away. His fingers traveled over her body, slowly exploring each curve, barely making contact. Chun loved to listen to her breath quicken or heart race as he caressed her. Each moan from Nisi's deep voice poured heat into his body. Living this strange existence made sense when they were together. Nisi was the only light in the dark world he traveled through.

He missed her, but understood why they had to work apart. The human race needed both of them working separately to get rid of this scourge.

"Nisi will be in town any day now," Chun said, scratching Ping under her chin. "She'll be happy to see you again." He still had a slight headache, and his shoulders, ribs and knees ached. Ping followed him upstairs to the first floor and sat patiently in the kitchen while Chun prepared her food.

Chun made himself two thick roast beef sandwiches after putting Ping's dish on the floor. Seizures always left him hungry.

He pulled the sub-compact computer out of the cabinet over the stove to review combinations of the words collected from other First vampires. The program shifted the words randomly into different groupings. Collected words were entered phonetically in the language used by the First and then translated into Navaho, a language Chun felt was more secure since few people knew it. It didn't seem to matter what language he spoke the words in. The sounds reacted with the First blood in his body. It took these two thing together to create a response.

He spoke them out loud, typing in his reactions to the word combinations.

"T'aadoo la'i yilkaahi." His fingers and feet grew numb, heat flowered over the tips of his nose, ears and neck.

"Naa nish aah." Left him flush, a little breathless and excited, the way he felt when he was around Nisi.

He did this, carefully, every day, in hopes of putting together the words in a pattern he could use to destroy all vampires, or at least Firsts. The only combination he avoided was the pattern of sounds of the First who originally attacked him. The two times he uttered them out loud produced seizures.

There was no way, at this point, to test the effect these words would have on Firsts, but a reaction in him had to mean something. No one knew why the ritual rejuvenated only those with First blood. Chun followed research on the internet about the positive effect of certain sounds and vibrations on healing normal humans. He couldn't help feeling that the answer to curing himself and destroying all of them lay in these words. Maybe if he collected enough of them he could rid the world of vampires. Maybe he could become fully human again and have a normal life with Nisi.

He tired quickly. Finishing his sandwiches, Chun checked the alarm system again and went to bed.

Adina sat in the corner of the rundown jazz club. The quartet on the low stage played riffs that reminded her of Coltrane. Music was one of human's redeeming moments. Jazz or rock or classical, she enjoyed the flow of music filling the air, the change of sound waves rippling and churning stillness.

"Do you mind?" a young man said, pointing to the empty chair opposite her.

For a moment she was going to tell him to move elsewhere, but she recognized his scent as the one questioning the vampire in the alley earlier. His long dreads were loose around his shoulders, his cinnamon-colored skin glowed with youth in the black turtle-neck sweater. This couldn't be a coincidence. What game was he playing?

She nodded and turned her attention back to the stage.

He turned around to watch the musicians and didn't say anything until the set was finished. When the group went on break, he ordered a Black Russian and offered to buy Adina a drink, though her glass of white wine was still full.

"I can see you're here for the music, not the drinks," he said.

"And what are you here for?" Adina said, her newly acquired sunglasses hiding her eyes, but smiling slightly.

"The music, a little human comfort." He clicked her glass gently with his glass. "Here's to music."

"And you assume I'm human?" Adina asked, still smiling.

"I don't like to use the word 'assume,' you know the saying 'making an ass of you and me.' But you do give the semblance of being human. Are you perhaps a ghost haunting the club?" he asked, smiling now.

"Perhaps something like that." Did he think flirting with her would be enticing? She tasted the air around him. He had something else going on. If she hadn't just fed, this one would be on the menu tonight.

"Are you an artist? Let me guess," she said, tapping her long red polished nails against her glass. "A writer."

"Bingo, you got me. And you, well, that's not going to be so easy." He leaned forward, squinting to see her face in the light of the small candle on the table. "A model or an international art dealer. Something unusual, not someone who works in an office building or anything mundane. You need the run of the whole planet." He took a sip of his drink. "Do you always wear sunglasses in the dark?"

She removed the glasses and set them on the table. "I'm sensitive to light. It's brighter than you think in here." His skin had the scent of someone about twenty-five years old, yet he maneuvered the conversation like someone older.

He lifted the sunglasses, then replaced them without touching her skin.

She raised an eyebrow behind the dark lenses. He was playing this very careful, in no hurry to make his move, whatever that was.

The next set started with a version of Miles Davis's 'My Ship.' Adina closed her eyes and listened to the trumpet, drums, and keyboards while breathing in the young man's scent. There was no cologne, just the natural musky odor of his body mixing with a slight fragrance of coconut oil from his long dreads. The heat of his body radiated through her. She imagined making love to him, his heat entering her cooling body. Hot lips on hers, his tongue, warm and wet, and in orgasm the sweet taste of his blood in her mouth and against her skin as her teeth ripped into his flesh. The trumpet caressed her thoughts, playing in between her images of them together.

She opened her eyes. He was engrossed in the music, his back to her. He nodded to the beat, his long dreads moving gently. The steady pulse of his heart mixed with the music, adding to her desire to taste him. The band filled the second set with versions of Miles Davis's work: 'Round Midnight', 'Now's The Time', 'Tempus Fugit', 'Summertime', 'My Funny Valentine', 'Nefertiti', 'Portia'.

Adina remembered an evening years ago, in this same nightclub, when it was the top jazz spot in town. Miles Davis played here and often sat in the audience to listen to others. She'd sat one table away from him that night, breathed in the smoky scent of his sweet dark skin and wondered at making him one of them.

She laughed softly to herself, making her tablemate turn and look.

"Sorry," she said, shrugging. Not that it would have been easy to get to Miles. He was never at the club alone. It was a challenge she'd considered worthwhile. To think, Miles Davis, still making music today.

Rapuluchukwu, leave it in God's hands. Not that she believed in the gods anymore, but she left Miles to his own mechanisms, to the errant hands of time and death. Now these young ones played his music, but without his passion, his focused wildness.

At the end of the next set, the house lights went up. The young man turned to her, lifted his glass in salute and finished his drink.

"As a ghost of this establishment, I don't suppose you could take a walk outside?" he asked.

She considered him for a moment, vibrant and attractive in the way that only the young mortals were with their taut, firm flesh, easy breath flowing through their bodies, unaware of their own mortality. This made them as appetizing to her as those at the end of their lives, the other end of the spectrum, so unwilling to leave, so desperate to hold on to one last breath.

"Not tonight," she said, crossing her legs and leaning back in her seat.

"Maybe another night?" he asked.

"Maybe," she said.

"My name is Michael," he said, holding out his hand.

"Adina," she said, taking his hand.

"A strong handshake, for a strong ghost," he said, kissing the back of her hand.

She simply smiled and watched him leave.

Whatever he wanted from her, he was willing to wait. His need for her was as clear in his eyes as his death. And there was something else, a flicker of desperation, a kind of hunger.

For a moment she imagined him nude, his strong body covered in bite marks, the blood trickling, dark juice over his cinnamon brown skin. She shoved the image away. The idea of gorging on him as full as she was now was almost as satisfying as doing it.

If their paths crossed again he would become a meal. After she played with him. Adina would show him what a real vampire could do, not like the weak Remade he had captured earlier. She licked her lips. He would be delicious. The words of the Whisper would settle nicely in his sweet body, his warm blood. Maybe she would take him to her place and bathe in his blood. She shuddered in anticipation.

She stood and stretched. This night was filled with surprises and there were still clubs and bars open to visit.

The next morning Chun worked out in the basement. These attacks always made his energy bunch and gather in knots. He went through two forms of tai chi, very slowly, leveling the energy in his body. Feeling more centered, he walked through his sword form, first with the light wood sword and then the steel sword. Finishing the form, a fine sheen of sweat on his face, Chun finally felt ready for the day, and more importantly, the evening.

"How about a walk before we go to work, Ping?" he asked the dog, who was sitting patiently at the doorway of the dining room. Ping ran to the front door and waited to have her leash snapped on.

While they walked, Chun listened to voice mail on his cell phone. A new client wanted an interview this afternoon. Chun returned the call. The nervous man didn't want to meet at his office, so they settled on a restaurant near the man's job. He wanted to talk to Chun about a missing person.

Chun made his money as a private investigator, finding lost things and people. He was very good at it, another side effect of the vampire infection. This day work supported his night job.

Back at the house, Chun showered and dressed in better clothes. "Let's go to work, girl."

He placed his steel sword in its leather case and carried it to his car, followed by Ping. It didn't take long to drive to meet his new client.

Jim Piper was in his early forties. Ron, his sixteen year old son was missing. Piper had gone to the police, but since the boy had run away before, he felt they wouldn't aggressively look for him. The father was convinced his son was in danger and wanted him found quickly. Chun was inclined to think this was another runaway incident, but knowing the streets as well as he did, he also knew there was real danger there.

Piper gave Chun a picture and, more importantly, a watch that belonged to Ron. Chun told the man he would call when he had something.

Chun put the boy's watch on and started at the bus terminal, then went to the train station, waiting for a sense of him, more than his face in the crowd. He drove to the usual places teenagers hung out, uptown and downtown, The Tombs, Gramacy Park, and Washington Square Park, taking Ping for a walk around each area. It was Ping's job to stay alert to their surroundings, since these searches were distracting for Chun.

A bolt of energy, like electricity, danced on his wrist near the South Street Seaport.

From an outside deck of the shopping mall he could see a group of teenagers skateboarding below on the side steps. Ping laid down at his feet while Chun closed his eyes and reached out with his inner sight. Taking slow breaths, he focused on the tingling around his wrist, and felt the surrounding air for its source.

The boy had been there hours ago, his imprint was clear. There was no sense of which way he may have gone. He looked at the boy's watch– 4:30pm—a half an hour of daylight left. He'd come back to the Seaport early tomorrow, hopefully the boy will return. The night would come soon and he would have to get back to his other job. He waited on the deck, slowly sipping coffee, watching the sun set. He'd forgotten there was beauty in the ending of a day, for him it heralded the nightly hunt, not a time to rest.

Adina moaned in torpor, the semi-conscious state that vampires laid in while waiting for the night to come. The Whisper sang in her head, in images, sprinkled with words.

. . . bodies torn open, a chaotic field of human remains, heads, arm, legs, hands, fingers . . .

. . . her naked, floating in a sea of warm blood, weightless and sated . . .

Fumiya, suffering.

. . . a wave of blood covers her, she is dragged down in the warmth, not suffocating, but drawing the blood into her lungs, her mouth . . . the blood is alive, squirming into her ears, between her legs, into every opening of her body, her back arches in orgasmic pleasure, her skin is stretched as the blood bloats her, filling her out like a balloon . . . she is going to explode...

Ayzize, let it come.

Adina jerked up out of the bed, eyes searching the dark. For what? She shook her head. Every night she woke to some phantom in the room. No one was ever there, just memories of the Whisper from her dreams, nightmares of torpor.

"Fumiya ayzize," she whispered, a burning surge dancing along her spine. She closed her eyes and moaned from the pain. She hadn't expected the Whisper to call her out so soon. Hunger stirred inside. She didn't usually feed two nights in a row. This happened if she spent time near another First. Maybe it was the influence of that creature from the alley last night.

A fleeting thought of holding off: no. She'd tried that before and could never control the maddening hunger and pain that came from denying the Whisper its place. She shook her head. No point in going through that again.

She didn't know why no First lived long without the ritual, but it was woven into the fabric of their extended existence. To deliver the words into the almost dead body of the victim, to drink their blood, to live. She smiled. Although people thought of vampires as the undead, she believed their lives were on another evolutionary level that unmade humans didn't comprehend.

Uwaezuoke, the world was imperfect, that was all she needed to understand. Whatever the reason, she would have to feed again tonight.

She dressed for the evening. Tonight she didn't feel like wearing black. The dark red leather bodysuit, with its deep v-neck and slit legs, matching boots and jacket and the sunglasses from last night would do.

She considered taking the human she held in her basement, but changed her mind. Something fresh would be better for the ritual. She didn't want to rush feeding on that one.

Chun sat on the deck of the seaport a few moments after the setting sun painted the sky in bands of purple, red and pink. On the lower deck the teenagers slowly dispersed. The missing boy hadn't shown up. Chun removed Ron's watch and put it in the leather pouch at his waist. The threads of Ron's energy detached as soon as Chun was no longer in physical contact with the watch. He couldn't afford to be diverted by the search while following the vampire.

Chun stood and stretched. He would come back earlier tomorrow to see if the boy returned. Ping stood up and yawned.

"Let's go, girl," Chun said to Ping. He drove home, and fed Ping, leaving her to guard the house.

Fortunately, it was a quick drive to Adina's house. He parked his car a couple of blocks away, with his sword strapped to his back, hidden under his large overcoat. He found a good spot in the alley across the street to watch her house with binoculars.

She didn't waste any time once the sun set. As in the past days, the vampire left her house not long after the sky darkened, hailed a taxi and sped away.

Chun waited fifteen minutes, making sure she didn't return before he entered the private courtyard. The gated fence between the house and street wasn't locked. He stood in the shadow of the large tree inside the fence. Weeds and wild roses overgrew the small yard, and ivy covered much of the walls of the house. His heart raced. He willed himself to calm down. He needed to focus. Was there a way into her house?

He closed his eyes and reached out. His augmented sight worked from the inside out, like three dimensional waves in water. Every movement of the objects within the boundaries of his widening circle–insects, wind through leaves, birds, people in the street, and the surrounding buildings caused ripples.

He took a deep breath and pushed to direct his attention on her house. There were no vibrations or the hum of an alarm system. He pushed deeper into the house. There was someone in the basement. A heart beat pulsed, making subtle waves in the air. It wasn't another vampire. A vampire's heart beat was slow, just fast enough to pump the mix of poisoned blood and the blood of their latest victim through the body.

Chun released his concentration. Why was she confident enough to leave the house with someone inside? He frowned. This didn't feel right. He had to keep his mind on his objective, to see if there was a way into her house. He hadn't come here to rescue anyone.

He moved to the side of the house, trying to avoid the wild roses that twisted around the edges of the yard. The windows were barred on the outside and shuttered on the inside. The shutters seemed metallic. He shook his head. This wasn't good. He worked around the outside of the house, but every entrance was barricaded. Even the windows to the basement had been sealed with bricks. He pressed his ear against the wall. Nothing. No doubt the house was soundproof—vampires liked to play with their victims.

He put his hands on the bricked window and reached out again with his senses. Someone was definitely inside. A steady heart beat thumped as well as the slow whoosh of air moving in and out of that person's lungs. Whoever it was, wasn't moving much; perhaps the victim was bound in some way or unconscious. He crouched against the house, hands tightened into fists.

He pounded his fists against his thighs, remembering the ultimate goal, the greater good. Besides, what could he do, dig into the earth and break through the walls to save one person. He stood. What if—? He took the missing boy's watch out of the pouch and held it. No. It wasn't him, none of his energy spiked near the house, inside or out. Chun took a deep breath and placed the watch back in the pouch.

"I'm sorry," he whispered, patting the bricked window. He reminded himself of one of the Noble Truths of Buddhism: we all experience suffering. The unfortunate person in the basement and he, for having to leave. If he took care of the vampire tonight, he could return.

Chun left the house. He didn't need a personal item to sense a vampire, especially a First. Her energy signature danced in the air, sharp-edged and bitter. Adina was hungry again. He frowned. This was unusual. Two days in a row. It was going to be a long night.

Adina walked the streets, savoring the movement of humans around her. As the sidewalks filled for a Friday evening painful hunger accelerated up and down her bones. Hundreds of years ago she'd satisfied herself early in the evening, wanting the burning to stop. But she learned to savor the sensation. Pain or pleasure, it was all one feeling. The longer she waited, the more violent the feeding, the greater the pleasure.

Each step sent a fiery wave up her spine, joining the growing hunger in her stomach. Each person she passed on the street, every woman, man and child, was the answer to her pain, the relief she needed. She could barely wait for lights to change at street crossings with people standing near her. Images tantalized her: tearing into flesh, blood flowing over passerby splashing on her. At one corner, she bit her own lip. Thick blood leaked in a bitter trickle into her mouth.

The night club she met Michael in last night was near. If she went in and saw him, she didn't think she could sit and listen to music with this hunger growing inside. As much as she wanted to consume him, she didn't want it to be fast. A cramp gripped her stomach. She grabbed a lamp post.

"Are you alright, Miss?" a man in a suit asked. He put his hand on her arm.

The blood surging through his body sang to her, like the river of her home land. She suppressed a growl.

"I'll be okay." He would do.

A woman came up to put her arm on the man's arm. "Can we take you to a hospital?" she asked.

Damn. "No, it's okay. I'll be fine, I just need to eat something." Adina pulled away from him and walked around the corner. Some of the sidewalk cafes of Greenwich Village still had tables outside, even though the evening air was cool.

Someone was in the alley behind her. One person.

She ducked into the alley. The narrow passageway ran through the middle of the block, winding through the backs of buildings and fenced-in gardens. The human was deep in the middle of the block, sitting against a pile of boxes, smoking a joint. He was young and healthy. Though his long blond hair hid his face, she could tell by his clothes and smell that he was probably living on the street. Perhaps a runaway. Even better—no one would be expecting him home tonight. She smiled and watched him, the burning and hunger intensifying.

Chun picked up her trail in the same neighborhood she had been in the night before. Odd for her to hunt so close to her last killing. She was getting sloppy, good thing for him. He stood in front of a leather shop, pretending to window shop so he could track which way she had gone. He followed her trail through brightly lit streets to an alley. Ducking into the darkness, he removed his sword from under his coat and carried it in his right hand, against the side of his body.

He sensed another person in the alley. Human. No doubt her next victim. His only chance was to catch her feeding. She would be too occupied to be fully aware of his approach.

Adina closed her eyes and let the sound and smell of the boy's body fill her senses, until he was no longer a human being but a web of blood circuits, veins pulsing with sweet fluid, stomach gurgling, heart pounding. She once cut one of them open, slowly stripping away skin and muscle, to see for herself what was actually within. The arteries and veins that spun through head, trunk and legs were quite beautiful. Unfortunately, humans didn't live long in that state.

This young one wasn't going to live very long at all. She growled. He looked up, eyes dazed by the drugs. She walked slowly towards him, stumbling a little.

"Hey girl . . ." he said, standing.

She easily pushed him to the ground and slid next to him, her hand still on his shoulder.

"Don't get up for me," she said, smiling slightly.

"I was just—"

"Yes, I can see you were just getting high," Adina said. " I don't have a problem with that."

"You're not going to bust me?" he asked.

"Not at all." She sat closer to him, the swish of blood rushing through his body echoed in her ears. Feverish, the blood hunger churned in her veins.

"Hey, do you want some? I think I have another joint in here." He rummaged through his backpack.

"Want some. Yes, but not that." She shoved the backpack away and pulled him across her lap.

"What —," he started to say, but stopped when he saw her sharpened teeth catch the moonlight.

"You look scared. Don't be. This can be very pleasurable. Well, at least, for me."

He tried to pull away and scream, but she handled him like a doll, putting her hand over his mouth and holding him down.

Chun stared in horror. For a moment he thought she had Ron, the missing boy, but the moonlight revealed her new victim was another teenager. As much as Chun wanted the words from her, he wasn't sure he could watch her kill the boy. He centered himself and gripped the sword in both hands.

Too late he heard a sound behind him, a hard object smashed into the back of his head. Everything went black.

Adina jumped to her feet, releasing the boy, who scurried down the alley as quickly as he could. Michael, the writer from the jazz club, stood over the body of a man, a piece of bloodied wood in his gloved hands.

"Well, looks like I got here just in time," he said, tossing the piece of wood aside.

"You're following me?" she said.

"I would say we were both following you. I suspect for different reasons," Michael said, kicking at the sword.

She looked down the alley where the boy had run, then back at Michael.

"You won't need him," he said. He walked up to her, took her in his arms and kissed her. She started to push him away but instead drank in his obvious desire. Then suddenly, she bit his lip.

He jerked but didn't pull away. She licked his lip, the drops of blood intensifying her hunger.

"You know what I am?" she asked.

"Yes, Adina. I know."

He kissed her again, wrapping his arms around her tightly. "It took me a while to find out your kind were real. It's surprising how much information is on the internet and the streets if you take the time and have credit cards."

Adina pushed him away from her. "I imagine you did more than that."

"Yes, I would do anything to find you," he said.

The moonlight flowed over his face. His pea jacket was open, the white shirt unbuttoned, smooth brown skin invited her bite. He was beautiful. She ran her hands over his chest. His heart beat strongly, his body firm and obviously aroused.

"You've gone through a lot to find me, why?" she asked.

"I needed to find a way to meet you, let you see I wasn't a threat. I'm dying. I know I don't look sick, but inside I am." He touched his head. "A tumor. The doctors say I might live one or two more years."

"What do you want?" she asked, even though she could guess.

"To be like you, to be Remade," he said.

"Indeed." She considered him. It had been hundreds of years since she had changed a human into a vampire. "I think we should get out of here. The young one might call the police."

Michael walked over to Chun and went through his pockets and found car keys. "He has a car. If we could find it—"

"I won't have any problem following the trail of his crude scent back to it," she said.

"Your place or mine?" he asked.

"Mine." She prodded Chun with her leather boots. "Let's bring him and his sword."

They had no trouble dragging Chun between them, like a drunk friend, to his car. They slipped him into the trunk and drove to Adina's house.

Chun came to tied to a chair. The back of his head hurt like hell. Adina had her back to him and was straddling a shirtless man on a chair. He thought at first the man was tied also, but could quickly see that wasn't the case. They were kissing. He closed his eyes and gently tried the bonds on his arms and legs. They were tight enough to keep him secure, but not so tight as to cut off his circulation. Very professional.

"He's awake," Adina said. "You might as well open your eyes, Chun. I can feel you're conscious."

He opened his eyes. "What did you do with the boy?"

"The boy? You mean in the alley?" she asked, standing. She picked up his sword and leaned on it.

Chun nodded.

"He got away," the man said. "A fair trade. We have you."

"Who the hell are you?" asked Chun.

"Where are my manners?" Adina said. She picked Chun's wallet up from the floor and read his name. "Chun Zhang, meet Michael Simon."

Michael stood and bowed slightly.

"I'm guessing I can thank you for my headache?" Chun asked.

"That's right. Couldn't have you hurting my Maker," Michael said, sitting on the black leather couch opposite Chun, drops of blood seeping from small wounds Adina had made on his chest.

"Maker?" Chun asked. "You *want* her to change you into a vampire?"

"Remade into something stronger than human, yes. Into something that can live forever–absolutely," Michael said.

"Why?" Chun asked, trying to buy time.

"Gliobastoma multiforme. A fancy name for inoperable brain tumor that's aggressively killing me. I have no interest in dying in a painful drugged haze. Why not live forever?"

"But—" Chun started to say, but Adina put her finger to his lips.

"Now, now, don't try to talk him out of this. He's very determined. You have no idea how determined." She turned to smile at Michael.

Chun felt a sudden surge of hunger, heat radiated from his groin, up his chest to his neck. He stared at her. Somehow he was picking up her feelings, sharing her reactions.

Adina dipped her nail into the bleeding wound at the back of Chun's head and licked the blood. She frowned. "Your blood doesn't taste right. You're only the latest hunter to follow me, but you're not quite human, are you?"

"It doesn't matter what I am," Chun said.

"Oh, but I think it does. I'd like to know before I kill you," she said.

Michael stood. "You said I could feed on him, after you Remade me."

"That's true, I did." She pointed the sword at Chun and winked.

Chun had a sinking feeling in his stomach. "You can't trust her, you can't trust any of them. She's going to kill you."

"You don't listen very well, do you? The tumor is already killing me. At least this dying is part of the transition to a different life. Besides who should I trust—you?" Michael said. "I think you would say anything to destroy her. That's not going to happen." He walked over and slapped Chun hard.

Adina caught Michael's hand before he could slap Chun again. "No need for that. Not yet."

She put her face next to Chun and sniffed him. "Definitely not all human." She looked into his eyes, holding his chin. "But you're not vampire. You have the blood of a First in you, don't you?"

Chun tried to jerk out of her grip.

"Yes. I see. Not very talkative, are you? You hunters are quite stubborn, but I can be persuasive." She brought his sword down, embedding it in the floor before him. Her face contorting in pain, she grabbed her stomach.

Chun winced, lurching in the chair. Pangs of hunger tore at his gut.

"You feel it also?" Adina asked. She caressed his face with a finger. "I taste an echo of my blood hunger in you."

He didn't want to. Why was this happening? This had never happened before. Maybe he had connected to her while he was unconscious. Whatever the reason, he wanted the hunger to stop.

"This will be very interesting for both of us," she said. "I'll bet you've never been this close when we remade one of you, other than the time you were changed."

Adina spun towards Michael, and pushed him onto the couch.

Chun tried to stay calm and centered, but squirmed in the chair in spite of himself, her craving pouring into him. He wanted blood. He'd never wanted blood before, but he'd never been this close to a First for so long.

"Watch and learn, hunter," she said, smiling at Chun.

"Is it time?" Michael asked.

"Yes," she said, caressing Michael's bare chest. "Past time."

She worked over Michael for the next hour. After a half an hour, he started screaming. She quickly ripped out his vocal cords, collapsed one lung. After that, the sounds Michael made were muted, more guttural.

Chun was disgusted by the sight but couldn't look away. Adina's yearning pulled him into the unfolding violence. The more she ravaged Michael's body, the deeper her satisfaction reflected in Chun. Her passion built into an indescribable wave of lust. Chun couldn't control the reactions from deep inside his body. The tainted blood wouldn't let him. Thoughts left him as everything became animal sensation. Her tongue against his skin, the thick warm blood sliding down her throat, blood slippery and slick under her hands. Chun's heart raced, his breath quickened, adrenalin flooded his body. Adina's desire dragged him to the brink of orgasm.

Towards the end, Michael turned towards Chun.

Chun could see terror in his eyes. Adina looked at Chun, smiled and turned Michael's face towards her. "Pay attention," she growled. "I have something to tell you."

She whispered, "*Fumiya ayzie, kambui sipo*," and ripped into his throat.

Chun tried to push away the sounds of her feeding but the contact with her remained strong. As Adina filled, he was engulfed in the same orgasmic high she floated in. A shiver ran through him as release came to both of them.

She was suddenly beside him. She ran her nail along the side of his face. Chun jumped.

"Don't tell me you didn't enjoy that, half-made," Adina said. She laughed, Michael's blood splattered over her arms and neck. She walked into another room, and came out with a wet towel, wiping the blood off.

Holding the blood-soaked towel near his face, she asked. "Want a lick?"

He turned away.

She laughed. "So, you don't drink." She sat down next to Michael's body and patted his thigh. "He really wanted it, you know. He believed

I'd remake him. It would have been a great disappointment for him to discover he wasn't going to live forever. The Remade can't. You have to agree I've done him a favor." She stretched and leaned forward, her elbows on her knees. "What to do with you? Perhaps make you part of my collection. I'm curious how you came about."

She untied some of the knots, releasing him from the chair, but leaving his feet and hands tightly bound. She threw him over her shoulder, grabbed his sword and carried him to the basement.

Adina dropped him to the dirt floor. A pervasive smell of death permeated the walls and floor. Many people had died in this place.

"You probably don't need the light, but not everyone here is special like you and I," she said, flipping on an overhead light.

There were four large trunks with grates on the sides in the center of the room. One was occupied, Chun sensing life, but not movement. The other three were empty.

"You know which one has my other guest, yes?" She waved her hand in the air. "Your sensing is crude, you know. It fills the air like the scent of rotten fish." Adina laughed again, her cheeks flush with Michael's life. She stumbled a little, as if high.

She unlatched the trunk and pulled an unconscious body out.

It was Nisi.

Chun squirmed backwards, "No."

"You know her?" Adina asked, propping the bound woman up against the trunk and sitting on the trunk next to her. She caressed Nisi's dreadlocks. "Do you have a vampire hunter's club, meet for drinks, give out assignments?"

Chun stared in horror. Nisi was bruised and marked with puncture wounds, her torn clothes streaked with blood. She must have put up a good fight, but her skill hadn't stop Adina from taking her captive and worse, feeding on her. Nausea rose in his stomach. He vomited on the floor.

"I'm sure she'd appreciate your gesture of disgust, if she were conscious," Adina said. "She's lasted quite a while, although I don't think she'll be with us much longer." She released Nisi's head from her hold. Nisi slid sideways and moaned, her eyes fluttered open for a moment. She looked at him, shook her head and passed out.

"Nisi," Chun said. He closed his eyes to concentrate. Her heart was still beating. She was alive. For now.

Adina lifted him from the floor to a standing position. "Why can you do that?"

"If you let her go, I'll tell you everything," Chun said.

She laughed in his face, dropping him to the floor. He couldn't keep his balance with his ankles tied. He fell to his knees. She stooped down, tipped his head up with a nail under his chin.

"Why would I let someone go whose life is dedicated to destroying me?" she asked. "Maybe I should remake her. What do you think? How would she fell about changing sides?” Adina laughed.

“But let’s forget about her and talk about you. You have the blood of a First in you. I can taste that much.”

She looked at his neck, ripped his shirt open to examine his chest and neck. She traced the scars with a finger, her eyes closed. “Hmmmm, let’s see. You were attacked by a First and somehow survived. Now you live with his blood mixed in with yours. The blood changed you: you run faster, hear better, see in the dark, feel around with your clumsy perception. Is that close enough?”

“Yes,” he said. His mind scrambled for a way to get himself and Nisi out of this alive. He flexed hopelessly against the rope around his arms.

“I wondered what was following me. I’ve never heard of anyone like you before.” She released Chun and sat on the trunk. “Still, the question is what to do with you? Unfortunately, I don’t like the taste of your blood. It doesn’t have the full body and sweetness of normal blood. You’re not a very good conversationalist. None of you hunters are.” She prodded Nisi with her boot. “You might be fun to play with. Maybe I could urge you to be more open. Or just open you up.” She giggled, still high on Michael’s blood.

“Now I see why the hunger came again. Your mixed blood called it out in me. Connects us now,” she said. “I don’t think it would do to leave you around for long.”

Adina picked up Chun’s sword, swung it through the air with one hand, the seven-folded steel singing over him. The sound reverberated up and down his spine. Vibrations, sound, the blood of a First. If he was affected, how would a First react to the words he had collected?

“*Adiilch’il,*” he said in Navaho. Be a crash of lightning. The beginning words from an effective section of the secret he had compiled in his notes.

She stumbled forward, letting the sword go. It clanged into the corner of the room.

Chun felt a surge of stinging pleasure through his wrists and feet. A stronger echo of the sensation snapped back at him from Adina. His heart skipped a beat; the words did affect her.

“What—what did you say?” She stumbled to him, went to her knees and grabbed him by the throat.

He repeated the phrase.

Holding him with one hand, she covered her eyes with the other, a shudder shook both of them.

“Where did you hear that?” she growled. “Did the First who attacked you say those words to you?”

“I have his words and others,” Chun said.

Her eyes narrowed and she shook him. “How many words?”

“More than I can remember. I keep them in a notebook at my place, here in the city.”

“What else do you know?” she asked.

“I know you need to use certain words when you feed, like tonight, they are part of the blood hunger. They are also part of the secret that makes you different than the Remade."

She released him. Chun fell onto his back. Adina walked to the corner to retrieve the sword. She held the blade to his neck.

"Kill me and others will know the words. I've made arrangements for someone else to get the book," he said, looking her in the eyes. "You know there's power in these words. Do you want to take the chance of another having this power?"

"What do you propose?" she asked, lifting the blade off his neck.

"We go to my place, I'll give you the notebook and walk away from all of this. Give up hunting. This mix of blood has given me more than extra abilities. It has made me sick inside. I'm tired of all the death." Tears filled his eyes as he looked at Nisi.

"Yes, I believe you are," Adina said.

It was true. At that moment, Chun wanted nothing more to do with this mission.

She turned her back to him and walked over to Nisi with the sword. Chun held his breath.

Adina dropped the sword, picked Nisi up and locked her back into the trunk.

"Don't think I trust you, but I want that notebook." Adina lifted Chun to his feet. "I don't care what you do with the rest of your life, as long as you give the book to me, leave this city and make sure our paths never cross again."

He nodded.

She carried him to the car and put him in the trunk. It was a fast ride to his house.

Chun rolled around in the dark trunk so his hands could reach a backup weapon he kept under the spare tire. He barely had time to slip the small knife in the side of his work boots before the car stopped.

She untied his arms and feet before taking him out of the trunk.

"We should go in the side entrance," he said.

"No matter how you've been changed, you're not stronger than me. There are many bones to break in the human body. You've seen how imaginative I can be in giving pain. Do I have to say what I'll do to you if you try anything?"she asked.

He shook his head.

He rubbed his wrists to get the circulation moving again, as they walked to his house. She kept her hand wrapped around the back of his neck. He had no doubt she could easily crush his vertebrae with one hand. His gait was shaky from nerves as much as from his legs being tied. The memory of Nisi in Adina's basement flashed in his mind. If there was any chance of saving Nisi, he had to stop thinking about her and be in the present moment.

He unlocked the door. Ping barked from behind the door.

"Just a minute," he said to Adina.

"You make sure it's under control or I will," she said.

"Okay." He opened the door a couple of inches. "Go to the basement, Ping."

She pressed her nose at the opening and barked louder, toenails scraping against the metal door. "Stop, Ping. Go to the basement," he said.

Ping whimpered but padded away from the door. Chun waited a minute before opening the door.

"I need to lock the basement door so she won't come back up," Chun said, when Adina held him back. He pointed to the open door on the other side of the kitchen.

Adina walked with him across the room. Chun looked down the stairs and could see Ping's eyes reflected the kitchen light.

"Good girl. Go to the box," Chun said, knowing Ping would obey their code word.

Ping growled low and walked away from the steps into the darkness of the basement. Chun locked the door.

"Okay, where's the notebook?" Adina said, shoved him against the door.

He pointed to the dining room. She looked away for a moment. Chun stumbled to his knees, snatching out the small knife hidden in his boot. As she reached down to grab him and Chun swung his arm up and down. The knife slashed through one wrist, then the other.

Blood spurted out. Having fed two nights in a row, Adina's body was rich with blood. The mix flowed thinner than her blood alone would have. Chun hoped this would happen. Every drop of blood she lost was an advantage for him, and he needed all the advantages he could get right now. Not surprisingly, he felt a stinging at his wrists. The connection between them was still strong.

She reached for him again, but Chun scrambled across the floor. He clawed under the small kitchen table and pulled loose a sword, half the length of the one lost at her house, turned and pointed it at her.

Adina didn't pay attention to the wrist wound, letting the blood spill to the floor. She laughed. "You can't be serious." She ran towards him.

He quickly turned and rolled out of her way, the short sword cutting across her thighs. Blood leaked from the gashes. His thighs burned, echoing her wounds.

"You'll never bleed me out through these little cuts," she growled. She threw the table at him. He ducked; the table slamming into his shoulder, throwing him against the wall. She rushed him, but Chun kicked the table at her and ran into the dining room.

She turned to chase him, almost losing her footing. The floor was slippery with blood, giving Chun time to get around the dining room table and grab another short sword from behind a cabinet. He stood in a low stance with a sword in each hand. She vaulted the table, expecting to land on him, but he moved faster than a human should have and slid under the table to the other side.

"You do move fast," she said, gripping the end of the dining room table. "Don't tell me you don't enjoy some of the side effects of First blood in your body?"

He inched along the wall towards the doorway to the living room.

"Still not talking? I will hear you scream tonight." She picked the table up and flung it at him. It shattered against the wall, but he was already through the doorway.

He jumped over the low couch to the middle of the room, took deep breaths to gather his energy. She was through the doorway in two breaths and shoved the couch aside. Only the trunk coffee table stood between them. Chun stood crouched, holding the two swords in front, pointed at Adina.

"Tell me where the notebook is and I'll kill you quickly," she said.

Suddenly Ping charged her from the hallway behind Chun. The dog had crawled from the basement through the hidden passageway as trained. She jumped into the air and landed on Adina, her strong jaws clamped on the vampire's neck.

The First tripped backwards to the floor, punched at Ping's head. The dog yapped in pain, unlocking her jaws. Adina flung Ping across the room over Chun's head. She landed against the wall and slid to the floor. She didn't move. Chun could hear her heart still beating. She wasn't dead.

"Not dead–yet, but she will be," Adina said, getting to her feet. Blood dripped from her neck. "After I kill you." She coughed and put her hand to her neck.

Chun coughed, and started to reach for his neck. Spikes of pain itched at a wound he didn't have.

"What will it be like to experience your death, I wonder. Let's find out," she said, taking a step towards Chun.

"*Niyiilkaah doo i ii aah*," he said in Navaho.

The words sent waves of pain and pleasure along his spine, his fingers and toes tingled. The effect on Adina was more intense. She flung her arms out to the side and screamed.

Chun sprung into the air. He landed with his feet on her chest, knocking her to the floor. Still in the grip of the words, she bucked to throw him off.

He repeated the words again. She growled and arched up, her hands reaching for his neck. Chun swiped outward with the two swords, cutting off her hands, blood gushed from her wrists.

The swords dropped to the floor. His hands were gone, his wrists throbbed, echoing Adina's pain.

No, not his hands, Adina's hands. He reached down to grab a sword but his hands wouldn't flex.

Adina growled, knocking him off her with her arms, spraying blood across the room. "That didn't work out the way you planned, did it?" she said. She tried to stand but the blood loss was becoming too great. Managing to sit up, she leaned against the living room wall. Blood poured from her wrists onto the wood floor in a widening misshapen circle. She tucked her wrists under her arms in a vain attempt to stop the blood flow. The thick dark liquid seeped down her sides to the floor.

Chun's energy dissipated but at a slower pace than Adina. His hands were still useless.

"You can't kill me," she said. "You would die too."

"It would be worth it," Chun said, crouched on his knees.

"Then who would save your precious Nisi?" she said, closing her eyes. "Ah, yes, Nisi."

He thought she had passed out, but instead she whispered, "Chun, come here."

The connection between them pulled at him, like a thick rope around his neck. He slid back away from her. "No," he said.

"I need you," she said.

He blinked. It wasn't Adina, it was Nisi, blood covered and begging, with open arms.

"Chun, please."

"Nisi?" he said.

"Yes, come here. I need you."

The tips of his fingers tingled. He leaned towards her. "But—"

"Please," she pleaded.

He had to save Nisi.

He shook his head. Nisi wasn't here.

He blinked.

Adina's eyes still closed, her head slumped forward, the lake of blood growing around her.

He blinked and shook his head.

They were home, in the hut he built for them. Adina was hurt. Someone had hurt her.

"Tacuma, come here," she whispered.

He would do anything for her, be anything. He loved her with every breath of his body. There was something wrong. His body didn't feel right, he was weak. This wasn't his home. Where was he?

"Home, my love, we're home." Adina's voice was barely audible. "Please come to me. I need you."

"Yes," Chun said, looking at her. It was the sweet girl he had married. She hadn't changed, still beautiful with a smile that pulled him into her eyes. Dark brown eyes that hid much, said everything.

Blood.

There was so much blood.

He slowly crawled towards her, aching for her, so hungry.

Nothing mattered except keeping her safe.

His hands felt strange, tingly, as if waking from a dream.

Why was there so much blood?

"Don't worry about anything, just come to me," she whispered. "Need you, hungry for you."

There were two swords between him and Adina. His hands curled around the hilts, he dragged them with him as he crawled.

Someone had hurt his wife and they would pay.

Blood.

A dog barked. Ping?

Blood.

His

    wife

          was

               dead.

Chun shook his head, took a deep breath and pushed out with all the psychic energy he possessed. The connection between he and Adina collapsed, the room came into sharp focus.

"No," Adina said, looking up.

Chun dove to her, and in a quick scissor action, cut off her head. He rolled off her body. Her head lay on the side, eyes open, staring at him, as her body twitched.

Ping whimpered. Chun laid the swords on the couch, and went to Ping. "Steady, girl," he said as she started to stand. Quickly checking the dog for broken bones, Chun ran his hands over her body. There was no serious damage.

"You're going to be okay," he said, giving her a hug.

Chun picked up Adina's head by the hair, and carried it, dripping blood, to the basement. Ping followed him, limping. He threw in Adina's head into the refurbished wood-burning furnace, pushed up the heat and watched it catch fire and burn. Ping rubbed against his leg.

"Good girl. It's all right now," he said, scratching behind her ears, his bloodied fingers leaving pink traces in Ping's grey fur.

He looked at his hands. Her blood covered them. The blood. The answer was in the words: the patterns of sounds and the blood of a First. He ran back upstairs, grabbed a jar from the kitchen, went in the living room and scooped as much as her blood into the jar as he could. He went through her pockets until he found the keys to her house.

Ping followed him and stood at the doorway of the living room, sniffing at the blood soaking into the area rug near her paws.

"Back girl," he said, pointing to the kitchen.

He quickly rinsed his face and hands in the kitchen sink, and threw on a black sweatshirt hanging on the back of the kitchen door. Hopefully the blood on his black jeans wouldn't be too obvious if someone saw him on the street. He had to get back to Nisi first, then he'd come back to clean up the rest of the body.

He looked at the jar of blood on the kitchen table and picked it up.

"Let's go get Nisi," Chun said to the dog.

With Ping in the front and the jar of blood in the back seat, Chun drove back to Adina's house.

He ran to the basement, carrying the jar, followed by Ping and used his discarded sword to break the lock on the trunk. Carefully lifting Nisi out, Chun put her on the floor.

She was still breathing, her heartbeat was weakening. She was fading fast. He wasn't going to make it to a hospital in time.

Nisi opened her eyes. "Chun."

He caressed her forehead. "Don't say anything, save your strength."

"Too late," she said.

Chun looked at the jar of blood next to the trunk. He picked it up.

"No, it's not. This is First blood," he said. "It could save you."

"No," she said, trying to lift her hand to push it away.

"You can't die, Nisi. I can't do this without you."

Her eyes closed. She went limp. He could feel the life seeping away from her. He laid her down and opened the jar.

"Please forgive me," he said and poured the blood over her open wounds.

He whispered, *"Fumiya ayzie, kambui sipo."*

The blood moved as if alive, pushing itself into her wounds and mouth. Tears poured from his eyes. This had to work.

Chun sat for what felt like an eternity, watching her prone body.

Ping whimpered nearby.

Finally, with a gasp, Nisi opened her eyes.

Holiday's Bite

By

W. H. Horner

"Move it, shit-head!"

He should have known it was coming, but the swat to the back of his skull still caught Brian by surprise.

"Knock it off, *Murray*. So the kiddies have to wait another five minutes after 1:00. I'm sorry I'm late!"

Large hands grabbed Brian's shoulders and spun him around. The mountain of a man that glared down at him certainly did not radiate holiday cheer. Murray's perpetually chapped lips were curled in their usual snow-white-enshrouded sneer. Dark, beady eyes stared at him from underneath bushy white eyebrows, while stale, fetid breath made Brian take shallow breaths.

"Listen, *elf*. You mess things up for me now, during the busiest week of the season, I'll break your legs like they're candy canes."

Brian swallowed the fear that rose in his chest. "Dude. Chill."

Murray jerked back and stared at Brian for a moment. Then a deep, rumbling laugh echoed from within his rotund midsection. "Just don't screw things up."

"It'll be fine," Brian said, continuing down the dimly lit hallway, his feet making a soft pat-pat in the ridiculous elf getup. He stared down at the bright green booties, hating the upwardly curling toes.

Murray stormed behind him, his hard-soled boots clomping on the concrete. When he wanted to, Murray could turn on the Christmas charm—he'd be all smiles and ho-ho-ho. A truly one-of-a-kind, convincing St. Nick.

The juxtaposition made Brian hate Murray all the more.

Can't be late on the rent again. Just grin and bear it another week, Brian thought. *Then I'll be rid of the homicidal maniac.*

Bursting out of the "Elves Only" door into the main sales floor of the Holiday Wonderland, Brian plastered his best happy elf expression on his face as Murray let loose with a Santa-laugh. It was all smiles and waving as they marched towards Santa's Cottage in the middle of the store, weaving their way through the aisles of Christmas decorations, knick-knacks, gift wrap, and toys—all to the deafening sound of the loudspeakers pumping out "Santa Claus is Coming to Town."

An entourage of children and their parents trailed after them to join the line already waiting for visits with Santa to begin. All of them willing to part with a ridiculous amount of cash for a crappy photo.

The girls were already at their places: Claire, the leggy one took the photos, waving the squeaky toy if the younger ones wouldn't produce a smile, and Beth, the short, busty one filled out the paperwork and took the money.

Murray sat his fat ass down in his huge red and green wingback chair, let out a "ho-ho-ho" and waved the first kid to his lap.

Thus began the drudgery.

Kid after kid sat on Santa's lap and recited their personal litanies of greed. Brian's job was to lead the shy ones and hand out candy canes as the kids left.

And always with a "Merry Christmas."

Murray had made sure on his first day that Brian would never forget that bit.

Four hours later, his mind more numb than he ever thought possible, Brian let out a sigh of relief as Murray set the "Santa's Getting a Snack!" sign up at the head of the line.

"I'm off to Blitzen's Buffet," Brian said.

Murray stomped in front of him. "Don't be late. Half an hour."

Ten minutes later, Brian sank his teeth into the best chicken finger he had ever tasted.

"I didn't know elves ate fried food."

The remains of the chicken finger flew from Brian's grasp and slid off the table.

"I didn't know they were so jumpy, either."

"Uhm . . . hi." Brian valiantly resisted the urge to grimace. *Uhm . . . hi?* What was it about a pretty girl that so totally disarmed him mentally?

And she was certainly pretty in a dark and mysterious way. Hair back in a ponytail, deep green eyes, smooth, creamy skin.

"Hi, yourself," she said, sidling up to him, stopping just before her hip touched his knee. "What's a handsome elf like you doing eating all by himself?"

"Lunch break. The big man's a slave-driver, but at least I'm allowed to eat."

"Yeah, you're looking kinda frazzled."

"That bad, huh?"

"I've seen worse . . . but not by much."

"Great. Thanks. You have a knack for spreading holiday cheer."

"Well," she said, rubbing her hip against his leg and sliding her hand onto his shoulder, "if you can pull yourself away from the glamorous world of all-you-can-eat heart attack for a few minutes, I can help get you back in the spirit."

She leaned into him, and opened her dark jacket, directing his attention to an inner pocket. Nestled inside was a plastic baggie full of enough weed to get totally baked.

"Woah. You're getting me in the spirit all right."

"Then come on," she said, running her hands down his hips. "Let's find someplace where we can get to know each other a little better."

What was he thinking? This went beyond irresponsibility. This was just stupid. She was staring at him, locking those deep green eyes with his. He was falling into them, feeling high already.

"Yeah," he said, barely able to hear his own voice, "the back hallway by the dressing room. We can sneak back there. Murray will be in his office right up till the last minute."

Her hand was in his before he knew it, and they were off, dodging through the crowd of shoppers. He was glad for the madcap pace. It kept his mind from wandering to where they were going and to the things her eyes—not to mention her hands, hips, and everything else—promised she would do.

They burst through the "Elves Only" doors, and charged down the dingy, dimly lit hallway, past the stock room, past an even dingier bathroom, past the dusty room where Murray and Brian changed. And then they were in a side hallway, hiding behind stacks of dusty pink and red hearts, Easter bunnies, leprechauns, and Uncle Sam cutouts.

Giggling and laughing, they rolled a joint and lit up. They shared a few puffs before the girl smiled her devilish smile and swung herself up and over him, straddling his legs, staring at him. She brushed his hand away from his mouth, moving the joint out of the way, and then she was kissing him, inhaling his smoky breath.

Her lips traveled down, caressing his jaw line, skimming down to his throat, kissing, sucking, kissing, sucking harder.

Then a burst of pain and sudden warmth, then a dull ache. "Oh God," Brian moaned. "I'm pretty sure you've left a mark."

"Yeah, but it's worth it, baby," the girl said, her voice coming from right by his ear. Then she moved back to his neck, working on him some more with her mouth while her hands eased their way down his chest, down his belly, lower, lower. . . .

From somewhere behind her, an enraged animal roared. Brian

reared back, slamming his head against the wall.

The girl fell backwards, giggling madly. "Oh God," she said, scooting past the large, bright red mass that had appeared behind her. "See you around."

"Wait!" Brian said, his hands reaching out. "I don't even know your name!"

Another giggle echoed down the hall and she was gone.

"What the hell is this?" Murray screamed, spittle flecking his beard, but the noise barely made a dent in Brian's buzz. "What the hell's the matter with you? We've got to—" Murray's eyes were wide, and he was staring at Brian's throat. "Good God," he said, taking a step back. "Get yourself cleaned up. You've got five minutes or you're fired, a week from Christmas or not."

Brian struggled to his feet and stumbled to the disgusting bathroom. Though his vision was blurry, and the mirror encrusted with filth, he could see that the girl had broken the skin. Blood was smeared across his neck from her lips, and it was running from several small bite marks.

"Psycho bitch!" Brian said, his voice coming out in a wheeze.

Grabbing a handful of paper towels, Brian thrust them under the running faucet, then jammed them against his throat and neck. The cold water and the rough paper stung, but he held it there until the pain dulled. The paper was stained red, but not alarmingly. She hadn't done too much damage.

Brian washed his hands before splashing cold water on his face to clear his head, then stuck a fresh paper towel to his neck as if he'd merely cut himself shaving. He went to the changing room and grabbed a green and red scarf and wrapped it around his neck and the improvised bandage.

Then he was running down the hall, racing to catch Murray before he reached the cottage. Brian caught him just before he opened the back door to the flimsy building.

"You barely made it," Murray said as he opened the door and then clomped to the front of the house where he let out a "ho-ho-ho" to indicate that Santa was back on duty. He glanced back at Brian. "Nice scarf."

"Yeah, thanks."

Despite the buzz he still felt, Brian fell into the routine as if nothing had happened, though the scarf itched him like mad, and it was really too warm to be wearing the thing. When Brian ran a hand over his forehead, it came away wet.

After maybe two hours, he caught Claire and Beth staring at him, talking back and forth between themselves. Checking behind him, he saw Murray locking him with a death-threat stare before flicking his eyes towards Brian's throat.

Then he realized that he'd been worrying at the scarf . . . no . . . the wound concealed underneath it. It felt like fire ants were crawling around on his throat, periodically biting him, sending hot pins and needles into his skin.

He tried to ignore the feeling, tried to keep his hand from probing the area, but it was getting worse. He definitely had a fever. Sweat poured down his face, pooled under his arms.

What the hell had she given him? Bad weed? Had it been laced with something?

Brian's stomach churned violently, releasing a gurgle that echoed even above the roar of excited children and shoppers. He fought the desire to vomit. Murray would kill him if he did that.

As if sensing his thoughts, Murray stood up after shooing a kid from his lap, and stood over Brian. "You're not looking well, *elf.* You're scaring the children." He leaned in close, his warm breath cool on Brian's face. "So get the hell out of here while you can still walk."

Brian nodded with very little conscious thought, then entered the crowd, one arm pressed firmly against his abdomen, the other raised so he could scratch at the scarf.

The store must have grown, since it seemed to take days for Brian to reach the back hallway and to make it to the dressing room. He managed to pull the slightly bloody scarf from his neck before the room spun and he fell to the floor.

His eyes closed with no resistance.

In the darkness, the girl was there, her confident hands roaming his body, her full lips toying with his. Her smooth body was pressed against his, and Brian moaned in pleasure as she sank her teeth into his throat with a savage jerk.

A crash brought Brian back to his senses, as Murray stormed into the room.

"I told you to get the hell out. You really are dumb, aren't you?"

Large hands picked Brian up and slammed him onto his feet. Something smacked into his face, forcing his brain to focus.

"Snap out of it!"

Murray raised his hand to strike him again, but Brian's hand arched upwards, grabbing the maniacal Santa's wrist, bending it backwards until Murray let out a scream and crumpled to his knees.

"You're breaking my arm, man!"

Something hot ignited in the back of Brian's mind, and his stomach growled again. He felt a hunger deep in his bones. And he could smell meat . . . blood . . . fear. It was all delectable.

Before he knew what he was doing, Brian gave into the primal urge. His head moved with the speed of a snake and his jaws clamped down on Murray's throat. With a tremendous jerk, Brian put an end to the larger man's futile struggling, covering himself in his first blood.

Murray slumped to the ground, his belly shaking like a bowlful of jelly, a spreading pool of blood encircling him. With a jerk, Brian ripped open the red jacket and began to feed.

Lo'Pontogo Madness

By

T.L. Randleman and Neal Levin

"More hydrogen mix to the forward balloon, Jonas!" Captain Norcent bellowed as I ambled up the wooden stairs onto the deck. "It's almost two *hels* below normal. Get someone up there and check that there's not a leak in one of the gaskets!"

He turned towards me with a smile, betraying the anger that laced his deep voice only moments before. "Ah, Simon. Just the person I was hoping to see. Those skymaps the university sent with you work like a charm. We should be at the island tomorrow, providing the wind continues to favor us."

I nodded absently at Norcent as he continued rambling on about crosswinds and updrafts, losing me with sky-naval jargon meaningless to someone unaccustomed to the inner workings of an airship. My gaze turned toward the horizon as I let his words flow over me. The view from that altitude was strikingly beautiful with vast bands of green, white, and blue in the distance. I glanced back at Norcent, his ruddy face expectant; he was waiting for an answer. Sheepishly, I asked him to repeat the question, motioning with a wave that the wind was in my ears.

"The university promised me that we'd get more instructions from you once we were closer to the destination. I'd like to discuss what we need to do now so that I can have the crew ready when we arrive."

"That's reasonable, Captain. We'll need to go over some papers that I have in my quarters. Shall we meet at your cabin in twenty minutes?"

I said goodbye to the view for the moment and slipped back downstairs to prepare for my showdown with the captain. He wasn't going to like what I had to say, but I couldn't blame him.

My quarters were ample for my current needs, though I wasn't sure I'd fit everything on the return trip.

For years, scholars had examined the journals and notes provided by Captain Cook, Joseph Banks and other naturalists. After years of proposals, the university deigned to accept my request to follow in their footsteps. I hoped to track down a few of the elusive creatures hinted at in the naturalists' ciphers.

I shuffled through my research materials pulling out those documents most pertinent to my meeting with the captain. Knocking over a pile of papers, I looked at the mess and wished that the expedition budget had allowed me to bring one of my aides. I glanced at my chronometer and realized my lateness. Satchel overflowing with bundles of maps and papers, I jogged to the captain's quarters.

His door was open and I could see the meeting had started without me. Norcent leaned over one of the maps that I had provided, and the lieutenant was next to him nodding at something. I paused in the entry, waiting to be noticed, but was instead shoved forcibly into the room. I fell to the floor, cursing as my papers went flying.

Bosun Adams hauled me to my feet, grumbling about people not having their air legs. My face felt hot and I flushed with embarrassment and anger. The bully was obviously still trying to take revenge for being bumped from his room at the start of the voyage. With a glare I began to gather my belongings.

Norcent and the lieutenant exchanged a significant look that I couldn't discern. Regaining my poise, I smoothed the folds of my frock coat and attempted to leap into my prepared speech, based in part on the one given at the award ceremony in front of the university when the Queen was in attendance.

"Captain," I said, pausing for effect. "On behalf of the university and myself, I wish to thank you and your crew for such speed and skill in the air. And I—"

The captain silenced me with a curt hand gesture. "Mr. Simon, in the air, we treat everything like a wartime effort. No grand speeches, just men completing their tasks as needed."

The captain steered us straight into planning without any introductions. It took several long hours to hammer out the details of the landing and subsequent expedition. My premonition of Norcent's reaction to the information was true to form; the man nearly went purple from an apoplectic attack when I told him that our target was known cannibal territory.

Everyone knew the story of *The Lady Ariadne*'s demise and her crew's fate in the stomachs of the savages. The sole survivor, who had escaped despite losing a hand to their stewpot, had been driven mad from the experience, but had at least lived to tell the tale. He had explained that the natives worshipped a bat god named Lo'Pontogo that devoured its enemies and instilled fear into all who survived contact with the tribe. It was a shame that I wasn't in possession of the transcripts of his naval interviews following the tragedy, but we would just have to make do with the information we had. What good was our science and technology if we couldn't defeat bloodthirsty savages, after all? We had no choice but to quash any attack made against us.

It was finally decided that we would land in a cove opposite the last known inhabitation of the natives. I would conduct my scientific experiments and specimen collection under heavy guard while gauging the reaction to our presence on the island. If all went well, we would then embark upon short expeditions into the jungle. Norcent and I were in agreement that wariness and caution were of the utmost importance. In fact, I was surprised that he intended to land the ship in the cove in the first place. I expected him to insist that the ship be anchored at two hundred feet and the skylift be set up to ferry us down to the ground, slow as that process might be.

I ran my hands through my hair, now longer than I liked it, and began to make the first of the never-ending lists that came with a position amongst academia. The sooner I finished with the paperwork, the sooner I'd be able to relax with a glass of whiskey and my own work.

The night passed sooner than I would have wished, and I woke still exhausted. Sunrise had not yet completely lit the sky when I was roused out of bed by a cacophony of shouts and bellows. The watch had just made the first sighting of land below. We had finally arrived. Hours passed as they made preparations and I contented myself by opening the porthole and letting the fresh smell of the tropics waft into the stuffy room, ruffling my journal pages as I worked. There was so much to do before we landed that I could hardly contain myself. I worked on and on, with no one bothering to inform me of how the preparations were shaping up.

An abrupt knock on my door startled me from my work and howled in frustration as I managed to smear ink all over my hands and marred the thick paper with large black stains. Two solid-looking marines entered and proclaimed that Captain Norcent requested my presence. I had barely enough time to grab my coat and my bag before I was rushed on deck towards a spherical glass and iron chamber; my ride to the ground. Clearly, I had been mistaken in my previous assumption that the airship itself was going to land. Or perhaps something had happened to change the captain's plans.

From either side of the deck, crew unraveled giant coils of rope and I was ushered quickly into what I had originally believed to be an observation dome. Brass seams, air tubes, and a single platform seat were all that adorned this magnificent contraption. Later, as I dangled and swayed, barely contained in this strange chamber, hundreds of feet above the ground, I had second thoughts of its magnificence. Sailors swung down ropes from all sides, scurrying like monkeys upon vines, uncontained by any such elegant protection as I had. Looking out upon the world, I simultaneously felt claustrophobic and agoraphobic. I recalled with some chagrin that the sailors called this contraption the bosun's chair, used derogatorily for ranking officers and dignitaries who couldn't climb the ropes.

Gusts of air must have been pummeling the outside of the sphere which was what caused it to sway so terribly; I could see the sailors' clothing being whipped about. Vexed or not by the crew's belittlements, I was suddenly quite glad that I wasn't hanging by a literal thread. I knew my fate was in secure hands as I was lowered. Finally able to slow my breathing and calm my mental state, I could enjoy the view of the bluest ocean I had seen in my life. Days of looking at nothing but the clouds below us had taken a toll on me. Even the island itself was breathtakingly beautiful. The white sand coves met the dense jungle which climbed up to a rocky mount.

The crystal blue water blended to a rich turquoise around the sandbar that jutted out to protect the natural cove. Palm trees dotted the horizon and ahead of us rose up rolling grasslands even more picturesque than the best memories of the untainted lands of my youth. Even the few lazy clouds only swabbed delicately at the mountain peaks, seemingly preferring to keep their distance.

Even from this skybound vantage, I could see that nothing looked like the landmarks portrayed in my books, a frightening thought considering all my time spent in study and calculations. I pondered the reasons for the disparity as the craft carried me downward. It felt as if much time had passed, but finally my descent slowed and I landed with a gentle thump upon the ground. I was somewhat surprised at how smooth the ride was once I was out of the crosswind. I had expected to be jarred to the very bone, but I was able to leave the craft with just a mild nausea. The tropical breeze quickly put me to rights as I surveyed my new surroundings.

The first thing I noticed was that Norcent had made the best of a bad situation. I immediately recognized that the cove was too shallow to land the vessel; even removing the dorsal sails, the rudders would extend more than twenty feet below the waterline. It was no wonder Norcent had decided to assemble the skylift.

Pairs of alert marines set themselves to patrol the beach at regular intervals, making certain no natives got the drop on the operation. In the meantime, a few of the men had set a roaring fire in order to smoke fish pulled from the waves in large nets. I spied Norcent inspecting a canvas pavilion tent that the men had pitched while I was inside the skylift. I walked towards him, shakily at first as my legs readjusted to the solid ground. Beneath the soles of my feet, the soft, white sand was littered here and there with shell specimens that I longed to stop and examine closely. A few of these made their way into my pockets, however, for later cataloguing.

"Captain, I'm amazed at what you've done in so little time. I confess this island seems to be different from the survey. Are we sure of the co-ordinates?"

"I noticed the same thing, but I've checked twice against the skymaps. It's the same, but the island seems to be very different. It could possibly be explained by volcanic activity, or maybe tidal waves. Whatever the reason, this is the island."

"Is there any native activity?" I asked while scanning the dark tree line. The hairs on the back of my neck prickled in a way that made me sure we were being watched by someone or something. Norcent shook his head and followed my gaze towards the darkness beyond the canopy.

"Nothing yet, but I'm sure we'll have some visitors later tonight. We'll be ready for them, I assure you. In the meantime, you'll want to get on with your work, so I've assembled a small group to keep you out of danger."

Norcent pointed a little farther up the beach where a small crate-filled boat was being unloaded with the miscellaneous items required for the expedition. There were two marines standing guard over three sailors who quickly made a pile well away from the incoming tide. One of the ship boys was busily assembling small cages for live specimens.

Letting them get about their business, I attempted to classify what I thought was a new species of tortoise, but the large fellow was pulled away from me and butchered for meat before I had finished my examination. The rude sailor could at least have given me a few more minutes with the gigantic beast!

Later that day, I was on my knees examining a particularly interesting lizard as it moved across the sand when a burly sailor stepped between my subject and me, effectively blocking what little light was left of the late afternoon sun. The lizard shot off, disappearing up one of the palm trees that fringed the beach. I sighed at the lost opportunity and turned my attention towards the sailor, noting the red hair, ruddy skin, and a crude brass prosthetic leg that was standard issue to Navy amputees. I glared and he ignored it, offering me a hand up from the ground. His grip was crushing, and his hand twice the size of my own.

"I thought I'd made it clear that I wasn't to be disturbed unless it was important," I said, brushing sand off my sturdy cotton trousers.

"You did, Mr. Simon." The sailor came to attention and saluted me as if I were one of his officers. "We spotted something up by the tree line.

Me and the men think you oughta take a look."

I followed with some anticipation, hoping the man would show me some naturalist wonder, but afraid that the better option had scurried away. Then we crested a sand dune and I saw the idol. Tears nearly came to my eyes as I began to appraise what I believed to be one of the wooden Lono idols found only on inhabited islands of the South Seas. I was more than happy to answer all the questions the seamen babbled. I was many things, but never stingy with information.

"But was it cannibals that made this thing?"

There I was stumped and had to shrug. "Natives made it for sure, but otherwise it's hard to say. These sorts of totems usually depict a creature that is either a food source for the tribe, or one that fills them with dread. You can see by the idol's sharp claws, narrow eyes, and vestigial wings that it is depicting some carnivorous creature, most likely their legendary bat god. Did you find any other tools or tracks nearby?"

The wiry sailor—Jonas, I came to understand was his name— stepped forward. "Not a thing, sir. Less undergrowth suggests a path, but we've found no tracks in the area save our own."

"Lack of other evidence would suggest this was a spiritual path. The islanders are likely to use it only for special rituals. I would say we are safer on the path than anyplace else on the island." The men visibly relaxed, although none of them shifted from defensive stances.

"Jonas, would you do the honor of leading us onward via this path? You men have already proved a great help."

The woods teemed with the wondrous sounds of creatures I hoped I would have the chance to see and examine up close. Ever fearful of encountering cannibals, the men stopped at every noise and did their best to aim at the source. In an effort to calm myself I pulled out my canteen and slowly drank.

Just then, a heavy weight landed on my backpack and something brushed the back of my neck. A ghostlike face appeared before mine causing me to let out a shriek as I threw myself to the ground. The men pointed their guns in my direction, but began to laugh. Then I noticed that the small ghost face belonged to a red-bodied monkey. A black skullcap and muzzle surrounded the monkey's white face.

The men put away their firearms, realizing the noises coming from the jungle were probably just the sounds of curious monkeys.

The monkey before me brought a copper object up to his face, and with a start, I realized it was my own trusted compass. The critter must have grabbed it from my pack. I called to the monkey and crept closer, but the moment I was almost upon him, he took off in a mad dash with my treasured tool.

I ran after the monkey, the men crashing through the woods after me. They shouted to dissuade me, but that compass had been with me for years, given to me as a gift from my father on my fourteenth birthday.

I should have expected the pit.

One of the first rules of jungle exploration is never to run after monkeys, lest you fall straight into a pit. I was just fortunate that there were no spikes at the bottom and that the only real injury was to my pride. The few bumps and bruises I sustained in the fall were nothing compared to my utter embarrassment at the situation.

The men all gathered around the top of the hole and peered down the short distance at me. Rabbie, the burly Scot, whistled through his teeth. Perhaps he contemplated just how much worse my fate could have been, but I dared not ask. He started unwinding a length of rope that he'd been carrying around his waist and lowered it down while the two other seamen pulled out their pipes, joking about the scientist in the hole.

"With all due respect, sir," Rabbie said with more than a little cheek. "The next time you feel the need to have a wee jog in a cannibal-infested jungle, wait until I'm back aboard ship. Preferably passed out drunk."

"I'll keep that in mind," I said as humbly as I could, reaching for the length of hemp rope that dangled just out reach. Rabbie eased it down another inch, and I had it. Moments later I was scrambling up the rope, using the earthen walls of the pit as leverage. As I crested the edge, several hands grasped me and hefted me to my feet, then gave me a good dusting off, as if to ward off any further misadventures. Jonas handed me my compass without a word. How he'd managed to get it from the monkey, I didn't ask, but I nodded at him gratefully as I tucked it into the inner pocket of my coat.

I felt at ease, here amongst these men. They were rough, but good men all. I looked forward to getting to know them in the next few days. If nothing else, perhaps they'd learn a little something about the natural world around them as I explored. I turned to speak to the marine about going back to the beach and something whistled past my ear. An arrow appeared as if from nowhere, and lodged in the man's throat. He gurgled and clawed at it, his brown eyes wide with surprise and the knowledge of his impending death. The light left his gaze and he collapsed at my feet, dead. Fear kept me rooted to the ground, staring as the blood pooled around the marine's head. Time seemed to slow to a crawl as a group of about ten natives burst from the trees, some with arrows at the ready, others armed with clubs and wicked bone knives.

The other marine got off two shots, the first into the face of an archer and the second one grazing the arm of the clubman that was set on killing Rabbie. Then the natives pulled him to the ground, the knife making wet, hungry noises as it stabbed into the man.

I heard Rabbie yell at me to run, and Jonas was grabbing my arm, pulling me towards the path that led back to the beach. I stumbled stupidly, smelling rich earth and the iron tang of blood. Other than the wet, painful sounds of battle, the jungle was eerily silent. No bird screeched, no monkey chittered, no bugs hummed in the heated air.

There was nothing I could do to help them. Rabbie and the two other sailors had cut the number of attackers in half. One sailor grabbed the marine's gun off the ground and was putting the bayonet to good use.

The last native archer turned and aimed directly at me, and I screamed. His black eyes were empty as he loosed an arrow that thunked into my chest a heartbeat later. The impact knocked me onto my back and I stared at the sky, expecting the pain at any moment, but it never came.

With a shaking hand I explored the wound as the battle raged around me. My mind raced as I searched in vain for blood. Then, realization that I'd cheated death; the arrow had embedded itself into the compass that I'd only moments before put into my breast pocket.

While I was focused on my miraculous survival more natives had arrived to replace their fallen allies. My companions killed a few more, but they were hopelessly outnumbered. Before long we were completely overrun and disarmed. Ironically, I had survived the arrow only to be destined for a soup pot.

I never felt more akin to fish than I did being brought to the native village. It was reminiscent of the meal the men had prepared on the beach and it wasn't a pleasant feeling.

The village was an immense sprawl, dwarfing expectations extrapolated from previous explorations. The jeering natives produced the odor of the great unwashed, but they unexpectedly kept their habitat clear of detriment. I had expected the area to have been overtaken by bones of their victims, but saw now that they utilized the remains in their tools and weapons. No hope remained that any of our remains would make it back to our homeland.

The village shaman spent far too brisk a visit at each of our cages. He lingered at my pen, but did not prod like he did with the others. Though his fearsome visage scared me, I wished for more time to examine his features. Like the textbook depictions of aboriginal holy men, this native went beyond the standard ritual scarification of his kin. Had I my sketchpad on hand, the journals back home would have lauded me for any images of how this man had grafted his flesh to emulate a bat.

The shaman spoke something in his harsh, guttural language. Every word seemed ominous as every motion of his mouth was visible with the skin pulled back away from his teeth. Whatever he said must have been profound, causing the rest of the natives to step away and ignore our presence.

The dread of our fate was amplified by our wait. It wasn't until hours later that we were sure none of the crew from the airship would come for us. With the sun low on the horizon, the natives once again grew interested in us. It was sudden: one moment we were motionless in our cages, and the next a warrior had flung each of us from our cages and forced us to the ground, held there until we expended all our energy in a futile effort to escape.

During the course of our imprisonment one of the sailors had perished. It had to have been a bite from something extremely poisonous, because I hadn't heard the man make a noise. I knew that if I made it through this, I would never forget the man's blank stare boring into me. None of the natives removed the body from where it was, but they seemed to be annoyed by our loss.

Our fear was palpable as we watched the receding torchlight. Our motion was limited by the vines that bound our hands and feet. The darkness of the mountain caves we had been taken to slowly began to cloud our vision. There was a haze in the light of the receding torches, and an overpowering stench of fecal matter mixed with the sickly sweet smell of nectar globules on the floor of the cavern. Before the last bit of flickering torchlight finally disappeared, the full darkness fell upon us and we struggled against our bonds in the hope of making for freedom. Near me was a large stone slab with sharp edges; wedged against it I gained leverage, but the rock sliced into my flesh almost as much as it did the rope. The sticky, sweet liquid of the nectar coated us as our weight burst its tiny nodules.

Out in the darkness at the edges of the cave we can hear hundreds of bats waking. Suddenly, I realized the horrible purpose of the nectar; bathed in the scent of the fruit, we would all be very appealing to bats.

Rabbie cradled his prosthetic limb. The rope at his foot was limp without the other limb to support it. "One of you help me with my hands. I still have a blade and other weapons concealed in this leg."

Using the bladed edge on Rabbie's leg we managed to free ourselves. He was still hobbling around, unbalanced without his limb, when I noticed the shadow of a bat growing larger and larger as it closed in upon us. By the time it was nearly human-sized it vanished from my vision. Strangely, I could recall no wall on which the shadow could have been cast. My companions convinced me it was just a trick of the light.

I began to explain a plan of escape using the flight path of the bats. Time was against us and the bats streamed around us, ripping our flesh and my plan apart. Assaulted by wings and claws, I couldn't tell in which direction I was traveling. My screams joined those of my companions.

In a short series of bewildering flashes of light, the room echoed with the thunderclap of Rabbie's derringer. A monstrous beast, akin in a less stylized way to the totem, had gotten hold of him and was thrashing him. Rabbie shouted many things, but the one word I recognized was "Run!"

Jonas had my shoulder, pushing me towards the end of the tunnel, but the sight of the bat god reduced me to a shuddering mass of flesh and I could do nothing but be propelled by his force. Rabbie was dying; the last sounds I heard before I lost consciousness were that of his weapon clicking on empty cylinders behind me in the darkness.

It hurts to be awake. My mouth and gums ache as if needles are stabbing the soft flesh, viciously trying to break the skin. My torn throat burns every time I swallow. I can't eat, and I can hardly drink. What little I can take is a thick broth or an overly sweet tea that would be soothing if the injury were less grave. The broth does little to alleviate the hunger that gnaws at my gut, however, and does nothing to satisfy my strange craving for extra-rare chops. I can't swallow more than broth, so it's just as well that there are no chops to be had on the ship.

My only respite is the laudanum. I can sleep and heal when in its narcotic grip, much to my great relief. The surgeon, an old sawbones named Plummer, doses me with as much as he dares. He says that he fears my side effects—cold, clammy, and pale skin, sensitivity to bright light, and slowness of breath and heartbeat—will worsen. Plummer speaks to me of long-term effects of the disease, but I've made it clear that's a worry for another time.

As for Jonas, he fell into a coma just hours after Plummer gave him a clean bill of health. Not surprisingly, the old surgeon is baffled, and as good as he might be at sewing up a wound, I don't think he is much of a doctor. He mumbles about new forms of rabies or other strange diseases while flipping through a large medical handbook, then frowns and prods Jonas, trying to find clues to his condition to no avail. It maddens him, and entertains me to no end. Jonas sometimes wakes during the day and unleashes an unearthly screech that puts us all on edge, until Plummer manages to sedate him.

The crew pretends to act cheerful whenever forced into the infirmary, but I know it's a poorly constructed act. When they think I'm asleep I can hear them whispering with the guards outside, telling terrible stories of what happened to us and worse, what we've become.

It seems that there has been a death or disappearance amongst the crew each night since we left that godforsaken island. Some of the men blame us, Jonas and I, for having brought a curse upon the ship. The superstitious amongst them have begun to wear garlic amulets and sprinkle salt on the floor as if to ward off evil.

A part of me is fascinated, but another is angry at their impudence and ignorance. Jonas and I are victims of a gruesome attack, not monsters from a horror tale.

When not in a poppy-induced haze or watching Jonas slowly die, I spend my time writing what dreams and nightmares I remember in my journal. The last three nights I dreamed that Jonas would rise from his cot around midnight and drift like a ghost out of the infirmary doors only to return fat, rosy, and bloated some hours later.

During a period of lucidity, I realized that Jonas rallies during the night and worsens during the day, as if his life-force ebbs and flows like the tide. Sometimes I wonder if my dream is really a dream at all, and then I am confronted with his still, pale form sleeping like death in the cot across the infirmary and I believe again that it must be the imaginings of a fever-induced haze.

More disturbing is a dream of being eaten alive by the cannibals' bat god, of being torn apart and having my marrow and viscera sucked from me as I scream into a dark place from which I will never return.

The margins of my journal are full of sketches of bloody and mis-shapen bats, along with other dark shapes that I don't remember drawing. I think I'm going mad.

I'm having another dream, only this time I'm being rocked gently in a cradle, having been newly reborn. The crash of drums and the screech of violins surround me, and I'm reminded of the ocean playing Mozart. My belly is full and I am content. My mouth tastes of iron and salt and I wonder if my desire for chops was somehow fulfilled. There is a bright light and I cannot open my eyes or I will be blinded.

I wake suddenly, not knowing where I am. I open my eyes and find them filled with stars. The moon rises overhead. The gentle rocking in my dream isn't a cradle at all, but a wooden rowboat. The still form of Jonas is swaddled in blankets opposite me. How we got here I don't know. With a groan I sit up and scan the horizon for the airship. There is water as far as the eye can see; we are on the open sea, drifting on the aimless tide. There is no airship. They've left us behind.

I attempt to take stock. Some magnanimous soul has left us a small supply of food and two jugs of water, enough to last us a few days. More importantly, there is a bottle of laudanum. I resist the urge to take my fill and continue searching.

My beloved compass is here, patched as well as could be expected, but in working order, along with a sextant and an oceanic map. They've also left my journal containing a wax-sealed envelope. Hands trembling, I open the note and read Norcent's words twice before I understand the horror of the situation.

He begins with apology and kind words regarding our future sur-vival. The crew, he explains, is on the verge of mutiny after the fifth body was found, with four other crewmen still unaccounted for. There is noth-ing for it, he says, because the only demand from the crew is that we, the suspected vampires, be killed, or barring that, put off the ship immedi-ately.

Faced with such a breakdown of discipline, he has little choice but to acquiesce to the demands of his superstitious crew, especially after the bosun's death and the disappearance of his sole midshipman.

I see now that Norcent simply hadn't had the strength to stand for me when it came down to it, and those other few who would have spoken up on our behalf had either died or disappeared. I think of Rabbie, who was a true friend to me despite the disparity in our roles.

Norcent's note claims that he will forever feel shame at his inability to help us, especially after being faced with evidence that backs up the crew's crazed belief. What the evidence is, he doesn't say, other than a maddening line about blood on our hands. Norcent believes that we have a chance to reach an island if we head southwest.

He signs the letter, with apologies and regards, humbly, Bors Norcent.

I crumple the letter in my hand and rage silently at the universe, Captain Norcent, and seamen everywhere. I silently wish for the airship to fall from the sky. It's clear that the crew is comprised of idiots without an iota of sense amongst them because they clearly cannot tell which of us is the purported vampire, after all. Granted, they must ensure that they rid themselves of the threat, but if they had given me time I could have proved I am not the killer. Or could I?

Am I so sure?

Night is now upon us. My companion stirs, and I realize that I can see him clearly in the darkness. He looks at me and his eyes become dark with fear. I want to explain that he's safe with me but I can't speak. It matters little in any case, because it is a lie. Jonas begins to scream and I reach for him.

The laudanum takes away the pain.

But not the hunger.

Tonight, at least, I'll feast like a king.

Box Lunch

By

James Chambers

Oblivion turned out to be silent and quite cold.
Johnny Sky had always wondered about that.

At least it only lasted three days. In that time the sensations Johnny had lost when he died returned to him by degrees. He gauged them by how clearly he could hear the clacking beetles and wriggling worms gathering outside his coffin. True, his senses lacked the same intensity he'd experienced in life, but it was enough to prove Madigan's promise genuine.

Johnny had died and come back to life—or, rather, "unlife," as Madigan called it, or sometimes, with a wink and a grin, "mi vida meurte."

Johnny remembered that night in Club Chattel when Madigan mounted his chair with exaggerated pomp and announced, "Johnny Sky, welcome to the chorus of the night. You have been chosen to rise alongside us in the dark majesty of our unlife." Then, slipping a bit like a drunk, Madigan clambered down and burst out laughing. The cold-faced men and women at the table smirked with tepid amusement. They had all been around a long, long time, and it took a lot to get a rise out of them.

Johnny, on the other hand, thrilled to Madigan's performance. It was the welcome he'd always imagined he'd one day receive; it left him speechless.

"Cat got your tongue?" Madigan had said. He'd gripped Johnny's shoulder and given him a reassuring squeeze. "Kid, no worries. You're in. You've paid your dues, and you're all right with us. We got what you want. A good death and eternity are yours for the taking."

Warm flashes of pride had filled Johnny's soon-to-be-forfeit soul. He had never felt so alive.

The bloodshed followed.

Johnny picked the night, and they made it as painless as possible when they bit into his flesh and drank away his life. They did it in a hotel room overlooking a parking lot and an industrial park while muted sex noises bumped and groaned from the next room. Johnny didn't care. Heat poured out of his body; cold streamed in. A neat, impenetrable darkness descended over him even as his mind sparked with short-lived anticipation of his new existence.

They left his body for the maid to find, and so Johnny Sky became undead.

He couldn't yet move in his new condition, but he sensed the latent power pooling in his corpse. Of course, the possibility of a trick had flashed through his mind. He knew stories of catatonic people being buried alive. He'd read about living people in Haiti tricked into believing they'd been brought back from the dead when really they'd only been poisoned into a deep stupor, buried, and dug up later. He'd heard about Japanese victims of poorly prepared fugu, alive but paralyzed to the appearance of death. And then there were rumors of organ thieves whose victims awoke up in bathtubs full of ice, minus a kidney. Much as Johnny trusted Madigan, a little part of him still wondered if it could all be real. But the way he felt proved it. He couldn't imagine being alive and feeling so empty yet so powerful at the same time.

He was dead for sure and goddamn glad of it.

If not for the paralysis and the fact that he was six feet under, he'd have gotten up, whirled like a dervish, and howled at the moon.

Instead, he waited.

An ethereal consciousness trapped in a featherweight husk floating on a dark tide, euphoric at finally achieving my destiny, he thought, allowing himself to wax poetic.

Finally, the reward I worked so hard for.

Johnny Sky would live forever.

Euphoric.

He rolled the word over in his mind and savored its elegance. Any time, now, Madigan would come exhume him and teach him to feed.

He could hardly wait. Feeding marked the last threshold.

Once Johnny consumed his first blood meal, he'd truly be a creature of the night, a lord of shadows with all the powers of charm and seduction to bend the world to his will. He wondered how to dress, whether or not to go Goth, or don some retro-Renaissance silk, or maybe Punk gear, or even a tux and cape like the classics. He could go professional in an expensive, tailored suit like Madigan, or cowboy like The Kid, who opted for an ebony Stetson and a bolo tie of jet and ruby. Then again maybe he'd dress like he always had in jeans and a long, un-tucked, red button-down shirt with a black leather jacket. It was a classic look. But no, he'd definitely trade up. He could sneak in anywhere, take the most expensive clothes he wanted, grab a fancy watch and a leather wallet. All of it would be his. So would all the women he'd never had a shot with. As long as he fed often enough, there'd be no problem getting it up and going at it like he was alive—Madigan had been clear about that. There were a few women in particular Johnny intended to visit: ex-girlfriends who'd dumped him because he wasn't quite smart enough, or handsome enough, or funny enough, and certainly never wealthy enough. Definitely that broad-shouldered brunette down at the art supply store who always called him "Jimmy" when he stepped up to the cash register. He'd show them what he'd become, get his hooks into them, get them hot and bothered, and then leave them to live their lives knowing what they'd lost out on when they turned their noses up at Johnny Sky.

That was real power.

Being dead was going to be good; it would be everything Johnny had ever wanted from life, and it would last forever.

He would leave all his failures behind him. Forget every dead-end garage band he'd ever joined. Shed his memories of the smirking dismissals and blunt rejections his poetry, short stories, and screenplays had garnered. He'd shrug off the humiliation of facing uncomfortable audiences on all those open mic comedy nights, and let go of his embarrassment on 1,253 straight failed auditions. So what if none of those paths had led him to his rightful fame and fortune? He'd never stopped believing he was bound for greatness. It was just a matter of finding the right path. And this one was perfect, because what was fame but a form of immortality.

His paintings had started him down the road, but it took seven years to earn acceptance from Madigan and his people. Johnny stumbled onto them by accident at a Halloween festival in one of the downtown clubs that showed his artwork. It was his second show, and already he'd earned a reputation for creating violent, visceral images. But even as a featured artist, he couldn't lay a hand on any of the many beautiful women dancing through the revelry. His intensity frightened them. Depressed and lost in the maze of darkened hallways, Johnny wandered into a private party room. Thunderous music and low light kept him anonymous, but he almost gave himself away when waiters brought in two men and a woman, nude and strapped into wheelchairs. He swallowed a scream when the party-goers bared their fangs and fed. Stifling his shock Johnny slipped away while the fresh blood distracted them. Their power amazed him; he ached to be like them. That night had been no accident, but a glimpse at his destiny.

All his failures made sense; fate had been preserving him for something much more magnificent than mortal riches.

It took Johnny months to track down the fringes of their community, and then he worked his way inward. He toiled and learned, kept his mouth shut most of the time, said the right things when he spoke, and said them to the right people. He noticed their interest in his work, so he kept on painting and sketching in his raw style. They began showing up at his exhibits, always in dive bars and drug clubs and coffeehouses, where Johnny's art was considered rebellious and edgy. Johnny demonstrated his sincerity in his work, displayed his commitment to their ways and his worship of those who had gone before him. He put his blood into every piece. He found that the promise of free booze and drugs was enough to attract a crowd of folks who wouldn't be easily missed, and his showings earned a reputation as choice feeding grounds.

Still, for the first year, they ignored Johnny almost as if he did not exist. For another two, they scorned him as unworthy. Then they tolerated him; he had earned their reluctant acknowledgement. And in the final year Madigan took him under his wing.

"Lot of the things I see in you, kid, I once felt," Madigan told him. "And your art is just—well, forget how people have treated you so far. They all find your work purely entertaining. It's so raw, so violent and bloody. You know we gotta love it. We don't see it like the living do, anyway. No. We see much more. And, man, but you know how to bring out the party folk."

From the inside, it all seemed so natural that Johnny almost forgot the years of lonely struggling. Almost, but not quite. Not until the night they took his blood and brought him over. That wiped it all out.

To eager Johnny it felt like weeks lying in his dark grave before a whispering voice came, along with the scratching of iron against soil. The digging noise seemed to go on and on as if it would never end, until just when Johnny thought he might explode from excitement, a weight slammed against the coffin lid inches from his face and shook the entire box. Minutes later the wooden shell cracked open. Stars speckled the far-off night framed by the rough edges of the opened grave. Madigan's smiling face loomed over Johnny.

"Put on your drinking shoes," he said. "Tonight's the night, amigo."

Madigan hefted Johnny from the coffin and slung him across his shoulders. Like a massive beetle he clambered out of the grave and surfaced in the cemetery. The warm air pricked Johnny's icy skin; the dark world sped by in a blur. It jumped with electric flashes, as every living thing in Johnny's sight sparked and flickered. The lights rose mainly from the trees and the grass, but Johnny spotted birds and squirrels, too, and even scintillating clouds of insects flitting against the black curtain of sky. It reminded him of the way he painted.

"Give yourself some time to adjust," Madigan said. "It can be disconcerting, but it's all good. In fact, it's all absolutely fucking great!"

Madigan glowed not at all.

He hurried down a soft slope toward a black limousine, eased Johnny into the back, and slid in beside him and closed the door.

Two gorgeous women in rumpled silk dresses slumped on the facing seat. One was dead; Johnny could tell by the absence of light dappling her body. The other seemed very close to death, her sparks quite dim.

"Told you I'd pick you up in style," said Madigan.

He thumped the roof and the chauffeur hit the gas. The jerking motion tipped Johnny sideways; he slid over and bumped his head against an armrest.

"Whoa, sorry about that," said Madigan as he righted Johnny. "Here. Have a little something to help get your legs under you."

Madigan grabbed the dying girl, brushed her hair away from her neck to expose a dripping throat wound, and then pressed it against Johnny's mouth. The blood burned his tongue, seared his throat, ignited a blaze in his guts.

This is what success tastes like, thought Johnny.

His entire body jumpstarted then shuddered like an engine failing to turn over. He clamped down tight and drained everything he could from the woman, but it wasn't enough. Not nearly. She'd been close to exsanguinated, and now fully awakened, Johnny's hunger raged for more, even as Madigan shoved aside the empty body.

"Good stuff," he said. "Do I know how to pick 'em, or what?"

Johnny's chest heaved. He licked a speck of blood from his upper lip.

"More," he said.

"It's coming when the time is right," promised Madigan. "That'll hold you, so at least I won't have to keep carrying you around."

Johnny raised his hands and stared at his pale fingers. He could move again, but he felt like he had the flu.

"Where are we going?"

"Dante's Hall," Madigan said.

This is it, then, Johnny told himself. *This is for real. The Hall is where everyone takes their first feeding.* He'd heard of it, but never seen it. He had no idea where or what it was, but he knew the rites of the undead took place there. In Johnny's mind Dante's Hall equaled the gates of Heaven.

Madigan read the awe in Johnny's face.

"Shit, kid, I know! How fucking cool is it? You've been working a long time for this. Hoping and dreaming. Just like a lot of people. Only not everyone makes it. We both know that. Lot of people lack the balls to chase their dreams or the smarts to do it right. And it's not only having the talent or the right perspective that gets you there. Fuck no. Lots of people better suited than you never even get this far because they just don't want it as bad as you. You got to get to know the right people, sure. But more importantly you got to know in your heart that no other thing will do, because you have to give up your life to it wholesale. See, it's the commitment that counts most. And Johnny, no shit, but you got that in spades. Most folks would've given up struggling the way you did, especially after being treated like shit for so long."

Johnny grinned. His mentor's praise felt incredible.

"But that's how it has to be," Madigan said. "We've got to keep our population down and maintain the integrity of our feeding grounds. So we're pretty damn picky about who and how many we let in. Tonight you get your shot."

"What'll happen?"

"You'll see."

The limousine exited the highway, prowled side streets, and traveled far outside the city, beyond even the suburbs. It crawled down lightless roads hedged by thick brush and high sycamores that blotted out the moon. Johnny spotted specks of light like *ignis fatuus* that signaled the presence of night creatures on the prowl.

"Thank you, Madigan," said Johnny. "For all you've done for me."

"You did it for yourself, Johnny. Maybe I gave you a helpful nudge in the right direction now and then."

"Well, thanks for that."

They turned down a gravel driveway and drove deep into the woods. The path terminated at a small parking area before a brick and stone mansion. The driver pulled past a row of luxury cars and stopped by the front door.

"Dump the bodies in the usual place," Madigan told the chauffeur.

He got out, rounded the car, and helped Johnny, who was unsteady on his feet but could walk. Madigan guided him toward the house. As they approached it he turned and took them along a brick path and around the corner. A stairwell of concrete and bluestone led to a basement entrance, where a crimson lamp glowed above a steel fire door. Madigan looked around to see that they were alone. Beyond the house stretched a vast yard draped in a thin mist.

"I like you, Johnny, so I'm going to give you some advice," said Madigan. "Whatever happens, don't forget that your limbs will grow back. Okay?"

"Uh, yeah, sure," Johnny said.

"Good, now I'm going to give you a little edge, but you have to keep this between me and you," Madigan said. He reached into his pocket and produced a dead rat encased in a Ziploc baggie. He took it out, slashed it with one of his fangs, pressed it against Johnny's lips, and squeezed. Johnny recoiled at the disgusting flavor.

"Drink it!" ordered Madigan. "I know it's cold and it tastes like shit, but it hasn't been dead that long. It'll give you a little more strength."

Johnny consumed the wretched fluid and wiped his chin when he was done. He felt a touch firmer on his feet.

"I'm pulling for you, Johnny. I'm not the only one. Like I said, folks find your art supremely, uh, entertaining. We kind of want to see where you'll take it."

Madigan ushered Johnny down the stairs and opened the door. Inside waited solid blackness adorned with a rendering plant stink.

"What is this?"

"This is your dream, Johnny. Now go in there and prove you deserve it."

"But what do I do?"

"You'll figure it out."

Madigan shoved Johnny through the door and slammed it shut after him. Johnny reached back, but there was no doorknob or handle on this side. He turned, took a shaking step forward, and stumbled along a narrow corridor defined by coarse brick. He heard scratching all around him and the low moan of a cold draft racing overhead. Murmuring voices beckoned him forward. The corridor ended, and Johnny tripped, nearly falling as he missed a step down; frigid hands caught him and propped him back up.

"Who's there?" said Johnny.

"Shut up! Shut the fuck up!" a man hissed.

"It's almost time," said another.

"What's happening?" Johnny asked.

"This is it," someone said.

Many others lingered in the dark with Johnny.

He asked, "Why can't I see you? Shouldn't I be able to see in the dark now?"

"Not enough blood," a woman explained.

"The first full feeding puts everything right," said another. "Makes you a fucking god."

"Then you become one of them," said someone else.

"Not you, dipshit. Me!" barked a voice. "ME!"

"No! I've got the edge. They gave me rat's blood," one snapped.

"Me, too," said another.

"And me."

"I said 'Shut the fuck up!'"

Johnny wondered how many were there. This was supposed to be his momentous night, his hour in the spotlight—the start of his new, glorious immortal existence.

Faint lights switched on overhead.

A loudspeaker crackled with a commanding voice that said, "Ladies and gentlemen, welcome to Dante's Hall."

The lights flared to brilliance.

"Y'all have proven you have something special inside you," the voice said. "You've pursued us, petitioned to join our special community, and demonstrated your desire and willingness to do what it takes to reach that goal. All of you have, in fact, given your very life's blood just to be here tonight. For that, I applaud you. So, go on and give all y'all a little pat on your cold, dead backs. Tonight is your night!"

Johnny's eyes adjusted to the glare.

There were forty, maybe fifty men and women gathered in a huge subterranean chamber, all of them blinking and holding their hands up against the light. Some wore rags, others fine burial clothes, and more than a few were naked. Everyone's flesh displayed the same cyanic tone, and they all looked weak and faint. An inch-thick layer of soft, gray dust furred the floor like fresh snow.

"Now if y'all will please relocate to the outer wall so that we can begin the ritual," the announcer instructed. "Place one hand on the brass rail there, and keep your dogs behind the red line. Just kick some of that there dust away and you'll see it."

Some complied. Others looked confused. Johnny shuffled into position and tried hard not to choke on his disillusionment. He didn't want to be like some graduation day sap cheering over a piece of paper they practically gave away to anyone who showed up. This was meant to be *his* night, *his* rite of passage, something sacred and rare. He had been *chosen.*

"Shake a leg!" the announcer shouted, spurring the stragglers. "Anyone not in position by the count of three will be...*removed.*"

Everyone hustled into place, and the voice continued: "At the center of this spacious arena are three large crates. Chained inside each is a living person, whose veins have never been tapped. That's right! They're young, they're clean, and they're hot to trot—or maybe they're scared half to death! I always get those two mixed up."

Now Johnny recognized the voice: The Kid.

He pictured that big, black Stetson and the devilish boots The Kid favored, the elegant bolo tie slung from his neck like a whip of venom.

"Here's how it goes. The first three of you to reach them box lunches and feed enough to open the red door and leave the room get to join us," The Kid said.

A spotlight shafted across the chamber. Johnny's eyes followed it to the massive iron door painted deep red on the far side of the room. Hinged at the top, its full weight had to be lifted vertically and held in order to exit. A picture window above it overlooked the chamber. Half a dozen figures waited there, watching. Johnny recognized Madigan among them, and some of those jaded elite who had been to his shows and who'd sat around the table in Club Chattel. He spied The Kid's silhouette, a microphone raised to his mouth.

"Rest a y'all who don't make it out get to sit tight down there till dawn, when we open up some windows and let that morning sun shine in," said The Kid. "But don't ya feel bad about that. It's a hell of a thing you managed just being here tonight."

What Johnny had taken for dust covering the floor was, in fact, the ash of all the failures who had gone ahead of him into true oblivion.

"I know how hungry you must be, so let's not delay," The Kid said. "In a moment we'll dim the lights. When they turn red, you may feed. Good luck to y'all."

The lights blinked out, leaving the observation room the only source of illumination. Johnny saw deeper into it now and observed the opulence of its furnishings. Many dark figures stood there like a gathering of noble statues, and in the low light their eyes and teeth gleamed like opals.

Lust for blood and eternal life filled the air, and it felt so common and brutal, Johnny wanted to lie down and give up. *This was what I died for*, Johnny thought, and with Madigan's words echoing through his mind, he asked himself just how badly he wanted it.

Shadows deepened.

Red lights flashed.

Johnny's voice became part of a savage chorus. The chamber filled with grunting, feral sounds rising from frail corpses fighting for the scraps of life that would sustain them and elevate them to greatness. Johnny made claws of his fingers, swung his arms, and forced his way toward the crates, and as teeth dug into his right shoulder and ripped his arm halfway loose from its socket, he remembered Madigan's advice. With a snarl he wrenched sideways so that his arm tore free and fell away, and then he plunged ahead into the tangle of decaying flesh that ripped and bit at him. He fought and shoved. He smelled the warm, waiting blood, almost tasted it on his lips. The galloping beats of the only three living hearts in the room thundered in his ears. He plunged his left hand through the chest of one of the others, then shook it loose and howled toward his destiny. His fingers scrabbled over wood. The side of the crates cracked, splintered, and fell away. Half a dozen others pressed against Johnny, and together, like some mutant amalgamation of cold flesh, they lunged ferociously into the crate, ignoring the terrified screams of the woman inside. They bit into her throat, her arms, her legs; they tasted her blood.

It was a race, now, to see who might drink the most the fastest.

Kashrut

By

Bernie Mojzes

There was a time when he'd have been tempted.
And he was.

But not, of course, for the same reason.

The girl grinned drunkenly as her eyes adjusted to the dim light. Her hips swayed in time to the throbbing dance music that pulsed through the floor from the club downstairs, and she leaned lightly on the doorframe for support, her body's curves haloed by the hallway's florescent lights.

"Hi," she said. "I'm, uh…" She hesitated. "April. My name's April. He told me you'd be up here. The Irish guy." She paused expectantly, then: "It's okay. I'm nervous, too. I've never… you know… Not for money." She stepped into the room and closed the door, lost her halo. Candlelight flickered across her features, softening her edges. Her face glistened with the exertions of the dance floor.

Toby breathed her in from where he sat on a low, cushioned sofa: perfume and sweat mingled in complex ways, heavily overlaid with the scent of cranberry and orange—she'd had several of whatever drink she was holding and the flavor was strong on her breath. From her hair and clothes, a sweetly subtle undercurrent of marijuana.

In ten years, maybe fifteen, she'd have traded the miniskirt and halter top for something more appropriate. Toby could picture her: squeezing into blue jeans just a bit too tight for her, waiting with the kids at the bus stop, and then dashing off to work. Or maybe she'd wear a suit to work. Or a lab coat. On her lunch break she'd read the latest diet book and eat a pint of Häagen-Dazs.

But that wasn't to be her fate. She'd been chosen for something far less enviable. And she didn't even know it. She came closer, close enough that he could have leaned forward and buried his head under her skirt. She ran her hands inexpertly over her breasts and stomach and hips.

"Would you like me to dance for you?"

The femoral artery runs shallow down the inner thigh. Her hands traced its path and back, and Toby's mouth watered. The vein in her neck pulsed alluringly. He focused instead on her belly button.

"Are you Jewish?" he asked.

"I could be." She laughed. "Hell, for this kind of money, I could be Hindu for the night."

"What's wrong with you, eh?" Toby pushed the girl away, then cracked her sharply across the shins with his cane. "Go! Get out of here!" He hit her again as she retreated, hopping in pain. Groaning, he pushed himself to his feet.

"You're fucking crazy, old man!" She fumbled with the door knob.

"Stupid *shiksa!* Coming in here and taunting an old man with something he can't have. Next time I see you I'll give you more than a lump on your shins!" He waved the cane at her, ignoring the protests from his knee. "Oy, kids today. What a world." He listened to her retreating footsteps and breathed a sigh of relief and regret. "What a life."

Still grumbling under his breath, he slowly worked his way down the stairs and out into the night.

A silent laugh crinkled Finnegan's eyes. "How was dinner?"

"Feh," said Toby irritably, waving the words away. Hand on the small of his back, he sank into his recliner, the only part of his old life he'd been allowed to salvage. He leaned back and closed his eyes and tried not to think of the girl's throat. *Don't think about the elephant in the corner.*

"You turned down my gift?"

"She was drunk."

"So?"

"So, I'm diabetic. All that alcohol could kill me. Not that you give a damn."

This time Finnegan gave voice to his amusement. "I paid good money for her."

"Good money. Hah!" Toby snorted. "Blood money, you mean."

"Same thing, my friend. Same thing." There was that wolfish grin Toby had learned to hate. "Don't worry, I'll find her again. You can have her sober."

"Why?"

"Huh? Because I paid her. She owes me."

"No. I mean, why me?" He ran his fingers through the wispy remnants of his hair. "Of everyone in the world you could pick to turn into…to curse with eternal life, you pick a sick old man with arthritis and kidney failure? With all those pretty young things out there, like that girl tonight."

"The pretty young things? Oh, they're fun to play with for a while. But the egos! They're like peacocks, all trying to out-goth each other. It happens to all of them. Sooner or later they all think they can be me. And then I have to find a new toy. But even that game gets old after a while."

"Just my luck." Toby closed his eyes and willed the sun to rise.

Toby poured twice as much bubblebath into the tub than he needed. He didn't want to look at his withered skin, at his sunken, hollow belly, at the ribs and hips protruding from his shrunken body. He didn't want to look at any of the flabby, useless bits. Undressing carefully, he removed his prosthetic foot and eased himself under the bubbles. His knees broke the surface: pasty, white twins. Nothing to be done about it. He'd complained about the size of the bath once.

"Then take a fucking shower," Finnegan had said. *What a* yutz.

He closed his eyes and let his head sink under the surface, let the tub grow still. Underwater, the gurgle of his stomach eating itself was impossibly loud. He surfaced angrily, rubbing suds out of his eyes. It had been over a week since Finnegan's grinning face had loomed over his hospital bed, over a week since he'd been turned into a vampire, into an abomination. Over a week since he'd eaten anything.

"You'll feel better after you feed," Finnegan had promised.

His last meal had been hospital food, a nearly inedible salisbury steak with lumpy, brown gravy and overcooked peas. A small cup of fruit salad. The nurse had promised it was kosher. He'd picked at it for a few minutes and wished himself dead, already.

"With this kind of food," he'd told the nurse, "who needs Dr. Kevorkian?"

She'd just patted his arm and smiled. "You'll feel better after you eat something," she'd said.

She'd lied.

"It isn't that easy, me boyo," Finnegan whispered in Toby's ear. He rolled Toby's inert body onto its back, ran his finger around the wound, over the skin stretched taut around the wooden stake. "Takes more than this to kill one of us."

He pressed the palm of his hand against the stake and pushed it around like a shift stick. Toby was as still as death.

"You feel that. Every damned inch of it. Every splinter. Every little twitch. You just can't move. You can't do anything about it. Can't do anything but feel."

He tugged suddenly, pulling the stake free. Toby gasped and sat up, clutching his chest. There was no blood.

"I'll keep that in mind," he managed.

"You do that." Finnegan tossed the splintered wood aside, poked a finger in the wound. "That'll heal up after you feed."

This time the girl—the one who called herself April—was crying. Toby could taste her fear, sharp and pungent, rising like a cloud from the bed where she lay trussed and gagged. It excited and sickened him.

"Again with the bimbos," he said, keeping his voice casual. "What is it always with you and the bimbos?"

Finnegan shrugged. "She's already paid for." He shouldered past Toby into the room. "Besides, she's not for me."

Toby limped across the room, leaning lightly on his cane, and helped the girl sit up. He pulled the gag out of her mouth and waited until she stopped screaming. "What's your name, dear? The real one this time."

She searched for clues in the old man's sympathetic eyes. "Amanda. Amanda Littleton."

Toby pulled a small pocket knife out of his pocket. "Tobias Seidman." He sawed at the ropes around her wrists.

"Mister Seidman, I'm..."

"Call me Toby." He took her hand and pressed it gently. The warmth of her skin surprised him. "Pleased to make your acquaintance."

"Toby. Right. Okay." She took a deep breath. "Toby, I'm sorry I called you names the other day. I'll give back all the money. I swear. Just please don't hurt me."

"I only wish it was so easy." Toby glared at Finnegan. "What's so funny?"

"You are. She is. You can't get comedy like this on TV. Except maybe *Fox News.*"

"It is *not* funny!" Toby poked him with his cane. "I'm eighty-five years old. I'm diabetic, I have a titanium hip and a prostate the size of Florida. I got gangrene on my foot and they had to cut it off. Two months ago my kidneys shut down." He turned to Amanda. "Who ever heard of a vampire on dialysis? You ever hear of such a thing?"

"Oh my God...you're both insane."

"You think that's insane? Look at this." Toby reached into his mouth and pulled out his teeth. "I haven't had my own teeth since Reagan was President. Now all of a sudden, this." He pulled his lips back to reveal sharp fangs protruding from his puckered gums. "I keep biting myself!" He tossed the dentures across the room. "Not that I even need teeth anymore. The last food I had was two weeks ago, and you know what it was? Microwaved peas. So mushy I could have chewed them with my gums removed. You'd think my mother came back from the dead just to cook my last meal."

Finnegan grasped Amanda by the hair and bent her neck to the side, exposing her throat. She whimpered. Toby's stomach grumbled involuntarily.

"Hardly your last meal," Finnegan said, tracing her carotid with a sharp fingernail. The blood coursed hot under the raised welt, and Toby realized he'd taken a step toward the girl.

"No."

"You're a vampire now. It's what you need. You don't have a choice."

"And Daniel did?"

"Who?"

Toby shook his head in disgust.

"Who the fuck is Daniel?"

"Daniel 6:16," Amanda said in a small voice. "Um. He got thrown in the lion's den."

Finnegan roared, slapping the bed with his open palm. "A Bible-thumper? This is too good!"

"I'm not," she protested. "I mean, I was. My parents..."

"Whatever." Already bored, Finnegan grasped Amanda roughly, pushing her toward the old man, throat bared. "Enough. It's time to feed. Take her now before she tells us her life story."

Toby backed up a step.

"I can't. She's not kosher." He shrugged.

"You're a goddamned vampire!"

"I'm a goddamned Jew first! And even if she had cloven hooves and chewed her cud, her blood still wouldn't be kosher." He looked in Amanda's eyes. "You don't chew your cud, do you?"

She shook her head.

"Good. I mean, who's to say what you people do? No, no, it doesn't matter. She's not kosher and that's that. So you can let her go."

Finnegan blinked. "What do you mean her blood isn't kosher?"

"'I will even set my face against that soul that eateth blood, and will cut him off from among his people.' It's, uh, somewhere in Leviticus."

Toby nodded. "The *shiksa* is a regular Torah scholar. Who would have thought it?" He held up a finger. "No, you listen. The soul is contained in the blood. You can't go around eating people's souls. It's just not kosher, any way you want to look at it. So, unless you can show me in the Torah where God makes an exception for vampires, forget it. Let her go."

"You're just not hungry enough yet. It's just a matter of time." Finnegan shrugged. "So I guess you get to watch, this time."

Toby's eyes went from Finnegan's face to Amanda's. "I'm sorry," he said, sagging heavily enough against his cane that the wood protested.

"I tried. But since you're going to die anyway.... Finnegan, maybe you could hold her up for me? I'm an old man with a bad back..."

"Really?" Finnegan's face held mock dismay. "I was sure we'd get another week or two out of this game." He pulled Amanda to her feet and held her still.

"I really am sorry about this," Toby said. And then he snapped his cane where he'd weakened it and drove the splintered wood forward with all his strength. It pierced Amanda's skin, pushed through the soft flesh under her shoulder and into Finnegan's chest. Pinned together, the two fell back on the bed.

"Don't move, dear." The scent of her blood was unbearable.

"You stabbed me!"

"I stabbed the *putz* behind you." He pulled out his knife. "I learned a few days ago that the stake only paralyzes. You pull it out and he'll be able to move again. So, stop squirming, already. Let's see. Corkscrew. Scissors. Toothpick. You'd think the Swiss Army would have a vampire-slaying tool."

"You'd think," Amanda said. Her face was pale.

"Oh well. I guess this will take a while." He began to saw at Finnegan's neck. "I also learned a few days ago that just because a vampire is paralyzed doesn't mean he doesn't feel what's happening. You remember that, if you ever need to kill a vampire. If you like him, maybe you get a nice sharp knife from the kitchen, yes? Either way, you have to take the head and throw it in the river. *In the daylight.*"

When enough of the tissue had been cut away to expose the spine, Toby took Finnegan's head in his hands and began to twist. The spine popped after half a turn, separated after a whole turn. He sawed at the remaining ligaments with the small blade. When it was done, and Finnegan's eyes finally dimmed, he pulled the cane free and set the blood-soaked wood on Amanda's chest, then pressed the knife into her hand.

He was shaking as he turned away from her.

"Thank you," she said. He heard her take a deep, shuddering breath. "It's over. Thank God." She hacked at the ropes binding her ankles.

"Over? Hah! That was the easy part."

"What do you mean?"

"I mean he wasn't wrong. It's just a matter of time." Toby turned to face Amanda, and the hunger was bright in his eyes. His fingers rubbed idly at the blood that had gotten on his hands, his eyes never strayed from the bloodstain on her chest. "Only one of us will walk out of this room."

He was between Amanda and the door.

It wouldn't have mattered. She'd seen how fast the old man had moved when he wanted, bad knee or not. Unnaturally fast. Running was only turning her back on him.

He looked pointedly at the broken cane lying on the bed, and she picked it up quickly. "I pray God it's you," he said, "or we're both damned."

They sat on either side of the bed, watching each other. It was a long time before either of them moved.

The Vampire Escalator of the Passaic Promenade

By

Hildy Silverman

Anthony DeLuca didn't want to be a mall security guard. He didn't hate it, but it wasn't exactly his goal in life. It was pretty easy work – just throw on the uniform, glower at teens, and tell older folks where to find the nearest restroom. It was also about as thrilling as, well, throwing on a uniform, glowering at teens, and telling older folks where to find the nearest restroom.

It didn't make a difference that he worked at one of the largest malls in the Northeast, New Jersey's own *Passaic Promenade*. Being in a huge mall just meant there was more room for Stupid to happen.

There was plenty of Stupid to go around in a big mall. People splashed their crotches with scalding *Celestial Stags* lattes and screamed for the nearest lawyer. Teens shoved each other to the floor and got trampled at pre-dawn Mall Madness sales at *Impress*. Kids attempted to slide flat-footed from the final step of the escalator onto the landing, only to have their perpetually-untied laces snagged by the machinery.

That one happened a lot, and resulted in a perfect storm of furious mothers, jammed escalators, and mangled sneakers. So far, no one had lost a toe or any other useful body part, although some blood had been shed on a few recent occasions. One kid got his butt cheeks munched after riding down while sitting, although by his wailing, you'd have thought a bear-trap had snapped off his whole damned hinny.

"Told you it wasn't a carnival ride," Anthony had muttered while prying the 'victim's' rump free. The paramedics came soon after and yelled at Anthony for doing their job. They gave the kid a lollipop.

Anthony wanted better than this for a career, or at least different. He'd started as a security guard when it was nothing more than a fairly easy summer gig between junior and senior years of high school. He figured it'd be something relevant to throw on his application to the police force. He still thought it would be, once he actually got around to filling out the application and went through with testing. The latest opportunity to do so had just rolled by last month and he'd almost been ready to go down to the station.

This was the fourth year he'd almost been ready. Next time, he'd do it for sure.

Yeah.

"Hey, Tony," said Peter Lincoln Roosevelt. He stepped out of *Celestial Stags* with a coffee cup tucked into one mitt-sized hand and a couple slices of lemon loaf peeking out of the other. Pete and Anthony often wound up on the same shift, ever since Anthony had gone full-time three years ago. "How'd the test go? Any word on your application, or is it too soon?"

Anthony shrugged. He'd long since given up on correcting Pete's use of the nickname Tony, which he loathed. He'd been called 'Tony Bologna' all through middle school and for freshman year in high school. No one had called him that after freshman year, because he'd grown about five inches over the summer, packed on twenty-five extra pounds of muscle, and beaten the living Stupid out of the last guy to call him 'Tony Bologna' in a very public and noisy fashion.

"Didn't make it down," Anthony said. He stared hard at a gaggle of blue-hairs down the hall ahead of them and mentally braced himself for Pete's response.

"What?" Pete's thick eyebrows arched like two caterpillars trying to wriggle off his forehead. "Come on, man, what are you *doing*?"

"I pulled, like, three double shifts the same week," said Anthony. He heard the defensiveness in his tone and cringed inwardly.

"And that was more important to you than joining the force?" Pete shook his head slowly. "Your priorities are all askew, my friend. They shot me down, but hey, at least I applied."

"Five times," Anthony said, under his breath. Aloud, he said, "Hey, I'll get there. I just needed the cash more last month. My rent's not getting any lower, you know."

Pete shrugged and his amazingly solid, perfectly spherical belly rose and fell like a bounced medicine ball. His hairy navel winked at Anthony from between the straining buttons of his pale blue uniform shirt.

"There's always something, ain't there?"

Anthony fiddled with the fastener that held his flashlight on his belt. *Snap, unsnap.* Like his temper at the end of a particularly long shift. Which this was. "Look, you want to pay my rent, I'll pass up the opportunity to work a double, no prob."

"Bull. And shit." Pete took a massive bite out of both lemon loaf slices. He gave Anthony a little shove and they headed off down the lower-level corridor of the mall.

The wide hallway was lined down the center with passably-realistic little trees in large, cracked terracotta pots. The employees of the stores along both sides of the hall were in various stages of end-of-day rituals – vacuuming around circular racks of clothes, taking jewelry out of window displays, taking in folding signs that begged, "SALE, SALE, HEY, BUY SOMETHING ALREADY!"

It all barely registered on Anthony's weary consciousness. Another close of day; another opportunity to regret his life.

"Tony, boyo, you ain't getting any younger." Pete mumbled around the remains of his snack. "You wait much longer, you're gonna be a forty-year-old rookie. And that'll just be sad."

"I'm only in my twenties," said Anthony. The weakness of his argument did not escape his notice.

"Time flies, buddy boy." Pete ran a hand through his thinning silver hair, leaving a few yellow crumbs behind. "It flies mighty fast."

"So I've heard." Anthony half-heartedly returned a vigorous wave from a *Jeans Junction* employee. The girl was a little mannequin of a thing, all of seventeen, with a major thing for uniforms. She giggled and turned to whisper something to a much older woman who was busy folding khakis. The older employee glanced up, smirked, and shook her head. Anthony looked away.

"Tony, you used to be all about joining the force. Remember what you used to say? 'This is my stepping stone, Pete. This is my proving ground.' What you proving these days, man? That you can stop teenagers from shoplifting out of *Muffy's* on a daily basis and that's enough to make you feel like you're protecting and serving?"

What could he say to that? *I am doing my part.* Why, just the day before yesterday, he'd rescued a woman's pump from the bloodthirsty escalator at *Dears* department store. She kept babbling on and on about how she had no idea how it could've gotten wedged in there.

When he'd managed to free her foot, the sole of her foot was dripping blood, but did he panic? Not in the slightest. He'd kept it together, talked to her calmly the whole time, and wriggled and strained until he freed her shoe from the teeth of the collapsed bottom stair.

Did he receive a tongue bath of gratitude? Nope. Instead, the woman bitched and moaned that the spiked heel of her *Jonny Foos* gazillion-dollar pump was chewed up beyond repair and, "good job, security drone," on destroying a shoe that cost more than his monthly salary.

Anthony's fingers curled into fists as he vividly remembered standing there, outwardly ignoring her rant and the snarky comments from onlookers while inside, he'd just wanted to feed her to the escalator again. Face first.

"Thanks for the pep talk. Maybe I should check the *Dears* wing for those kids zipping around in Wheeleys again." He turned on his toe and marched off in the opposite direction from Pete.

"You could do better!" Pete called after him. Anthony paused, but didn't look back. "It didn't work out for me or some of the other guys hangin' around here, but you...? Yet here you are, just draggin' your heels, giving up without even trying. I ought to punch you in the face until your brain kicks in and reminds you there's more to...hey. Hey, Tony! Come back, man, don't be like that."

Anthony clenched his jaw and kept right on walking. His own father was dead and he already had a married, employed older brother to nag him about his lack of direction in life. He didn't need his work buddy to *yenta* at him, too.

He turned the corner to head down the side corridor toward *Dears*. At which point, a woman ran into him at a full sprint. She'd raced up so fast that all he saw was a blur of movement out of the corner of his eye before she collided with him. His head rang and his lungs protested their abrupt deflation.

Nevertheless, his reflexes kicked in enough for him to grab her arms before she went flailing away into one of the stubby, artificial evergreens.

"Help me, Jesus. Help me, sweet baby Lord!" She grabbed his forearms and stared up at him. Her dark brown irises were surrounded on all sides by bloodshot whites and he feared her eyes might roll right out of their sockets.

"Ma'am, can I help you?" He recited the words automatically, even as he wondered at what could've driven her into such a tizzy.

"It ate him! The damned thing just sucked him up!" Her acrylic nails dug into his skin right through his thin polyester shirt.

Anthony winced and tried to dislodge her gently, to no avail. "I need a little more information..."

"Are you deaf?" she screeched. Though he wasn't yet, she seemed determined to make him so. "My Jerome, my sweet Boo-boo. It just sucked the life right out of him." A sob choked off her tirade and tears filled her bulging eyes.

Oh, good. She's bugshit crazy. "Show me," Anthony said, wearily.

The woman mercifully released one of his wrists, but maintained an iron grip on the other as she half-tugged, half-led him down the corridor to the *Dears* anchor store.

Once inside, Anthony saw a group of mall-goers clustered around the bottom of the Down escalator. A couple had cell phones in hand and were punching buttons or shaking the devices, which apparently weren't responding as commanded.

Not this again, he thought. This escalator malfunctioned more often than any other in the whole bloody mall. A steady diet of children's feet and hard resets were most likely to blame. Not to mention the primo *Jonny Foos* it had digested the other day.

Anthony pushed his way through the small gathering of looky-loos with the woman's help. He found himself staring at the tarnished, all-too-familiar moving steps as they collapsed into the floor, one after the other, grooved metal flattening and gliding into the teethed mechanism at the bottom. Nothing seemed amiss, except for what appeared to be a black sweatshirt shirt and blue jeans casually tossed onto the metal floorplate that marked the escalator landing.

Anthony reached for the sweatshirt. A combination of groans, mutters, and giggles arose from the onlookers as he picked it up, uncovering the embossed name of the escalator's manufacturer on the floorplate, *Trans-Sylvan.* The shirt resisted his efforts. He tugged, hard, and heard a rip as the sleeve tore free, its cuff snagged on one of the escalator's teeth. Anthony patted down the rest of the sweatshirt in his hand. It felt like the dark-stained, moist cloth was wrapped around something rubbery.

Then he saw something drooping down the back from the neckhole. It looked like an empty blow-up doll's head.

Anthony scowled. Great, exactly what he needed to polish of his day. "Is this some kind of a joke?" he demanded.

"No! That's my Boo!" wailed Jerome's girlfriend.

Anthony pulled up the deflated kickball of a head. There was awfully realistic, tight curly hair attached to the top of it. He stared at the gray face and his stomach threatened to eject the food court corn dog and fries he'd eaten for dinner.

"Jeeze. Us." Anthony's eyes traveled down to the withered, hollow arm sticking out of the torn sleeve and he all but tossed Jerome's sweatshirt and empty skin to the floor. How was this possible? He eyed the escalator and his blood froze in his veins.

It was one thing to nibble on a few feet, nip the occasional ass cheeks. It was an entirely different thing to suck out one of his mall patron's entire insides.

"Jer-*ome!*" Jerome's girlfriend was apparently incapable of communicating at a decibel level below eleventy-three. "We was just going on down the escalator to shop for p.j.'s and one minute he was in front of me and the next he was..." She waved her hands as if casting a spell.

"And you say it — the escalator — pulled him in?" Anthony took another step back from the mechanical staircase. It kept thrumming along as if nothing were amiss. The only thing out of place was the empty sleeve wrapped around the bottom set of teeth and the thud-thudding sound of the stairs collapsing under it, to begin their endlessly recycled run back up to the top floor.

He gave the escalator a dirty look. This was a pretty blatant move.

The escalator had never done much damage before. A little shoe leather, a little blood. He thought back to the woman the other day and remembered the outsized amount of blood on the bottom of her foot. He'd assumed she'd sliced it when her shoe jammed, but come to think of it, he hadn't seen a gash, only a narrow line of smaller piercings. Could they have been...bite marks?

"I know what I saw, Mr. Security Man," hollered Jerome's banshee. "Jerome just stood there, shaking and moaning, and then he just fell down like a pile of laundry. It hollowed him out, like...like...."

An observer with a keener grasp of similes offered, "Like a Slushee sucked out of its cup by a fat kid with a wide straw."

"*Some* of us tried calling the real cops," another offered, glaring at a couple of his fellows, presumably those who hadn't whipped out a cell phone at the first sign of trouble. "None of 'em would dial out, for some reason."

The rest of the crowd murmured and nodded their agreement. "I even tried one of the land lines, behind the counter over there," another woman said, pointing. "Not so much as a dial tone."

Jerome's bereft girlfriend nodded and hiccupped. Loudly. "I mean, I heard escalators could be dangerous, maybe grab a foot or something."

"It's developed a taste for blood," Anthony said, under his breath. He closed his eyes and shook his head. *Ridiculous. Totally nuts.* He opened his eyes, watched the stairs cycle down again and again.

Crazy or not, the situation was clear to him, *this sucker's graduated from tasting a few toes to murder.* Plus, just to make it all worse, the entire communications grid had decided to commit suicide at the same time.

Unless it wasn't suicide. Anthony shook with a sudden, bone-deep chill. The escalator had to be stopped.

"There was that one at Penn Station," one of the looky-loos volunteered, a round, middle-aged woman. "A little girl's shoelace got stuck along the side and it nearly sliced off all her piggy toes. Al, you remember that, right? Al? Remember that?" She elbowed a short, thin man by her side, who nodded like a good boy. "Al. Say you remember that."

"I remember that, Sylvia," said Al.

"One of them escy-lators darn near took off my sister's best friend's cousin's foot once," a burly man with a Western shirt and thick mustache drawled. "Peeled the soles of his shoes clean off, it did."

"This one time? At Bridgewater Commons? My sandal? Got pulled right off my foot, you know?" A girl with impressively large hair cracked her gum to punctuate her testimony. "And you know what was the worst? They were brand-new? From Coach, can you imagine?"

Anthony took a deep breath and released it slowly. "Okay, people, I need you to move along now. If you could...?" He nudged the Marlboro Man aside and crouched beside the escalator. "Thanks." He flipped up the protective plastic covering over the red emergency Stop button and gave the button a jab. He found it amazing that not one of these geniuses had thought to hit it already.

"Um, like, don't you think we tried that?" said Jersey Girl.

"That's why they pay him the big bucks," some comedian added. The rest of the crowd snickered in appreciation.

Anthony felt the fine hairs on his arms and the back of his neck rise. Some of it was irritation, but most of it was because, no matter how forcefully he jabbed the Stop button, it didn't stop the escalator from its relentless roll. He still heard that low sound as each step was swallowed into the mechanism below, a vaguely mechanical thumping that he was sure he'd never heard from any escalator before. It didn't seem to be related to the sleeve jammed in the bottom, either.

Damn it. If he couldn't shut down the escalator, he couldn't get Jim from Maintenance to pry up the floor covering and get to the mechanism within, take it apart, and eliminate the deathtrap. *This is going to be a problem*, Anthony thought.

He stood up and faced Jerome's girlfriend, whose mascara now ran in black rivers down her cheeks. "Ma'am, I'm very sorry," he said, "but, um, could you tell me exactly what happened? I mean, did you see what it, er, *did* to Jerome?"

"It sucked him empty!" She jabbed a faux French fingertip down at the metal floorplate. "It was crazy. One second he was half-off the thing, the next his feet get stuck. He bends over to tug 'em free, but then…" She shuddered. "He started shaking and yelling. I saw blood, right under his shoes. It kept flowin' down with the steps, just runnin' down and down. Then he just…*deflated*. There wasn't anything left. It happened so damned fast!" She broke off and buried her face in her hands. Her shoulders heaved with each earsplitting sob.

"Aw, the poor thing." Sylvia all but shoved Al across the room in order to reach Jerome's girl. She put an arm around her shoulders and patted her. "It's okay, sweetheart. You're probably better off without him. Men are such burdens."

Anthony eyed Al warily, concerned that the guy might hurl himself to a preferably quick death-by-escalator. "Folks, I really need you to clear out." He used his most commanding tone of voice. "If you could just go about your business and…."

"What're you gonna do, arrest us?" The Comedian from before, who Anthony could now see was a bruiser of a mountain of a very large man, barreled forward from the back of the crowd.

"Yeah, right? 'Cause you're not the boss of us?" Jersey Girl snapped her gum in approval of the Comedian.

The rest of the group muttered their agreement. Anthony was just calculating how many volts from his Taser it would take to bring down the Comedian when someone shouted, "Look!" and pointed.

He swiveled and saw to his horror that someone was coming down the escalator. "Hey, Tony," Pete called and waved. "I got a squawk that there was some problem with the escalator. I blocked it off on the upper floor and figured you might need a hand down here."

"Pete, no!" Anthony ran forward, but rocked to a stop before his toes crossed onto the landing of the escalator. He signaled like an airstrip employee warning a turbo-prop out of the path of a 747. "Go back up, go back up!"

Pete just looked at him, one shrub of an eyebrow cocked. "What're you talkin' about? Everything's fine upstairs, that's why I'm coming down to help you out."

"Don't help! I don't need...Pete, for God's sake, just go back!" Pete was almost at the landing.

The crowd behind Anthony muttered. A couple of cries of, "Yeah, go back!" crossed with other shouts of, "No, come on down! See how that works out for ya!"

Anthony hated people sometimes.

Pete's step started to fold down. The thump-thumping from deep within the mechanism controlling the escalator grew louder. Anthony felt the floor rumble in tune under his feet.

He had no choice. He ground his teeth together and leapt.

Anthony landed on the step just below Pete. He wobbled, but Pete grabbed him by the elbows and steadied him. "Whoa, man, what're you doing?"

"Pete, the escalator. It's dangerous." Anthony grabbed Pete's meaty arm and began pulling him backward against the flow of the stairs. "Come back up with me and I'll explain it."

"Ohhhhh-kay." Pete shrugged and gave him a look of, 'you be crazy.' Nevertheless, he started back up the escalator and Anthony let out a small breath of relief.

Until he felt the escalator accelerate.

"Hm. That's weird." Pete looked down. "Do you feel that?"

"Damn it all," Anthony muttered. He started taking the steps two at a time. "Pete, move it. We're in trouble here."

Pete frowned with confusion but also started taking the steps two at a time.

The escalator sped up some more.

There was no mistaking it this time. The thudding from below was joined by a loud grumble, as if generated by a very large, very empty stomach.

Anthony broke into a jog. He was halfway up to the top, with Pete puffing along behind him. But the escalator just kept on accelerating, pulling them down faster than they could run up.

"What in the crappity-crap is going on with this thing?" Pete gasped. He dropped to all fours and tried to propel himself forward. Failed.

"It's...malfunctioning," Anthony said, "badly." He glanced over the side and calculated the likelihood of breaking a leg if they leapt over the side to the floor below. He decided it was almost definite. Then again, they could heal from broken legs. From being slurped hollow by a mechanical monster? Not so much.

"Tony, man, I can't. Keep this. Up." Pete's round, red face glistened. His breath came in tight wheezes.

"We're going to have to jump for it," panted Anthony. He had to sprint just to stay in place. The escalator all but whirled beneath him, causing him to stumble and grab onto the moving rubber handrail for support. It was going much slower. Normal speed, actually.

"Jump? Are you high?" Pete said between wheezes. "I ain't jumped anything, anywhere, since I was under two hundy. When I was *twelve!*"

"Hang on. I've got another idea." Anthony grabbed onto the rubber handrail. He hoisted himself onto it, until he clung awkwardly to it by his knees and hands. He hovered in place, compared to the relentless flow of the moving stairs. Apparently, the entire escalator wasn't possessed, only the steps. "Dude, hop up on the railing and ride it down. Just don't touch the..."

With a groan of protesting machinery, the escalator steps abruptly collapsed flat. Pete tripped and slammed facedown on the resultant conveyor belt. Screaming in horror, he slid full-tilt down the rest of the escalator to the bottom.

"Pete!" Anthony grabbed for Pete's shirt, his belt, his size 14-Wide loafer. All flew past him too fast, just grazing his fingertips. He watched helplessly, heart in his throat, as the big guy tumbled away.

The metal floorplate groaned and, impossibly, opened. It stretched wide, wider, a gaping maw. Spiked metallic teeth sprouted up from the floor and down from the plate, stained with red. They clanged together in anticipation as the big security guard rolled toward them, fingernails clawing uselessly over the flattened slats underneath him.

"No! *Pete!* Damn it, no!" But there was nothing Anthony could do. Pete fell into the hellish mouth and the teeth clamped together. They pierced him like multiple Ahabs spearing a single Moby Dick. Blood flew and splattered the crowd, which had toppled back screaming and panicking when the floor lurched open before them.

Anthony screwed his eyes shut and clung to the slowly moving handrail. He heard one last moan from Pete, one rasping cackle from the escalator.

Then there was silence.

He opened one eye, just in time to see that he was nearly at the bottom. Anthony threw himself sideways off the moving handrail and landed on the floor, well away from the bottom of the escalator.

The *Trans-Sylvan* floorplate once again rested flush against the floor. There was nothing to mark the horror he'd just witnessed but the blood spatters dappling the clothes of the few remaining, stunned onlookers and the strips of pale blue fabric flapping between the floorplate and the escalator. The moving stairs were back, too, as if they'd never been anywhere else.

Anthony stared blankly at the escalator. His eyes roved slowly back to the remaining members of the crowd who hadn't sprinted straight out the nearest exit.

The Stupid, sometimes it hurt.

He cleared his throat and said in a low, measured tone, "Time to go home, folks."

Not one person contradicted him this time. The Comedian was gone, had probably been the first to dash his macho ass out of there. The others just turned and obediently shuffled off, too shocked by what they'd witnessed to do anything but follow directions. Anthony sorely wished he could join them.

But he couldn't. He had a job to do.

He glared at the escalator and told it, "I'm coming right back, you son-of-a-whore."

He went to the nearby Lingerie department and got on the Intercom. A test squawk let him know it was still functional. *Guess the beast doesn't care if its food talks amongst itself, so long as it can't call out for help.*

He announced, "Dears has to close a bit early tonight, a minor gas leak's been detected, please visit our mall's other fine stores, thank you so much for cooperating and come back soon, m'kay?"

The store manager hustled out of his office to confront him, but one look at his face and the older man decided maybe this was a good night to shut a half-hour early after all.

Soon, he and the other supervisors had rounded up the employees and few remaining shoppers and ushered them out. Anthony told them to pull down the night gates over all the doors and they reluctantly obeyed.

He breathed a small sigh of relief when he heard the last gate clang into place. Apparently the thing wasn't powerful enough to control the mercifully old-fashioned manual doors and gates.

Not yet, at least.

It was just him and the escalator now. Anthony walked slowly back over to the escalator. He reviewed the ghastly image burned into his mind, of dingy steel fangs chomping down on his buddy. And laughing. *Laughing.*

This metallic piece of Hell swallowed up Pete's body like the rest of this thrice-damned mall devoured the big guy's dreams long ago, Anthony thought. *Well, I'll be damned if I wind up like Pete. An empty shell, robot-walking through my life until some stupid, wicked thing puts me out of my monotony.*

If he had to go out, it was going to be while finally *trying* to do something. He had to bring this impossible monster down.

Anthony approached the languidly rolling mechanical stairs and unsnapped the tether on his Taser. And hesitated. "Yeah, good plan. Electrocute yourself shooting an arc of electricity through metal." He took his hand off the weapon.

Okay, so what were his options? He had a flashlight, but artificial light obviously didn't bother the escalator, so that was useless. He wished he had a gun. Even without silver bullets or whatever the myths said worked on otherworldly bloodsuckers, it still might have affected it.

As for fire, well, while it was tempting to just to burn the whole *Passaic Promenade* until nothing remained but the toxic waste dump on which it'd been built, he doubted the local firefighters — and cops — would agree. He'd just wind up in jail for arson and the fiend would still be there, rolling along, waiting for its next unsuspecting victim to take a ride down from the Hardware department.

What did that leave him? His nightstick. It *was* wood, but what did that matter? He couldn't stab something in the heart if it didn't have one.

Anthony straightened up abruptly. He listened, hard. There it was, deep inside the mechanism, that weird thudding that didn't belong. It had a pattern, of sorts. Thump-*thump*. Thump-*thump*. He placed a hand against his chest. And grinned. *Maybe...?*

Now, the only question was how to get in there?

Anthony knelt beside the floorplate. He flexed his fingers, reached for the edge — and paused. The thing had sucked poor Jerome's life right out through his feet. No reason to feed it ten fingers through which to do the same to him.

He looked around. A crowbar then; something to pry the plate up without risking flesh and bone. Anthony closed his eyes and visualized the floorplan of *Dears*. The Hardware department was upstairs, to the left.

He walked around to the Up escalator, crouched down, and used his flashlight to cautiously jab the Stop button. This one obediently stopped the moving stairs and he took them two at a time to the top. After a little rooting around in Hardware, he found a flat-edged crowbar and ran back down the Up escalator to the bottom floor.

Anthony approached the demon escalator, slapping the crowbar against one palm. He grinned and said, "Suck on this." Then he jammed the flattened edge into the floorplate and shoved.

The floorplate didn't budge. He added his full weight, groaned and strained. It didn't even wobble.

"Oh, that's not fair." Anthony shoved the flat-edge of the crowbar under another seam between the plate and the floor and heaved. He nearly toppled over onto the escalator, but the floorplate remained stubbornly fixed in place. The thumping below skipped a merry beat as he stumbled.

"Damn it!" Anthony glared at the floorplate. There was no way it should've remained stuck. He'd watched Maintenance Jim pry up floorplates a half-dozen times to rescue kid's shoes or effect minor repairs. He knew he was doing it right. Then again, he'd pushed the Stop button like a pro, and that hadn't worked, either.

Anthony felt his ire rise. He hoisted the crowbar and slammed it down on top of the metal plate. It clanged, but didn't dent. He swung again with a furious howl, and struck it so hard that the reverberation numbed his arms. Again, the only reaction was a louder thudding from below, accompanied by a barely perceptible rasp that just might have been a chuckle.

Anthony whaled on the floorplate. He shouted and cursed until his voice shredded into a hoarse echo of itself. He knew it was a ridiculous, pointless waste of energy, but the feelings that churned inside him demanded release. An outburst had been building for a long time, well before this godforsaken evening, but current events stirred his every frustration, rage, and grief to a rapid boil he was helpless to contain.

Finally, the crowbar flew out of his nerveless fingers and cartwheeled away into a nearby mannequin, knocking it onto its plastic *tochis*. He doubled over, gasped for air and clutched his knees, eyes blurry with tears. "I'm sorry, Pete. I'm so sorry, bud."

What am I trying to do here? he thought. His efforts were doomed to fail. He shouldn't even bother, when all he'd likely accomplish was getting eaten alive. He should just get the hell out, call his Uncle Angelo the priest, or maybe the real police to deal with the creature. Just be realistic and let a pro handle the situation.

No, damn you. He caught his breath and stood up straight. *Not this time.* He had to step up, or he never would. Sure, he'd live if he just walked away, but he wouldn't be able to bear the life that followed. Not anymore.

There *was* a way into the machinery and whatever-else lay beneath the floorplate. He'd seen it. The question was how to survive long enough to get done what had to be done?

Anthony picked up the crowbar from where he'd flung it. Then he went back up the safe escalator. He took a right into Housewares. Found a big-ass kitchen knife in one of the butcher blocks. He took out his nightstick and whittled the tip to a nice, sharp point. It took everything he had to keep his hands from shaking long enough to finish the job.

He walked over to the Down escalator. It rumbled an invitation.

Clutching his newly-fashioned night-stake in one hand and the crowbar in the other, Anthony took a deep, cleansing breath. "It's now or never time," he said. Then he strode onto the moving stairs.

At first, nothing unusual happened. He just rode down. Remembering how the thing had simply sucked Jerome empty, Anthony realized he had to challenge it, or it might not open up for an attack. So he crouched down and jammed the crowbar into the side, as if trying to wedge the stairs and keep them from moving.

He heard a metallic groan. The escalator sped up a bit and a glance down showed the floorplate had risen to reveal a slit of blackness between it and the floor. Anthony's pulse slammed in his ears until he couldn't be sure whether the loud thumps echoing through the store were coming from inside his head or down below.

He reached for the handrail, and made as if to hoist himself up again. With his hands full, it made that a lot more difficult to accomplish.

A grinding scream and the floorplate lifted up, again revealing gore-stained teeth. Anthony sat down on the step and watched as the teeth *clang-clanged* together. Apparently the mechanical beast hadn't filled up on Jerome and Pete. It seemed as eager to swallow him up as if it hadn't fed in weeks.

"Come on, you bastard. Come on." Anthony heard his voice crack but fought his every instinct to run away or even just scream. Instead, he clutched the crowbar in his right hand until his knuckles cracked. The night-stake he held tight against his chest. Its work would come after he survived this.

Assuming he did.

Anthony forced his eyes to remain focused on the gleaming maw. He timed the clashes of the steel fangs – *one-two-open, one-two-open.* He calculated the width of the mouth when it opened its widest to when the teeth scraped shut. He shuffled all the information together as he reached the bottom and came up with the only possible conclusion.

"Aw, fuck it." Anthony rose to a low crouch, then jumped.

As he shot over the gaping orifice, he thrust the crowbar down into the side of the monstrous jaw just as it tried to slam shut. He felt something incredibly sharp slice into left leg, and warm dampness glued his slacks to his skin. Nevertheless, he managed to bend forward in time to execute a forward roll and came up just a few precious inches beyond the hoisted landing.

Anthony groaned and rolled up his left pant leg to survey the damage. It looked as if one of the teeth had scraped a landing strip in his flesh from the top of his knee down to his ankle. It welled blood and throbbed enough to make him want to cry for his mommy, but he'd survive. He rolled down his pant leg and struggled to his feet.

The mouth was still stuck open, though it strained repeatedly to shut itself. Metallic groans accompanied each attempt. Anthony took a small step closer and cautiously squinted into the dark interior, careful to keep his head out of tooth-snapping distance.

The thumping he'd heard before was deafening now and the floor beneath him bucked with each pulsation. He snapped his flashlight free and shone it down into the depths of the escalator.

It lit up the expected machinery – gears and pulleys, the turning conveyor of stairs, all the usually trapping that made an escalator run. But there was something else, something lodged in the middle of all the standard inanimate paraphernalia. Anthony's gorge rose as he strained to steady the beam of his flashlight on the black-red, pulsating organ in the midst of the machinery.

"Gotcha," Anthony whispered. He laid the flashlight on the floor, his eyes never leaving the outsized heart beating between the still-moving escalator parts. He didn't dare lose sight of it, lest he wind up shoving his hand into a crank or gear. He must not miss.

Anthony picked up his makeshift stake with both hands, braced himself on his knees, reared back, and rammed it down deep into the center of the rubbery, throbbing heart of the escalator.

Blood shot straight up, a geyser of gore. He just managed to jerk his head to the side to avoid a direct hit in the face. As it was, the gruesome fountain quickly soaked him from head to toe. He had to blink rapidly to clear his eyes.

Did he only imagine the scream that followed? It was louder than anything he'd ever heard in his life. It made Jerome's girlfriend sound like she'd been on Mute. He clenched his teeth together, sent electric pain shooting through his jaws and straight up into his brain.

Anthony hauled back on the stake until it released with a sucking snap. He jabbed down again, was deflected by a gear. He swore, aimed, and stabbed again. *Nailed it!* Blood pooled around the heart, filled the cavity around it, and covered the equipment that kept the monster rolling with foul lubricant.

The screech of metal and monster echoed and reverberated around him. A nearby glass display case shattered. Mannequins wobbled and a couple toppled over. The entire floor heaved and bucked underneath him like a rodeo bull with a cattle prod jammed in its bunghole. But still, Anthony stabbed, again and again, not allowing his blood-stung eyes to lose sight of their target for a second, ignoring the agony in his ears, his torn leg, and his over-strained shoulders.

Abruptly, it all stopped.

Anthony nearly fell forward into the mouth as the floor beneath him froze back into immobility. The grinding scream cut out so completely that, for a moment, he thought he'd been stricken deaf. The relentless roll of the moving stairs ceased. He looked down at the heart...and found he was stabbing at empty air between gears and pulleys. It was gone, as was the blood pool that had surrounded it.

Anthony looked down at his shirt front, at his immediate surroundings, and blinked at the absence of crimson gore. The only blood that remained came from his leg wound.

He let his arms drop to his sides. It took everything he had left not to let the sharpened nightstick tumble from his hand. He slowly climbed to his feet and limped around to examine the front of the mouth.

It wasn't a mouth anymore. It was just a bent and battered floorplate, stuck in the air by a crowbar rammed into the corner between it and the floor. The fangs were gone.

"I did it," Anthony said. Then, "Wait, did I do it?" He blinked a few times and looked again. Escalator stopped – *check.* Teeth gone – *check.* Heart gone – *double-check.* Nothing but proper machinery lay beneath the open floorplate.

"Hey, I *did* do it!" He gave a couple of fist pumps and whooped. "Yeah I did. Go, me. Go, me." He performed a little end-zone dance, until he caught sight of himself in a mirrored pillar. He stopped and flipped his judgmental reflection off.

He hobbled over to the steel gate that barred the door to the parking lot from would-be thieves. He took off his ring of keys from his belt with trembling fingers and fumbled around until he found the right one. Then he raised the gate, opened the door, and hobbled out into the fresh New Jersey air. Well, the air anyway.

Anthony carefully locked up behind him. He'd have enough damage to answer for in the morning without leaving *Dears* vulnerable to outside evildoers overnight.

The sound of approaching sirens filled the air. One of the departed looky-loos must have eventually thought to call the authorities once they got outside the escalator's blockade.

Geeze, but how would he explain the mess inside? Pete's disappearance? The mad stories all those freaking gawkers were bound to start spreading about Jerome and him and the escalator?

He shook his head and shrugged. "Who gives a crappity-crap?" he asked the night sky. It offered no answers. So he came up with his own.

He made his way to his old 1998 Corolla. Stripped off his uniform; hissed a bit as the pant leg grazed his open wound. He folded the uniform neatly and laid it in his employee parking space, along with his key ring, utility belt with flashlight, Taser, and other equipment. Except for his night-stake. That was his now. He'd earned it.

"You could do better," Pete told him. Damn skippy he could. He *would*.

Anthony gunned his engine just as the first police cars and EMTs roared into the parking lot. He shot over to the partially-concealed service lane and headed for the highway, leaving the so-called first responders, the *Passaic Promenade,* and its demons far behind.

Love and Other Excuses

By

Terri Osborne

Diana Sveglio's entire life changed in the year of our Lord 1604, when she was just twelve years of age. "Diana," her mother, an aging woman named Viviana had said, "your father's business just will not allow us to keep food on the table for us all."

The girl had made a valiant protest, even suggesting that they move to one of the farms outside the walls of Florence, but it was to no avail. Her father was a barrel maker, but his business had taken a turn for the worse since many of the local wineries had begun hiring their own coopers instead of going to the specialists in the Oltrarno. Viviana had tried to take on maidservant duties, but that had left no one to watch young Diana. A young girl, alone, in an artistic community in the shadow of Pitti Palace? Diana could feel her mother's fear. If the family were to survive, something had to be done.

Viviana argued with Diana's father Giacomo for days over the decision, but ultimately, there was nothing to be done. There were no other Sveglios in Toscano. Viviana had been an only child. She had hoped for more children, but there were to be no more. Viviana's answer had been to consign her own daughter to the service of the Coteanno family, whose vineyard lay between Firenze and the town of Prato to the northwest.

"Mother, will I see you again?" the girl asked, trying desperately not to sound as distraught as she felt. If she could manage to be strong, perhaps it would be easier for her mother...perhaps.

"I do not know, Diana. You know I only want to ensure you are fed and cared for."

"I know." She understood, but at the same time didn't. How could anyone give their only child away to complete strangers? Family came before survival, before everything in the world. There was only one person more important than family, her father had always said, and that was God.

"Why can I not go to the convent?" she asked. "God will protect and feed me."

"You are not meant for the convent, child," Giacomo said from his place in the small kitchen's doorway. "I will not lose another to God, and certainly not my own daughter. No. You will go where I tell you, child. You will do as you are told. Please, for once in your life, *figlia cara.*"

Trying to hide her surprise at his response, Diana's eyes fell to the floor. "Yes, father."

A knock on the door brought an English man named Robert into Diana's life. He was older, much older than he appeared. His dark hair was shorter than the normal style, with strands that stood on end in the front. There was white in that darkness, though, almost as though salt had been spilled inside a pepper mill. He had gentle, caring green eyes, something Diana noticed the moment her mother had brought him into the room. "Diana," he had said, his accented voice something completely new for the young girl. "I have come to bring you to the Coteanno estate."

Somehow, the idea of going away with a grandfatherly old man that she'd never met before was a thought that piqued her interest more than her fear. Why would an Englishman be working for a vineyard in Toscano?

Viviana cried, but allowed Robert to take her daughter. Her father, not surprisingly, escaped to the safety of his workshop while his daughter was taken away. As Diana walked outside, the bare ground beneath her thin-soled shoes was warm from the bright sunlight. She couldn't help but think how strange it was that the last day she would ever see her family could be so beautiful.

Robert ushered Diana into the elaborately-carved oak carriage, closing the door behind her and allowing her to get comfortable in the plush velvet-covered seat before climbing into the driver's seat and ushering the four black stallions to cart them away.

The ride was long and bumpy, and as Diana watched the landscape pass her window, she began to realize that while Firenze may have been a cultural center, there was much more to the world than her tiny corner of the Oltrarno. *There is so much to see.* She felt as though she were just scratching the surface of the potential future that her circumstances had doled out. Before her father's patrons had stopped visiting, they had spoken of lands far and wide, of beginning treks down the Silk Road in

Venice, and ending up in far flung China. China had sounded so exotic. Would she be able to see it now? Diana's blue eyes widened as they passed one enormous tree after another, until finally, they reached the wide fields of the vineyard. Row after row of vine-covered, x-shaped supports stretched into eternity. "How large is this place?" Diana wondered aloud. Would she have to clean it all? Or, perish the thought, work these massive vineyards? Her hands ached just at the thought.

The carriage turned down a tree-lined path, and after a few more minutes, they came upon the main house of the Coteanno estate. The multicolored brickwork was magnificent, with the squared-off front door and at least a dozen windows that Diana could see. The windows, interestingly enough, looked new to her young eyes.

The vineyards may have stretched on forever, but Diana also saw a wide, freshly-cut swath of the grounds. Her heart leapt at the thought of playing within. She wondered if there would be other children. Her stomach dropped as she realized that she'd forgotten to ask that question. *Oh, God. What if I'm the only child in this entire vineyard?*

As the carriage rolled to a halt, the horses neighed, and the entire frame bounced as Robert got out of the driver's seat and came down to open the door for her. "Signorina, permit me," he said, offering her his arm to help her climb down.

Swallowing hard, Diana looked up at Robert. "What is expected of me, signore?"

"That will be up to Signore Coteanno, young one."

Robert led her into the house, down a long, cold corridor that was nothing but stonework and tapestries on the walls. She stared at the tapestries as they passed, trying to remember each scene. One she recognized as a variation on The Last Supper, a painting her mother had told her about after a trip to Milan. "Signore, what are all of these tapestries?"

"Do you always ask so many questions, child?"

"Yes," she said, not wanting to lie. "Papa would get angry with me, as well."

Robert stopped, and then dropped to one knee to look her in the eye. "I am not angry with you, Diana. You have endured much today. Not many would be so inquisitive after being taken from their home."

"I understand the need," Diana said, trying her best to put up a brave front. "Mama cannot feed us all. Signore Coteanno will take care of me if I work for him?"

The man smiled, and she found it an odd comfort in the midst of it all. "Yes," he said. "Signore Coteanno needs a new girl to work in the kitchen. Are you capable of that?"

Diana nodded, one lock of black hair falling into her face. "Si, signore," she replied, trying to keep her relief at not having to work those immense fields from reaching her voice.

With that, Robert took her into an enormous great room. Ornate walnut cabinets adorned each of the room's four walls, with more tapestries hanging beside them. A refectory table ran through the room's center. Four large, scrollwork-carved armchairs encircled the table, each with what looked to be tooled leather seats and backs. Diana had only ever heard of such finery in furnishings, having grown up with hard wooden benches and barely-padded beds. In the chair furthest from the door sat a man who looked no older than her father, with robust, healthy cheeks, brilliant dark eyes, and black hair that was long on the top, but short on the sides. There were flecks of gray hair at his temples, the only thing she could see that belied his age. He took one look at her, and smiled a broad smile. "You must be the Sveglio child," he said, his voice smooth like the velvet of her mother's favorite dress. "Diana is your name, no?"

"Sì, signore," Diana said, promptly following it with a curtsey. She couldn't help but feel inferior at the worn feeling to the fabric of her thin dress as she released her skirts. It seemed so much less in the presence of both her new employer, and the finery that surrounded them. "I apologize for my state, signore."

Antonio's smile took on an oddly sad tone. "Child, I've seen far worse in my time than you. Far worse." Raising his eyes to Robert, he said, "Take her to Gianna. Have a dress made for our newest family member immediately."

Family member? Diana tried to hide her confusion, but failed. "Signore?"

Antonio stood, walking over to her and taking her small hand in his. "Diana, I consider anyone in my service to be a member of my family. Robert is like a father to me. Gianna is a daughter; as, now, are you."

And with that simple statement, Diana was embraced by the Coteanno family as none had ever done for her before. Diana's new father made sure she had the best of everything, even going to far as to employ a tutor for the children on the estate. Her classes were scheduled in between the time she was to be turning the meat spits over the fires in the kitchen. It was long, arduous work, but after a while she managed to grow accustomed to the schedule. She would go to sleep right after the dinnertime cleaning, waking with the sun and beginning work on the breakfast preparation with the other kitchen helpers. Studies came between meals and classes.

How Diana studied. "Do you believe you will be allowed into University?" the other children asked time and again as she would turn down yet another opportunity to play in that wide expanse of yard outside the main house. As she considered the vineyard, with all of the possibilities that Antonio Coteanno had placed before her for the simple price of a day's wage, she found that no answer would come. Every possibility was one that interested her. A proper education was something not normally meant for women. But what if it *was* for her?

The promise of a larger education than she had ever thought possible was one that she could not ignore.

One day, shortly after her sixteenth birthday, as she came out of the small building on the estate where the tutor held the classes, she saw Antonio standing at the edge of an upstairs balcony, watching the children as they came back to the house. There was something prideful in his stance, almost as though he were watching his own children after school. Only, there was something even more intense in that gaze.

And Diana realized that she liked being on the receiving end of such a look.

"You are of age now, Diana," Gianna told her when she asked about such things. "You are no longer a child. Antonio looks upon you as he would look upon any woman he finds pleasing."

She was surprised to think of her patron in such a manner. Of course, she had encountered boys her age on the estate who would give her similar approving looks, but someone of Antonio's years? The idea of an older man in her life as anything other than a father figure had never occurred to her before that moment. She was only sixteen. She needed to concentrate on finding someone her own age.

Gianna dark eyes and round, gentle features gave her a look that managed to convey both envy and sympathy. Diana began to wonder what Gianna knew that she didn't.

One night, Diana was roused from her sleep by the sound of a carriage outside her window. She crawled out of bed, walking across the room she shared with Gianna, and carefully tucked her head around the corner.

There, she was greeted by the sight of three dark figures coming by sheltered candle light into the house. Gianna's soft snoring served as background noise for the conversation taking place outside. Curious, Diana stepped softly across the wooden floor, so as not to rouse her sleeping roommate, and slowly pulled open the door just enough to get an earful of the conversation taking place downstairs. Fortunately, the large house allowed only the most secluded conversation to be held in any form of privacy.

"We need help, signore," she heard one man say. His voice was rushed, almost nervous. "Our house is under siege from the duke. He insists we owe him fealty, yet we are not subject to Toscano rule."

"And if I help you, what will you give to me?" Antonio said, his own voice a well-practiced calm.

"What do you wish, signore?"

There was a break in the conversation, during which Diana heard Gianna's snoring grow softer. Diana said a quick prayer that her roommate would not choose that point to wake up.

A prayer that was answered as the snoring grew back to its previous volume.

"I wish," Antonio began, "for one fourth of your annual harvest for as long as you are under my protection."

"It is done," another of the men said without hesitation. "It is a small price to pay instead of half our harvest to the duke."

"I will send two of my best men with you. The next time the duke tries to collect his tariff, he will find a surprise waiting. And that surprise will wait as often as necessary, for as long as necessary."

"Grazie, signore," the first man said, sounding almost pathetically grateful, "grazie. We are forever in your debt."

"Yes, you are."

She could hear the three men talking again as they walked back out toward their carriages. Then she heard gasps.

Padding back over to the window, Diana saw two other men appear as if out of the air. Something about the two men raised the fine hairs on the back of her neck. Even in the dim candlelight, they looked paler than the first three men. The men who came seeking assistance looked...they looked terrified by the new arrivals.

One of Antonio's men raised their eyes to Diana's window, and she quickly ducked behind the stone ledge. But she had seen enough, even in that short glance.

There was something unnatural about that face. It was nothing like Antonio's. This was pale, drawn, and appeared to be the face of death itself.

He will find a surprise waiting.

As Diana crawled back into bed, she tried to eliminate that spectral visage from her mind, but it wouldn't be so easily dismissed.

On her nineteenth birthday, Antonio gave her a necklace that was beyond anything she had ever seen before. It was made of bright white pearls, with glimmering sapphires and ornate gold drops. "Signore," she said, "this is...quite extravagant. I am not certain what to say."

"Grazie will be sufficient, my dear," he said.

"Grazie, signore."

But that wasn't enough for Diana. She stared at the gems in her hand, knowing they were fit more for a queen than gracing her own inadequate neck. The blue of the sapphires would match her eyes, yes, but what did Antonio have in mind for her?

Diana's hands shook as she reached the necklace over her head and slipped it into place. "Signore," she said, "what is going on?"

"Diana," Gianna whispered, her dark eyes strangely fearful, "be quiet."

Quiet was something that Diana had never been very good at. "No.

I must know. Whenever a boy has shown interest in me, it is never for more than one dinner. The next time I see him, he acts as though someone has threatened him if he speaks to me. Many of the women my age are already well-married, signore. Something is going on here, and I wish to know why my life is being controlled in such a manner."

"The impetuousness of youth," Antonio replied. "Though you are not as young as you were when you came to live with me, are you?"

"Of course not."

"What do you want?" he asked.

"I don't understand."

Antonio Coteanno rose from his chair, walking across the length of the great room to where she sat. He looked down upon her with that same strange look that he had used years before. "You may have whatever you want, Diana. You are an educated young woman. The world is yours for the asking. What do you wish to do with your life?"

Diana's brow furrowed. She had never actually come up with an answer to that question. For a poor peasant girl from the Oltrarno, it was one she had never in her life expected to even be asked. "I don't know. What is it that you do?"

"I make wine. You are aware of that."

"You do more than that," Diana replied. "I've seen the men come into the house and ask for your help. I've also seen them leave, usually with relief on their faces, only to see it quickly replaced by fear. I've seen things that I didn't think existed, signore. Who are the men you send to help those who seek your assistance?"

Antonio steepled his fingers against his lips, slowly beginning to pace the front room. "You have seen them?"

"Yes."

"They are men in my employ, Diana. Men who have promised to help me in return for my patronage. Not unlike you, my dear, or Gianna, or any of those with whom you study every day."

Diana turned her gaze toward Robert. "What about him?"

Antonio gave the butler a long look. "He is my oldest and dearest friend, Diana. I owe him my life."

"Yet you keep him as you have me?"

Robert began to stand, but Antonio stopped him with a hand. "I do nothing of the sort," Antonio said. "I will make you this pact, my dear. If you have not found your soul mate by your twenty-seventh birthday, I will give you all of the answers you seek."

"Why that year? I will be too old to marry by then."

"The power of numbers, my dear. The Father, the Son and the Holy Spirit. Three times three times three. The New Testament has twenty-seven books to enlighten us. If God himself requires twenty-seven books to bring us to the Revelation, can we truly expect to understand anything in youth? I believe only when you reach that age, you will be able to comprehend what I have to tell you."

Diana stared at him, not quite certain whether he was serious. "You think I that will wait eight years for you to answer my questions?"

"No," he replied, in a voice as flat as the table's surface. "I think you will continue to seek those answers. However, whether you find them remains to be seen, no?"

Antonio had been absolutely right. Eight years passed, and Diana's romantic luck continued to be as poor as her parents' financial straits had been. She was beginning to grow weary of only seeing men once, and then having them disappear as though they'd never existed.

But something changed in that intervening time, as well.

Diana began wandering the fields, taking part in the annual harvest of the grapes and making a nuisance of herself to learn about the process of making wine. She wasn't certain what drove her to such learning at first, but in time, she realized, if she were going to spend more years of her life on the vineyard, perhaps she could learn to leave her own mark on it. A wine all her own, with her own special touches. She was beginning to understand how the nuns in the convent felt when they mentioned their calling. She even began experimenting with cuttings from the vines, mixing and matching until she had created a wonderfully sweet, robust black grape all her own. When she took the first taste of the vine's fruit, it was like a mix of honey and the most succulent grape she had ever tasted. It was magnificent. The challenge for her was not to eat every fruit from the vine. Somehow, she knew this grape would make an equally-magnificent vintage.

On the eve of her twenty-seventh birthday, a knock came at the door to her room. Gianna had long since been left to a room of her own, for which Diana had been eternally grateful. When Diana answered the door, she found Antonio standing there, that same beneficent look on his face that he'd given her from the balcony over a decade before. "Yes, signore? What is it?"

"The moon is high," he said. "It is the morning of your birth, is it not?"

"Could this not wait until sunrise?"

Antonio's left eyebrow rose. "Perhaps. But I thought you should have the entire day to consider my offer."

"Your offer?"

"Yes. I believe I promised to give you the answers you sought, if you hadn't found your soul mate by this day."

Diana rolled the sentence around in her mind. Yes, he would provide answers, at the price of a mate for her soul. Was it possible that she hadn't found that yet, because it had been there all along? She tried to shake the idea out of her mind, as she still thought of Antonio as more a father than a lover, but it refused to leave. So, she shoved the thought into a nice, tight box in the back of her mind, hoping it would stay there for as long as necessary. Still, she needed more information. "What is there to consider?"

"The price to be paid for such knowledge."

She watched his face for any sign of what he was talking about, but not even his eyes reflected the gravity she could feel hanging on his words. There was something beyond what he was saying, something that held half-truths, mystery, and death.

"What are you?" she asked. "I have been in this house for over a decade. Where most everyone else has aged, you and Signore Robert still appear the same as you did when I first arrived."

"How do you consider me, Diana?"

Damn, there it was again. "What do you mean?"

"Don't evade the question. How do you consider me?"

Diana stared at him, trying to form an answer in her mind. Yes, she did care for him, quite deeply, but was that love? How did someone who never knew what love felt like recognize it when it happened? Was it her mother's attempt to find her a better life than she could provide? Was it Gianna's protective, maternal nature? Was it the kindred spirit she felt in the people who surrounded her every day in the kitchens? Was it the caring and concern to take in a perfect stranger when their parents couldn't? "I don't know, signore," she said, trying to put everything back into its tidy place where it had been for so very long. "You took me in when my parents could not care for me. You gave me an education that I likely would not have had. I suppose I am in your debt."

"A debt that you have more than repaid, my dear," he said. "If you wish to remain here, you are welcome to do so. But it must be a choice made of your own free will."

Diana blinked at that. "What would I do, signore?"

"You may call me Antonio. You are no longer my servant, Diana. You earned your freedom long ago."

She canted her head sideways. "Why did you not tell me of this?"

"I understand you have been working with the vintners on ways to possibly improve our wines. You could always continue that work." His eyes wandered around the room. "Perhaps a woman's touch is what is needed to bring life back into this old vineyard."

"That is a possibility," Diana said. "But why would I need to consider anything to remain here and do what I have been doing?"

Antonio smiled, and it was a smile the likes of which she'd never seen before. There was love there, far more than the paternal love that she was used to seeing in him.

"I have been alone for a long time, Diana," he said.
There was a wistfulness to his voice that she knew could not be imitated. The pain in his soul managed to worm its way into her own, and she felt a loneliness like she had never thought possible. That was when she ventured the question that had been in the back of her mind for at least

ten years. "How long?"

Antonio reached up and his fingers gently caressed her cheek. "Too long. If only she had lived now. I might have been able to save my Isabella."

"How old are you?"

He pulled his hand back, standing as straight as he could manage. "Would it frighten you if I said I was born in the year of our Lord 1432?

"Is it something you would be inclined to do?" she asked, trying—and failing—to lighten the moment. Diana quickly did the math. Unable to hide the shock from her expression, she said, "You are 187 years old. How?" Then it occurred to her. Those spectral visages that had protected those two men years before, the ones she had been unable to forget, they could only be one thing. "*Vampiro.*"

"Yes, my dear. That is what we are, and that is what I offer you. An eternity at my side."

Her brow furrowed, as that word took on a far different meaning than it had only moments before. "Eternity?" The idea of centuries spent in the place that had become so much more of a home than anything her parents could ever have provided? It did have a certain sense of appeal. "We would be damned to hell, would we not?"

A small smile turned Antonio's lips. "Ah, but think how long we could keep the devil from getting his prize," he said, raising a conspiratorial eyebrow.

"And how would we live?" Diana asked. "Is that why so many human servants are brought in, Antonio? Are they to feed you and the others?"

"Of course not." He gave her a questioning look. "Have any of the others touched you?"

Diana shook her head. "I merely wonder how a family of *vampiro* could exist around Firenze without the duke finding out?"

"Oh, the duke knows of the Coteanno family, my dear. Of that I am quite confident."

That got a skeptical eyebrow from Diana. "He knows what you are?"

"There, he may not be so certain."

Her eyes fell to the floor between them, and she whispered, "I don't think I can say yes, Antonio."

"No?" His voice was shattered, like a beautiful stained glass window ripped to shards. "Why?"

Diana took a step back, still keeping her eyes on the floor. "Love."

His bare foot came down beside hers, an odd warmth in the chill. His fingers reached around her left hand, not letting her get any further. "Love? You know I love you, Diana."

"Of course," she said. "But I do not know if what I feel is love, or merely obligation."

He shakily asked, "What does it matter? You could grow to love me."

She quickly turned her gaze back to him. "How would I know? You have not given me a chance to find out if I am even capable of love."

"I promise you every chance in the world. Whatever you wish."

Her eyes met his, and her resistance began to weaken at the beauty in that heartbroken darkness. "And what if I wish another later?"

He blinked several times, and she realized that the thought had never crossed his mind.

"What if I agree to this, but in a hundred years I fall in love with another?"

Antonio swallowed, "Then I would have to allow you to follow your heart."

"But would you?"

He took a deep breath. "I do not know. Please, Diana. I do know that I love you, and I will protect you. I will do anything you ask of me."

Diana felt her heart race, and then slow once more. "You said that I needed to make the decision of my own free will. All I ask is that you respect my decision."

Antonio's hand gently cradled her cheek. "You do not love me?"

"As a child loves her father? Of course. As a wife loves her husband? I do not know."

Diana turned her eyes away from Antonio for a moment, and found herself able to think more clearly about his offer. An eternity at the side of the man who had taken a poor cooper's daughter and given her a life her parents could never have managed. An eternity at the side of a man who obviously cared for her, and whom she realized she cared for as much. There had been a softness to his touch, one that she only could recall from her mother.

Antonio reached for the door's handle, pulling it closed as he backed out of the room. "Please, spend the day thinking of the possibilities I offer you. If you do choose to join me, today will be the last sunrise you have for quite some time. I suggest you enjoy it."

As the door closed behind him, and the sun slowly crept out of its own slumber, Diana wondered how much the world around them would change if she chose not to see it awaken once again.

That evening, Gianna—her round face even more robust thanks to pregnancy—her husband Eliseo, Robert, and Antonio all gathered around the refectory table in the great room. She had grown quite thankful for the fact that the ear pulling portion of the birthday tradition had gone by the wayside when she'd reached adulthood. Her earlobes ached at the memory.

Still, the birthday meal was one that she always took great pleasure in consuming, even though the number of courses was usually reduced from the norm. The risotto with a white wine and Parmesan was a harmonious explosion of flavor on her palate, one she would never turn down whenever Cook chose to make it. Of course, whatever white wine

Cook chose from the family cellars dictated so much of the flavor. Judging by the elegant complexity of the taste, an excellent vintage had been chosen, as usual. She made a mental note to thank Cook for his thoughtfulness when the evening was done.

When she finally got to the meat course, Diana took a slice of her steak, watching the blood drip from the rare meat as she lifted it from the plate. She stopped the fork before it could reach her lips, her eyes drawn to the brick red center of the meat.

That was when she realized it. Rare meat had been her favorite for as long as she could remember. Robert had introduced her to something from his homeland called black pudding, its peppery tone mixed with the onion and coriander was a taste whose mere thought made her mouth water. Granted, she had tried to ignore the fact that it was made with pig's blood, but that didn't change the recipe. She already was a consumer of blood.

How would joining her soul to Antonio's make that any different? Where was the line that kept humans from becoming food alongside the cattle?

She slipped the piece of meat into her mouth, realizing that she'd been staring at it for far too long. The peppery marinade that Cook loved to use brought tears to her eyes. Blinking quickly, she turned her eyes to Antonio. He didn't even try to hide the fact that he'd been watching her, almost as though he knew the thoughts going through her mind.

Had he had the same thoughts back then? How *had* he been turned? What was the process like? Did it hurt? What would she do after? Who would be her first kill? Would she be consigned to work with the enforcers that Antonio sent out to those who sought his favor?

So many questions, and not an answer to be found.

You have a way to find out, but are you willing to put your life on the line for it?

That question repeated in her mind for the rest of the dinner. As the cake was brought out, candles lit and songs of celebration sung, she still couldn't decide on an answer.

For a few moments, she allowed herself to watch Gianna and Eliseo, and she saw that same abiding certainty that she'd seen in Antonio's eyes. There was obvious love there. They would protect each other; keep the other safe, warm and content for as long as God gave them. And, really, what more could a woman ask for in a husband than that? But with Antonio, she had even more; she had that most coveted of power, freedom. Freedom, for all eternity, to live a life she had never even aspired to when she'd been born.

Your life has been devoted to this place, these people. If it lasts eighty or a thousand years, what would be the difference?

Indeed, had she not already knit her soul to this family, and to Antonio in particular? What difference did it make if he were human, or something else entirely?

Your mother cannot complain. You don't even know if she's alive, do you?

But, as the last vestiges of the cake were consumed by those who were able to eat human food, she still couldn't devise an answer that didn't involve consigning her soul to eternal damnation.

If it were eternal damnation at Antonio's side, would it truly be that horrible?

That night, as she was dressing for bed, the same gentle rapping came at her door. Pulling a woolen shawl over her muslin-draped shoulders, she padded across the room and hoped the light woolen fabric of her nightgown were enough to ward off the cold.

Somehow, I believe it's going to become much colder before the night is done.

As she slowly slid the door back, it didn't surprise her in the least to see Antonio standing there. He wore the same tunic and cowl he'd had on at dinner, but there was something different about him. There was the faintest hint of a glow to his skin, one that was very similar to the one she'd noted in the *vampiro* he'd sent out all those years ago. "Yes, Antonio?"

"Diana," he said, his voice a soft velvet that seemed to wrap itself around her spine and gently cradle it. "Have you considered my offer?"

She couldn't keep the soft smile from her lips. "Yes, I have." There was just something about his eyes, about the way he looked at her, that told her she would be protected.

Forever.

The corners of his lips turned at her response. "You have?"

"Yes."

He gave her an expectant look, one that suggested he'd been anticipating her answer all day. "I ask again. Will you spend eternity with me?" As though to reinforce his point, he leaned forward and brought her lips to his. The kiss was surprisingly soft, gentle, and every bit the kind of kiss she would have expected to share with her husband.

When their lips separated, she whispered one word, "Yes."

The View Never Changes

By

KT Pinto

Before I became a vampyre, I was a real son-of-a-bitch.

I spent most of my time sleeping, eating, and hanging out in dark alleys where most creatures feared to tread. During most of my youth, I ran with a bad crowd that terrorized the streets, chasing down those that we believed had no right to be anywhere in our zone.

I amused myself by trapping those weaker than me in corners and make them beg for freedom. I would seduce females to do my bidding and them leave them a lonely shell.

True, it doesn't sound much different from being a vampyre...

Then I woke up one morning to find myself lying on a bed in a halfway house. I really don't remember how I got there. I saw a couple of others lying on beds scattered around the room, but none of them stirred. I lay in that bed for quite some time, staring at nothing and trying to remember what the hell happened. I had been running through the nighttime streets, having some fun by overturning tables full of imitation Rolexes and bad artwork. I had met a couple of my boys in front of boarded-up building, and we decided to do a little exploring.

I don't remember much after that. Images of broken vials and empty bottles flashed through my mind, but I just couldn't connect them all into a full picture of what happened. I could remember running; I still tasted the fear in my mouth. But fear of what, I couldn't imagine. I stared at my bandaged limb and wondered what had happened. Had I fallen? Had I ripped the skin on some metal? Or was it wood? I looked over the rest of my body and – except for some scrapes and bruises – I was no worse for wear.

So where the fuck was I?

I stood shakily, testing my legs as I put my weight on them. I didn't land in a big old heap on the floor, so I guessed I was good.

The sun shone brightly in the room, hurting my bloodshot eyes as I made my way through the beds. The beds' occupants were cleaner than I was, but had that same look to them. They were strays, like me.

I followed voices to an obnoxiously cheery kitchen, where a plump woman dressed like something out of the '50s was taking a tray out of the oven and chatting with other wayward souls who were around the room, eating large bowls of what looked like stew.

"Well, good morning!" she said when she spotted me in the doorway. "Did you sleep well?"

I tilted my head at her in response, but then my stomach growled, distracting me. I actually couldn't remember the last time I had eaten.

I must've had that look on my face, because the woman put the tray down and rushed to my side. "Oh, my poor dear! Look at me rambling on while you must be starving, you poor thing! Let me get you some food!"

I stood a little aside from the others as she scooped some meat and gravy into a dish for me. I was not a social butterfly to begin with, but I knew better than to bother the starving.

I don't know if I picked my head up at all once she put the dish in front of me. I can't tell you if the food was good, because I was so hungry. I almost felt like myself by the time I finished the second bowl. I then drank the water she gave me like I had been in the desert for a year.

"I'm sorry it's only tap water here," she fussed, refilling my drink. "There's no room for that fancy stuff in my budget, I'm afraid."

I wondered if the woman really didn't know how wonderful her simple fare was. I also wondered if I had the same blissful look on my face that everyone else in the room did. I figured I did, since it was the first time in months that my stomach was actually staid.

The woman started collecting the empty dishes, nodding to the front door. "Why don't you all go outside with Shaji and get some fresh air while I clean up this mess?"

I glanced at the small man standing at the door. He looked fit, but I had a feeling I could easily outrun him once we got outside. I mean, the food and bed were nice and all, but I had to get back to my boys, to the streets.

So imagine my surprise when we got outside and – beyond the large gated yard – all I saw were acres and acres of trees in any direction.

Where the hell was I?

"Come, come," the man called Shaji beckoned. "We have nice set up for you here. We have track for you to exercise. We have rocks to sit on if you want quiet time and we have jungle gym. We also go for long walks trough the woods and sometimes we hunt. You like here."

A few of the others went bounding off, obviously familiar with their surroundings. The rest of us kind of huddled in a group, wondering what they should do. I finally decided to do some exploring; maybe I could find a hole in the gate or something and then make my escape at night...

And then I saw the track. It was a few miles round with a separate section for hurdles and sprinting. It was better than anything I had ever seen in the city.

Shaji stepped up behind me. "You like running, yes?" He opened the gate. "Here. Go run."

It was an amazing feeling to be running without guys in uniform chasing me. I was starting to think that this might be a good place to crash after all.

One night, I was woken up by a lot of talking throughout the beds. Someone important was driving to the halfway house that night and it was rumored that they were planning on adopting one of us. I snorted indifferently and rolled over in my bed. Why in the world would I want to be adopted? I got three meals a day and a bed, and could exercise as much or as little as I wanted. And Flora and Shaji were great people. Why would I give all that up?

I heard some rustling as, one by one, the others got out of bed and started preparing for their visitors. I buried myself deeper in the covers and tried unsuccessfully to block out their noise. I was trying so hard not to listen to them that I didn't hear Flora walk over to my bed until she was sitting next to me.

"Everyone seems all excited about the approaching guests except you, love. In fact, you haven't seemed excited about anyone that has come to visit our happy home. Now, you know that you are more than welcome to stay with Shaji and me as long as you want, but you must remember that there's more out there in the world but our quiet forest and my world-famous stew. You are too feisty a creature to be satisfied with this kind of living. Why don't you come meet these people? If you don't like them, that's fine, but you'll never know what you're missing if you stay in bed all day."

With that, she stood and walked away and I was left with the annoying feeling that she was right. Never in a million years would I had ever believed I would be happy living where I was and – if I really thought about it – I knew I wasn't completely content.

I sighed and dragged myself out of bed. I figured it wouldn't do any harm to make an appearance. I stretched and shook the sleep off of me as the rest of the household went towards the front door. Once I was certain they had all left, I made myself look presentable and then followed them to the porch.

As I found a spot in a dark corner, we heard the sound of a large car coming up our leaf-covered road. Many of the younger residents gasped as a dark purple limousine pulled into view. Even I had to admit I was impressed by the gleam on the vehicle as it rolled to a stop in front of the building.

But I was more impressed by the passengers. The first was a man of slight frame with the oddest eyes I had ever seen: one blue, one green. He was dressed in a dark gray suit with very small pinstripes, and a black shirt with a startling white tie. His shoes shone like the car, and his blond hair was slicked back as if he had just got out of the shower. Even with of his small size, he radiated strength and danger. He also showed old-world class as he turned back to the car and held his hand out to the person inside.

Smooth, very smooth.

The woman he helped out of the limo looked like something straight out of the 1980s. She was wearing stretch pants with a long peasant shirt and construction boots. She looked like Earth Mother meets Goth chick. Her thick hair was piled on her head in a fountain ponytail, and her chunky jewelry made a sort of music as she moved.

He led her towards the porch as if he were assisting royalty to the throne. I thought at one point he was going to pull a cloak out so she wouldn't have to step in the mud. By just looking at her, though, you could tell she was of hardy stock; she was just letting him lead her because he wanted to, not because she worried about getting dirty.

The man gave Shaji a sturdy handshake, and a slight bow to Flora; she beamed at him in return. "Welcome to our happy home, Mr. Morningstar!" She held out her hand to the woman. "And you must be Ms. DeCumpania." The woman smiled and gave them her own hearty handshake in return. "Please, come in for some refreshments! You've had a long trip. Even in such a luxurious ride, I'm sure you can do with some homemade pie."

The woman smiled; I noticed her eyes were traveling across the porch, taking us all in. "I can never say no to pie."

She suddenly turned, her eyes narrowing as she looked at the cab of the limousine, where I saw a shadowy form behind the wheel. The man followed her glance for a moment, then guided her into the house.

Weird.

I watched the others move about nervously as the visitors enjoyed Flora's hospitality. It was odd to see them all on edge; I guess the limo was giving them the jitters. For some reason, people equated money with happiness.

People are stupid.

I stayed in my dark corner of the porch and stared at the front of the limo. That silent exchange had piqued my curiosity; what had made the woman turn around like that? There hadn't been any more movement, but I knew that someone was there... and he was not happy.

My legs had begun to hurt from staying in one position for so long, so I decided to take a peek through the kitchen window. The couple was seated at the table with a bunch of folders spread out in front of them. It took me a moment to realize that they were looking at files about us; I didn't even know we had files. Flora was rummaging through the fridge, and I could still hear her friendly chatter through the closed window.

When I glanced back at the couple, my eyes met the woman's. She was staring straight at me, and I felt myself being drawn into her dark chocolate orbs. I shook my head, trying to clear it, and when I looked again she was studying a file with the man. I jumped slightly as the front door opened and Shaji came out with a full key ring. I knew what that meant: he was going to open the gate to the track. I followed on his heels as he walked across the yard to the gate.

"You all too nervous," he explained as he unlocked the gate, "Go have some fun."

I nearly pushed Shaji down as I ran into the yard and started jumping the hurdles. It was always a rush for me to feel the breeze in my face and my muscles pumping...

I don't know how long I had been running, or how long they had been watching, but when I slowed down to a trot I saw them standing by the gate. The woman's eyes were wide, with a smile on her face that gave me the shivers. She pointed to me and whispered something to the man. He watched me for a few moments then – begrudgingly, it seemed – nodded.

Flora, understanding the situation as easily as I did, beamed at me as she escorted the couple back inside. Shaji walked up to me as my breathing slowed to normal. "Come. You must get cleaned up while they sign your papers."

As I walked back to the house, I noticed all the sad and depressed faces of my fellow orphans, who all wanted this adoption much more than I did.

Oh well, sucks to be them.

I stood by the limo, cleaner than I had ever been in my entire life. I watched as all the other urchins skulked back into the house. None of them wished me well, none said goodbye; that's the price to pay for being a loner, I guess. I felt chills down my back as I waited, and I knew that whoever was in the driver's seat was staring at me... and not in a friendly way. I resisted the urge to make faces at him, but cocked my head slightly as if I were listening to something in the distance.

I was still in that position when Celeste and Luci came out of the home with Flora and Shaji in tow. When Flora saw me all shiny and clean, she ran past them and grabbed me in a big hug.

"I knew you were destined for greater things," she gushed; then she started sobbing into her handkerchief.

Shaji wrapped his arm around her waist and gave me a smile. "You do OK," he told me, then escorted her back into the house. I watched them for a moment, then looked back at my new guardians.

Luci glanced at Celeste. "Are you positive about this?" he asked.

She rolled her shoulders. "Sure, why not?"

"My darling," he said as he held the door open for her, "I have a feeling you have not thought this through."

"When does she ever?" came a voice from the front of the limousine. It was deep, a male's voice, that seemed both worldly and youthful at the same time.

Celeste jumped across the seats with a snarl. "You are in my good graces just barely, Kitten. I'd say you don't push your luck."

She then turned to me. "Come on in luv, don't be afraid."

I crept into the limo and slid into the seat next to her. She patted her lap for me to rest my head. For some reason, I obeyed.

Luci got in and closed the door before saying, "Well, isn't this a pretty picture?"

"Vanity," she said to the driver, "start moving. I can't hold out much longer."

The limo moved without a sound at the one called Vanity eased it down the country road.

"Celeste," Luci said, "think about this. You don't know what will happen to him. It's never been done before."

"That we know of."

He raised an eyebrow. "Does that really make a difference?"

"Not really. No."

I looked from one to the other, confused. What in the world were they talking about?

Don't worry, pet

I jumped slightly at the sound of her voice in my head.

This will only hurt for a bit... and then a new world will be open to you

Before I could ask anything, I felt a sharp pain in my neck, and she began drinking my blood. I tried to pull away, my legs flailing as I felt myself getting lightheaded. But she had a firm grip on me; I couldn't get away. I saw lights flash behind my eyes, and my limbs were getting too heavy for me to move.

Everything started to get dim, and I saw my sad, pitiful life play out before my eyes. I mean, for a dog, it wasn't that horrible, but in the grand scheme of things...

What? You didn't realize I was a dog? Well, I'm not anymore. I am a hunter. A fierce predator of the night who preys upon the weak and unsuspecting...

Well, maybe I am still a dog, but now my bite is much worst than my bark.

And yes, I am still a real son-of-a-bitch.

Cauterize the Wound

By

Jeffrey Lyman

January 1869, Amsterdam:

Professor Solomon Van Eyck entered the College of the Atheneum Illustre one bitter, January morning to find his demonstration cadaver missing. None of the professors would admit to the absence, and his interrogation of the cleaning staff elicited nothing further. The woman's corpse had been on the table when the doors were locked the night before. Now it was gone.

Standing in the lecture pit beside the empty table he clenched his fists, looking up at the seats above him. The pranks of the students had gotten out of hand and something needed to be done. He had better not find the body in a closet somewhere, or worse, violated. Though perhaps a case of syphilis was what the perpetrators deserved.

Furious, he strode to the offices of the Rector Magnificus, Professor Dr. Willem Moll, in the Agnietenkapel. Professor Moll rose from his desk with a smile as Solomon entered, obviously delighted by some news. "Professor Van Eyck," Professor Moll bellowed, his smile broadening further. "I believe that we are well on our way to transforming the Atheneum Illustre into a University. Won't that be wonderful? It may only be a few years now. *The University of Amsterdam.*" He spoke proudly. It had long been his dream to make the Atheneum into a true rival of the University of Leiden.

Solomon bowed, honoring decorum before voicing his grievances. "You have been our College Master for twenty-three years, Professor Moll. It will be an honor to see you University Master."

Professor Moll tossed aside the missive that delighted him so, perhaps one more letter of support from the city fathers. "But that is not why you come to me, Professor Van Eyck. What can I do for you?"

"Someone," Solomon stated, "has stolen my cadaver. I must have a subject for my lecture, which is to start momentarily." Both men looked out the window at the tower-clock across the square. It was ten minutes until the hour.

"That is, indeed, serious," Professor Moll replied. "We will find you a suitable replacement immediately and make further inquiries afterward."

And thus Solomon had the unpleasant task of sharing a corpse with Professor Hoogh, who would be lecturing on the bowel system in the afternoon and so had not disturbed the circulatory system of the arms, which Solomon was reviewing.

A more thorough search in the afternoon failed to produce the missing cadaver, so he was forced to work late preparing another subject. He refused to share a body with Professor Hoogh two days in a row. Not with bowels everywhere.

The new corpse, an otherwise healthy pauper who had sold his body to the College for quick money, had died in a fall the day before. Solomon worked quickly and precisely with his scalpels, peeling back swatches of skin to expose the major veins and arteries, all the while nursing his anger at this waste of time. He tried to ignore the faint scratching of rats, so much like fingernails, back below the raised seats. Wherever there were bodies there were rats, he told himself. He hated rats. Vermin. Their bites were so infectious. Their teeth sharp. He shivered.

Eventually the constant noises got to him and he walked to the small access door, low on the wall of his teaching pit. It led to the crawlspace below the student seats and he had checked it earlier to make sure that the pranksters hadn't stuffed the missing body there. They couldn't have taken her far. Carrying around a dead, naked prostitute was hardly inconspicuous. Especially a body that had gone through two lectures under his scalpel.

He yanked open the access door and stuck his head in, thrusting his candle out in the void. "Hey!" he shouted. The scratching stopped, replaced by the scurrying of tiny feet from deeper in the darkness. The candle illuminated a few feet, a couple of wooden supports, dust, spider webs. Rats and confining places! Two things he loathed.

He examined again the dust of the floor just inside the door. It had been disturbed. He hadn't seen it earlier in his anger and urgency to find a replacement body. He looked more closely. The scuff marks didn't bear the hallmarks of crawling boys dragging a corpse, but someone, for some reason, had been in here. He dipped the candle back and forth, examining the dust. Well, they would not make him the butt of their jokes in his own lecture hall!

He pushed forward into the cold, stale air of the space, and immediately his breathing grew faster, loud in the muffled darkness. He had to control his body. There was nothing to fear here. Just rats and maybe the corpse of a prostitute. He lifted his right knee to bring his leg through the door and ran straight into a spider web. Sputtering and sneezing and slapping at his face, he backed out and slammed the door. It was late and he should be home. His son needed him more than ever these days with the sickness. The cleaning staff could look under the seats tomorrow.

On his way out, he stopped by Professor Broen's office and knocked softly.

"How many today?" he asked softly when invited inside.

"Three new cases with mild symptons," Professor Broen said, "and two more bodies in our morgue. Don't worry, Solomon. We'll find a cure."

Solomon nodded and took his leave and hailed a carriage home. Nothing was incurable, he told himself over and over. Nothing was beyond the minds of such men as were gathered in the Atheneum Illustre and the University of Leiden.

It took him a long time to fall asleep, and when he finally slept he was restless. He awoke in deep darkness, certain he had heard something. He lifted his head, loathe to expose his skin to the freezing night air, and peered around his bedroom, listening. The moon had set and the room looked like a faint etching on gray slate. Nothing moved. No sound repeated itself, but something had awakened him.

Elizabeth stirred in her sleep beside him and pulled the blankets tighter around her throat. He looked over at his wife of twenty-four years. Her black hair, striped with gray now, was tangled around her head. "Rest easy, Elizabeth. I'll be back."

Frigid January air oozed in through the gaps and cracks of their old house; her father's house. Fortunately the iron bed-warmer below the bed was still hot enough to have kept his slippers warm. God, it was cold! It burned his nose when he breathed. He swung his legs over the edge of the bed and shivered violently until he could wrap a heavy woolen robe around himself. He pulled his nightcap down tighter over his ears.

He grabbed a candle nub from his desk and lit it from the embers of the fireplace. The pages for tomorrow's lecture lay ghostly on the black-lacquered desktop. His new cadaver had better be there when he arrived in the morning, he thought in a flash of irritation, a carryover from the day.

The floorboards creaked under his feet as he checked on Marya. His daughter was still asleep. Lawrence, his son, recently home from medical school, was not in his bed. Solomon grew immediately concerned.

The talk of Amsterdam lately had been of nothing but this new *sleeping disease* that Solomon feared was taking Lawrence. It had claimed dozens of victims in the last two months – death being preceded by increasing exhaustion, anemia, and hallucinations. His demonstration cadaver, the prostitute who had gone missing, was one of the victims.

Solomon hoped it was just a lack of energy brought on by the cold and darkness of winter. Nevertheless, he kept lengthy notes on his son's condition and plied him with every herb or powder he could think of or that Professor Broen suggested.

The professors at both the Atheneum and the University of Leiden had been hunting for a cause, methodically yet with growing urgency. The theologians were equally busy seeking signs of God's displeasure. And though Solomon mocked them, the theologians were having more success in finding a cause. They blamed the Jewish refugees who had been streaming into the city from Antwerp over the last few years.

On top of this sickness that had everyone pestering the hospitals or crowding the churches, a dozen men had been discovered in various parts of the city with their throats cut and their bodies drained of blood. The police had been unable to apprehend this bizarre killer and these two items dominated the gossip of the fashionable circles. It was lucky that the winter was so unnaturally cold. The populace didn't have the energy to panic.

Solomon proceeded downstairs, his breath billowing as clouds of steam, and stopped as he rounded the final corner of the staircase. The fire in the parlor had been built up.

"Who's there?" Solomon demanded sternly. "Lawrence?"

Father," came a rasp from one of the two wing-backed chairs facing the fire. "I'm sorry to have awakened you."

Solomon strode forward and skirted the chair. When he saw his son he gasped, nearly dropping his candle. "Are you all right?"

"I couldn't sleep," Lawrence whispered. "I dreamed of a great moth fluttering at my window."

Lawrence was as pale as snow, his lips a faint slash between sunken cheeks. His eyes were swollen, with great, dark circles beneath them. His hair was wild from the pillow, and Solomon could swear there was more gray in it than a month ago when he first returned home. More alarming was that Lawrence was fingering a heavy, gold Cross, about four inches tall, suspended from an ornate, double-interlocked, gold chain around his neck.

"Lawrence, where did you get that?" Solomon had not raised his son to believe in superstitions.

Lawrence met his eyes for a moment, and then glanced down at the cross. "The jeweler's shop at the corner of the Market Square."

"Why?"

Lawrence smiled. "I'm dying, Father." Solomon winced. "I have the *sleeping disease*," he continued. "I am exhausted, and yet I don't sleep. The sleep I do find is populated with nightmares."

"There will be a cure." Solomon was convinced of it. "Don't worry.

The greatest minds of the city are working on it."

"Perhaps the theologians are correct and God is punishing us."

"God has no place in science!"

Lawrence chuckled, then winced and slipped the Cross gingerly out of sight under his robe.

Solomon duly noted his son's weakness as the young man closed his eyes for a moment and clenched his jaw. He would write it down later in his journal. As well as this sudden interest in religion. Perhaps it was worse than he feared. Lawrence was slipping into the final stage of the disease – the endstage punctuated by hallucinations.

Not speaking, Lawrence struggled to his feet, keeping his hand protectively against the cross under his robe. "I am returning to bed," he wheezed. He began to limp towards the stairs and Solomon stepped up next to him. Lawrence gripped his father's shoulder tightly for strength.

"I understand that the marvels of our age have made you a devout atheist, Father," Lawrence whispered, "but in my time in medical school, I saw things that convinced me otherwise."

Solomon laughed, though he tried not to. Lawrence grimaced and Solomon felt that he must apologize, if only because of his old son's condition. "I am sorry Lawrence, but God is a tale your grandparents told you as a baby. This is the age of wonders and it is best to let superstitions die."

"They say there is an unholy beast at the source of this plague."

Solomon shook his head, saddened. "You've been listening to gossip. That is not proper for a young man of your standing."

"They say he was a man once, and that he sold his soul to the Devil."

"Like Dr. Johannes Faustus?"

"Not like Faust. This thing had no need of gold or relics in exchange for his soul."

"What then?"

Lawrence stopped and looked at his father. "Immortality."

"Immortality? Now what would the Devil gain by such a compact? This man would never go the Hell. The Devil could never collect."

Lawrence started up the stairs. "The gifts of Satan come with a price. It is rumored that if the man, this thing, cannot continue killing, then he has failed in his half of the bargain. His soul will be forfeit. They say it is a hunger in him."

"And you believe this fantasy is at the heart of your sleeplessness and nightmares?"

"Not all killers leave a mark."

Solomon forced himself to keep silent as he and his son slowly mounted the stairs. It was absurd, thinking a murderer could cause sleeplessness and anemia. The public was desperate for a cause. But everything would be fine. Solomon remained confident in this.

As they parted at Lawrence' door, his son met Solomon's eyes. "Faust was saved in the end by Gretchen. Perhaps this beast will one day return to the light at the hand of a woman." And then he closed his bedroom door.

"You're cold," Elizabeth murmured as Solomon climbed back into bed beside her, and she moved away from him. He didn't tell her of his conversation with Lawrence. Their son's weakening condition upset her terribly. He blew out his candle and stared into blackness. Immortality! Foolishness, though he could see the attraction in such fairy tales. Death was an ending like the quenching of a flame. To cheat it was a wonderful fantasy indeed.

Traveling to the Atheneum by coach in the following morning's darkness, Solomon marveled at the frozen canals. He had rarely seen them freeze so hard in his life. The children, on their way to work in the factories, were playing games on the ice; trying to chase each other but falling instead. He had not wanted children originally, and had only had two at Elizabeth's insistence. He found he liked them more than he had expected.

Such sentimentality was unbecoming, he knew, but there it was. And it was clouding every thought he had about the *sleeping sickness*. So much so that he made a detour to the morgue before going to his lecture hall. No new bodies had been brought in during the night. He walked between the older ones laid in rows on the tables – men and women and children, frozen and lifelike even days after death.

His new cadaver was still in the lecture hall when he arrived, so the irritation he had been brooding over cooled a bit. He attempted one more cursory look for the missing body, stared at the door to the underside of the seats, and then turned away. He would wait until after the thaw. Then the prostitute would be easily located from her stink.

He finished preparing the body just as his students trooped in, and continued his lecture on the circulatory systems with his hands dappled with blood. He used his scalpel like a pointer, speaking up to his students in the bleachers. The rats below the seats were, for the most part, quiet today.

He rushed home as quickly as he could in the later afternoon and sought his son immediately. Lawrence was sitting in a chair against the wall with his eyes closed. Elizabeth murmured, "He didn't sleep well last night, so he took laudanum and slept the day away. He is only recently up and about." She looked up into Solomon's eyes, worry and fear stamped across her face. "Is he going to be all right?"

"He'll be fine," Solomon grunted. When she continued to stare, he drew her into his arms. "He is ill, Elizabeth, but we're working on a cure. He'll be fine."

When she reluctantly left, he drew a chair near to where his son dozed. Lawrence' thick hair hung lank around his head, and his necktie hung loose. He opened his eyes, and it seemed to Solomon that the draught of laudanum had not yet run its course.

"How do you feel today?" Solomon waited as Lawrence attempted to sit up straight.

"I'll live. Thank you for your help last night. Without you I would slept the night near the fire."

"I want to talk to you about that while dinner is being prepared. You spoke a great deal of foolishness last night, and I don't want you upsetting your mother and sister. Your mother is worried enough without tales of beasts and compacts with the Devil."

Lawrence didn't reply for a long while, but eventually said, "I may have spoken too freely and I apologize. I won't repeat myself in front of mother."

Solomon remained stern. "And this demon who prays on our city?"

Lawrence sat up straighter. "I know, I should not listen to gossip. It is unbecoming for a young man of my station." And then he slouched back down.

Solomon nodded. He left him there and retired to his desk while the preparations for dinner continued. Tomorrow's lecture would be a continuation of today's on the circulatory system, wherein he would open the throat of the cadaver and demonstrate the tremendous vessels that transported blood to the brain – the center of thought. Man was a thinking animal, and Lawrence' fear of and belief in the supernatural was a primitive instinct that Solomon Van Eyck could not abide.

Additional Laudanum gave Lawrence another good night's sleep, and he felt well enough to accompany Solomon to the Atheneum the following morning. They parted company once inside, Solomon to his lecture hall, Lawrence to the morgue. Solomon had told him of the bodies down there, and Lawrence was keen to help in the investigation of a cure, though he previously hadn't had the energy.

Between morning and afternoon lectures, Solomon stopped by the morgue to see how his son was getting on. The mortician told him with a thinly disguised smirk that Lawrence had left after just an hour.

"And why is that funny?" Solomon demanded.

"Nothing, Professor Van Eyck. I've just never seen a graduate of the medical school who was so weak-stomached at the sight of a corpse before."

"My son is not weak stomached!" He wasn't. The boy had never been put off by anything.

"Of course, of course, Professor. But our coterie of poor souls here certainly had him upset."

Solomon finished his afternoon lectures in a distracted state, and he was sure later that he had missed several important veins.

Dinner that night was mutton stew, as it was every Tuesday, and Elizabeth and the children made small talk. Solomon didn't join in. He watched his son. The young man certainly ate heartily enough, but soon after excused himself to his bedroom. After dinner, Solomon mounted the stairs and knocked quietly on Lawrence' door.

"Yes?" came the muffled response, and Solomon turned the knob and entered. Lawrence was sitting on the edge of his bed in his night-clothes, shivering, staring out of his bedroom windows at the dark night.

"Did you see something?" Solomon asked, stepping up to the diamond-paned glass and looking down on the street below. Along the way, someone dressed in heavy furs hustled along before turning off onto a side street. It was another cold night. Would January never end?

"No, nothing," Lawrence replied, but his voice was distant.

Solomon went to him and met his eyes, examining his face. His son was barely awake. He might have fallen asleep sitting there and frozen to death. "Into bed," Solomon ordered, and Lawrence complied. Solomon checked the bed warmer and it was still giving off plenty of heat.

"You didn't remain long this morning at the College," he said.

Lawrence shuddered. "All those bodies. I couldn't look at them."

"They're just bodies."

"They looked so alive."

"Yes, I know. They all died of extremely low blood levels, and some have theorized that decomposition is being delayed by this lack of a fluid medium in the body. I think it's just the cold."

"No, it's not the cold." Lawrence' voice was growing fainter, and Solomon stepped forward to hear. "I felt like they were still alive, just sleeping. I thought I could hear a blackbird caged by the ribs of each, struggling to break free. It was horrifying. I couldn't listen to that pecking and fluttering any longer."

Solomon ground his teeth. It was getting worse. He feared that Lawrence couldn't survive many more days. He would have to talk to Elizabeth tonight. Prepare her. He closed his eyes. How could he prepare her? How could he prepare himself? His son wasn't supposed to die. There had to be a way to save him.

He placed his hand on his son's head for a moment before turning to leave, but Lawrence reached up and gripped his wrist weakly. "Science won't explain away all mysteries, Father," he whispered.

"Lawrence!" Solomon was insulted. How dare his son criticize the science that Solomon Van Eyck based his life on?

"I am sorry, Father, but sometimes belief in something larger is the only path to the truth."

"Deliberate research and the scientific method succeed where superstitions will always fail."

"No." Lawrence opened his eyes. "Listen to me. I have been thinking on the gossip you hate. I wondered how this demon-man could have gotten access to me. I did not remember permitted anyone into our home. Then I recalled the foreign Prince.

Solomon frowned. "What is this?"

"Prince Leonid Nikolayevitch Barashkov, of Petrograd. When he and his grandfather first arrived in Amsterdam, he made the rounds of the noble families. It was during the day, so you were at the College."

"I remember your mother mentioning that." Elizabeth's family was of the noble class, so they occasionally had foreign noblemen introducing themselves.

"He frightened me, though I don't know why. I have dreamed of him several times since then. Maybe he is the demon itself, or an emissary preparing the way."

"That is nonsense. Go to sleep and don't dwell on such dire thoughts."

It only took a moment for Lawrence to fall into the breathing patterns of sleep, and Solomon watched for signs of nightmares. Nothing. His son was a peace. As he turned to go, he caught sight of the gold cross around Lawrence' neck. Determined to prove to his son that this was all nonsense, he gently removed it and dropped it into his pocket. Such trinkets were not necessary for a good night's rest.

A short while later, his daughter Marya retired to her room for the night. Solomon waited in the parlor for everything to quiet down with impatience, because it was Tuesday and he and Elizabeth always made love on Tuesday nights. They had mutton stew on Tuesday, and they made love. It had been so ever since they were married. Tonight he would talk to her about Lawrence instead. He just needed to think of the words. She would weep, and he might too.

He sat in one of the winged-back chairs in front of the fire, warming his toes and allowing his scarf to slip from his throat. He had gotten down one of the medical texts of Galen, hoping that the Greek master physician might have listed an illness with similar symptoms to their current scourge. Something to save Lawrence. Others had read through the books already, but Van Eyck's knowledge of Greek was superior to his fellow professors. In Latin he was their equal, but he excelled at Greek.

Elizabeth, descending the stairs, said, "It is time for bed, Solomon."

Solomon looked up at her. He loved her very much. He struggled for the words. "Elizabeth, we need to talk about Lawrence."

She froze at the bottom of the steps. "Talk about what, Solomon? You said he would be fine."

"Elizabeth. We are racing towards a cure, but I don't know that we will be in time." A tightness in his throat threatened to choke off his words. "We have not spoken of this aloud, but it is the *sickness*. I can't deny it any longer."

She paled, still standing at the bottom of the steps. Her hands clung together. "You said he would be fine." Her voice trembled and the tightness in his own throat grew worse. She turned and ran up the steps.

"Elizabeth!" Solomon leapt up and raced after her. He reached her just as she grasped the doorknob of Lawrence' bedroom and the door swung inward. The first thing that Solomon noticed was that the room was freezing. He couldn't figure out why Lawrence would have opened his windows.

Elizabeth bustled forward and pulled the windows shut, almost losing them for a moment as a gust of wind tried to snatch them from her hands.

Solomon looked down at his son. Lawrence lay placidly under a mound of blanket, eyes closed and darkly ringed like a badger's. Suddenly he sensed that something vital had gone from the boy; some spark had faded. That realization startled him. Until this moment he had thought of the terminus of life like a gas lamp as it is shut off: no flicker, no afterglow, just an end and then darkness. But staring down at Lawrence, it didn't feel like that. It felt like a tide pouring back into a vast sea, leaving behind the smooth, washed sand. *He's dead*, he thought, stunned. *He's not breathing.*

"I can't imagine how these windows got open," Elizabeth whispered.

"Elizabeth," Solomon choked. He sat on the edge of the bed and took his son's cold hand.

"What?" She put her hand to her mouth in silent horror, and then ran to her boy. "No," she howled, the tears coming. "You said he would be fine!"

"I just left him an hour ago." Tears glazed his eyes. "He *was* fine. He was sleeping peacefully."

"What is it?" Marya said from the door. She ran to her mother.

Solomon wiped his eyes. It was too soon. His boy was dead too soon. The professors and doctors had not been fast enough. They had failed. He felt hollow, like the moment after the orchestra stops playing and silence falls.

He staggered to the recently closed window. Movement caught his eye. Down below, in the winter street lit by gas lamps, was a man in a top hat and cloak. He was walking away down the center of the street. Behind the him dragged a shadow of something not man-shaped. "What is that?" The shadow billowed and rippled like a sheet in the wind. Solomon shook his head and wiped his eyes again. Sometimes the gas lamps distorted shadows.

He looked to his boy and then back out to the now empty street, his anger finally beginning to fill the nothingness that had eaten away his internal organs. Elizabeth cradled Lawrence in her arms and rocked and moaned softly. Solomon welcomed her keening. Silence was worse. He rubbed his arms. He didn't know how to grieve. He wanted to sob like his daughter, but he could not.

He lifted Lawrence' Cross from his pocket and fingered the edges. Such a small thing.

He clenching his teeth, remembering the fairy tales his mother had once told him. The power of the supernatural would be greatest in the night, but could be held at bay with religious icons. Had he killed Lawrence be taking this Cross?

He dropped it back into his pocket. No. The disease was just a disease.

Solomon Van Eyck walked into the College of the Atheneum Illustre just as the sun rose. He had not slept, but had stayed with Elizabeth while she held Lawrence. The morticians had come now and were transforming the front parlor to hold Lawrence' body for the wake.

Solomon couldn't watch them. He had gripped the cross in his pocket and numbly answered questions directed to him until he'd had to flee the house. Grief now completely filled the place where science and probability used to dwell, and that grief had not abated on his long, cold walk to the College. He wouldn't be able to do his lectures today. He would have to tell Rector Magnificus Moll.

As he walked down the cold and echoing hallway of the Atheneum, the college mortician hurried past him, obviously angry. The man stopped short as he recognized Solomon.

"Your cadaver was stolen, wasn't it?"

"Did you find it?"

"Two more bodies went missing from the mortuary last night. Rector Moll is terribly upset. He has called an assembly of the boys for eight o'clock. We cannot allow these pranks to continue."

"No, we can't," Solomon said absently. He didn't really care right now if the boys were stealing bodies.

Standing in his lecture pit beside his latest body, he touched the cold and semi-hard skin. Lawrence's hand had felt like this last night. Faint light descended from high clerestory windows above, but gloom still draped the pit. Solomon lit a candle.

The scurrying claws of rats below the seats distracted him, so he strode to the small access door on the wall and pulled it open. He thrust the lantern out in the dark void. "Hey!" The scratching hesitated for a moment in the gloom then began again.

Solomon forced his shoulders in, and then his legs, and crawled through thick cobwebs and dust, waving the candle about. Cobwebs didn't matter. There was something in here and he needed to see it with his own eyes. Lawrence' gold cross hung heavy in his pocket.

He prayed that she wouldn't be here; that science and reason still mattered. But no. She was there. In the far recesses of the crawl space he found his missing cadaver.

A young, naked prostitute surrounded by dozens of rat corpses. Her left arm ended at the elbow, the white end of the humorous glistening in his candle's light. He himself had removed her forearm not three days before in order to demonstrate the vessels running through the joint. A tremendous patch of skin was missing from her inner thigh where he had presented the femoral artery. In all parts of her body the skin and muscle had been peeled away by his scalpel. She was a patchwork doll, and she glared at him with an evil fury.

His anger flickered and then rose to meet hers.

Crippled, she lurched at him. He snapped free one of the smaller wooden boards of the seating structure. Equally calmly, determined and methodical, he slashed at her main arteries and veins with the broken end of the board, pushing her back as she rabidly tried to advance.

She had been empty of blood when she died. He reasoned that a need to replace her blood had brought her back. The vascular system was her weakness. He slashed the stick across her throat and she fell.

She lay on her side, staring up at him with animal confusion, her throat hanging open. She was no longer capable of attack. He crawled close and drove the stick between her ribs and into her heart, quieting her eyes.

Then he sat back against a post and truly cried. Tears fell and froze on his collar. He had to get home, to his parlor where even now Lawrence was being laid out in his best suit. His son couldn't be allowed to return like this, crouched in a hole and eating rats. Solomon needed to go, but he couldn't yet make himself move.

He gazed at the prostitute, her dull eyes the proper filmy shade for death, her hair matted and dirty. Her destruction had been a mercy. So would Solomon's desecration of Lawrence' body. There would be others across the city – including the ones down in the Atheneum morgue. He must cauterize the wound before it turned gangrenous.

Lawrence had told him; had warned him! He had even given a name - Prince Barashkov. Solomon would visit the Prince's home. Perhaps this man was the source of the scourge. He lifted the Cross from his pocket and hung it around his neck.

Then he stopped. Perhaps Lawrence had been too far gone in his hallucinations and it was just a disease after all, albeit a peculiar one not yet explained.

Solomon had failed his son because he had refused to consider something that defied logic and reason. But just because it could not be explained, did not mean that it had to be supernatural. Solomon simply lacked the language to describe it. Even as he destroyed the victims of the disease, he would study them. He would solve this mystery.

This was the Age of Reason! There was no place for a supernatural explanation for this prostitute or for Prince Barashkov, certainly not that of a Faustian bargain. But it could stand as a preliminary hypothesis. Science would explain and illuminate the remainder.

Solomon lifted his lantern high and crawled back toward the distant hatchway.

If At First You Don't Succeed...

By

C.J. Henderson

"There are but two roads that lead to an important goal and to the doing of great things: strength and perseverance. Strength is the lot of but a few privileged men; but austere perseverance, harsh and continuous, may be employed by the smallest of us and rarely fails of its purpose, for its silent power grows irresistibly greater with time." *Goethe*

The fanged thing drew closer, all of its senses alive, all of it ready to take the plunge, to throw itself fully into the life it had dreamed of for so long. Its prey seemed trapped, helpless, with nowhere else to run, with no further tricks to play. The mere human had been bested at all turns—strength, speed, endurance—the pale-skinned thing approaching had proven itself to be his master, and now as per one of history's soundest axioms, it would take the conqueror's spoils.

"Sounds good so far."

"Yeah, then what happened? Did it kill ya?"

"You know," said the tall, deceptively charming man holding court there in the Narkane, "that's why I hate telling stories in bars."

"What happened about what—where? Why aren't you dead? What's the story?"

The grinning newcomer approaching the table there in the world's most supernaturally sensitive tavern was a tall, thin gentleman with intense blue eyes and a sense for the amusingly horrific. As all at the table greeted him with civility, if not open friendship, the older man said, "All right, lads, don't keep an old man hanging—what's going on now?"

The intense speaker who had been telling the story began an attempt to catch the newcomer up to speed, but the others at the table protested, claiming it was too good a tale not to hear from the beginning. When he reminded them they had all heard most of it already, and would now have to hear it all again, everyone concerned agreed it mattered little. As one of them put it;

"Who cares? Your stories always get better with each telling anyway, Marv. Introduce the professor all around, and let's hear it again."

Giving in to the will of the majority, Marvin Richards, head anchor and main producer of *Challenge of the Unknown*, the only network news show dedicated to covering the strange, the bizarre, and the supernatural, introduced noted professor Zackery Goward to those at the table not already of his acquaintance, and then relaunched himself into the telling of one of the strangest and most bizarre supernatural stories of his career.

"I'm telling you, that's what it looks like to me."

Richards frowned. He knew enough about the various beyond realms to know how things worked in the world. Yes, there were indeed such creatures as vampires roaming the Earth. But, they were not the opera-caped blood leeches of Hollywood and other modern soft-core pornography mills. They were, in their actuality, a breed of thing far more horrible and dangerous. For one thing, they were not affected by sunlight, did not sleep in coffins during the day, turn into bats, command rat or wolves, shrink from the sight of mirrors, or the thought of eating in Italian restaurants, et cetera.

What made them unique, and in any way vampires in the way most people understood the term, was that they did indeed steal the energy of the living to prolong their own lives. But, there was nothing romantic or in the least bit sexy about the manner in which they did so. No, real vampires could only be labeled as monsters for they murdered their victims while staring them in the eye, choking them, beating them, stabbing them to death. It was that close proximity to their victims which allowed them to steal their individual life essences, but it was the ruthlessness of their personalities which allowed them to hold onto it.

Many people murdered others at close range, and for a brief time felt the energy of their victims coursing through their veins. But, claiming of that energy also meant taking the spirit, personality and memories of the slaughtered party into their minds. Most murderers would reject the accusing voices within their heads, surrendering the extra power and extended life gladly rather than live with their victim's voice within their brain for all eternity.

That was why there was no great plague of vampires, as would have been the case if another was created every time one of their number got hungry. And it was exactly that idea, the notion of a plague, a veritable army of super-strong, flying, invisible bloodsuckers that had Lieutenant Evan Delvecio, as well as his main toe-tagger, one Sergeant Anton Thorner, in such a frazzled state of anxiety the morning in question.

"For God's sake, Lieutenant," said Richards, deciding finally to be amused at the big, bald-headed man's show of concern. "You know there's never been a proven case of blood drinking vampires in the history of the world. So what gives? Why are you wasting your time with this?"

Every major police force had someone that handled their jurisdiction's "Twilight Zone" cases, as they were unofficially called across the country, and New York City was no exception. Delvecio and Thorner had a great deal of latitude when it came to watching out for their town. And, in truth, they kept things remarkably quiet, all things considered.

"Despite your expertise," Delvecio answered in a dry, bitterly sarcastic tone, "and our relative inexperience, this may be something different."

"I'm a big fan of the different," said Richards, always willing to bend with the breeze if there were a story in the air. "Just how different are we talking?"

"Listen, newsboy, I brought you here for one reason," Delvecio said in a calmer voice. A hint of dangerous secrets in his tone, one the anchorman responded to like Pavlov's dachshund, the officer said, "Anton, take our lad here down to the basement and show him what we've got. Then we'll see if he wants to act a little more cooperative."

Richards protested that he was always ready to cooperate, but Thorner informed him he would be of no help to them until he saw what they had in the basement. The newsman, of course, had to catch hold of himself before he said anything antagonistic, professional enough to remember that the police often had little interest in helping anyone but themselves, and of course, the public. It was a notion Richards found quaint, but understanding the social mores of various cultures did often help him produce his show.

And, he thought, getting a look in the basement right now probably won't hurt, either.

Arriving in a practically ancient sub-basement minutes later, a thick-blocked, low-ceiling affair not used regularly since a short time after the War Between the States, Thorner spoke with one of three armed guards outside a thick iron door. After that he motioned Richards forward as one of the guards pulled a large metal ring from a drawer in the desk behind which he was sitting.

The newsman noted that the ring only held six over-sized, antique keys, most likely fitting the six thick, but narrow, antique doors there in the cramped underground room. As Thorner prepared to open the now-unlocked door, he slipped a paper face mask over his mouth and nose. He then handed one to Richards, advising;

"You'll need it." Not one to be impressed by theatrics, the newsman turned him down, answering that he preferred to get the full measure of whatever it was he was about to be shown. He was certain Thorner was smiling under his mask as he put his broad back into opening the door. When the pair entered, they were greeted by two tables. Upon each an extremely pale young woman had been strapped down. Both appeared unconscious. Each was festooned with bundles of fresh garlic.

Against one wall was a third woman who, even paler than the others, had been chained by her wrists and ankles, as well as at the waist and neck. She was also draped with garlic bulbs, but far fewer than her companions. Richards noted that unlike the others, she was not unconscious. A moment after his observation, the woman sighted Thorner and immediately began a spirited diatribe of foul and bitter comments, none of which would have been fitting for the anchorman's viewers, unless, he thought, he could secure a cable special.

Still, he wondered, what was this little tour of Thorner's all about? Why were these woman being restrained? And, moreover, why were they being held in such a primitive, barbaric fashion? After all, it was the twenty-first century, he reminded their jailor. People had rights.

"That what you think," asked Thorner smugly. "These people have rights? Okay—why don't you go talk to them about it?"

Richards stared at the officer for a moment, then moved toward the woman chained to the wall. He did not do so hoping to refute Thorner. The newsman had been around long enough to know when someone else was bluffing. No—he did so because he knew the officer was not bluffing, because there had to be something remarkably compelling about the three women before him.

"It wasn't, you know, that I thought the police would never hold anyone against their will without the right to do so," Richards told those at the table, "it was just that I knew they'd never show the proof of it to a newshound."

"What about the face mask," asked Goward. "Why were you offered one?"

"Because they were right about everything. The women, all of them, were vampires. Movie vampires—women bitten on the neck by something that killed them, drained their blood, and turned them into creatures of the night.'"

"Marvin," asked Goward, "really—are you quite certain?"

"Zack," answered the anchorman, "they had the bite marks. They had no reflections, no pulses, didn't give off any breath if you put a mirror to their nose—believe me, I checked it all. When I started moving the garlic away from the ones on the table they started waking up. But something was wrong—well, since there is no such thing as this kind of vampire, 'wrong' might not be the word I want, but anyway ..."

"Marvin, old boy," the professor asked once more, "the face masks?

"Oh, it was because of the smell coming from the women. You see, they were decomposing."

Everyone at the table watched Goward, wondering if the older man would have something to say in response. He was, after all, a highly respected professor of philosophy and theology at Columbia University, and was often called in on supernatural cases by the police, the media and private sources to render opinions. That he had no comment at that time to add to the mix sent a small shiver through the table. Noting such, a smug Marv Richards went back to telling his story.

The anchorman stared at the woman chained to the wall, one hand over his mouth to help block the smell of her rotting flesh. White-skinned, fanged, wild for the taste of blood, she was for all intents and purposes a vampire straight out of fiction, except that she was dead, not undead.

"I don't get it," the newsman said to Thorner over the vampire's curses. "Why are they rotting? And for that matter, why are these chains working? Why doesn't she just turn into a bat and fly away?"

And with those words, a dark silence fell over the room, the way it does when a television repair man asks if anyone checked to see if the set was plugged in. Before either man could react, the woman in chains began to concentrate, pouring all of her focus into following Richards' suggestion. Before their eyes, the woman's body began to mutate, slim clean arms growing hair, armpits beginning to web-over, ears expanding, face flattening—

"Jesus-Holy-Christ-on-a-crutch," muttered Thorner. "They hadn't done it because they hadn't thought of it, ya big gasbag!" Throwing himself across the room, the sergeant slammed against the door, ordering those outside to open it ASAP.

"Freak show!" The sergeant screamed at the top of his lungs. "Get in here—now, goddamnit!"

"He means it," shouted Richards, his eyes not leaving the woman chained to the wall. As he watched, his eyes remained unblinking as the transformation continued. By its end, the woman had been completely transmogrified. Slipping all of her bonds, she now tested her wings, slowly beginning to take flight even as the door finally swung open.

"Fire," Thorner ordered, "take it down!"

The two guards entering pointed the shotguns they had been given in case such a need arose. As the snarling, eagle-sized mammal came flapping toward them, both fired. The resulting explosions covered the back wall with blood and hair.

"And my brothers, let me tell you—what a mess." Richards shook his head sadly, telling those at the table, "Movies, you know, they turn into little bats—not this chick. No, she has to turn into a thing as big as a German Shepherd. And, like it didn't smell bad enough in there already."

The newsman quickly told the others how the resulting smell caused him to add to the wall decorations by leaving behind the Caesar salad and melon bowl jumble he had apparently wasted time having for lunch. All of them temporarily deaf from the shotgun blasts in such a tightly confined space, in quick order the men retreated, the door was locked once more, and the guard was changed so all affected could retreat to the outside to massage their ears. Delvecio joined the group of them on the front steps of the precinct house. As Richards began to look as if he could hear once more, the lieutenant waited until no one was passing by, then asked in a whisper;

"So, ready to take the idea of blood-sucking vampires a little more seriously?"

"Yeah, I'm thinking you might have something there."

"Gosh, that's awfully big of you."

"Are you kidding," answered the anchorman. "This story is bigger than the Burning Bush. If I had film of what I just saw, what a gyp—say, think we could degarlic one of the others, try and get a replay ... man, would that be cool."

"Wouldn't it also be a cross between entrapment and murder?"

Like all newsmen, Marv Richards hated when things like the law, or simple human decency, got in the way of a good story. Admitting that the lieutenant might have a point, he said;

"Well then, what's up, Kojack? Why'd you bring me here if all you're going to do is throw a blanket over the desert table?"

"Gosh, but you're colorful," answered Delvecio. "You've gotten plenty of freebies outta my office. Time for some payback. We're keeping a lid on this because we need to try and figure out how it can even be happening."

"And you expect me, who's never seen anything like this, to have the answer to it?"

"No," answered the lieutenant. "But you have a network of agents and stoolies and contacts just like I do. Bring me something I can use and you'll get a forty-eight hour jump on everyone else."

"That's no good for me," countered Richards. "We're a news magazine. We need time to develop and advertise a special. You give everything you have out to the CNNs of the world and we'll be left crying in the dust."

"Bullshit," responded Delvecio. "You know as well as I do that you'll have your lead team start cobbling ground work as soon as your cell phone is in tower range. You'll sit down, get made up all pretty and then do a lot of different calm, reflective talking head segments your editors can piece together around whatever footage you bring them, and when the story can be released you'll be on in less than twenty-four hours."

"I can send a crew into that room Thorner just brought me out of—right?"

"You can send one person in, and they will be accompanied by a police editor. One unauthorized shot and they get bounced."

"I'll still need a guarantee of sixty hours exclusive before you open the damn gates."

"Sixty, forty-eight, what's the difference?"

"If I take your offer the network will think I'm rolling over for the man. If I beat you back an extra half day, I look like a hero. And to show my appreciation, I'll shine BPLs on the police."

"On the police and the mayor's office," countered Delvecio. The pair haggled a bit further, but their deal was set. Something that made Goward ask;

"Really, Best Possible Light promises for the mayor's office? This mayor? Were you really that desperate?" Goward took a swig of his Baggins Brew Dark Ale, giving the anchorman the chance to confide;

"I needed the time and didn't figure the mayor's office to end up anywhere near things. Life is filled with compromises, you know."

As everyone at the table agreed with Richards' last, sad truism, he began outlining the next steps in his story. While the police went up and down every ladder they knew how to climb, the anchorman began rattling all the trash cans at his disposal. At the same time, Richards and his top writers began a concentrated effort, pouring over everything the police already had, centering their approach on the first three victims.

Thorner and the anchorman worked together at a break-neck pace, narrowing the hunt for what they had labeled "Vampire X" as much as they could. It seemed the only chance they had that in any way might possibly prevent the next attack from ending in the creation of yet another young female corpse whose day planner was filled from one end to the other with "scream some more about wanting blood." Try as they might, however, none of them could find any kind of solid connection between the three victims that might give them a lead on where to start searching for their twenty-first century Dracula.

Finally, their break came during an all night one-more-time-over-the-facts session, one born more out of desperation than any kind of actual hope for productive results. The lives of the three young women were checked backward and forward, not only by the cops on Delvecio's team, but the senior production team members Richards had brought along with him. Nothing worked.

The women had nothing in common.

Well, Richards explained to his audience, not "nothing." There were always some similarities upon which to build. All three women were attractive. There was that. But, outside of that, there was nothing beyond the fact they all lived in New York City—a town with a mere eight million residents. But then, as the digging continued, cops and production assistants working side-by-side, finally, an over-weight, greasy-haired fellow with exceptionally pale skin made an observation.

"We're lookin' for anything these three women might have in common, right—no matter how small?" When he was assured that was the case, he answered, "How about the fact they all worked at the same place at the same time?"

"What're you jabbering about," demanded Delvecio with a snarl. "They don't work anywhere near each other. The one's a clerk way uptown. One's—"

"Not full-time work. Look, you see this one, she got a check for five hundred dollars from Venture Limited. And this one, here's a check from Big World Entertainment, and the third one's got one from the Atlantic Graphics Corporation. They all got paid for workin' the same place on the same weekend."

"But for three different companies."

"Three different comic book companies," added the pasty-skinned youth. "And the dates they worked, that was the weekend of the big comic convention at the Javitz Center, you know, back in February."

All conversation ceased. When it started again, the police began a series of checks to confirm what the young man in the black T-shirt had brought to their attention. In short order, it was discovered that the three young women had indeed all been hired as models to walk around the convention center on that particular weekend dressed as super-heroines. Finally, with something of a lead to go on, the police had thrown themselves into a new line of attack. This suddenly reduced the possible suspects from eight million to something slightly under twelve thousand—still an impressive number, but one more easily handled.

And, the proof in that was the speed with which the NYPD was able to narrow the lesser figure to one far more diminutive. Pulling in the promoters of the show, it took a mere hour and twenty minutes for the numbers to drop from 11, 957 to six. Examining the convention from all angles, it was quickly deduced that the most likely place for anyone to have come in contact with all three of the women in question was the costume contest. They could not have taken home any of the big prizes since their uniforms were not homemade, but it was good for their corporate sponsors if they did a superheroine skit to entertain the comic-book buying public, and so, all three of them had appeared on the same stage at the same time.

"Three," said one of the promoters, a slight trace of question in his voice, "hell, there were more than three."

In short order, the promoters quickly named all the other super-heroines who had been in attendance that day. Between the professionals type players, such as their "vampire" seemed to favor, and the amateur talent, there had been no less than fifteen girls and women who had taken the stage during the contest. Immediately, Delvecio began barking orders. Men were sent in teams of six to find each and every still living contestant. The heavily armed teams were to either take their targets into protective custody, or if refused, to stake out their homes and to watch them every minute of the day, no less than four members of their team on duty at all times.

As the police rapidly emptied the room, Marvin Richards sat back in his chair, fingers knitted behind his head. His smile was wide, his pose expansive. The anchor was happy at that moment, for finally everything seemed headed his way. They had their break. It seemed obvious their villain would strike again soon, and when he did, this time the police would be there to pin back his opera-caped wings. And, when they did, he would have the ratings buster of the century.

"You look happy, Mr. Richards," said the intern. Feeling egalitarian, the anchor agreed that he had not experienced a happier moment in years. Knowing he had been the cause of such bliss, the pasty young man continued, saying;

"So, have you put any thought as to where this kind of vampire might have come from?"

"What do you mean, George?"

"You know my name, Mr. Richards?" When the anchor nodded, the young man blushed, beaming with pride for a moment before adding, "well, you know, the Hollywood vampire, everyone at the show knows that's not how it works. But, here it is, we've got one. Why do you think that is?"

"Well, obviously I've been giving that whole idea some thought. All I can figure, and this is after considering everything we at *Challenge* have come across over the years, is that this joker—whoever he is—must have made his way to the dreamplane."

"The dreamplane ..." George said the world with a mixture of surprise and reverence.

"Yeah, you know, we've seen it a dozen times. Anyone who can actually reach the dreamplane when they're sleeping, who can consciously understand what's going on, can wish for anything they want there. It just takes complete and utter faith in one feeling they deserve what they're asking for."

"That's for sure ..."

"Yeah, forget God. I mean, let's face it ... the dreamplane is how prayer actually gets answered. It's the energy field of the universe, where those with a pure and perfect faith can get the energy to do anything. Those that believe, who haven't got a shred of doubt in their minds, their prayers are answered. Now, how someone gets it into their head that they should be a vampire—sleep in a coffin full of dirt, never see their reflection, drink blood, not be able to go out in sunlight, fear garlic and crucifixes, yadda, yadda, yadda—what kind of loser is that?"

"I guess it depends ..."

"On what," asked Richards. Not actually paying a great deal of attention to his intern, his mind distracted by some of the data he was reading concerning the other women their vampire might have seen at the convention, he answered, "How many bad porno vampire novels the guy has read?"

"Maybe the guy sees himself as something more than the average guy. Like he deserves something more, after a terrible home life. Maybe he had a mother that treated him bad, a dad who wasn't around much. Maybe he lived his whole life being told he wasn't worth anything, that he wouldn't amount to anything. Maybe while his mom beat him and humiliated him and made his life a living hell, he was dreamin' of a way to get past all of that."

"Well," mused the anchor, still not paying very much attention as he continued studying the fact sheets on the other women, "it's still kind of pathetic. I mean, if you're going to dream yourself up a life, why not dream yourself up as king of the universe?"

"Maybe that's what he did, Mr. Richards." The intern's voice getting excited, he rambled, "Think about it, look at the people we meet doing this show. The women especially, they're all flipped for vampires. Look at all the porn with vampires, they're not monsters anymore. The best looking movie stars play them, and why not? They're heroes. Super-powered Heroes who slaughter their enemies with ease, and who get never-endin' oceans of sex with the hottest women in the world. And when they're done with them they just throw them away."

Richards looked up from the sheets of notes he was studying. George's eyes had gone all dreamy, a faraway look of smug contentment curling the edges of his lips. His own eyes scanning the top sheet in his hand once more, the anchorman pushed his chair back from the table slightly as he asked;

"George, are you trying to tell me something?"

"Yeah, I guess." Richards gulped. The intern was still pasty and sloppily over-weight. "It came to me when you first heard about the dreamplane from that freelancer that didn't work out. You decided it was too risky to let the world at large know about it, cancelled that big special you were planning. That got me thinkin', you know?"

There was nothing about the lad that suggested power or sexual prowess, strength or cunning—certainly not a dark and abiding evil. And yet, as he spoke, Richards began to put together a singularly chilling truth.

"My whole life, it's just been one big rat burger—you know? My she-ape of a mother, that bitch, that whore, always pickin' at me, ridin' me—pushin' me. I never had no chances, no breaks ever came my way—nuthin'. Until I hooked up with this show, and learned the way things really are."

In horrifyingly quick succession, George told the anchor the high points of his life—how he had realized he had been given the life he had for a reason, how he had survived his mother's insane cruelty by concentrating on the salvation he knew would one day be his. Year after year, he waited, he prayed, but nothing came his way, until—

"And then, after I'd been working here at *Challenge* for about six weeks, that's when we met, and you told me the secret of life."

"I told you the secret of life?" When the greasy young man merely nodded, Richards added, "Didn't know I knew it."

"I was tellin' one of the other interns about goin' to church," said George softly, not actually hearing the anchor's words, "and you gave me a friendly rap in the back of the head and you said, forget prayin' to the clouds. We make our own reality in this world. You want something, you just reach out and get it."

The intern kept talking, telling of how he concentrated his dreams, night after night, until finally he reached the dreamplane and remade himself. He told of using the cache of the convention to get the names and addresses of all the girls at the show. There had only been one he wanted, but the convention center did not know which girl had been hired to play which character.

"I'll find her, though," said George with a wickedly self-pleased grin. "After all, I've got the police out finding them all for me right now."

"George, my boy," said Richards with barely a trace of the bone-rattling terror he was feeling. "Have you thought this thing through—really?"

"Sure, Mr. Richards," answered the intern eagerly. "Once I've got the right girl by my side, why then everything will be perfect. Those first three, they were mistakes, but once I've found the one I want—then I'm going to pay everyone back." And with those words, the door opened and Lt. Evan Delvecio walked through, gun drawn, badge around his neck. Service automatic drawn and aimed at the intern, he shouted;

"George McCullen, I arrest you in the name of the law!"

"You can try."

As the intern stood from his seat, Richards threw himself from his own chair even as Delvecio, Thorner and several other officers began firing at the approaching McCullen. Knowing he had only minutes to find out if the one theory he had was correct, the anchor threw himself into the hallway, his mind closed to the sight of bullets passing unrestrained through the intern's sloppy body. Ignoring his laughter as well, Richards accosted officer after officer, trying to find where the other potential victims of the vampire had been taken within the station house. He did not know what had tipped the lieutenant to the possibility of McCullen's guilt, nor did he care. Now all he wanted to do was find the one woman he believed could end the raging conflict behind him before it escalated to include the entire world.

After only a few panicked inquiries, Richards discovered the location of the women in question. Before he could reach them, however, he heard what he could only believe to be the sounds of George descending the police house stairs after him. Racing to the holding rooms in question, Richards found himself panting. He was a star, he thought indignantly, he was not made for such exertions. Putting out a hand, he steadied himself against the nearest wall. And, in that moment of respite, George McCullen appeared.

"Hello, Mr. Richards. Thanks for finding the girls for me."

The anchor could tell that his time was over. Although the intern still seemed the same pudgy dweeb, there was nothing in his manner that suggested he was about to do anything except slaughter Richards, take the woman he wanted, and then plunge the world into a mad and perpetual darkness.

Richards backed against the door to the holding room, he and it the only two things between the vampire and its prey. As the anchor wheezed for breath, the fanged thing drew closer, all of its senses alive, all of it ready to take the plunge, to throw itself fully into the life it had dreamed of for so long. Richards was trapped, helpless before him, with nowhere else to run, no further tricks to play. The mere human had been bested at all turns—strength, speed, endurance—the pale-skinned thing approaching had proven itself to be his master, and now as per one of history's soundest axioms, it would take the conqueror's spoils.

"George, Christ sake," gasped the anchor, "you don't want to do this."

"Of course I do," answered the youth. "The fact I can do it ought to prove how much I want to do it."

And then, as the monster's hands reached for Richards, he threw his weight sideways, twisting open the knob to the door he had been blocking with his body. Falling inside backwards as he stumbled, he screamed out—

"Evelyn, Evelyn Matiskloski—I've got a really bad boy for you!"

And, as most of the women in the room screamed, or threw themselves to the walls, clawing them to reach the high-set windows, a tall woman with eyes and a smile as cold and hard as iron, slapped her hands one against each other making a sound like the whip crack of God and demanded;

"On your knees, maggot!"

To which the snarling, charging George McCullen responded by sinking to the floor and touching his sweating forehead to the cold concrete, his smile one of complete and total ecstasy.

"And that," asked a somewhat surprised Goward, "is that?"

"Yeah," responded a grinning Richards, taking a swig of his long-ignored Scotch as if in triumph. Smacking his lips with an almost obnoxious self-satisfaction, he said, "Com'on, Zack. A smart guy like you. You had to see that one coming."

"I admit, knowing what I do about comic books these days, I had my suspicions," said the professor. "Coupled with what he said about his background. But really ..."

" But really' what," asked another of their little group. "What the hell happened?"

"Mr. McCullen, world-beater extraordinaire," answered Richards, "Was just another schmoe looking for mommy." When dissatisfaction arouse from around the table, Goward offered;

"The dreamplane is not a land easily conquered. It takes discipline, and extreme desire. It also takes an absolute purity of purpose. The only thing strong enough within Mr. McCullen's life to allow him entry there was the sad relationship with his mother."

"Mom abuses baby boy," added Richards. "He wants a life, wants to grow, wants to become a man, have sex, et cetera, but also, he wants mommy. He was able to make himself into an actual throat-ripper because in our twisted society, men who use women like toilet paper have become a sexual ideal in some circles. But, notice even when he took on superpowers, he still remained a little fat nothing."

"In other words, fellow happy inebriates," said Goward with a smile, "Mr. McCullen did not want to become a world beater. He simply wanted to find his way back to that which he missed the most—mommy."

"But," came a new voice from the table, "then what was all that with the women from the comic convention."

"Mistress Bitch," answered Richards. Finishing his Scotch with a mighty swig and signalling for another, the anchor said, "She's one of those 'is she a hero or isn't she' type characters. All dressed in skimpy, tight black leather, she's remarkably vicious, cruel to everyone she meets, overwhelmingly sexy, but supposedly a virgin. In other words, the wet dream of every comics reader out there." As several at the table frowned, Richards added;

"Present company accepted, of course."

"So, what happened to the guy? I mean, she cracks her whip and he falls in line for the moment, but what are they going to do with him?"

"They gave him to her," answered the anchor. When most at the table refused to let the simple answer suffice, he added, "Delvecio didn't see what else could be done with him. Super strong, super fast, able to turn into a puff of smoke or a bat—God only knows what else—they gave him to the Mistress Bitch actress as a slave. Since it doesn't look to be all that much of an act with her, it looks like he'll be under control for a good long time."

After a long moment of silence, one of Richards' guests finally mused, "Wow. So essentially, this guy reached godhood by mixing perseverance with a bad upbringing."

"Let' not undercut perseverance," chided Goward. "As C.H. Spurgeon said, by perseverance the snail reached the Ark."

"If we're going to be quoting," added another at the table, "perhaps one for the other side of that equation. Like what Sid Harris said about mothers ..."

"Oh, you mean," interrupted yet another, "that bit about having a child doesn't make one a mother any more than having a piano makes one a musician?"

"I think you're all heartless," said the only woman sitting at the table. When called upon for an explanation, she answered, "you jabber on about this fat bastard, making jokes because he'll be a slave to this black leather mommy figure for the rest of his life, but what about the women he killed? What about them?"

"Why, didn't you notice," asked Richards. "I got them jobs here at the Narkane. Heck, one of them's been waiting on us all night."

And, as the curvaceous, but still decaying zombie gal returned with their latest orders, another rose to tell a story of their latest encounter with the monstrous horrors that frighten all. And, as he spoke about his IRS audit, all about them drinks were served, pretzels were munched, swamp creatures hit on demons, Cyclops talked about the difficulty of getting a really good prescription, hedgehogs cheated at cards—as they always do—and unicorns danced, as they did every night at the Narkane.

Tripp's Raid

By

John Sunseri

"Last chance to change your mind, Sarge," said Carlson.

"Do it," said Tripp.

Carlson nodded. He held up the hypo and squirted a spray of liquid from its tip, the plasma glistening in the darkness of the tent. Tripp sat back on the camp chair and swallowed drily. He was terrified.

The medic took a step forward and with his free hand guided the sergeant's head back and to the left. Tripp took one last look at the world—not much to see, actually, in the dim of the tent—then closed his eyes. He felt Carlson's hand leave his chin, but kept his head steady. He could feel the pulse throbbing in his neck, his heart thumping in his chest. It was chilly in this part of the world at this time of year, but he was hot with fear and anticipation. Sweat slicked his armpits, trickled down the crack of his ass.

A sudden sting beneath his ear as the needle pricked, and instant pain as the plasma shot into his maxillary artery. He spasmed, trying hard not to jerk away from the syringe, but it only took a second and then the medic had withdrawn it anyway. Tripp's eyes sprung open and he gargled a thin, strangled squeak of agony as the cold shot into him, wrapping his skull in pain. He could feel the pathogen spreading downward as well, seeping quickly into his chest, his pecs twitching in protest.

"Good luck, Sarge," said Carlson, backing away. He put the syringe on the camp table and quickly exited through the flap, the heavy fabric flapping behind him. Tripp, even through his momentary paralysis and whole-body agony, could smell the night air perfectly, the tang of smoke from the campfires, the slight bite of the autumn chill, the dried dung and silage from the nearby fields.

Jesus, he thought. *It's so fucking* quick.

And then all thought fled, and he surrendered to the pain. Outside, Carlson and the transformation squad nervously fingered their weapons as the howls began.

When he regained consciousness, Tripp had barely enough strength to lift his head. All his sweat had dried, but he could smell its sour residue, the salt and urea. Through the ache, the maelstrom in his mind, he thought disjointedly about the fact that he would never sweat again.

He opened his eyes, then quickly squinted. The lone bulb hung at the apex of the tent frame, only twenty watts but it seemed like an inferno to his new eyes. The interior of the DRASH, so dim and shadowy to the sergeant just minutes before, was as bright and clear as broad daylight. Tripp looked at the table where the doctor had set the syringe, and he saw a slight discoloration where a bit of the plasma had leaked. He saw the weave of the tent's walls, could see the motes of dust that had settled into the mesh. Across the space, from ten feet away, he saw a fly crawling along one of the support struts.

He could count the facets in the fly's eyes.

"Sarge?" came a voice from outside. It was little more than a whisper, but Tripp felt it in his ears as though it was booming from an amplifier. He winced. His body ached, as though he'd been worked over by professional thugs. Every muscle burned, every joint was a tip of fire. The pain was different than any he had ever experienced—more diffuse, more intense. But the pains he had learned to live with before the injection—the constant throb in his lower back that had been a reminder of his college football days, the low tension in his jaws where his wisdom teeth were coming in—had disappeared. And he knew that the agony he now felt would disappear, too, later this evening. He would never again be bothered by toothache, by mosquito bites, by lumbar aches.

"It's over," he said in response. His voice sounded strange—deeper than it ever had been. His new ears were hearing it on every register, sensing vibrations that he'd never been able to sense before. "Come on in."

One of the soldiers entered first, his modified pistol sweeping the flap open. Tripp looked at it, the hunk of metal, and saw a slight scratch on the barrel that would be invisible to the weapon's owner. He smelled gun grease. He smelled the wood and controlled another flinch. Worse than the wood, though, was the chlorine odor of the holy water.

And worse than that was the smell of the soldier's blood. *So strong,*

Tripp thought. *So very strong.*

He wondered if he would make it through the hunger, or if he'd die here instead, riddled with wet bullets of ash and hawthorn. He rose from the chair smoothly and quickly and the grunt paused, wariness and a touch of panic on his face. Tripp could hear the man's heart quicken, saw a bead of sweat appear on the man's temple beneath the bristle of his scalp. And beneath everything else, above everything else, was the rich, intoxicating smell of the soldier's blood coursing through his veins.

Tripp held out his hands. It was difficult—he wanted to fly across the space in the shelter, use those hands to rip open the soldier's throat. But he fought the dictates of his body, tamped down the ravenous hunger and simply stood in the universal gesture of harmlessness.

Carlson came in next, and then the other two soldiers. They stood at the flap, waiting.

"It worked, Doc," said Tripp, his mouth turning up in a slight smile, then opening wide, lips curling back. He showed them his fangs.

"You should be feeling better in a few hours," said Lieutenant Reeves.

"I'm fine now, sir," said Tripp. He wasn't a hundred percent, but the initial disorientation and pain had greatly diminished. They stood in the open air, under the stars, and a couple of torches flickered nearby. Tripp saw everything clearly, could see into every shadow, his vision better than any human's on Earth. He could see out into the countryside past their bivouac, the endless fields and copses of this foreign countryside. Behind him, the hill rose up into the night sky and he craned his neck back so that he could see the top of the crag, hundreds of feet up. Each individual star was a blaze of flame, and the fingernail crescent of the autumn moon was as sharp as a razor blade. He could see the dark part of the moon as well, and it looked different to him than it ever had in his thirty years—he saw *all* the craters, even the ones that telescopes couldn't make out. Mars wasn't out, but he knew that the next time he saw it, he would be able to differentiate between it and every other point of light in the sky.

Reeves looked at him, and Tripp sensed that the man wasn't afraid of him. No surprise there—the lieutenant had been fighting the wars for five years and had killed more than his share of vampires in that time. Tripp had been there alongside him for the last six months, and had never seen the man tense or taut. The difference this time was that Tripp could smell the rivers of blood spilling through Reeves's body, dank and delicious, only a skin's-breadth away.

"Good," said the lieutenant. "Your team is waiting for you."

"Yes sir," said Tripp. Reeves began to walk again, and Tripp followed, breathing through his mouth and trying not to give in to the hunger. He didn't salivate—he *couldn't* salivate—but his thoughts were full of carmine need, red-splashed desire. He shook these thoughts aside and tried to focus on the task ahead. He was an officer, a leader, and his new physical form must be dedicated to battle and violence, his new urges sublimated beneath the weight of duty.

They'd bunked the vampires a hundred yards away from the main camp, near a craggy overhang in the hill. Tripp had been here several times over the last few nights, meeting his new squad and feeling out the mood of the team, testing to determine whether they would easily accept his leadership or whether the loss of Sergeant Smith four nights earlier in a hail of mortar fire was still too fresh a wound to salve. Tripp and Reeves had decided, finally, that the exigencies of their current situation warranted a quick promotion no matter how sensitive the vamp soldiers were to the newbie coming in.

But in their meetings, Tripp and the Suck Squad, he'd sensed (beneath the rage and sorrow) a level of curiosity on the part of the night warriors equal to his own. He'd tried to take their measure, and they'd certainly tried to take *his*. With his new senses, he understood that the men of his team had probably understood him on an almost-cellular level, knew exactly what kind of dirt he had under his fingernails and the smell of his breath all the way down to his lungs. But in spite of the sensory advantages the Squad possessed, they still couldn't know what was in Virgil Tripp's mind, nor he what was in theirs.

He'd find out in a hurry.

Kostic was the big one, a hulking vampire fully six foot eight and bulking well over three hundred pounds. He was also the armorer, though he wore no armor himself. Tripp had examined the flak jackets the vamps wore into combat and they were a marvel of the art—way too heavy for a normal human to wear and still hope to perform effectively in a firefight, but for all their weight and bulkiness, they were flexible enough to allow the vampires to move as though they were unencumbered. *Goliath suits*, they were called, and though Tripp wasn't a big fan of the name (he remembered his First Samuel, from the days he was studying, playing football, and trying to get laid at Our Lady of Sorrows back home in Cleveland), but he definitely admired the workmanship of the body armor. Kostic preferred to fight armored in nothing but his skin, his speed and his ferocity. He, alone among the Suck Squad, had scars. The rumors said that whenever he took damage in a fight, he treated the wounds with holy water rather than let them heal preternaturally, rather as a gang punk would shove cigar ash into a wound to make it heal badly. Whether or not the rumors were true, Kostic was an impressive specimen.

"Hullo, Sarge," he said, nodding as Tripp and Reeves entered the vamp camp. There was no campfire, of course, but they'd all know the human lieutenant would be coming, so they'd turned on a couple of bulbs.

"Hello, soldier," said Tripp. Reeves stopped at the edge of the circle, but the new sergeant continued on into the ranks of men awaiting him. Rank meant certain things in the modern army, but when it came to vampire squads, human brass tended to stay out of the loop whenever possible. This was Tripp's team now, if he could win it.

The other vampires stood in a circle around him. Tripp did not fear them, but his combat instincts kicked into a higher gear. He knew, without modesty, that he had been the best fighter among the human soldiers here in enemy territory and taking the war to the aggressors, but he was unsure about how well those honed talents would translate once he took the pathogen. He showed nothing of his higher alert, but he knew now that the squad could tell things about him that he hadn't considered possible before he had become one of them—he casually swiveled his vision around the circle and noted slight dilations of vampire pupils, the almost imperceptible tightening of fists, a shift in musculature as two of the soldiers went from parade rest to tense readiness to pounce.

"Men," he started, choosing his word carefully. They were none of them men anymore, but they fought alongside humans. Species differences apart, they were a common army, with common goals.

"Men, you know that time is short," he continued. "You know what the enemy has done, and you know the challenges that face us. You also know that Sergeant Smith is dead beyond any chance of recovery."

Some of the vampires shifted. They had been a squad for three years now, occasionally losing a soldier and gaining a replacement, but Smith had been their leader that whole time, until he'd fallen victim to a Sunlight Shell, and they'd followed him with a dedication that came not only from discipline but from a kind of love—love born of respect and the knowledge that Smith could have killed any one of them at any time. He had been a vampire of the highest strength and skill, and that meant a lot to a species that tended toward self-sufficiency and autonomy. Had the war never started, each of these soldiers would still be back in America, spread out over various hunting grounds and rarely, if ever, interacting with their brethren. Smith's charisma and strength had kept them together. And now here was Tripp, attempting to take the legend's place.

"The mission remains," said Tripp.

"Lieutenant," said Kostic, turning away from his new squad leader and facing the human. "We can take it from here."

Reeves looked at Tripp, and there was the slightest fraction of a moment in which the latter considered spinning on his heel and leaving with his superior officer. Instead, he gave the man a tight nod.

"As you were, then," said Reeves. His arm came up in a salute, and Tripp saluted back, and then the man was striding away, back toward the human camp and the torchlight. Tripp watched him go for a second.

And then he was facing the gigantic armorer again.

"You know the drill, sir," said Kostic. "I accept your authority, but we've got a new guy and he's not sure about you."

"Yes," said Tripp, looking around the ring of vampires. He knew which one it was, too. He'd seen the Mi-8T come in bearing ammunition, supplies and personnel, and he'd known that there'd be a replacement for Private del'Assandro, the vampire who had died with Sergeant Smith under the onslaught of the enemy barrage.

The soldier stepped forward, and Tripp let his senses explore the man. Young—maybe twenty years old, and would never grow older—but his bearing suggested that he'd seen combat before. Many of the vampires who had been fighting for the duration of the war had begun as simple monsters who had realized that they needed to resist the adversary or have America overrun by an enemy who would not suffer them to exist, and though those combatants had been as strong, fast and relentless as the rest of their species, they hadn't had the discipline or will to submit to military command, and many of them had died under the guns and arrows of an opponent who knew how to destroy them. Those that survived, though, grew wise quickly, and with their help the tide had eventually turned, and now Tripp and his squadron, and the rest of the platoon, were standing on enemy ground readying for the final push toward the capital.

And the new private seemed to be one of those blooded soldiers that had gotten them there.

"Step forward," said Tripp, looking at the new man.

He did. "Private Brauckmiller, reporting for duty, sir," he said. Tripp took a closer look at him. Blond hair trimmed to the scalp (would it ever grow back? Tripp wondered. He wasn't an expert on bloodsucker physiology yet, though he was sure he'd learn everything he every wanted to know if he survived the war), long, thin fingers, a slim build that reminded Tripp of the guys who used to front New Wave bands when he was a child. Slap a couple of tattoos onto Brauckmiller's arms, some eyeliner and mascara onto his thin face and give him a synthesizer, he could have made a million dollars back in the day.

But there was that posture, that aura of competence about the man, that gave Tripp plenty to think about. Back home, maybe, Brauckmiller would cruise the bars looking for blood and would attract the hell out of the young girls. The goth chicks would eat him up; at least, until the tables were turned in the alley out back or whatever den he'd set up for himself. Then they'd die, but they'd die in the throes of almost-religious ecstasy.

For a second, Tripp wondered how he'd feed himself when he got back home. The cat was out of the bag, and the vampire out of the closet, and once peace regained a foothold in the world there would be a lot of debate about the returning troops, whether to attempt another assimilation as had happened so many times in the course of America's history, whether to segregate (*or whether to eliminate,* thought Tripp, but shoved the idea aside. They'd worry about peace if and when it came). But then he was back in the moment, his senses on full alert.

"Brauckmiller," nodded Tripp. "How'd you get here?"

"Transferred in from the 10th Mountain, Sir. Third Brigade Combat Team," said the private.

"Impressive," said Tripp, meaning it. The 10th Mountain boys had been the van of the initial assault on Charlie Country, and they were still running around the mountains shaking out terrorist squads and digging out enemy vampires. "Do you accept my authority?"

"I think I want to test you out, Sir," said Brauckmiller.

So there it was.

The two vampires faced off in the circle, neither moving. Brauckmiller had stripped down to the waist, and Tripp could see the smooth play of muscles in the young man's thin chest. He still looked like a New Wave musician, a Thin White Duke, but without his shirt on he also looked powerful, feral.

Tripp kept his clothes on, making sure the other vamps could see his sergeant's chevron. He shook his fingers, staying loose, trying not to tense. He didn't blink, or breathe. He just stared into the young vampire's black eyes and waited for the assault.

Brauckmiller stared back. He didn't bother baring his fangs or using any of the other intimidation displays that the vampires used when facing the enemy who hated and were terrified by them. He bounced up onto his toes once, twice. Tripp's mind raced, considering which way he would dodge when the rush came, visualizing blows and counterblows. Most disturbing of all, the hunger—the blood thirst that was now churning in his guts. Vampires could drink of other vampires. Tripp wanted to taste Brauckmiller's blood.

Cursing inwardly, he forced his brain to shut the hell up, and tamped down the tides of desire in his belly. This would be no typical fistfight, and it was useless to plan ahead as though he were taking on a drunk in a Shaker Heights dive.

The rest of the Squad watched silently. Kostic had a half-smile on his face, his head set a bit forward of his shoulders, looking at the two combatants with mild interest, as though he were watching a pretty good ball game on television. The other vampires were more eager, and Tripp knew that their own blood thirsts were roiling within them, the prospect of wounds and carnage both dreadful and exhilarating. He hoped that it wouldn't come to bloodshed—Brauckmiller was one of his warriors, and he didn't thrill to the idea of hurting him too badly.

He's not my warrior yet, he reminded himself. *And what if he hurts me?*

And then it began. Brauckmiller didn't tense, didn't telegraph his move in any way, but suddenly he was halfway across the circle in less time than it would have taken for Tripp to blink. Tripp didn't dodge. He put his weight on his heels and braced for collision.

As the private, with breathtaking speed, closed the rest of the distance, Tripp whirled and there was a riflecrack *slap* as Brauckmiller, his momentum carrying him, was spun past his victim. A normal human would have stumbled and crashed to the ground—Tripp had used this *harai goshi* move many times, and that's what invariably happened—but Brauckmiller was far too quick, far too coordinated to be dropped so easily. He caught his fall with one hand on the ground and instantly sprang up, leaping feet in the air as Tripp's leg swing came toward him, jumping over the attack and falling, hands-first, arms spread wide, directly at the sergeant.

Tripp wasn't there. He was rolling, feeling the grit of the ground, for a moment smelling the thin, small blood of whatever insects burrowed in this alien dirt, and then he was back up and feinting toward Brauckmiller, who had instantly recovered from his missed attack. The younger vamp (younger in mien only, of course) dodged away.

The two vampires were moving at such speeds that only a second and a half had passed since the time the private had launched his attack. Humans watching would have been atavistically terrified—nothing moved as fast as the two forms were moving. The human eye couldn't track them, and the only response a human would have had—could possibly have had—was a sudden rush of fear hormones that would make the blood taste exquisite when sipped.

Tripp went on the offensive. He closed the distance between them and dove into a tackle. Brauckmiller leaped again, and Tripp's hands—claws, really—grazed the kid's combat boots. Even such slight contact was enough—the new strength in Tripp's fingers spun Brauckmiller out of his controlled jump, spun him fractionally.

Tripp pressed the advantage as the private grunted and attempted to right himself, but vampires, for all their strength and speed and ferocity, were still bound by gravity, and there was nothing for the private to grab onto to correct his delta-v. Nothing but the sergeant. Instinct caused Brauckmiller to whip his hand out, still turning in the air, and Tripp, with a lunge that would have made a cobra wince in impotent envy, grasped his opponent's wrist.

After that, it was over. Tripp slammed the private to the ground, followed him down, landed hard on the kid's stomach with his knees. A human would have died, his ribs crushed, the air leaving his body in a pneumatic *whoof* along with his life. Brauckmiller didn't cry out, but he was momentarily stunned, his lips curling away from his fangs, his eyes wide and surprised. Tripp whipped his arm down, his forearm cross-barred across the private's throat, and with inhuman strength forced the vamp's head two inches into the hard ground.

"Yield?" he asked. And part of him wished that the kid *wouldn't* yield, wouldn't give up. His head was inches from Brauckmiller's throat, and he envisioned himself dipping down and ripping into the flesh there, tearing out the windpipe, feeling the hot splash of blood down his own throat. His excitement was almost sexual, though he felt it not in his groin but in his guts.

"Yield," whispered Brauckmiller.

And then it was over. Kostic clapped once, the sound of his hands sharp and clear in the cold night, and the rest of the Suck Squad—*his* squad, now—nodded.

"Welcome aboard, Sarge," said one of them. And Tripp rose, releasing the other vampire, helping him to his feet. Hunger raging, lust a tsunami, blood thirst howling in him like a hurricane, yet he shook his opponent's hand and nodded. It was over.

"How'd you sleep?" asked Kostic quietly.

"I dreamed," said Tripp. He didn't take the binoculars from his eyes. The starlight and his new, superhuman senses, combined with the technological wonders of the Oberwerk binocs were enough to give him a clear view of their target from even this distance. He could see the guards patrolling. It made him ravenous. "I didn't know I'd still be able to."

Kostic snorted. "I hope your dreams are better than mine, Sarge. I usually just dream about food."

"Me too," whispered Tripp, smiling slightly. Of course, 'food' meant something different now than it had three days ago. Back then, back when he'd been human, food was MREs and whatever the soldiers could scrounge from the scorched earth they marched over. They'd caught a pig a week ago, slaughtered it and cooked it over a sheltered fire. Tripp could remember the hot grease of the roasted shoat running down his chin, the taste of the pork, the almost orgasmic joy of hot, fresh meat after weeks of reconstituted spaghetti and chow mein.

The remembrance disgusted him.

He lowered the Oberwerks. "Twenty or so guards. Agree?"

"Aye," said Kostic, taking back the binoculars. "Ten patrolling, the rest in the bunkhouse."

"Minefield between us and the target," said Tripp. "Laser eyes, probably a direct line to their headquarters, definitely some Sunlight Bomb IEDs where we can't see them, and for all I know they've blessed the whole reservoir."

Kostic laughed. "Wouldn't that be something?" he wondered. "All that water, nor any drop to drink."

Tripp thought the idea funny as well. Their enemy was not Christian, and an imam couldn't very well turn water into vampire poison. But they may have shipped someone in for the purpose. Religion was all well and good, but war was war, and you did whatever you could to win. If that meant dealing with the infidel, Charlie would do it.

"Okay, so we don't take a dip while we're there," said Tripp finally. In quick, drop off the Horse..." he trailed off. This wasn't going to be pleasant at all. They were joking, as all soldiers through all times have done, laughing in the face of danger and death, but tonight Tripp was going to lose some of his men. It was inevitable. And it wasn't funny, not in the least.

"And then we go home and fuck all the women," finished Kostic.

Tripp chuffed some humorless laughter. "Yeah," he said. "That's one thing I'm definitely going to miss."

"You get used to it," said Kostic. "After a while, you start wondering what all the fuss was about. And besides—we've got something better than sex."

Tripp nodded. He would discover that for himself. Tonight, probably. One of those sentinels he'd watched through the binoculars was going pop his cherry. "Let's do it," he said.

Kostic nodded, and let out a subvocal rumble. Instantly, the rest of the Squad was there. They'd been hiding in the shadows of the low hill, waiting patiently for the hour Kostic and Tripp had been doing recce. "All right, boys," said Kostic in a voice too low for human ears. Tripp and the rest of the vamps could hear him perfectly, though. "Let's saddle up."

They raced through the night in single file. Tripp was third back, Kostic in front. The big vampire was best at sensing traps, and thus far they'd managed to avoid any mines. They were moving so fast that Tripp felt the still air of the night as though it were a whipping wind on his face. He wore light armor (though it was still heavier than any human could have handled while running) to protect against claymores—the enemy had taken to loading the vicious little bastards with wood, and vampires had died when the little hardened, weighted splinters had torn through flesh and nicked hearts. But thus far they'd been lucky...

Kostic, in the van, stopped suddenly. The file halted as well, throwing up clouds of dust as their feet skidded on the dry dirt. Tripp looked up, wondering if there were any modified Predators up there in the black sky, but seeing nothing to indicate that any observers had noticed their abrupt halt.

The big vampire waited as Tripp made his way up to the front. "What?" asked the sergeant.

"Something," said Kostic, nostrils wide, eyes darting this way and that. "I don't know..."

And then they all heard a whistle as something rose up into the sky. "Cover!" shouted Tripp, spinning around and diving to the ground. His hands were blurs as they tore at the dirt, pulling up clods and clots of earth, sending a cloud of dust into the air around him. Most of the other vamps were doing the same thing, and it was as though they were a team of dogs frantically scrabbling at the ground to catch a rabbit.

The Sunlight shell exploded above them, brightening the sky. Tripp felt an agonizing pain as he kept digging, kept throwing up dirt. They'd created a good haze to hide in, but still the UV rays of the firwork bomb managed to fight their way through the smoggy cloud. Tripp heard several screams as his men took damage, and he felt the back of his neck bubbling and boiling as a stray ray of artificial sunlight lanced across him. He dove into the hole he'd made and began pulling earth down on top of himself, tasting dirt and shit and fear as he quickly covered all his exposed flesh. The light in the sky, barely visible through the haze, began to fade, to gutter, but the pain continued—it felt like acid eating through the nape of his neck, into the flesh and bones beneath. His skull was on fire.

And then the darkness reclaimed the world and the shell went out.

"Shit," Tripp moaned. "Is everyone all right?"

"They know we're here," said Kostic, his voice rumbling.

"No crap," agreed the sergeant. "Everyone—sound off!"

"Brauckmiller," came a voice from the dirt. "Thompson," came another, and "Jackman", "Garvey", "di Vittorio", all the way down the line. Two voices that should have come...did not.

"Where's Briggs?" asked Tripp. "And Zuke?"

But he already knew the answer. There was no time to waste—the enemy would be loading another shell into the hidden howitzer, and they had to be gone from this spot in the next minute or so. But Tripp and Kostic scurried to where their fallen comrades had to be.

Briggs was a mess. He'd not managed to create any shield against the deadly radiation, and he looked like he'd melted—runnels of bloody flesh spilled across the ground, his uniform had been shredded in his final, frantic spasms against the artificial sun, his skull shone through the black, blistered remains of his forehead and hair. It smelled like death. Tripp grimaced and turned away.

"I found Zuke," said Kostic, his voice subdued. Tripp didn't want to look, but forced himself to move toward the shadow of the big vampire.

Zuke had protected the Horse with his body. He'd been flayed by the merciless radiation, his back split open and boiled, his spine gleaming in the starlight through all the black and violet hamburger his flesh had become. But underneath him was the canister.

"Take the anthrax," said Tripp quietly. "And get behind me."

Kostic rolled Zuke over, revealing the dead vamp's face. Tripp would have recoiled if he'd let his instincts take over—Zuke had died screaming, and his flesh had drawn taut over his skull. His eyes were gone—he'd apparently looked at the bright light, and the vitreous humor had instantly vaporized. His fangs were completely extended, whiter even that his bloodless face.

"Got it," said Kostic, easily lifting the heavy canister with one hand.

"Let's get this done," said Tripp, and began to run again. They moved cheetah-fast, race car fast, through the night, and more whistles rose behind them.

The guards were on full alert, but it didn't matter—the vampires tore through them like the Chicago Bears through a Pop Warner team. Tripp felt bullets bounce off his armor and roared as he closed with the enemy, ripping their guns from their hands, and then their hands from their arms. His blood was up, and he laughed as the men screamed and shit themselves. The stench of offal, of blood, the rich savor of terror filled his nose, and he tore off one man's head and lowered his mouth to the jetting stump of his neck, drinking in the hot fluid, feeling energy course through him, howling in delight as the other man tried to run. Tripp let him get a few steps away, then leaped through the air, arms spread wide. He whipped his hands together at supersonic speed and crushed the man's chest as though it were paper. He kept laughing as the man collapsed, watching the insane panic of the soldier's eyes as he realized he was dead. Laughed as he died.

"C'mon, boss!" shouted Kostic. "Quit playing with the poor sonofabitch!"

Right. They had to deliver their package.

Around them came other screams and the roar of heavy arms, sending lead and wood through the night. Tripp gulped in ecstasy, tasting the fear hormones, the rich glutinous glee of blood, the joy of death and dismemberment—but he forced himself to continue.

They'd covered the reservoir. A thick cap of concrete and steel sat atop the water, but a couple of focused grenades took chunks out of the hard shield, and then a couple more got through. Tripp's enhanced senses could hear something in the distance...

"Planes," said Kostic, beside him. Blood covered the big vampire— he'd taken out a soldier of his own—and he still carried the Horse. "Get this done."

"Right," said Tripp. He reached into his pocket and took out the vial. Smiling with glee, he uncorked it and spilled the contents into the blackness of the hole in the reservoir cap, hearing the droplets patter onto the water inside. The reservoir was the only source of water the capital had. By tomorrow, the city's denizens would be drinking from it. They'd have no choice.

And now for the Horse.

"You're a good man, Sarge," said Kostic. He didn't smile.

"Give me the canister," said Tripp. The giant handed it over, and Tripp felt its weight. Thirty pounds of stainless steel and enough anthrax to wipe out half of Asia. Right now, he felt as though that would be a good thing—but their plan was better. More effective. More horrible.

"You know what to do," said Tripp. They had no more time—already, jets were roaring over them. Armies were being sent. Anyone who didn't leave now, wouldn't be leaving.

"Good serving with you, Sarge," saluted Kostic. He pulled out the gun, aimed it at his commanding officer. It was one of the enemy's guns, loaded with hawthorne bullets that were soaked with holy water.

"You too, soldier," said Tripp. "Go fuck all the women."

And then the man fired. Tripp felt the wood tear into his torso, and if he thought the sunlight on the back of his neck had been bad, now he knew better—this was pain such as no one had ever felt. Satan on his lake of fire hadn't suffered so much.

Tripp's vision turned blood red, but he saw Kostic whirl and sprint away. Maybe he'd make it to safety, maybe he wouldn't. But that wasn't the point—any of the Suck Squad that made it home was a bonus, and if they were all cut down here at the reservoir, so much the better for their plan.

Tripp knew how it would look when the enemy cleared the area and found him. There was a hole in the reservoir, there a dead vampire officer, there a canister filled with deadly poison—but the vampire had been killed before he could contaminate the water. They'd feel a horrid chill as they realized how close they'd come to having their water supply poisoned with anthrax, and they'd run some hasty tests to make absolutely sure that it was safe to drink.

But they wouldn't test for the vampire virus. They *couldn't* test for it—they didn't know what it was and wouldn't recognize it. Only America had isolated the stuff.

And by late tomorrow, the few drops that Tripp had dumped into the water would have multiplied and spread, and shortly after that the enemy would begin turning. They hated and feared vampires so much that they were ready to commit genocide to wipe them out.

Tripp laughed through his agonies as he picture the enemy's capital on the next day—new vampires being born all over town, most of them realizing what was happening, none of them able to stop the transformation.

All of them hungry, all of them trapped with each other.

It would be pandemonium. It would be beautiful. It would be Hiroshima squared. And none of them would escape—the Army had the city bottled up, and was ready with napalm, Sunlight Shells and a ring of thousands of soldiers ready to cut off anyone who tried to escape.

You don't fuck with vampires, thought Tripp, *and you don't fuck with America.*

It was his last thought, and he died grinning.

Pig Boy
the Vampire

By

Rowena Morrill

At four a.m. when the door slammed shut,
Out stumbled a dark, burly figure.
He hitched up his pants to cover his butt
Which forced out a belch, reeking liquor.

He was leaving a Goth club heading for home.
Slumped in a cab, his thoughts started to roam
To the girl's snow white face framed by spidery hair.
She was clad in slashed leather leaving lots of her bare.
Pierced with lip studs and ear plugs, a ring in her nose,
This delectable morsel was the one that he chose.

Zenobia had watched as he singled her out.
What she saw as he was swaggering about
Were caterpillar eyebrows crawling over dark eyes.
Rampant black hair had his head tyrannized.

A pendulous lower lip lolled over his chin.
A second chin ballooned underneath.
His overhanging belly made it hard to see his feet.
Zenobia thought "Pig Boy" was the perfect name for him.

But Pig Boy was cunning. When he noticed her wince,
He slowly sidled near her in a deferential stance.
He admired her choker of black widow pearl.
Is that Jewelry by Astra? A phantastical girl!

He ordered many drinks and one sip at a time
She found him amusing, her defenses all down.
Little did he know she was smashed on heroin
When he urged her to a hidden, plush divan.

With his eager slashing fangs he nearly wrecked her
Drinking deeply of her flowing, crimson nectar.
Ah, he was replete with his narcotic red repast.
Such blood soon had him wasted, high and all aghast.

He couldn't possibly remember his address.
Driving by a basement, he thought he saw a coffin.
He fell out of the taxi, squirmed over the grass,
And smashing a window he squeezed himself in.

Tucked in the casket at a funeral home Pig Boy passed out.
Blood seeped from the corners of his open, snoring mouth.
Because it was Sunday, there was no one around
When out lurched Pig Boy who'd awakened at dawn.

At once he found a pallid woman sleeping on her back.
All hung over and bewildered, he sank fangs into her neck.
He slurped, gulped, devoured and completely inhaled
Formaldehyde, glutaraldehyde, methanol, and ethanol.
He slammed smack on the floor as his brutish heart failed
Sending Pig Boy below to Swine Wallow once and for all.

Cannibalistically Incestuous Vampire Penguin from Coney Island

By

Diane Raetz and Patrick Thomas

It had been a long night and I stumbled toward the shower, dropping clothing across the apartment as I went. Janey would yell in the morning, but I didn't care. With dawn fast approaching I was desperate to get the stench of a night of 'investigative reporting' with Stan and his beard off of me. Stan had been such a bastard during the attempted stake out that I'd been tempted to bite him. I would have except I was afraid that his greasy food and lice infested beard would bite back. I couldn't afford to lose any blood. Being a vampire has its downsides. Dehydration is one. Plus, um, yuck. I shivered. Hanging around Stan in an alley trying to see into a Women in Black research facility was bad enough. Having his beard bite me would be worse than I could possibly imagine. Disgustingly enough he actually puts the lice in there so he can pass himself off as a homeless man more effectively. My editor is a far more dedicated reporter than I am.

I didn't bother turning on the light—I can see in the dark just fine. I leaned into the shower without bothering to pull the curtains and turned on the water. As the room began to fill with steam I reached back and took off my bra. "Hey Dollface. Turn down the water temperature, would ya? It's getting hot in here." A whistle and then, "Nice bazongas,

Doll. Forget about turning off the water. Instead hows about getting in here and rocking the boat with me?"

"What the hell?" I screamed and jumped ten feet into the air, crashed into the ceiling and wound up in the sink. Vampire startle reflex is a little extreme. "Who the..." I curled my body up into itself, trying to hide my nakedness, and looked wildly around.

"Dollface. Sweetheart. You okay? I didn't mean to scare you. I thought you saw me, sweetie pie." The voice was coming from down, way down. Down, at the bottom of my shower, barely two feet tall, was a talking penguin. I blinked a couple of times, but the penguin didn't disappear. It had to be a Monday.

"What the..." I didn't get to finish my question. My roommate Janey and her boyfriend Chet burst into the bathroom.

"What's wrong?" Janey had a bat in her hand and looked ready to use it.

I pointed mutely to the bottom of the shower, but I was too late. Instead I heard, "Whoa there, big boy. Take it easy now..." Chet—all seven foot two inches of him—in all his naked; hairy but naked, glory had the penguin dangling from his hand.

"My eyes," I cried trying to curl up into a ball on the countertop. I didn't know what was worse—having spent the night with Stan's beard, a talking penguin in the bathtub or seeing my roommate's sasquatch boyfriend naked. I opened my eyes, flinched as I saw the naked man in front of me, and my head hit the mirror, shattering glass all over me. Lack of a reflection really throws off depth perception. Yup—it was definitely a Monday.

Moments later, we were in the living room, the curtains drawn firmly against the approaching dawn. Better yet, we were all dressed. Janie was in a sleeping shorts set, Chet in a pair of pajamas covered in frogs that he loved, me in my most comfortable sweats and I'd even put a bow tie on the penguin. I'd suggested it as a joke, but he agreed and preened as if he were in a tux.

"Call me Humphrey," he said.

Best of all, I had a wineglass full of goat's blood in my hand. I didn't want to like blood—but I was a vampire. It was later, rather than sooner, that I'd accepted the cliché *Blood was Life*, but I'd become a believer a few months back when I was helping save the Spear of Destiny from some less than retired Nazis. Since then I'd learned to appreciate the nuances of blood. In my humble opinion goat beat pig, cows and chicken's butts. It didn't come close to human blood—but then again nothing did. On the other hand I could buy goat's blood in a butcher shop. Human blood—not so much. The Red Cross gets a little suspicious when you offer to buy blood from them. My roommate had made an occasional emergency donation, but wasn't about to become a regular dinner treat. Besides—ew!

Janey and Chet were each scarfing down a slice of cold pizza. Actually Janey was scarfing down a slice. Chet had folded three slices into themselves and was inhaling the triple combo the way that I longed to. God I missed pizza! Bizarrely Humphrey was staring at my wine glass of blood the way that I was looking at the pizza. With naked lust.

"Want some?" I held out the glass to the penguin and swore I saw a tooth at the edge of his beak. Did penguins have teeth? It was really more of a fang.

"More than you know Doll. More than you know."

I shrugged and got up to get the bird a bowl of blood. Once I got past the talking bird part, blood wasn't that weird. Although, honestly, I thought penguins ate fish, I wasn't an expert. My instincts were telling me that Humphrey was more than a bird, but I was ignoring them with all my might. I didn't *need* to know, but the reporter in me wanted to know. There might even be a story in it.

"I can't drink it." The disgust was clear in my avian visitor's voice. "Ever since I got stuck in penguin form all I can eat is..." The shudder started in his silky black head and went all the way to his webbed feet, "raw fish. Blech."

"Stuck in penguin form. Blood. Don't tell me."

He told me anyway. "You got it, Dollface. I'm a vampire."

Janie started laughing uncontrollably. "Vampire penguin. Vampire penguin. You're a vampire penguin." There was a hint of hysteria along with the fun, "Big foot, vampires, Women in Black... what next?"

She had a point. Even *The Wayward Star* couldn't come up with the weirdness that had been my life since I got bitten by John Johnson. Well, except for the fact that I faithfully chronicled all my adventures for the paper. Since we were a tabloid in the glorious tradition of the *Weekly World News* my stories fit in just fine between the Area 51 and the Elvis is alive on Mars stories. Jezebel Lovecraft, my alter ego at the paper, even had a vampire advice column called "*Don't Cook With Garlic*." It was popular, but not nearly as popular as the mysterious *Dear Cthulu* column. I didn't have a clue who wrote that one. It just popped up periodically in the paper—the typesetting changed to accommodate the Elder God's words of advice.

"Don't laugh, Birdbrain," my featherless friend snapped, bringing my thoughts into focus. "It isn't like I asked to be stuck as a freaky fish feeder forever."

I sobered down instantly. The first time I changed, it was into a pig, and it scared the bejesus out of me. I had no idea what happened or how to turn back. What would I do if I was stuck as a pig in Hoboken unable to think clearly or speak? "Hey!" I said the obvious hitting me on the head. "I can't talk when I take an animal form."

"Yeah well, this wasn't exactly a normal transformation," Humphrey confessed. "And it gets easier with practice."

I settled into my chair more comfortably, ready for a story. "What happened?"

"I'd followed this broad into the aquarium down in Coney Island, you see..."

"Can we not do that?" Janey scolded.

"Do what?" Humphrey seemed genuinely confused.

"Not call women broads, or chicks or dolls? It's demeaning." My roommate went to her first protest when she was in her mother's arms. She'd been conceived in Washington DC after an Apartheid protest. I think she absorbed feminism with breast milk.

"Look Chickie." She growled at him. The penguin seemed to smile. "Where I come from calling a Broad a Dame was a compliment."

She groaned and I shoved her—gently. "Let it go or we'll be here all day. He's probably one of those old timey vampires who can't modernize."

"I heard that."

"I meant you to." He hadn't shown up in my bathroom by mistake. He wanted something—I knew the signs. My column in *The Wayward Star* attracted the paranormal community to me like moths to a flame. I was the only out and about vampire in New York. The few vampires I'd met hated me for it, but hey. I hadn't asked to be turned. So screw them.

I'd never seen a penguin roll his eyes before. "I was down at the aquarium following this broad—" Janey cleared her throat and he corrected himself, "—this dame." Another throat clearing. "—this LADY with great gams into the penguin exhibit. She definitely saw me—she walked away from me with more curves than a figure eight and I was hoping for a little boogie woogie with the dame dressed in black."

"Black?" I asked sharply. I didn't like where this was going.

"Like a jail-bait widow," he confirmed. "Curves in all the right places, blond as the sun and wearing black down to her unmentionables."

"Damn it." The Women in Black were in play.

"You got a problem with black undies? What do you like? Pink?"

"Not the underwear, the entire outfit. When did this happen?"

The penguin shrugged. "Six or seven months ago. Year tops. It's hard to tell when you're living as a aquarium exhibit."

"That's got to suck, but this blond—was she about twenty four, twenty five, spoke with a Long Island accent and wore really expensive shoes?" Why was I asking a man about shoes? I only knew that Loralei's shoes cost a fortune because she told me so.

"An Able-Graber like a Sharecrop with money on a Friday," I figured he was agreeing with me by the fact that he was nodding. I had no idea what the rest of the sentence meant.

"Loralei. I'll bet anything it was Loralei." Growing up she was my next-door neighbor and my mother's ideal good child. I spent half my life wondering why I was involved in a sibling rivalry with a girl who wasn't in my family. Now I was a vampire and she was a hunter. Funny how things work out.

"I follows this dame into the penguin exhibit and we're all alone. So I gives her my best line from back in the day, 'Hey Sugar, are you rationed?' and the moll takes out a peashooter and sticks it in my stomach. Now as a fanged feeder, the peashooter shouldn't hurt me, but this dame tells me it's a water gun filled with holy water. The Big Guy and me—we don't jive. So I think fast and jump in the water."

"Vampires can't swim." I found that one out the hard way.

"I knows that." Humphrey's brow wrinkled up. "But I figures I could wait on the bottom until the dame gets tired and goes home."

Janey cleared her throat and the penguin rolled his eyes again. "The LADY got tired..." he said with a sigh.

"If we're talking about Loralei I'd go with broad," I muttered to myself.

As Humphrey made a honking noise that I thought might be a laugh, Janey poked me in the stomach. "It's still disrespectful to women."

"So is Loralei breathing," I replied. Stealing slang along the lines of the way the featherless fowl spoke, I added, "She needs to take a dirt nap."

"Yeah, like that it'd go over well with your mom," Janey pointed out.

Chet scratched his massive head with his paw like hand. "I don't understand anything that is going on here." 1920's slang was not his forte. Then again, he was having enough trouble with the modern version. A drawback of growing up in the wilds of Canada among the bigfoots. Or would that be bigfeets?

"I'll catch you up later," Janey promised.

I waved my hand in a circle. Humphrey got the hint to keep talking. "Thanks Dollface. So there I was, under the water and the dame wasn't leaving. Water makes me sick..." I could relate. "So I gets this idea. I'll take a snack on a bird in a monkey suit." He straightened his bow tie.

"And then change into a penguin. You'd hide better in the flock, be able to swim, and feel better. Humphrey—that's brilliant."

"Thanks. At first it works like a charm, see. I takes my snack, I changes and in a minute I'm playing flipper flapper with this bird..."

"Humphrey!" Janey was genuinely appalled, "Does flipper flapper mean what I think it means?"

I swear the bird gave her a cheeky grin. "What do you think it means, Chickie?"

"EWWWWWWWWWWWWEEEEEEEEEEEEEE that's disgusting!" Janey stormed off making retching noises like she wanted to vomit.

I stared down at Humphrey. "You didn't really.... Not really."

The bird winked at me. "What, swim?" He asked innocently, "Of course I did."

"You're a bad, bad person," I told him with a shake of my head and a reluctant grin. There weren't too many people who could upset Janey as much as Humphrey managed to.

"I tries my best," he bowed as though seeking applause. "Anyways, I sees the broad in black with a different peashooter. I thought it was one of those Taser shooters without the pea, and figured I could take the electric shock better as a fanged fighter than a featherless fowl. So I starts to change and BAM a silver liquid comes out of the water shooter she was packing. Wham, bam, thank you ma'am, and I'm stuck in flipper form ever since.

"Why did she leave you there?" I asked. That didn't sound like Loralei or the other Women in Black that I knew. The ones I'd encountered were relentless in their need to eliminate vampires.

"I gots lucky. Just as the dame finishes spraying the pool with water a uniform walks in and yells that the pool is closed and she has to leave. They has a fight and then the uniform threatens to call a black and white. The moll leaves then comes back a few hours later, see. But the tuxedo suit helps me out—she can't tell which bird is me. So she tries to catch as many birds as she can—but an alarm goes off and she scampers. I tries to change into a vamp; but I'm stuck. The silver poison is still in my system.

"That morning the broad in black comes back to the aquarium. She sprays the silver liquid into the drink again. I can't change out of the tuxedo suit while she's shooting us because of the big ball of death in the sky. She leaves. That night I tries to change. Nada. This happens every day for months. A couple of times she tries to smuggle herself inside the aquarium, but the guards always catch her. So we're at a stalemate. She keeps me a bird, but she can't catch me. Then, one night, I sees your by-line in *The Wayward Star*. I does some research and finds out you're legit. So I makes a break for it, and here I am."

I had so many questions: How'd he find me? How does a penguin do research? Didn't anyone notice a penguin walking around Hoboken? How'd he get into the apartment? But one was at the top of my list. "Didn't the penguin keepers notice an extra bird?"

"Dollface—them bird keepers don't like the bean counters. They keep the bean counters in the dark when they can—and with me they could. What would they say to the bosses? That they FOUND another bird? They report a missing or sick bird. A new healthy bird that just appears learns tricks right quick and makes the audience happy? That they forget to tell their bosses."

I thought about it for a moment. Yup—if I worked in a normal place I'd "forget" to tell my boss things too. But at *The Wayward Star* the weirder things get, the happier my bosses are. It's one of the perks, along with making twice as much as I would at the World's Most Pompous Daily. The downside is that I get to cover stories with unanticipated side effects—like getting me turned into a vampire. Or having a naked penguin in my shower. Little things like that happen to me more often than they should-which is to say, at all!

"Janey," I yelled. "We need you."

"Not to help that Jackass," she yelled back.

"But Janey..."

"He's a womanizing jerkoff. He doesn't deserve help. Plus—with a bird. That's bestiality… the poor bird."

Humphrey tugged at the bottom of my shirt with his beak. "I was a bird too. That's why it was flipper flapper action and not just flapper."

"That poor bird being assaulted by… by a reprobate!"

"Old Sally likes it," Humphrey sounded aggrieved by Janey's accusations. "Heck, after the first time, she came looking for it."

"And think of the children," Janey continued to yell through the door.

"What children? She didn't have no babies, just a bunch of yolk sacs."

"Where do you think baby penguins come from?"

"The mama penguin."

"No! They're birds. They hatch from eggs," screamed Janey.

"Oh. Now I feel a little bit bad," said Humphrey.

"Why's that?" Janey asked.

"Well, Sally gave me a bunch of eggs."

"The father penguin is supposed to sit on them and help hatch them!"

"Well nobody told me nothing like that. I figured it was a courting gift, like flowers or candy," said Humphrey. "Now I feels really bad I ates them." His voice was so innocent that I looked him up and down suspiciously. When he was sure Janey wasn't looking, he winked at me.

"You ate the eggs? You killed your own babies? You ate your own penguin babies?"

Humphrey shrugged. "They tasted good."

Janey let out a scream. Humphrey tried to hide a grin.

"You're a cannibal! Worse, you ate your own kids. You're a cannibalistically incestuous vampire penguin!"

"Hey, I just ate those eggs. I didn't have no relations with them," said Humprey.

"I'm not helping a cannibalistically incestuous vampire penguin. I won't do it," said Janey.

"I'm sure those kids would have wanted you to if they made it to hatching," Humphrey said consolingly.

"You aren't helping," I hissed at Humphrey. I rubbed my hands over my eyes. This could take all day, and dead or not, I wanted a nap. "Janey—I'm not asking for help for Humphrey. I'm asking for help because I believe the Women in Black are involved."

"You mean they finally got a vampire that deserved everything they could dish out?"

"Janey!" I was genuinely shocked. "You don't mean that!" The Women In Black tortured vampires. Loralei—aka "Lee" who I'd known my whole life—tried to feed me holy water at my mom's barbeque after finding out I was a vampire. The stake out I'd been on was to try to get information on vampires that I believed were being held for experiments somewhere in a church basement. I hadn't found the church yet. Janey knew all of this.

She marched out of her room, neatly dressed in a pair of jeans and a yellow tee shirt. "No, I guess I don't mean that. But, the bird is still gross."

"I can't argue with you about that," I agreed while thinking to myself that I actually could argue with her. I'd argue that it must be very hard for a person—for a vampire— to adapt to the changing world. From the way Humphrey spoke I'd guess he was at least a hundred years old and hadn't exactly kept up with modern terminology. Maybe in my copious spare time I should run a sensitivity class for vampires.

One fast rundown later Janey had an infinitely sensible suggestion. "If he's been poisoned by whatever the 'silver liquid' is, then let him stay here. Twenty-four hours from now it'll probably be out of his system and he'll be able to change at will."

"Say Chickie," the bird said from the floor. "That's a pretty good idea. I'll stay in the bathroom." He turned to me, "Dollface, you'll get me some raw fish for grubsteak, will ya sweetie?"

"Other people might need to use the bathroom," I said mildly. I had minimal toiletry needs. I used the shower for warmth and ran a wash-cloth over my non-reflective face, but being dead I really didn't digest food or liquid.

Janey rolled her eyes. "If you're worried about me, don't be! I'll be staying at Chet's as long as the Benny Hill wannabe is staying at our apartment."

Chet suddenly looked up like a deer caught in headlights, his eyes wide as saucers. "Huh? But..." I knew his objection. Chet had a full football scholarship but still shared a double at JHU with another freshman on the football team. The room was tiny, the men were huge and to my best count Chet hadn't slept in his dorm room for at least a month.

"Doug will just have to deal," she stormed into their bedroom as Chet followed.

"But I don't even have a bed there anymore," he said.

She turned like a woman possesses and metaphorical fire poured from her eyes. "What. Happened. To. Your. Bed." Each word was ice.

"I wasn't using it and Doug wanted more room." Poor guy seemed so confused, so unaware of what he'd done to upset Janey. Men can be so clueless sometimes, regardless of species. Add to that the as yet un-known—to us—dating habits of the North American sasquatch and Chet was worse off than most guys.

"You. Can't. Move. In. Without. Talking. To. Me. First." Janey was beyond pissed.

"Some of my clothes are at the dorm," he reasoned. "And I like sleep-ing here. I like being with you. You make me happy." He was so earnest. So innocent. So naive.

Neither Humphrey nor I were even slightly surprised when Janey's

"AAARGH!" shook the living room and she stomped into the bedroom slamming the door behind her.

"What did I do?" Chet stood there like a big dope looking like his world had just blown apart.

"You didn't ask," I told him as I brushed past him to Janey's room. Janey was going to need to talk, and as her best friend it was my job to listen.

"Should I ask now?" The poor Bigfoot was genuinely confused.

"You explain," I ordered Humphrey. "I'm busy."

"If I understood how a doll thinks I would have been handcuffed a long time ago and not a bloodsucking siphound."

I was finally getting a handle on his slang. "So you were turned by an unhappy girlfriend."

"I was barney-mugging a fire alarm instead of paying attention to my blue serge. The moll turned out to be a siphound and next thing I knows I wakes up dead."

"Yeah, I got almost none of that."

"I cheated with the wrong dame," he clarified.

"And the lady in question was a vampire who turned you. Got it." I was at Janey's door. "You know you aren't the person to explain relationships to Chet. Why don't you watch some television instead?"

"Cat's Pajamas," he agreed.

I didn't know what Humphrey wanted to watch, but I knew what was going to be on television. Chet was addicted to sports. All sports. Dollars to donuts ESPN was going to be on in 10, 9, 8... yup. Bees Knees.... Damn it, now Humphrey had me thinking flapper talk when I wasn't talking with him.

Janey was no surprise, flung face down in her bed. "You okay honey?" I sat on the edge of the bed and rubbed her back.

"No," she announced tragically. "Not at all." I waited and she cried, "How could he do this to me?"

I laughed to myself. "What, move in without asking you? Not take you to dinner and talk about wanting to move to the next step?"

Janey's "Yes" sounded decidedly watery.

"Oh Janey, Chet's different. He's this weird, exotic creature that we took home, Naired to death and turned into a real boy. But honestly, he doesn't know the right thing to do when it comes to normal relation-ships. You know that."

She rolled over. Her eyes were red and watery. "I rented *Love Actually* and we watched it together. *Love Actually*!"

What the hell was she drinking? I was the one who drank blood. Janey was the sane, sober and sort of normal one in the group. Didn't she get the memo? "Did you think he was going to learn to understand relationships by watching a movie?"

"No. Maybe. No. Yes."

I rubbed my temples. Could vampires get headaches? Because I think I had a pretty good-sized one starting right between the eyes. "Honey, you know better. Love isn't what they show at the movies."

"I know. But..."

"But it'd be nice if he bought you a chocolate heart on Valentines Day or brought you a rose for no reason at all, right?"

"He bought me buffalo wings! For My Birthday!!!!!!!!!!!" The wail was a cross between a cry and a laugh.

I stifled my own laugh, "Maybe he likes buffalo wings?" I offered.

"It's his favorite food."

"And he wanted to share it with you," I said encouragingly. "That's sweet. Kind of weird, but sweet."

She sat up and looked at me with sad, puppy dog eyes. "Do I want kind of weird but sweet for the rest of my life? Do I?"

"Janey, why are we talking about the rest of your life? You're only twenty-four and have barely started your PhD in forensic anthropology. You've got school, internships, digs, travels to other countries ahead of you. You don't have to decide anything now."

She gave me the 'what are you, stupid?' look. "Hello! Living together!"

"Hello! You've already been living together. For months. And you didn't seem to mind this morning that he hadn't gone home for ages."

"But it wasn't real. I mean we weren't really living together until I found out that he doesn't even have another bed. I mean, where's he going to go if I kick him out?"

"Well," I said slowly. "I guess Doug would have to give up some of his space and Chet would live in his dorm room again."

She sniffed. "That wouldn't be too bad."

"Of course, if you two weren't together he'd be out on his own. A single guy prowling the campus with Doug as his wingman."

"He wouldn't... I mean I still WANT Chet. I'm just not sure about the living together thing."

I knew I'd caught her attention so I went on deviously, "As the best wide receiver in JHU history—not to mention the fact that he's seven foot tall and built like a brick outhouse." With a face like a caveman, but I left that out of my assessment. "I'm sure a lot of the coeds have been noticing Chet. So, even if you two were still dating, he might go to a frat party with Doug." Being on the football team I assumed the pair had carte blanch to attend frat parties. "Where half naked sorority girls will hit on him. But you wouldn't mind that, would you?"

"The Hell With That!" Janey stood up and squared her shoulders, "I'd claw the eyes out of any woman who even thinks about hitting on Chet."

I stood back and let Janey slam the door open. "Chet get your clothing."

The guy looked up from some golf game that looked like it had been filmed in the seventies. I mean the guys were wearing plaid pants and argyle sweaters. That can't be today's golf fashion... can it?

Chet stood up and shuffled his feet towards the bedroom; his massive shoulders slumped. "Okay." It was clear that Humphrey had found enough common English to explain about break ups. The bigfoot clearly thought one was coming his way.

"Not those clothes," Janey almost screamed at him. "The clothes from your dorm room. You're moving in. Effective immediately."

"But. Huh?" He was completely confused and happy at the same time. A smile shone on his homely face.

"No half dressed drunk sorority girl is going to be climbing all over you while I'm off working in the lab. Do you hear me?" Janey yelled at him.

Chet ducked his head meekly, "Yes dear." And then, "What sorority girl?"

It was pretty funny to see Janey reach up and grab Chet by the ear. When he straightened she was dangling off the floor, but she still managed to march him into their bedroom where she was hopefully planning on teaching him a couple of things about life. In between bouts of serious sex.

Humphrey looked at me admiringly. "Bees knees, Doll-face. Bees knees."

I took a sip of blood, leaned back in my dad's old recliner and smiled smugly. "I know. Today I'm cooking with gas."

Three days later

It was another long night of investigative reporting. More vampires were missing. Stan's greasy, slimy beard was full of fresh lice, chicken bits and chocolate shake. Eight hundred variations of "This story is big!" and "This is the big time, babe!" had me longing for a hot shower. Instead water was flooding out from under the bathroom door. Cold water. Ice cold water.

"DAMN IT!!!!" My scream was loud enough that Janey and Chet came running out of their bedroom. Nude. Well mostly nude. They appeared to have been victims of coitus interruptus and playing with a colored glow-in-the dark condom. The number one thing I never needed to see in life was Chet's 'ahem' glowing purple.

I slapped my hands over my eyes and then peeked. Chet was massively built and let's just say that he didn't disappoint. I guess that wives' tale about big feet only proved that some of those old wives were pretty smart. For a moment I was almost disappointed I didn't have a Chet. Almost.

"You peeked!" Janey yelled at me.

"Um…" I literally had nothing to say.

"You're my best friend. I can't believe you peeked!"

"Well," I reasoned, "it's purple. How often do you see a twelve inch long, one eyed, one horned purple..."

"Nobody looks at my boyfriend but me!"

I have no idea what I would have answered because this was the moment that Humphrey chose to open the door—a flood of water preceding him. I took a step back from Janey—I mean she was human and therefore probably couldn't hurt me, but she was also pissed and I didn't need a slap in the face—hit some ice and landed on my back. Damn it! It wasn't Monday. It was Thursday. Thursday was supposed to be Ladies Night and one dollar martinis, not sasquatch penii and bird brained vampire penguins. AAAAAARGH! I had had enough!

An hour later I was sipping very expensive yak's blood in my dad's old recliner. I'd bought the crimson cocktail for my birthday dinner, but I needed a pick me up. Janey, Chet and Humphrey had cleaned up the winter wonderland that the Humphrey had created out of my bathroom.

"Angela?" Janey approached me with caution since I was still brooding.

"I don't want to talk about it."

"We didn't mean..."

"I landed flat on my back in a puddle of ice water after seeing your boyfriend's glowing purple light saber."

"I'm sorry..."

"Humphrey flooded Noah's apartment," I said. He was one of the neighbors I liked.

"I know," her voice was soothing.

"He saw Chet encased in a glow-in-the-dark purple condom." My voice had more than a hint of hysteria in it.

"I know," she agreed. Was she stifling a giggle?

"Humphrey was smoking a cigar. How do we explain a cigar smoking penguin to the neighbors?"

"A new circus act," she offered. Yes, that was definitely a giggle.

"We owe Noah repair money." I was still sunk in gloom. It wasn't just the flooded bathroom, the penguin that had moved into our home or the sasquatch who was my roommate's boyfriend. It wasn't even that I was a vampire. I mean I wasn't thrilled about the all blood diet, but living forever and leaving a good-looking corpse did have its advantages. It was the look on Noah's face when he saw what was inside the apartment. When had my life become such a freak show anyway? Oh yeah—the day I'd been turned into the walking dead without my consent.

"After Humphrey changes back into a vampire, we'll make him pay."

"When's he going to change Janey? When? I can't take much more of this."

"Soon," she promised. "Soon." Then she turned to Humphrey, "You've got to stop these antics."

"I'm not all wet and I won't be left holding the bag," Humphrey flapped his wings indignantly. "I turns the Dapper John into an icebox because I needs to. I'm a penguin not a cake-eater. I needs the cold."

"He's right," I agreed reluctantly. "He does need to be in the cold. He's a chinstrap—they're born and bred in Antarctica." Everyone looked at me, "What? I did some research on our featherless friend here. If he gets too warm for too long he'll get sick."

"You could have kept the ice and water to the bathtub!" Janey wasn't happy.

"You try living in a coffin by any other name and tell me how you like it," he retorted.

"About as much as I like living in an apartment with a sideways fridge and a wisecracking penguin," she shot back.

"A sideways fridge?" This sounded like a new disaster I hadn't walked in on. I had a mini fridge in my bedroom for my blood. Having it in with the food grosses Janey out.

"Short, fat and fangless boy over here toppled the fridge over this afternoon."

"Hey!" He had the gall to sound hurt. "I was just trying to grab some grub."

"You broke the refrigerator, dumped all my food out across the floor and I came home to find you in the middle of a disgusting mess of milk, juice, soda, raw meat and fruit! Which I had to clean up!"

"I's hungry." Innocent was not a look that worked on Humphrey. When Janey growled—actually growled—he added, "I didn't mean to break the icebox. I's trying to reach my food when the whole thing fell over."

"You were eating raw fish in the middle of the mess."

"No use letting good food go after bad," Humphrey said sounding remarkably like my mom for a minute.

Janey face was almost as red as my yak blood. "Aargh."

I got up and walked over to the wall and banged my head against it. Repeatedly.

"What are you doing?" Chet asked.

"I figure it'll feel better when I stop."

Chet furrowed his massive brows. "But why would you want to start in the first place?" he asked. "I mean your head didn't hurt before you banged it, right?"

"Riiiiightttttt," I agreed flopping back down into the recliner and picking up my wineglass of blood again. I didn't know how to explain the concept to Chet so I didn't even bother. You either "got it" or you didn't. He didn't .

I took a deep breath of air and a gulp of blood. "This has got to stop."

Humphrey made a sniffing sound. "I's knows when I ain't wanted." He opened the accordion fold hall closet with his beak and took out an overnight bag, pulling it awkwardly with both flippers, but he did manage to drape the strap over his chest. He walked toward the door, dragging the bad behind him. "Yous won't have old Humphrey to kick around any more." His dramatic scene was cut short by him trying to figure out the best way to open the door with flippers. I was watching with interest, still not having figured out how he ended up in my bathroom in the first place.

Instead of making the effort, he looked up at Chet. "Hey ya big lug. Gets the door for me."

Chet jumped up and opened it. Humphrey got to the frame. "I's is going out into the not so cold but still cruel world. Not sure how a penguin..."

"A cannibalistically incestuous vampire penguin," added Janey.

"A good hearted penguin is going to survive out on the streets of Hoboken, but I'm sure I will somehow." Not bad acting for a high school play. A little over the top for my apartment.

"Hey, Humphrey," I said.

The penguin stopped and looked back like he was ready to come back in. "Yeah Dollface?"

"That's my bag. Leave it, but feel free to keep the bowtie," I said.

"Oh." The penguin looked dejectedly down and slipped the strap off. Now he looked genuinely sad. "I guess this is goodbye then.

"Oh stop the bad acting and manipulation, Humphrey." I was annoyed rather than sympathetic to the little man. Besides my mother was the heavy weight champion of guilt and I had grown up with her daily manipulations. The penguin wasn't even a contender. "We said we'd help you and we will."

"Doll-face you are the bees knees! I don't mind sayings as how I was beginning to get the Heebie Jeebies that yous was going to give me the bum's rush. Buts now everythings all Jakes."

I rubbed my temples. "Everything isn't Jakes," I said faintly. "But we're going to do our best to get you turned into a vampire again. Then you're going to pay for all the damage you've done to the apartment. Are we clear?"

"Applesauce!"

"That better mean yes." I turned to my roomie. "Okay Janey, why hasn't Humphrey turned back into a vampire?"

She bit her bottom lip for a moment and looked up at the ceiling. "The poison isn't out of his system."

"How long is it going to take?" I asked, unable to hide the frustration in my tone.

"How the hell should I know? I don't even know what he's been exposed to."

"Well, then we need to figure that out then don't we?" I said.

The stiff shoulders, wrinkled brow and generally pissy attitude disappeared as the annoyed woman who had been cohabitating (badly) with a male chauvinistic penguin disappeared and the scientist came to the forefront. "I'll need blood," she said slowly. "I can run the samples in the lab after hours and see what's in Humphrey that shouldn't be." She looked at me. "And I'm going to need a sample of your blood too. As a control."

I didn't mind giving blood. I never had... I was one of those sick kids that was perfectly happy chatting away with the doctor as he shot needles into me. A few years back in high school I broke my arm. I asked the doctor for a local instead of general anesthesia so that I could watch the operation and then I wrote a column for the school paper on the whole thing.

Sadly Humphrey didn't seem to have the same sangfroid as I did when it came to needles. "I'm no piker but I'm not spifflecated neither. You must think I'm a real Rube if yous is planning to stab me with a needle."

"Humphrey I won't hurt you," Janey said with more patience than she'd exhibited since the fowl floated into our lives.

"Says you!"

"Says John Henry University," Janey shot back. "I'm getting my PhD there."

"In what?" Humphrey stared at her through squinted eyes.

"Anthropological Forensics," Janey said proudly.

He squawked, flared his wings and back peddled into the side of the couch, "No way, Mrs. Grundy. You pokes dead people. Yous going to hurt old Humphrey if yous pokes me."

"Um, Humphrey," I interjected mildly, "You're already dead. So am I."

"But nots dead and buried," he unarguably told me. "I's is supposed to have a long and happy death. Not being pricked and prodded by a blue nose nurse!"

"That Blue Nose Nurse will take good care of you," I retorted and then asked, "Wait. Blue Nose Nurse?"

"Smarty pants."

"Ah." I was getting the hang of Humphrey talk, but that one confused me.

"Don't worry," Janey drawled. "Humphrey will give us blood when the time comes. Otherwise he'll be stuck forever as the homeless tuxedoed bird."

"Homeless?' Humphrey squawked.

"Sure," she looked at him with the coldest expression I'd ever seen on her face, "I don't know about Angela, but I'm not planning on living indefinitely with a cowardly destructive bird."

"I'm no coward!" As I glanced around the room I noticed that he didn't say anything about the destruction he had wrought.

She looked him up and down. "Yeah, right! I've drawn blood from four year olds that made less fuss than you." Janey worked as a part time as a Phlebotomist in college which sure beat the sixteen different part time jobs I'd had in four years. The one I would die before telling my mom about? The time I conducted surveys asking Playboy and Playgirl subscribers what kind of content they wanted in the magazine. You Do Not Want To Know The Answers.

"I's can take anything you can give."

"Fine."

"Fine."

Crap—it sounded like two year olds arguing. I was about to say something, but Janey very calmly got up and walked out of the room. After waiting for about thirty seconds I flipped on the television and was deep into Sports Center when Janey marched out of her room with what looked suspiciously like a doctor's medical bag. "Okay short stuff. Put your money where you mouth is. Wing out."

"Now?" I swear if it was possible for a penguin to go white with fear Humphrey managed it.

"No time like the present," Janey said with an evil grin.

"Roger that," I heard the bird say to himself. "Yous can do this." As he was giving himself a pep talk and fear was wining.

"Oh for heavens sake!" Maybe Janey found it fun to torture the man, bird, vampire... whatever, but I didn't. Phobias are phobias. "Do me first. Maybe if he sees how gentle you are..." With that I gave Janey a look that said plain as day 'don't screw this up' and held out my arm.

"You take away all my fun," she complained, but she gently wiped my arm with alcohol—despite the fact that as far as we know I'm not subject to infections and then slid the needle in to draw blood.

"I barely felt it," I told Humphrey.

"Sweet Cheeks likes you," the bird told me with impeccable logic. "Hers and me, we's not as tight."

"What I would like is to be called Janey, not Sweet Cheeks!" Janey came close to the bird, waving the needle in the air. "Is that really too much to ask for?"

"Sorry um Chicky um Janey." If the chin strap penguin could sweat he would have. "Um, sorry. Sorry." He gulped and held out a wing.

As Janey tried to grasp the wing Humphrey flinched back. "Oh for the love of..." She grabbed at the wing, he pulled it back and she went sprawling into the couch. It was Lucy, Charlie Brown and the football conducted against the foul stench of phobia.

"Sorry," the bird honked. "Sorry. He held out his wing again muttering to himself, "Yous is not a cake eater. Yous is not a lounge lizard."

Janey—approaching cautiously this time—had the needle within an inch of Humphrey's wing, only to have him roll with semi aquatic vampire speed away from her. This time she managed to stay on her feet to listen to his, "Sorry. My bad. Sorry."

I rolled my eyes. Phobia is nothing to laugh at, but at the same time, come on. Humphrey was a *vampire*. Surely a big bad vampire had encountered scarier things than donating blood.

Another attempt had Janey flying into the couch as Humphrey flapping wing tossed her. I would have been mad, but the whites around Humphrey's eyes were so big it was clear the bird was in a state of outright panic. Unfortunately Chet didn't see it the same way. A dive, a "bam" that sounded like it was right out of an old Adam West Batman television fight and the couch was in two pieces, Chet was holding his head and I could almost see the stars I was sure were spinning around his head. Humphrey was under the dining room table, wings wrapped around himself shaking back and forth muttering.

If we didn't need Humphrey's blood, I swear I would have given up. But a potential lifetime of flooded bathrooms, broken refrigerators and Noah's shocked and appalled expressions gave me the where withal to take a different approach. "Hey, Humphrey," when I had his attention I wiggled my hips in a lame imitation of what I thought a stripper might do and slowly played with the button on the top of the pink oxford I'd put on hours before. When I was sure I had his attention I slowly—so slowly—popped it open and then stroked the skin revealed, before opening the second button.

"Day-me. She's a real Sheba." The bird sat stock-still and unmoving under the table.

I took my attention off of Humphrey for a second, still gyrating away, to flick my eye from Janey to Humphrey and back. I heard the bird's wings flutter and locked my eyes and hopefully vampire mojo back on the manimal hoping that Janey got the hint. Another button open—this one showcasing my slightly grayed bra. If I'd known I was going to do a strip tease for my friends and a scared penguin I would have worn a newer, lacier bra. Still, the target of my dance didn't seem to mind the view. At least not if "Applesauce!" was a compliment.

Another button and I heard a yelping noise from Humphrey. "Eyes on me," I ordered him and imitating some movie or another flipped my hair down and back up again.

"Yowzer!" That one didn't need translation.

I played with the next button hoping that Janey had taken enough blood. I had no intention winding up naked. Shirtless, with a bra on, was a far as I was willing to go.

The shirt was off. I flicked my eyes over to Janey and she was pulling what appeared to be the third syringe full of blood out of Humphrey when I was hit by a flying tackle and a blanket? "Oomph!"

A big, not so hairy sasquatch was sitting on my back. Sounding remarkably like my mother, except about two octaves lower, Chet said, "No. This is not right. You should not undress for that animal. You are a good girl."

"I was trying to distract Humphrey," I whined back.

I found myself wrapped in a blanket by two very strong male arms. "You are a good girl," he repeated implacably.

I looked into eyes that met mine squarely and realized that I had gotten that most dreaded of things. A big brother.

"Well," Janey said brightly when we were all untangled from the fight on the floor. Noah's knocking on his ceiling telling us to be quiet only added to the fun. "Tomorrow night we go to the aquarium. Humphrey, you can get us in, right?"

"What!!!" Humphrey and I screamed at her together.

"Well," she said with a smile that clearly hid her ruthless edge. "I need samples of the water and penguin blood from real animals-ones that that aren't wimpy vampires. I can find non-contaminated penguin cells on file at JHU, but I'm going to need to do some comparison work with contaminated penguins. And I don't think the aquarium folk are going to let me come in and take blood samples in the middle of their shows, do you?"

I crawled under the table where Humphrey had been and rocked backwards and forwards crying to myself, "No. No more penguins." I had images of tens of Humphreys all doing their skittering best to avoid Janey's needle by dancing, sliding and diving their way into disasterville.

When I dreamed of being a reporter I thought that my career would take me to the front lines in Iraq and Afghanistan. I thought I'd be in Hollywood interviewing the glitterati. I thought I'd be interviewing people whose family members had been killed, lost their homes to floods or fire, turned one hundred or won the lottery. Never in my wildest imagination did I think I'd be breaking into the Coney Island aquarium with a sasquatch, a forensic anthropologist and a talking vampire penguin. I mean it sounded like the start of a joke, not what my reality was supposed to be. Oh dreams, I hardly knew ye.

The next night

It was surprisingly easy to break into the aquarium. Apparently Humphrey had used his vamp mojo on the guards so they kept a very close and careful eye on the penguin habitat. We arrived, he said hi and told them to go take a break and they listened. I was disturbed and jealous at the same time. No one should have that kind of power over another, but I imagined what I could do with it. A raise, sale prices all the time, cute guys fanning me... No, that was part of how John Johnson got me. Better to remain a mind mojo amateur. Less likely to use it.

Humphrey had, in his escape, accidentally made a hole in the electrified fence that kept the flightless waterfowl inside their exhibit in the aquarium. He told us cheerfully, "It's Aces in there for the birds. Three squares, clean water and no big bad. No fear that Old Sally and the other chickies will try to go over the wall." I shuddered thinking about the havoc that would be caused if Humphrey's assessment of the situation was wrong and penguins were running amok in Coney Island; but he proved to be correct.

I was expecting one big building, but most of the exhibits at the

Coney Island aquarium were outdoors and that included the penguins.

I went in first and put plastic bags over the security cameras. The guards would leave us alone, but better not to leave video evidence. I didn't show up on camera, but Janey and Chet would. Then we snuck in quick and quiet. The penguin exhibit was separated into water and land sections. Chet helped Janey over the top fence into the habitat and followed after. Humphrey and I managed ourselves.

The penguins had been sleeping on the ground snuggled up together, but seeing us decided it would be safer in the water.

"How are we going to get their blood?" I asked.

"Don't be pointing your peepers at me, Dollface. I's take you here, but I's ain't helping you pincushion Sally and the rest," said Humphrey.

Janey leaned over and tried to grab penguins as they swam by with no success.

"Let me try. I learned how to fish salmon by watching the bears," said Chet. In bear fashion he bent over and tried to swat penguin after penguin, with no luck.

"Guess penguins are faster than salmon," I said.

"Smarter too," admitted Chet.

"I guess it's up to me," I said, figuring my vampire reflexes would be enough to catch one. Pity nobody told the penguins how it was supposed to work. I guess that was why Humphrey hadn't been caught. I never was one to quit something easily, but on my second try one actually popped up in front of me and stopped to look at me. I reached closer and the penguin paddled one stroke backward, splashing me in the process. "Hey! He did that on purpose!"

"She," said Humphrey. "That flapper is Sally." The penguin waved at her. Either she actually waved back, or just liked splashing me. The way my life was going, I was willing to bet the penguin just wanted me all wet.

"She, he or it, we need her blood," I said leaning over to get ready for a grab, but the edge was wet and I slipped in.

Vampires swim almost as well as rocks and like a good vampire I sunk to the bottom. The legend about vampires not being able to cross running water isn't exactly true. We can do it; it just makes us extremely ill. Showers, even a tub I can handle. Anything bigger and I get bad. Bad inside and bad outside.

I hit the floor of the penguin pool; suddenly starved and nauseous at once, mixed with a hangover easily a dozen times worse than the baldest one I ever had as a human. I felt something like this everyday on the PATH when I went to work in Manhattan. This was much, much worse. On the PATH, I was dry and able to close my eyes in a feeble attempt to ignore the miles of water above the tunnel. Immersed in it, I couldn't ignore it as it pushed down on my skin, matching me itch and burn like I was being eaten alive by fire ants. Then it got worse.

The water moving through the filters was like being battered with acid. The currents made by the black and white blurs that rocketed by, showing off their swimming ability didn't help either.

My mind wanted to shut down, to make the pain go away, because the worse the pain got, the worse the hunger became. I would have feasted on a penguin's blood if one was kind enough to come close. None did.

I fought to try to stand, to swim. I knew how, but apparently it wasn't like a bicycle. Vampires did forget. I tried to stand and walk. It's not like I needed air. The gentle water movement felt like an undertow and knocked me back to me knees.

I wanted to curl up and die, but I was already dead, so I settled for just curling up into the fetal position. I contemplated sinking my hangs into my own arm, to see if my own blood would help.

"Dah Dah Dah DAAAA!!!! It's Super Penguin." Humphrey swam next to me waving his wings around. I didn't have a clue how I understood him. I just did. I hurt too much to talk but I managed a cross between a moan and a grunt.

"Hydroitis really getting to you?"

I groaned and growled something incomprehensible. Humphrey said with complete accuracy and more than a little bit of kindness, "Baby's all wet." He held out a wing and I manage to grab it. My head felt like it was in a blender on puree and I didn't know which way was up or down. The vampire penguin was strong enough to pull me to the surface and seconds later I was lying on the dry part of the environment feeling like I'd been kicked in the stomach and head—repeatedly by an angry mule.

I sucked in some air, driven by some vestigual reflex. The pain was better but the hunger gnawed at my guts like a living thing trying to eat its way out.

"Blood," I begged more than demanded, but only barely. I could barely see, it was like looked through a kalidoscope and although I could feel ground under me, it still felt like I had put on the Cyclone rollor coaster next door as it crashed down from the top of the Empire State Building. My skin hurt like someone was using I cheese grater on me. It felt too hot, too tight. Like I would burst if I didn't get...

Damn it, I'd never been jonesing this bad, not even when I turned.

I sensed more than saw my trio of friends looking down on me. "We didn't bring any," Janey confessed. "I didn't think that you'd need any."

"How could you forget? I always have bagged blood. You always make sure I have some."

"I forgot."

"No, you didn't. You brought some. You all did. It's not in bags. Now get it out of you and into me," I yelled, only hearing what I saw after the words had exited my mouth. "I didn't mean that." My belly felt like the hunger had gnawed its way through my stomach and into my abdominal cavity. "Yes, I did. Feed me now.

Humphrey waddled next to me. "Angela, you can have my blood if you want it, but you shouldn't need it. You just have to focus to beat the hydoitis. It's tough, but you can do it."

Part of me realized that he suddenly wasn't speaking in flapperese. The speak nonsense was an affectation. The rest of me didn't care.

That same part that noticed the change in speech said there was a reason not to have the penguin's blood, screamed it was a bad idea. The part eating me from the iside out didn't care. I had permission. There was no reason to hold back. My fangs elongated, my skin tingled and I could all but taste the penguin's blood in my mouth. Still on hands and knees, I lunged towards Humphrey when Janey screamed, "Wait!"

Chet dove football style into the featherless fowl. The pair tumbled into the pool. Several of the penguins actually came over to defend Humphrey by pecking at Chet's face and eyes. Humphrey herded most of them away from the bigfoot. To Chet's credit, he only defended himself, not hurting any of the flightless birds, even though he tended to sink when he used both hands.

I didn't have any of that self control. I was inside my own head screaming not to hurt Janey but the bitch had taken away my food, my medicine to make the pain go away. How dare she!

I turned on her, slowly crawling toward my best friend, nothing but hunger on my mind. I moved like a puppet, controled by my body's need. In my mind's eye I saw me feeding on her, that precous red liquid gushing down my throat, making it all better. I saw Janey's face.

"Hey, um Angela... your eyes are red. And um...."

I saw her laying dead after I'd drunk my fill and for the briefest moment my hunger was replaced by guilt and despair. It was enough to stop me, just long enough to mutter a single sylable.

"Run."

Humphrey honked from the pool. "Do what she said and go slowly. Otherwise the running will make her run you down like any predator chasing prey. She's going scrootched on blood." The penguin made like a torpedeo right at me. Chet shook off the last bird pecking at him—I think it was Sally—and swam my way. I didn't care. Janey had what I needed, what should be mine. Mine. She stole my blood and now she had to replace it. It was only fair.

"Angela, please. Don't!" Janey sounded small. Helpless. Pathetic. Prey. The perfect dinner. Stopping was no longer an option. God help me, I'm not sure there was any part of me left that wanted to stop.

"Dah dah dah!!!!" I was knocked into the water by a two foot singing bird. "Super penguin to the rescue!"

I sank to the bottom. Again.

This. Was. Not. Happening. It started again. Agony overwhelmed pain and this time I stood. I felt the water current burn me, but it wasn't as bad as what was eating my insides. I reached out and caught a penguin.

Finally. Something close enough to eat.

I pulled it to my mouth but was hit in the gut by an underwater missle and knocked backwards into the pool wall.

"Sorry, Dollface. I can't let you go eating Sally. Now calm down and we'll get you fed."

This had to stop. I had to eat now, not in a minute. I pushed off the wall behind me and caught Humphrey. I bit him before he got away, but what came out wasn't life. It was sludge. Blood flavored, silver tainted poison. Just the taste made my mouth burn. Yuck. I flung him up and out of the water. I heard later he landed in the beluga whale tank.

I was distracted enough that Chet managed to get behind me and wrap one over sized arm around my neck, the other around my chest and arms. Stupid bigfoot was smart enough that I couldn't bite him with that kind of a hold. I felt the sensation of being lifted up and out of the water. The sasquatch managed to walk us both up the side of the pool using his feet and toes.

I felt blessed dry air. So much easier to feed. Chet was big but I was stronger. I head butted him and managed to flip him back into the pool.

"Would somebody feed me already?" I screamed. I caught the scent of two humans and again felt a rapidly approaching missle. Humphrey leap into the enclave and in some bizzare penguin kung fu kick knocked me over the wall and onto the concrete outside the penguin habitat.

I climbed back into the penguin pen, determined to get my blood out of Janey's veins and the penguin stood in front of her, his little flippers held out like he was an old time boxer.

"I'm bigger, stronger and hungrier than you. Think you can stop me?" I asked.

"No, but I'm pretty sure I can." Even in my beaten and bewildered state I knew that voice. It was my former next door neighbor—the object of a sibling rivalry that was just wrong. How can you have a sibling rivalry that's with the next door neighbor? "Who knew tonight would be so rewarding."

Loralie Lee, dressed in an all black wet suit and looking like nothing so much as a James Bond babe with her flawless hair, body and Crest smile, stepped out from behind the bleachers—gun trained firmly on me. Well maybe she looked like the James Bond villainess. I mean the gun was trained on ME. Another idiot trying to stand between me and blood that was rightfully mine. Her smile was frightening in its sincerity, "Thanks for getting rid of the guards and disabling the camera. I was prepared to do something high tech like cut the power. Who knew a couple of shopping bags would do the trick? It wasn't so much the cameras, but those damn guards. You made them into security the secret service would have been pround of. Sadly, I wasn't authorized to kill any humans. Innocent ones any way. Luckily your roomie and boytoy don't qualify. After all, they are aiding and abeting not one, but two monsters."

My answer was a terribly coherent, "Grrrrr." I thought about telling her she was wrong, that Chet wasn't human either, but she didn't deserve to know. She was standing between me and my blood. Then it occurred to me that she was standing between me and her blood too.

Sweet. A warm, hot meal and I got toget rid of Lee to boot.

"Hey that's the moll that..." Humphrey shut up fast.

"Two freaks for the price of one." There was nothing friendly, nothing sane, in Loralie eyes. She was too stupid to see anything different in mine. Her funeral, my happy meal. She gestured at Humphrey. "Get over next to Angela. I'm taking you in."

Instead of moving towards me, Humphrey started slowly advancing on Loralie. "Say chicky, what ya pointing a peeper at us for anyway?'

Her hand moved a little. "I wouldn't. This is loaded with blessed silver nitrate mixed with holy water. It might not kill you, but it'll disable you until I can get you into lock up. And I assure you vampire—it has been tested on others of your ilk. And weres." She giggled. "It works even better on those furry freaks. They burn like a moth in a flame." Her eyes rolled back like she was in estasy. "Now go stand next to Angela before I do something you'll regret."

"Blessed?" Janey asked faintly from where she was lying on the pool's edge.

Lee gave Janey a look of contempt. "We have priests who work for us since we've convinced them that you guys are evil undead creatures and all. One out of control with pain and hunger vampire can convince anyone that you guys are demons that need to be stopped."

"How despicable." I was glad to see Janey still couldn't be won over by Loralie -even after I'd tried to kill her.

As Lee was distracted by Janey, Humphrey inched closer to the Woman-in-Black. He was no more than fifteen feet away when she became aware of his stealthy movements. "Stop right there, short stuff."

"Jeez lady. I wasn't doing no harm and I'm not spifflicated. I's wants to make sure that yous don't take me for a ride, see. I's is not ready to get..."

"Of course I'm going to take you for a ride, you dumb fool!"

Humphrey's short neck gobbled a few times, "What. Wait. No need to give me the bum's rush..."

"What the hell are you talking about, you short, nasty little loathsome bird"

"I's is not ready to be bumped off. I's is things to live for."

With a sickly sweet voice and a smile that was truly happy she said, "Oh I'm not going to kill you. I'm calling for a pick up. And then you and my childhood bestie over there are going to the lab where we're going to find out someday what makes vampires work and what hurts them. Holy water is a given, but did you know that any blessed liquid works?" She giggled again like she was talking about her first kiss. "I had a priest bless some pig's blood and when the vampire drank it, she blew up! Can you imagine? Next we're going to see what happens if we bless a pig before butchering. If it works the way we expect, butchers all around the world are going to find a new low cost source of pork—and then "Bam! No more nasty little vampires!" She looked at me and said with total sincerity, "We're also experimenting with converting garden equipment into stake launchers. Maybe we'll get to test it out on you."

Humphrey had inched closer. Now he screamed, "No!" and launched himself at Loralie. She was fast. Fast enough to fire off the gun twice. Not fast enough to get out of the way of a charging vampire penguin. She went down with Humphrey lying unmoving across her. The smell of burning flesh was covered by the sweet potent smell of Lee's blood.

Perfect. The penguin had even opened the wrapper for me. I was speed itself. Lee didn't react as I raced to her delicious neck. Nothing, no orgasm, no love, no food, no front page byline ever felt so good as that salty cocktail of crimson blood trickled over my lips and down my throat.

Yummy, yum, yum.

The beast inside me quieted. My skin stopped screaming at me. I felt like I was getting a full body massage and orgasm all at once while I ate at the ultimate all you can suck buffet. It was heaven. I could have kissed Loralei for giving that all to me, but not till later, until I was done. I wondered if it was as good for her as it was for me. Probably not. Pity. I debated taking up smoking because I had no idea what else I could do after something like this.

"Angela, Angela!" A large male hand shook me. Without lifting my head, I smacked it away. No bloodus interruptus.

"Oomph," a voice said somewhere in the distance. The hand was gone. And blood was still flowing down my throat. Mmmm. Keep them coming bartender. I'll have another.

"Angela. Angela, you can't." A female voice was talking to me. It was damn rude to interrupt me. Whoever it was should know that more blood would make me more betterer. Blood made everything better. "Angela, you don't want to kill Loralie."

"Go way," I said, gurgling as if I was about to stop to talk to some twisted idiot who wanted to make me stop the single greatest experience of my life. All the pain inside me was going far, far away.

"Deep Throat, listen to me."

I tore my mouth away from the woman lying at my feet and snarled, recognizing my best friend, "I told you never to call me that!" I hated that nickname ever since I wrote an expose of the dean at college and what certain female students did to get out of trouble.

Janey slapped me across the face. Hard. Brave and stupid. "You can't kill Lee."

I blinked from the shock of the blow. Why the hell wouldn't I finish when there was more blood there just for the taking? Yummy, orgasmic blood.

But with the blood came back the parts of my mind that weren't the predator parts. I wanted to smack Janey for taking away by bloodgasm, but she had blood. Fresh new blood for more bloodgasms. The thought make me ill. I couldn't. I hurt Janey when I turned and I could have lost her forever. I was not going through that again. I'd leave her alone, but I never liked my sibling rival. I could live without her. Life would even be better I reasoned. It took longer than I want to admit for my brain to catch up and tell me that the way I had been think was very twisted, self serving and wrong. Then I remembered what she'd done to my little friend.

"Lee killed Humphrey. She doesn't get to live after killing him. I'm drinking her dry. She deserves worse for what she did. Poor silly little Humphrey. He didn't deserve to die." I picked up Loralei and shook her like a rag doll, then screamed. "He didn't deserve to die you heartless bitch. But you do."

"Angela, no. She didn't kill him Humphrey. He's just hurt."

I looked next to her. Humphrey wasn't moving and Chet has his hand on Humphrey's neck.

"No, he's dead! Lee killed him, so I get to kill her, drink her. Guilt free."

"No such thing. As evil as she is, you'll hate yourself in the morning because she did not kill him. He's hurt," she said honestly. "But he isn't dead." Then she said with a cunning I'd appreciate later, "Maybe you can help him stay alive."

"Alive?" I was beginning to believe her. As more blood hit my brain, it started to work like that of a person instead of a monster. "He's alive?"

Chet said from his position next to Humphrey, "Yes. But he doesn't look too good. His heartbeat is really, really slow."

I looked down at the Loralie. She was pale and looked unconscious, but I suspected that the faint might be an act. Actually part of me hoped it was. Loralei had turned into a foul, loathsome woman, but my mother still loved her. She'd never forgive me for killing her favorite almost daughter. I winked at Janey. "Maybe I'll feed Lee to Humphrey. She still has enough blood left to be of some use to Humphrey…"

"No. No!" Lee squirmed frantically in my arms. "You can't. No. Please…." The babble was incoherent but fairly clear. She didn't want to be Humphrey's dinner.

"And then all I have to do is figure out what to do with the corpse. Janey, do you know where we can put a corpse?"

"Weeeeellll I guess we could taxidermy her. Think your mom would notice at the Labor Day barbeque?"

"No!" My ex almost sibling twisted so violently she managed to tear herself half out of my grasp. Startled, I dropped her onto the floor. She hit with a clunk and as she tried to scramble away. I caught her by the ankle and lifted her up so she dangled upside down. There were some plusses to being a vampire.

"Angela. You must do something now. Humphrey's heart is beating slower," said Chet, holding the tiny penguin in his giant hands.

As much as I was tempted to, I couldn't feed Lee to Humphrey. I had no idea how much blood I'd taken, how much blood Humphrey needed and how much blood it was safe for Lee to donate. Plus she was scared out of her wits and despite myself I felt bad. "Oh Lee Lee," I muttered, more to myself than to her, "What have you become?" She'd been a spoiled princess of a child but I never expected this.

I hardened my heart. I couldn't let Loralei go unsupervised. So I conked her head against the floor and hoped I was gentle enough that I didn't cause any serious brain damage. She slumped down, unconscious. As a precaution I pocketed the gun of deathly fluids.

The penguin's chest was a raw bloody mess. Burnt in places, oozing blood and guts in others, it was a horror to behold. Worst was the bite I'd taken out of him. It wasn't the worst wound, just the hardest for me to look at. There was a catch in my voice I couldn't hide as I called, "Humphrey?"

Not surprisingly, there was no answer.

Janey joined us. "Oh man, that looks bad."

"Yeah," I sniffed. I had to stop myself from shivering and pull myself together. "He needs blood."

Chet moved his hand and bloody gunk gushed from Humphrey's throat. "I do not believe he will be able to swallow it."

"I so totally would have been justified in killing Loralie for this," I said. Even as I said it, I knew it was a lie only a monster would believe and I knew moments before, I would have believed it entirely. I bit into my own arm. Blood poured down my hand and flowed onto the mangled mess that was my little friend. "Hopefully this will help."

I turned to Chet and Janey. "He might need more..." I didn't even know if vampire blood would help. I mean my blood was already dead, so how could it possibly add life? How quickly did blood go from my digestive system to my circulatory one? Did it even work that way or was it broken down some other way? I needed a vampire physiology class.

"I'll go next," Chet said somberly. "I liked the little bugger."

I hated the fact that Chet was talking about Humphrey in the past tense, but as I gazed down at the blood mess that was my funny little friend, I let the unthinkable creep into my head. And I hated Loralie more than I thought possible. More than I did when I thought draining her dry was the cat's pajamas. Great, I was thinking in flapper speak. Humphrey had really gotten to me.

Humphrey's body convulsed and he screamed in agony. I moved my arm away, afraid I was hurting him in some way. He screamed louder. "No," Janey moved my wrist directly into the penguin's mouth. "I think he needs more blood."

"He sounds like he's dying," I sobbed.

"No. Wait. Maybe." Janey's dithering wasn't making any sense and then she screamed, "Ah ha!"

A thin bead of silver grayish liquid was dripping down Humphrey's body. "Is that..."

Janey nodded her head, "He's expelling the poison."

"So he's going to be okay?"

Janey bit her lip. "I don't know to be honest. We just have to wait and see." There was a tear on her face. "I hope the sexist pig pulls through."

It started as a small trickle but soon became a river pouring out of Humphrey's body, mostly through the wounds. His body convulsed over and again. The liquid left scorch marks wherever it rose in his body. I made the mistake of touching it. "Aaargh" I screamed at my finger burned black in one second. "Wipe it off of him," I begged as silver nitrate plus continued to pour out of the bird as screams of agony ripped out of his torn throat. Chet pulled his outer shirt off and started cleaning the bird.

When it stopped coming out, he was completely still. The agony over, blood and guts oozed now out of open wounds that seemed free of poison. Blood still dripped down my arm into him, but it didn't do any good.

His eyes opened. "Here's looking at you, kid," he gasped. His eyes fluttered closed and he lay motionless.

Great. Humphrey Bogart as an exit line. The flightless fowl would choose that moment to get classy. My eyes red with shed bloody tears I shot back with, "It's the start of a beautiful friendship."

"We're losing him," Chet said unnecessarily.

Janey's busy brain hit jackpot. "Humphrey change," she demanded. "It'll help."

"What? He doesn't have the energy."

I don't know if she was challenging me or Humphrey, "The bird brain who managed—without hands mind you—to convert our bathroom to an ice palace doesn't have energy? Yeah, right."

Humphrey didn't move. "Damn. He really is bad." She thought for a second. "Humphrey—" It was a coaxing tone. "If you change for me, I'll make sure you see the best chest this side of the Mississippi."

His eyes opened a crack. "Airbags?"

"Bozongas," she confirmed gravely.

I can speak from experience that changing shape, is, at the best of times, agony. Bones, muscles and tissues reshape into things they were never meant to be. To try and change when mortally wounded, that must have been torture. And I learned tonight torture might make him as dangerous as I was minutes before.

But somehow, and I don't know how, he found the strength. His screams were silent as his skin slit and his back arched, bones forcing the body into a shape that was human; bloody, bruised, slashed, naked and... me? Humphrey had changed into a naked me. It made sense. We can only change into things we've recently tasted the blood of.

"Breasts," he said happily as he collapsed against the floor panting.

"They are okay," Janey drawled dismissively. "But certainly not the best set I've ever seen. Not by a long shot."

"Hey, I've never gotten any complaints." I glanced over to the girls that were staring back and me and looked quickly away. Looking at my naked breasts on someone else was just too weird for me to think about. They were pretty damn good though.

"The pair I'm thinking about are much firmer and twice the size," Janey said in a confiding tone. "And I promise I'll show them to you if you'll just change one more time."

"Applesauce!" He closed his eyes and the outline of the other me started to get blurry and then nothing happened. Humphrey collapsed unconscious.

I lunged towards him. "Humphrey! Are you okay?" Stupid I know but instincts don't change because the person is a vampire. I shook him but nothing happened. I slit open the almost closed wound in my arm and allowed blood to drip into Humphrey's mouth. It trickled out the side, useless.

"Chet, would you?" I couldn't bring myself to ask Janey. Chet held out his arm.

I slashed his arm with my fang. I tried hard not to take a taste since Chet hadn't offered me blood—he was trying to take care of Humphrey— but a drop was on my fang. A yummy, life giving, unfreaking believably fantastic drop of blood. "Wow," I said softly to myself. Now that was a fine vintage.

"What's that?"

"Um—nothing." Janey would NOT appreciate me lusting after her boyfriend's blood. But Oh My God it was so good it was hard not to jump him for another taste—especially as blood trickled, uselessly out of Humphrey's mouth.

"Is he going to be okay?"

Janey was attempting to sound positive as she said, "He should be. He was much worse before and he…"

Humphrey's body spasmed and shook. He arched into the pain, his body changing into that of a short muscular man, maybe five foot six with a dancer's body and an Errol Flynn mustache, a center part and honey blond hair. He looked like a picture out of the nineteen twenties come to life.

"Dollface, you're aces with me!" He bounced up, hugged me and kissed me.

"Aces indeed!" I stood staring, speechless. Being kissed by a naked Humphrey was something else. Something else indeed. It was a good kiss. When I broke it off, Janey was looking at Humphrey wide-eyed. If I didn't know better I'd swear my roomie was crushing.

When Humphrey held out his hand it was engulfed by Chet's much larger one. "Bees Knee, Big Cheese. That hootch of yours is something else! If you want to sell your giggle juice, you'd get a C-note."

Chet was, as usual for his conversations with Humphrey, looked confused. I rescued him by saying, "I don't think we want Chet selling his blood to random vampires, but thanks."

He turned next to Janey. "Well Sweet Cheeks?" A grin twinkled in his eyes, "Where are these amazing breasts you promised me?"

Although she tried to be outraged, she couldn't keep the smile off of her face. Or her eyes off his. She slowly walked over to Chet and removed his soggy t-shirt. "There," she said happily as she stroked Chet's chest. "Aren't these the best breasts you've ever seen?"

His chest was hard, hairy and not at all feminine. "Do you take me for a cake eater, Mrs. Grundy? Those buds aren't no bug eyed Betty's. They're Joe Brooks."

"I got about half of that and I have to agree with him. Chet's a masculine man and those are definitely not breasts."

"Oh I disagree completely," she replied. "Gray's Anatomy defines breasts as the 'human mammary gland' and the front part of the body from the neck to the abdomen. And as far as I'm concerned this is the best mammary gland I've ever seen."

Humphrey began to laugh. "You slayed me with a lollapalooza and I fell for it like a Rube."

Chet on the other hand looked remarkably pleased as he leaned down and kissed Janey. He probably thought he was whispering, "I'm glad you like my body baby," but he was pretty loud.

She kissed him back. "I do. I really do." But I caught her looking out of the corner of her eye at the former penguin.

"Petting party," Humphrey leaned back to enjoy the show. It seemed to turn on Janey and Chet was too overwhelmed by the kiss to care.

Since watching my best friend make out with a guy who had blood I'd love to suck was more than a little bit gross, I decided to take care of my sibling rivalry turned psycho killer but she was gone. "Where's Loralie?"

It wasn't hard to figure out what had happened. There was a faint blood trail to the street. From there she she'd either driven, been picked up or caught a taxi. But that was okay. I'd learned something very valuable. Lee was far more involved in the plot to kidnap and torture vampires than I'd believed. I'd thought—hoped maybe—that she was a minor flunky in the ranks of the Women-In-Black. Clearly she was a full operative. And that was in my favor. I knew her parents, her fiancé and I was kind of dating her brother. I knew she worked at New York's Most Prestigious Daily. Sooner rather than later, she'd show up somewhere. And I'd be waiting.

In the meantime we had some issues to resolve. I was soaking wet, as were Chet and Janey. Humphrey was wearing his birthday suit and was covered in bloody gunk. All and all, not a great look for any of us.

Granted we had the van, but it was going to be a wet, squishy gross ride home.

And then I saw it. An all night consignment pawn shop. I suggested my cohorts search the penguin pen for clues—specifically anything that Loralie might have left behind. They could spare me for ten minutes or so.

The lady behind the counter had long thick curly red hair, glasses and a butterfly tattoo. Oddly enough she was singing *Spread a Little Sunshine* from *Pippin.* At her feet was a brownish dog that came over and enthusiastically began sniffing me. Revamp that. I was in an open consignment shop in Brooklyn at two o'clock in the morning. Odd did not begin to describe this shop owner.

Since she didn't say anything I began browsing, the dog close on my heels. It was easy to find clothing for Janey and I—we were both pretty normal size. There was only one choice for Chet—a pair of 3X sweatpants and a tee shirt. I'd picked up unisex sweatpants for Humphrey when it caught my eye. A pale green tuxedo and pink ruffled tuxedo shirt. The damn vampire had trashed my bathroom and destroyed my fridge. He had to pay. Credit card out, I decided that whatever the cost, the tuxedo was mine. Well, up to $1200 at least. Then my card would be maxed out. I used the shirt to cover and pick up something special for Janey and threw it on the pile

She took one look at the tuxedo I was holding. "A remake of *Grease,*" she guessed ignoring the fact that I was dripping wet.

"Yeah, um, that'll do."

"I played Rizzo in 1988," she confided.

"Oh?"

In response she started singing "*Look at Me, I'm Sandra Dee.*" She was, to my inexperienced ear, very good. Mid song she cut off and hollered, "Jordan."

Out of the back room came a large teenager who looked like he'd just escaped from a strict Amish upbringing and dove into a sweats as soon as he'd left Lancaster behind. The shave and haircut were apparently going to happen later. "Yes Esther.'

"My *Pippin* baby," she confided in a stage whisper. Since he didn't respond I didn't ask either. I assumed he'd been conceived when she was performing in *Pippin.* The alternative didn't make sense. He didn't have a hunchback.

He just stood there and stared at her with an expression of righteous embarrassment teenagers mastered ten minutes after the dawn of time. "Could you please pack everything up? Make sure to use extra tissue paper on the tux. We don't want it to get damaged."

"Uh, huh." The non loquacious young giant gave me a shrewd look and then said, "One thing about living in Brooklyn I never could stomach. All the damn vampires."

His mom responded with, "At least they don't drink wine. Leaves more for me"

I grabbed my bags and took off like the proverbial bat out of hell. Maybe they were vampires. Maybe they knew about vampires. Maybe they were vampire groupies or more likely they wanted to kill us. I didn't know and I didn't care. My plate was full and I didn't have room for another mystery in my life. At least not that night.

I walked back into the penguin pen to discover Janey and Humphrey squabbling over a penguin egg.

"No, you can't have it," yelled Janey. "You'll eat another one of your children."

"But I don't wants to make like a chow hound. I wants you to have it. Make sure it hatches okay and then bring it back for Sally and the rest to raise." Humphrey held the egg out to her sincerity all but oozing out of his pores. He was up to something. "Please, takes it."

Janey was actually speechless. "I'll take good care of it."

"I's knows youse will."

I handed out clothes. Janey gingerly put down the egg just long enough to get changed. Behind Chet.

Humphrey looked at his tux. "What's with the monkey suit, Dollface?"

"Payback's a woman doing your clothes shopping. And drop the flapper speak. I know you don't have to talk like that," I said.

"Don't have to. Likes too," said Humphrey.

"And you know we're not equipped to take care of an egg back at the apartment, right?" I said.

"I's knows. What Chicky don't knows is that's not a real scrambler. It's a display to teach the kiddies. It ain't never gonna hatch. You ain't gonna rat me out, are you?

"I'll think about it," I said.

"By the way Dollface, I owes you. The biggest. Thanks for extraditing me from that predicament," said Humphrey.

"Applesauce!" I said brightly.

I knocked on Janey's door about an hour before dawn. She snuck out into the hallway, leaving Chet asleep in their bed. "Crazy night," I said as I motioned her into my room.

"Uh huh," she agreed sitting on the edge of the bed.

Words no one ever wants to say. Words no one ever wants to hear. "We need to talk."

"What? You're breaking up with me?"

I thought I'd hit her gently, but from the way she tumbled against the pillows I might have been rougher than I'd thought. "No stupid." I paused for a minute and then brought up the thing that was bothering me the most, "Tonight was pretty scary, huh?"

"Yeah," she sat cross-legged on my bed, "Who would have thought that Loralei could possibly be as nuts as she is?"

"That's not what I was talking about."

She ignored me. "I mean I know she's a self centered, self absorbed blonde, but...."

"Janey," I interrupted her, "We can't ignore what almost happened. I lost control and almost *bit* you. I could have done did worse."

"Nothing happened," she told me firmly. "I'm fine."

I rolled my eyes. "Janey I could have killed you. I was completely out of control."

"You didn't."

Her faith in me was touching. And stupid. "Thanks to Humphrey. Next time someone might not be around."

Janey kicked me in the shin. "Angie—listen to me. You didn't bite me. You didn't hurt me. You fought the blood lust long enough for Humphrey to knock you in the water. From now on we'll just make sure that we always have a bag of blood with us when we go out, okay?"

I shook my head. "Not good enough." I went over to the dresser and took out a well-wrapped package from the consignment store.

Janey took the bag with interest alight in her eyes. "What's in it?"

In the bag was a box; inside the box was another box, and then tissue paper and then finally a jewelry box. "I want you to wear it—always."

It was a Celtic silver cross on a leather string. When she started to say something I held up my hand to stop her. "I want you to be able to defend yourself against me at all times. This should be able to stop the monster inside of me."

"This isn't necessary."

"It is to me." If she didn't protect herself, I wasn't staying. I was resolute and after a moment of dithering she slid the necklace over her neck and tucked it in her shirt. "Good. Now don't take it off."

"Okay. Listen, I've got to check on the egg," she said. I had to fight back a grin. "Turns out Humphrey wasn't so bad. For a sexist pig."

"Or a cannibalistically incestuous vampire penguin from Coney Island," I added.

"That too," she agreed and walked out of the room.

I spent a long time staring at the ceiling. Janey was safe—that was good. But I'd gotten a chance to see how far blood lust could take me and I was scared at how far it had taken me.

Still, I had already called Stan. I had two days to write it up, but he practically guaranteed me the front page.

Author Bios

Jonathan Maberry is a New York Times best-selling and multiple Bram Stoker Award-winning author, magazine feature writer, playwright, content creator and writing teacher/lecturer. Novels: *Ghost Road Blues* (Pinnacle books; Bram Stoker Award), *Dead Man's Song, Bad Moon Rising, Patient Zero* (St Martins Press; in development for TV); *The Wolfman* (NY Times bestseller from TOR,), *The Dragon Factory* (St Martins Griffin), *The King Of Plagues, Rot & Ruin,* (Simon & Schuster) and *Dust & Decay.* Nonfiction: *Vampire Universe* (Citadel Press), *The Cryptopedia* (Citadel, winner of the Bram Stoker Award for Nonfiction); *Zombie CSU: The Forensics of the Living Dead* (Winner of the Hinzman and Black Quill Awards and nominated for a Stoker Award), *They Bite!,* and *Wanted Undead Or Alive.* Marvel Comics: *Black Panther, Wolverine, Deadpool, X-Men, Fantastic Four,* the NY Times bestselling *Marvel Zombies Return, Doomwar,* and *Marvel Universe vs Punisher.*

Danielle Ackley-McPhail has worked both sides of the publishing industry for over fifteen years. Her works include the urban fantasies, *Yesterday's Dreams, Tomorrow's Memories,* and *The Halfling's Court: A Bad-Ass Faerie Tale.* She has edited the award-winning *Bad-Ass Faeries* anthology series, and *No Longer Dreams,* and has contributed to numerous other anthologies and collections, including *Dark Furies, Breach the Hull, So It Begins, Space Pirates, Barbarians at the Jumpgate,* and *New Blood.*

Brad Aiken is Medical Director for Rehabilitation at Baptist Hospital in Miami. Author of numerous science articles, SF short stories and books, he is also a recipient of the Navy Science Award, NASA Research Award, Army Science Award and Air Force Physics Award. Info on his latest book, the nanomedicine thriller Mind Fields, and award winning short stories can be found at bradaiken.com.

Linda D. Addison, award-winning author of *Being Full of Light, Insubstantial* (Space & Time Books) is the first African-American to receive the HWA Bram Stoker Award. She has fiction in *Dark Matter* (Warner Aspect), *Dark Dreams* (Kensington), and *Dark Thirst* (Pocket Book). Catch her in "Dark Faith" (Apex Book Company) and *The Big Book of Necon* (Cemetery Dance). Her work has been listed on the Honorable Mention list for the annual *Year's Best Fantasy and Horror and Year's Best Science-Fiction*. She is a member of CITH, SFWA, HWA and SFPA. Her site: www.lindaaddisonpoet.com.

W. H. Horner is publisher and editor-in-chief of Fantasist Enterprises, an independent publishing house specializing in fantasy and horror short fiction anthologies, novels, art, and music. His latest anthology is *Blood & Devotion: Tales of Epic Fantasy*. William is an adjunct faculty member with Seton Hill University's MFA in Writing Popular Fiction program, and is the founder and director of the First Writes, a writing group that meets in Wilmington, Delaware. For more information about William and his freelance editorial and design services, please visit www.wh-horner.com, and to learn more about his projects with Fantasist Enterprises, please go to www.fantasistent.com.

T.L. Randleman grew up in Texas and made her escape soon after she realized that there was a great big world out there. In 2000 she moved to New Jersey, where she presently resides with her husband, Neal, and their two cats. Tina's favorite color is red and she loves to travel. This is her first published story.

Neal Levin is a game designer, author, and publisher. His work in game design includes credits with: Ambient Games, Bastion Press, Dark Quest Games, EN Publishing, Mystic Eye Games and Top Fashion Games. Neal lives in New Jersey with his wife and two furry children. He is a member of the Garden State Horror Writers, EPIC, and SFWA. He is the Aquisition Editor for both Dark Quest Books and ADF Books.

James Chambers' short story collection, *Resurrection House*, was published by Dark Regions Press in 2009. His tales of horror, fantasy, and science fiction have appeared in *Bad-Ass Faeries, Breach the Hull, Dark Furies, The Dead Walk, Hardboiled Cthulhu, No Longer Dreams, So It Begins*, and the magazines *Bare Bone, Cthulhu Sex*, and *Inhuman*. He is also the author of *The Midnight Hour: Saint Lawn Hill and Other Tales*. His website is www.jameschambersonline.com.

Much to his embarrassment, **Bernie Mojzes** has outlived Lord Byron, Percy Shelley, Janice Joplin and the Red Baron, without even once having been shot down over Morlancourt Ridge. Having failed to achieve a glorious martyrdom, he has instead turned his hand to the penning of paltry prose (a rather wretched example of which you currently hold in your hands), in the pathetic hope that he shall here find the notoriety that has thus far proven elusive. Should Pity or perhaps a Perverse Curiosity move you to seek him out, he can be found at http://www.kappamaki.com.

Hildy Silverman is the publisher and editor-in-chief of Space and Time, a four-decade-old magazine featuring fantasy, horror, and science fiction. She is also the author of several works of short fiction, which include, Picky (Dark Territories, ed. Gary Frank and Mary SanGiovanni, Garden State Horror Writers, 2008), Witch Way to the Mall? (ed. Esther Friesner, Baen Books), and Bad-Ass Fairies (ed. Danielle Ackley-McPhail, Mundania Press). She is on the literary programming committee of the Philadelphia Science Fiction Society and vice-president of the Garden State Horror Writers.

Terri Osborne has far too many things on her plate, but she wouldn't have it any other way. "Love and Other Excuses," one of many stories of the *Realms Next Door*, is her first venture into original dark fantasy. She is currently at work on the first *Realms* novel.

She has a resumé of critically-acclaimed media tie-in fiction. Her Stargate: Atlantis novel *Portals of Discovery* , the memoirs of Dr. Elizabeth Weir, is due in 2011. She has traveled to the 24th Century with several *Star Trek* crews, as well as the First Century CE with *Doctor Who*.

She is a regular contributor to syfy.com and has contributed to Star Trek Magazine over the years.

Terri lives in New York City with two insane cats. Find out more at her website at terriosborne.com.

KT Pinto couldn't stand where her family had moved once they left Brooklyn, so she started killing people. Once she ran out of room to hide the bodies, she decided she had to find another outlet for her frustration.

That's when she started writing... KT is the author of *The Books of Insanity* series, of which the first two books—*Celeste* and *Vanity*—are published by Mundania Press.

Her fantasy super hero series, *Sto's House Presents...*, is slated to be published by Dark Quest Books in 2011.

For more information on KT, go to www.ktpinto.com.

Jeffrey Lyman (www.jdlyman.com) is an engineer in the New York City area. His work has appeared in the anthologies *Sails and Sorcery* from Fantasist Enterprises, and in *Breach the Hull* and *So It Begins* by Dark Quest Books. He was co-editor of *No Longer Dreams* in 2005 with all the lovely editors of this current volume, and is a 2004 graduate of the Odyssey Writing School.

C.J. Henderson is the creator of the Piers Knight super-natural investigator series and the Teddy London Occult Detective series. He has written scores of books and/or novels in his time, including such diverse titles as *The Encyclopedia of Science Fiction Movies, Black Sabbath: the Ozzy Osbourne Years,* and *Baby's First Mythos.* He has also written thousands of short stories, comics and non-fiction pieces, a body of work various segments of which have now seen print in some thirteen different languages. Pleasant, gifted, sleek and informed are just some of the words rarely used to describe this powerhouse storyteller. For more information on this self-proclaimed king of the festival, to read more of his work or to simply comment on his story in this volume, please travel to www.cjhenderson.com. Tell him Zarbinkle sent you. For no particular reason.

John Sunseri lives and works in Portland, OR. He is the co-author (with David Conyers) of the upcoming collection *The Spiraling Worm* for Chaosium, and is currently editing an anthology of cross-genre Lovecraftian fiction for Permuted Press. He's had over forty stories published in various magazines and anthologies.

Rowena Morrill is one of the best known names in the world of science-fiction and fantasy illustration. During a career that has spanned over two decades, her paintings have appeared on hundreds of book covers, on calendars, portfolios, trading cards and in magazines such as *Playboy* and *Omni.* Books of her own work have included *The Fantastic Art of Rowena, Imagine* (in France), *Imagination* (in Germany), and *The Art of Rowena.* She has also been included in many anthologies, such as, *Tomorrow and Beyond* and *Infinite Worlds.* Rowena began her career in New York City where she lived for sixteen years. She presently lives in upstate New York gaining creative inspiration from the beautiful countryside. *Pig Boy the Vampire* is among her first literary publications.

Diane Raetz has had several short stories published, co-authored a vampire novella in *Flesh & Iron* and is the co-author of *Mystic Investigators: Once More Upon A Time.* She helped create the YA series *The Wildsidhe Chronicles.* Diane is the editor in chief of Padwolf Publishing and the upcoming web magazine *Uncast Shadows.*

Patrick Thomas is the author of one-hundred and fifty plus short stories and twenty books including eight books in the popular fantasy humor series *Murphy's Lore; Fairy With A Gun; Dead To Rites*; three books in the *Mystic Investigators* series—including *Bullets & Brimstone* co-authored with John L. French and *Once More Upon A Time* co-authored with Diane Raetz. Patrick also writes the syndicated satirical advice column *Dear Cthulhu* and the first two collections—*Have A Dark Day* and *Good Advice For Bad People*—are out now for those searching for the meaning of life or a good laugh. He's also co-edited *Hear Them Roar* and the *New Blood* vampire anthology. Drop by his website at www.patthomas.net.

Artist Bio
(Interior)

Linda Saboe started to draw seriously at age two, continuing on until it became apparent that her children enjoyed eating on a regular basis. So she got a job. Now that her children can feed themselves, she quit the job and started drawing again.

Linda works in oil paints, paper and digital drawing, polymer clay and, most recently, rabbits. In addition to *New Blood*, she is the illustrator of *The Evil Gazebo, The Halfling's Court, Bad-Ass Faeries 3: In All Their Glory,* and *Dragon's Lure.*

She does not enjoy writing bios.

To see more of her work, visit www.croneswood.com.

The shout has echoed throughout history, "Barbarians at the gate!" Words that strike terror in the hearts of civilized peoples everywhere. If we have learned anything from our past, it is that history repeats itself. So on a grim day in the future when less civilized aliens attack us will we cry, "BARBARIANS AT THE JUMPGATE!"

Award winning author and editor Bruce Gehweiler has gathered together for the first time fifteen fresh tales of science fiction and fantasy adventure that hearken back to the golden age of science fiction. Join C.J. Henderson, Patrick Thomas, Danielle Ackley-McPhail, John Sunseri, Robert E. Waters, James Chambers, Bernie Mojzes, James Daniel Ross, R. Allen Leider, Neal Levin, Lawrence Barker, and Darren W. Pearce on a wild ride through towering imaginations and an uncertain future as great civilizations fight against hordes of Barbarians… in the future!

Hidden from the eyes of mankind they lurk in the shadows. In remote parts of our planet they survive the passage of time. Brave men and women seek out these unknown creatures in a search for truth that is muddled in legends and folklore-scoffed at by modern science.
These are the tales of cryptozoology, the study of hidden and unknown animals.

CRYPTO-CRITTERS
VOLUMES 1 & 2

Got Blood? We do and as everyone knows new blood is simply the best. With these pages we have wonder and fangs aplenty including a cyborg vampire in space, steampunk vamps, a werewolf PI, a vampire escalator, blood suckers in love, a study in orthodox vampirism, the undead at war and of course a cannabilistically incestuous vampire penguin from Coney Island. And that's just the begining.

Join New York Times Best Selling Author and multiple Bram Stoker award winner Jonathan Maberry, Bram Stoker Winner Linda Addison, fantasy legends C.J. Henderson and Rowena Morrill, award winners Danielle Ackley-McPhail and Brad Aiken, alongside some of the best writers in the business - James Chambers, William H. Horner III, Neal Levin, Jeff Lyman, Bernie Mojzes, Terri Osborne, K.T. Pinto, Diane Raetz, T.L. Randleman, Hildy Silverman, John Sunseri and Patrick Thomas - as they bring you tales of vampires you never dreamed existed and others that will forever haunt your nightmares.

BAD COP...
NO DONUT
edited by
John L. French
**Tales of Cops
Behaving Badly**

In this book you will find:
Good Cops gone bad
Bad Cops gone worse
Police in the city
Sheriffs on the hunt
Cops on the beach
Cops on the take
Fights to the death
Ninjas and nunchuckas
Hookers and dealers
Good guys and bad guys
And the Devil's own cop

featuring the talents of:
– James Chambers – Gary Lovisi
O'Neil De Noux – Quintin Peterson
C. J. Henderson – Michael A. Black
– Ron Fortier – Patrick Thomas
Michael Berish – Vincent H. O'Neil
– Austin S. Camacho – Wayne D.
Dundee – John L. French
– Art Monterastelli – James Grady

*"A ride-around with some of the best cops
and best cop writing in the business!"*
-David Black,
author of **The Extinction Event** &
writer for **CSI Miami** & **Law & Order**

Private Eye Matthew Grace
always believes his clients,
tries to anyway. That's not
easy in a city where almost
everybody lies.
Grace should know, he's
told a few himself – always
in a good cause of course.
In the end it will be up to
Grace to make the right
choices, ones that will
lead either
to a second chance
or no chance at all.

**"TERRIFIC!
JOHN FRENCH
IS THE REAL DEAL!"**
-Daniel Stashower,
author of THE BEAUTIFUL
CIGAR GIRL and THE TELLER
OF TALES: The Life of Arthur
Conan Doyle.

MIND FIELDS
Brad Aiken

Renegade NSA agent Trace
McKnight infiltrates the lab of Dr.
Fletcher to steal her nanomedicine
research in order to develop a
mind-control weapon. Fletcher
enlists the help of Baltimore police
detective Richie Kincade, and the
pair soon find themselves caught
up in a web of espionage that
places them directly in the cross-
hairs of the seditious NSA agent, a
man feared even by those within
his own organization. As
McKnight's plan unfolds, Kincade
realizes that he and the good
doctor have just been pawns in a
game that neither of them were
prepared to play, but that won't
stop them from playing to win.

*"Aiken's brilliance as a writer weaves a
strikingly vivid tale of scientific
advancement that leads to a terrifying
vision of the future. The resulting
rollecoaster ride of action and suspense
kept me on the edge of my seat
throughout the entire novel! "*
- Melissa Minners, **G-Pop**

More anthologies from Padwolf Publishing

THE DEAD WALK AGAIN

edited by
Vince Sneed

Zombie tales from James Chambers, D.J. Kirkbride, John French, Nate Southard, C.J. Henderson, John L. French, Nate Southard, Steven A. Roman, D.J. Kirkbride, Adam P. Knave, Bruce Gehweiler, Laszlo Xalieri, Patrick Thomas, and Jack Dolphin

EPITAPHS

edited by
Edward J. McFadden &
Tom Piccirilli

With stories by Linda D. Addison, Mike Allen, Trey R. Barker, Warren Newton Beath, Tippi Blevins, Dan Clore, Corrine De Winter, James S. Dorr, Rhonda Eikamp, Cindie Geddes, Harrison Howe, Gerard Daniel Houarner, Randall Ivey, Michael Laimo, Natalia Lincoln, Edward McFadden, Adam Meyer, K.K. Ormond, Wendy Rathbone, Michelle Scalise, Vera Searles, Sue Storm, Honna Swenson, G. Warlock Vance, & Thomas Wiloch

THE 2ND COMING
The best of Pirate Writings Vol. 2

edited by
Edward J.
McFadden

With stories by Linda D. Addison• Paul DiFilippo• Tom Piccirilli • Mike Resnick • Josepha Sherman • Allen Steele • Patrick Thomas •Brendon Adams • Kathryn J. Brown • G. William Cromer • Steve Hamilton • J.L. Hanna • Anthony J. Howard • Brett Hudgins • Mary Soon Lee • Lyn Lifshin • Edward J. McFadden • Brian Plante • Arthur J. Scott • Christopher Stires • Jeffrey Valka

TIME CAPSULE

edited by
Edward J.
McFadden

They come from the past to conquer the future of Science Fiction, Fantasy, and Horror. Paul DiFilippo Manages to Destroy all Brains Edward McFadden & Tom Piccirilli guide us to Year 1 After the world is forever altered Sue Storm takes us Under The Lizard Trees & Ed McFadden Catches The Big One

More books from Padwolf Publishing

WORLD TREE RPG

by Bard Bloom and Victoria Borah Bloom

A MARRIAGE OF INSECTS

a novel of The World Tree

by Bard Bloom

THE STARSCAPE PROJECT

by Brad Aiken

DECONSTRUCTING TOLKIEN

by Edward McFadden

THE WILDSIDHE CHRONICLES
Books 1-6

*by
Patrick Thomas
(books 1-2)
Judith Tracy,
(books 3-4)
Tony Digerolamo
(book 5),
Myke Cole
(book 6)*